DEATH SWATCH

"New readers won't have any trouble jumping in at this point, and longtime fans will feel like they've reconnected with a friend. The characters are suitably eccentric and the mystery very involving."
—CA Reviews

FRILL KILL

"[A] sprightly . . . mystery. Childs rounds out the story with several scrapbooking and crafting tips plus a passel of mouthwatering Louisiana recipes." —*Publishers Weekly*

MOTIF FOR MURDER

"An entertaining whodunit . . . The heroine is a plucky, strong, and independent woman . . . The original steel magnolia."
—*Midwest Book Review*

P9-DCB-888

Praise for the Scrapbooking Mysteries

GOSSAMER GHOST

"This mystery comes alive with the sights and sounds of the French Quarter as its residents revel in their favorite holiday . . . Plenty of parties, colorful characters, and the brutal murder of a shop owner make this mystery pure, scary fun."

—*RT Book Reviews*

"In *Gossamer Ghost*, Childs gives cozy fans everything they want: an armchair mystery, likable characters, and loads of entertainment. There are plenty of suspects and false leads, but this mystery isn't just about clues or scrapbooking; it's also about New Orleans and BFFs. Carmela and Ava enjoy the festivities and entertain the readers as Ghostesses on the Ghost Train. Dressed as Ghost Brides, the two really throw themselves into it . . . It's a spooktacular ride you can't miss. *Gossamer Ghost* is the perfect Halloween treat." —My Shelf

"I love it when Childs keeps me guessing, and she certainly did with this one." —Debbie's Book Bag

GILT TRIP

"Chutzpah and coincidence play large roles in Childs's . . . Big Easy romp." —*Publishers Weekly*

"Exactly what I look for in a cozy! It had an intriguing crime, a unique cast of characters, and a terrific setting . . . also a lot of humor thrown into the story." —Booking Mama

continued . . .

POSTCARDS FROM THE DEAD

"A wonderful whodunit as this time the heroine vows to not investigate but feels compelled when the postcards start coming. Carmela and Ava are brave buddies who team up in search of the person sending postcards from the dead."
—Genre Go Round Reviews

SKELETON LETTERS

"An addictive murder mystery which would have Miss Marple at a loss for words . . . The novel offers plenty of laughs as well . . . The amateur detectives are witty and resourceful fashionistas whom readers will wish they could jump into the novel and befriend. *Skeleton Letters* is a hit and brings the charm of the Big Easy to life in this delicious murder mystery."
—Fresh Fiction

FIBER & BRIMSTONE

"Catching the real killer is a job, of course, for NOPD Lieutenant Edgar Babcock, Carmela's main squeeze, but the detecting chops of artsy Carmela and her saucy sidekick, Ava, totally steal his thunder. Scrapbooking tips and recipes for dishes like Candied Fruit Banana Bread and Dr. Pepper Tickle-Your-Ribs Spareribs round out a volume sure to please cozy fans."
—*Publishers Weekly*

TRAGIC MAGIC

"Fast-paced with plenty of action, *Tragic Magic* is a terrific scrapbooking amateur-sleuth mystery." —*Midwest Book Review*

Gossamer Ghost

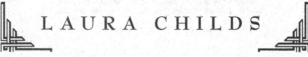

LAURA CHILDS

BERKLEY PRIME CRIME, NEW YORK

An imprint of Penguin Random House LLC
375 Hudson Street, New York, New York 10014

GOSSAMER GHOST

A Berkley Prime Crime Book / published by arrangement with the author

ISBN: 978-0-425-26667-0

PUBLISHING HISTORY
Berkley Prime Crime hardcover edition / October 2014
Berkley Prime Crime mass-market edition / October 2015

PRINTED IN THE UNITED STATES OF AMERICA

10 9 8 7 6 5 4 3 2 1

Cover illustration by Dan Craig.
Cover design by Lesley Worrell.

Acknowledgments

✂

A major thank-you to Sam, Tom, Amanda, Troy, Diana, Nancy, Bob, Jennie, Dan, and all the designers, illustrators, writers, publicists, and sales folk at The Berkley Publishing Group. You are all such a wonderful team. Thank you also to all the booksellers, reviewers, librarians, and bloggers. And special thanks to all my readers and Facebook friends who are so very kind, supportive, and appreciative. I truly love writing for you!

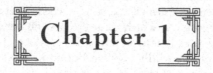

Chapter 1

IT was Halloween again in New Orleans. A week-long, rabble-rousing celebration that just seemed to get bigger, badder, and crazier every dang year. A time for would-be werewolves, witches, fairy princesses, goblins, Venetian lords and ladies, and zombies to dust off their costumes, throw on a wig, howl at the moon, and paint the town the bright red color of fake vampire blood.

Carmela Bertrand, the owner of Memory Mine Scrapbook Shop in the French Quarter, was no exception. This year she was debating the merits of wearing a medieval lady's costume for the week leading up to Halloween, a Scarlett O'Hara dress for her friend Baby Fontaine's annual masquerade ball, and a sexy witch dress for the ultra-fancy Pumpkins and Bumpkins Ball.

After all, what's a girl to do when she has dozens of party invitations and is dating one of the hottest police detectives in the Big Easy?

Well, for one thing, it wasn't so easy.

Right now, late Friday afternoon, with streetlamps just beginning to glow in the darkening purple haze of a French Quarter evening, Carmela was still hunched at her computer trying to figure out which classes to post on her Facebook page. She'd already offered several Paper Moon classes that had proven to be wildly popular. But now she was racking her brain for something different, a couple of fun crafty sessions that would tickle her customers' fancies and really get their creative juices flowing.

Maybe a stencil class or a class on painted fabrics? Painting on velvet clutch purses and pillows could generate lots of excitement among her die-hard scrapping ladies. The other thing might be . . .

She stood up fast and hustled out of her tiny office and into her retail area. Pulling open a flat file drawer, she peered inside. *Yes!* She had a huge inventory of square and oval jewelry findings. Neat little square frames, as well as hearts and elaborate ovals that you could slip a tiny photo into. So maybe she could offer a Charm and Pendant class? That could be loads of fun.

Carmela nodded to herself, liking the idea more and more, as she rushed back to her office and typed in her new class. There. Done and done. Creating a personalized charm or pendant was almost as fun as creating a miniature scrapbook page.

Feeling satisfied and a little relieved, more than ready to call it a day, Carmela grabbed her handbag and suede jacket and headed for the front door. Rushing now, she smoothed back a strand of honeyed-blond hair from her short, choppy bob and did a little quickstep. Not quite thirty, Carmela was at that point in her life where she was still young enough to be bubbly, but old enough to be serious. A freewheeling Southern conservative with inquisitive blue-gray eyes, fair complexion that rarely saw the need for makeup, a nose for getting into trouble, and a serious penchant for chocolate.

We could even make charm bracelets, she thought to herself as she turned and locked the door behind her.

As Carmela stepped out onto Governor Nicholls Street, she inhaled deeply and smiled. Evenings in the French Quarter never failed to give her pause and an overall feeling of sweet contentment. After all, who wouldn't love to gaze up at a purplish blue-black sky that served as a dramatic backdrop for two-hundred-year-old brick buildings? Or wander through courtyard gardens with pattering fountains and giant froths of jasmine and magnolias? And if you stopped and listened carefully, you could more often than not hear the haunting low notes of a jazz saxophone bumping along on a breeze from the river.

Of course, the French Quarter had its crazy hurly-burly side, too. Lest you think it was a perfect little slice of heaven, you couldn't forget the voodoo shops, absinthe bars, strip clubs, and touristy T-shirt and bead shops. But for every one of those crazy shops there were dozens of quaint oyster bars, jazz clubs, elegant restaurants, historic old homes, French bakeries, and haunted hotels. All there for your delicious enjoyment.

Feeling upbeat, Carmela paused outside her own quaint little bow window with its display of finished scrapbooks, memory boxes, Paperclay jewelry, and altered books. Just gazing at all the finished crafts gave her a keen sense of satisfaction. A feeling of accomplishment for having found her happy little niche in the world.

Over the past few years, Carmela had managed to build Memory Mine into a thriving business. No thanks at all to her ex-husband, Shamus "The Rat" Meechum. He'd bugged out after their very first year of marriage, leaving her to figure out how to negotiate a lease, write a business plan, and obtain a bank loan. And the rat (yes, we're making a point here) even hailed from one of New Orleans's premier banking families, owners of Crescent City Bank.

But Carmela had taken the risk, worked her proverbial buns off, and figured out how to entice and build a customer base. And, wonder of wonders, her efforts had not only paid off monetarily, but she found she *enjoyed* being a small-business owner. One of many here on Governor Nicholls Street with its plethora of gift shops, antique shops, and what have you.

What have you.

That thought caused her to pause outside the front window of Oddities, the shop that served as her next-door neighbor and with whom she shared a common brick wall. Oddities was a strange little business run by an even stranger man by the name of Marcus Joubert. The shop had sprung up two years ago like an errant mushroom and was aptly named. Because Oddities carried an eclectic and macabre mix of merchandise. There were taxidermy animals, Victorian funeral jewelry, steampunk items, beetle and butterfly collections, antique furniture, old medical devices of indeterminate usage, albums filled with black-and-white photos, and any number of bleached-white animal skulls and bones. She'd even once spotted an apparatus that looked suspiciously like a thumbscrew.

Tonight, under the soft glow of streetlamps, her curiosity getting the best of her, Carmela stopped and peered in Oddities' dusty front window. And saw a pair of old leather goggles, a piece of scrimshaw, a collection of Chinese vases, and a top hat and antique dagger.

For some reason the top hat and dagger struck her as something Jack the Ripper might have had in his possession. Might have even treasured.

Kind of creepy.

Then again, it was the week before Halloween. So perhaps Marcus Joubert was trying to set a theme?

Carmela was just about to turn and walk away, hike the few blocks to her cozy apartment, when she was suddenly aware of a funny and slightly ominous set of noises emanating from inside Oddities. What she thought might have been a muffled scream followed by a dull thump.

Huh?

She stepped closer to the window and tried to peer in, to see what was happening in the back of the shop. No luck. A rainbow of lights from the street reflected off the glass, creating a glare that made it almost impossible.

Still . . . she'd heard something, right?

Carmela, who was generally practical in nature but was blessed (or cursed, some might say) with a giant dollop of inquisitiveness in her DNA, decided it might be smart to investigate.

After all, what if Marcus Joubert had suddenly taken ill? What if the sounds she'd heard were him staggering and falling? Could he be lying in there right now? Struck down by a heart attack or some other ailment and unable to call out for help?

Carmela put a hand on the brass doorknob and turned it slowly. Nothing doing. The door was securely locked.

No problem, she had a key. Joubert had given her one in case of emergency—and this just might qualify as an emergency. If not, then no harm done. She'd take a quick look-see and lock up tightly. No one would be the wiser.

Quickly pulling out her key fob, Carmela found the little brass key and stuck it in the lock.

And that's when her bravado and good intentions suddenly came to a screeching halt. Because when she opened the door, the shop yawned at her in complete darkness.

Oh my.

Carmela stood there for a few moments, feeling unnatural warmth wash over her, as if a space heater had been left on, and hearing a monotonous ticking from an old grandfather clock in back. As a few more moments passed, she realized the shop wasn't completely dark after all. There were a few dim lights scattered about the place. Pinprick spotlights glowed from the rafters like bat eyes, illuminating a suit of armor and a wrought-iron candelabra. A stained glass turtle-shell lamp cast a dim orange glow on a shelf alongside a set of frayed leather-bound books. And way in the back, sitting atop Joubert's rickety rolltop desk, was a faux Tiffany lamp.

Unfortunately, none of the lightbulbs seemed to pump out more than ten watts of power. It was like walking into a dark cocktail lounge without the benefit of strong liquid refreshments.

Carmela took two steps in. "Marcus?" she called out. "Are you okay?"

There was no answer.

"It's Carmela from next door. I thought I heard something . . ." Her own voice sounded shrill to her, but also seemed to be absorbed quickly into the gloom and darkness. She advanced a few more steps. "Now what?" she muttered to herself. What should she do? What was going on? She prayed it wasn't some weird Halloween prank that was being played on the unsuspecting next-door neighbor.

"Joubert?" she called again. "Are you in here?"

There was another muffled noise. From where? Maybe from the back of the shop, she decided.

Could it have been the soft snick of the back door closing? Had someone been in here with her for a few moments and just now slipped out the back?

A cold shiver traveled up Carmela's spine and a little voice in her head, the one that sometimes whispered, *You're taking too big a risk*, told her to get out now.

A prickly feeling, as if she was being watched by unseen eyes, made Carmela crank her head sharply to the left. And she suddenly found herself staring directly into the grimac-

ing face of a stuffed capuchin monkey that was perched
precariously on a shelf, condemned forever to wear a hideous
purple vest and matching fez.

Startled by the snarling mouth and beady eyes, Carmela
whirled away from the monkey, caught her toe on the edge
of an Oriental carpet, and started to stumble. Her arms
cartwheeled out in front of her in a last-ditch effort to catch
herself from falling. And, in so doing, flailed and flapped
against the front doors of a tall wooden curio cabinet.

As her splayed-out hands thumped against the thin
wooden doors, they rattled like crazy and the entire cabinet
seemed to teeter forward on its spindly legs. Terrified that
the entire piece was going to fall over and smash something
odd or precious, Carmela tried to grasp the cabinet and
steady it. But as she felt the weight of the cabinet slowly
tipping toward her, as her fingers fumbled against the brass
handles, the cabinet's doors slowly creaked open.

And then, like a corpse spilling out of Dr. Caligari's
closet, the dead, bloody body of Marcus Joubert suddenly
came lurching out at her!

Carmela took a step backward in shock and protest. No
matter, the body tumbled relentlessly toward her in horrible
slow motion. There was a low moan, like the stinking sigh
of a zombie, as a final bubble of air was released from the
deep recess of its lungs. And then Joubert's body flopped
cold and bloody and unwelcome into Carmela's outstretched
arms!

Chapter 2

"*Noooooo!*"

Stunned and horrified beyond belief, Carmela screamed at the top of her lungs. She shoved Joubert's body away from her with as much strength as she could muster, made an awkward jump sideways, and crashed into a small metal table topped with glass figurines. A tiny lion plunged to the floor, a rearing horse tumbled over backward and shattered, its head and right leg flying off.

And still Carmela continued to scream.

When nobody showed up to help, when nothing seemed to be accomplished by her loud screeches of protest, she let out a garbled cough and closed her mouth with a snap.

Joubert is dead. Right here in front of me. Oh dear oh dear oh dear.

Her mind churned wildly, like a rock tumbler gnawing away at bits of agate and sand.

What just happened? What should I do?

She grimaced and looked about nervously. The suit of

armor was certainly no help. The capuchin monkey hadn't made a move. A weird, beady-eyed cat head stared relentlessly back at her.

I . . . first I have to pull myself together.

That decision made, Carmela really did try hard to collect herself. To stifle her fear and revulsion, to try to figure out . . .

Wait just one minute.

A frightening thought had suddenly formed like a cartoon thought bubble inside her brain.

Is Joubert dead? Is the man really dead?

Carmela scrunched her face into a look of distaste. Of course, there was only one way to find out and it wasn't very pleasant. Still, she supposed it had to be done. Slowly, methodically, Carmela took a few steps forward until she was all but hovering over Joubert's body. He'd landed on the floor in a heap and looked fairly lifeless, like a rag doll that had been slung across the room. Grimacing, she saw that the front of his white shirt was shredded in some places and stained wet and dark with blood. Had he been stabbed? That seemed most likely.

Stabbed, then stuck inside a cabinet? Why?

Shuddering, hating that she was forced to do this, Carmela reached slowly down until the tips of her fingers brushed against the pulse point at Joubert's throat. Correction, what *had* been his pulse point. Because now it felt utterly cold and devoid of life.

That was enough for Carmela. She fled the death and darkness of Oddities, ran out onto the street, and then hastily retreated to the relative safety and security of her own shop.

Slamming the door hard, Carmela quickly latched it, even as she tried to still her racing heart. Then she gazed, unbelieving, out her front window and tried not to let her imagination run wild. Tried not to go completely bonkers and let a movie version of what might happen next crank through her brain. Because in her personal horror show—and this was most definitely a real-deal horror show—Joubert's stiff and blood-soaked body would come lurching after her.

No, Carmela told herself. *Get a grip. That isn't going to happen.*

She was pretty sure—really, more than a little sure—that the man was dead. Therefore, she was going to handle this crisis with calm and dignity. Or as much shaky composure as her frayed, overwrought nerves would allow.

Pawing frantically through her handbag, Carmela hastily located her cell phone.

Definitely got to call for help.

But instead of calmly dialing 911, Carmela's shaking hands fumbled the phone. Feeling stupid and more than a little helpless, she watched it tumble to the floor and spin wildly on the wooden planks. As she lurched after it, her toe accidently struck the phone and sent it sailing beneath one of her display cases.

Dang! Dropping to her hands and knees, Carmela wondered what else could go wrong.

She fished around under the case until she finally managed to grab hold of her phone. Then she stood up and feverishly punched in a familiar number.

The first person she called, of course, was her boyfriend, Detective Edgar Babcock. Luckily, her call was answered on the first ring, because her request immediately devolved into a disjointed ramble, delivered with staccato urgency and more than a few tears, pleading for Babcock to please come quickly because something really, really terrible had happened. The second call she fired off, once she'd pulled herself together in a vague sort of way, was to her best friend and neighbor, Ava Gruiex.

That done, Carmela walked slowly to the back of her scrapbook shop, gazed at her floor-to-ceiling shelves filled with albums, paper, stencils, and shadow boxes, and wondered just what on earth could have happened next door. Oddities wasn't exactly the kind of shop a thief was likely to break in to. Inventory ranged from the strange to the bizarre and, from Carmela's recollection, nothing had ever seemed particularly valuable. In fact, if a thief was going to make a big score in the French Quarter, there were dozens of antique shops, estate jewelry shops, and upscale art galleries filled with extremely valuable merchandise.

So what on earth had happened? Had it been a burglary? Was there anything in Oddities worth stealing? Or had it simply been cold-blooded murder committed by a couple of crazy stickup artists or hopped-up tweekers?

PREDICTABLY, AVA WAS THE FIRST ONE TO AR-rive at Carmela's shop. She flew in like a witch on a nuclear-powered broomstick, managing to look worried, gorgeous, and perfectly pulled together in a spangled purple sweater, tight black leather pants, and studded leather cage boots.

"*Cher!*" Ava cried breathlessly. "What happened?" The shapely ex–beauty queen fluttered a hand to her chest as she gazed worriedly at Carmela. Her mass of raven-black hair was poufed out around her expressive, fine-boned face. "When you called you were babbling like a crazy lady. Something about your hair? So naturally I came a-running."

Carmela was fighting back a bad case of nervous hiccups and still stumbling over her words. "Not hair, I was trying to tell you about Joubert!" She made a hasty circular motion with her hands. "You know, the shop owner next door."

Ava eyed her carefully. "Something happened?" She paused, trying to assess the situation. "Something bad?"

Carmela nodded excitedly. She was still having trouble stringing her words together, but was relieved that Ava was finally able to comprehend her terror.

"Excuse me," Ava continued. "Was this something that could be construed as . . . harassment?" Ava had never been particularly fond of Marcus Joubert. Had never really trusted him.

Carmela continued to bob her head nervously. Then Ava's words clicked with her and she said, "Um . . . what did you say?"

Ava placed her hands on slim hips and narrowed her eyes into a catlike scrunch. "Please don't tell me that lecherous old coot made a pass at you," she said in a low growl. "I've always found something smarmy and unsettling about . . . Oh. And you've got blood on your sweater. Oh no. What *happened*?"

"No, Ava," Carmela choked out. "It's not what you think." She held a hand out. "The thing is . . ." Carmela forced herself to bite down hard to keep her teeth from chattering. "Joubert is . . . well, he's dead!"

Ava's finely groomed brows rose in twin arcs as she stared at Carmela. "Dead," she said in a flat tone. Then she seemed to finally comprehend what Carmela was saying. "Wait a minute, you're talking *dead* dead? As in not among the living?"

Carmela nodded frantically. "That's it exactly. I heard these strange noises after I locked up. Coming from his shop. So I went inside to check on Joubert." She gave a shudder. "I had a key . . ."

"You went *inside* that creeped-out shop? All by yourself?"

"Because I thought Joubert might be *hurt*. Because I heard . . . well, anyway, that's when I found him . . ." Her voice trailed off as she recalled the bloody scene inside the shop.

"Holy Coupe de Ville," Ava whooped. "Did you *see* what happened?"

Carmela shook her head vigorously.

"Then what do you *think* happened?"

"I'm pretty sure Joubert was stabbed," said Carmela. "There

was . . ." She wrinkled her nose, repulsed by the remembered image of his dead body catapulting out at her, an image that was now seared into her brain. "There was blood. So much blood. All over." Suddenly remembering how she'd shoved the dead body away from her, she held up her hands, which were smeared with traces of dried blood. "You see?"

"Did you call Babcock?" Ava demanded. "Is he on his way?" She'd finally jumped into hyperdrive, too. "The police are coming?"

"Yes. Of course."

"Who else knows about this?"

"Nobody," said Carmela. "Just us. And the police."

Ava chewed at her bottom lip. "It sounds like you did okay, honey. You pretty much kept your head in spite of what happened over there. But for now, until the police arrive, let's work on getting you cleaned up." She put a hand out and pulled Carmela toward her. "Poor dear, you're an awful mess." She sat Carmela down on a rolling chair behind the front counter, grabbed a pack of wipes from her purse, and carefully swiped at the blood.

Carmela sat numbly as Ava cleaned her off. Of course, when the damp wipe hit her bloodstained hands, the blood began to smear all over again, reminding her of a scene straight out of a horror movie . . . like a dead body being reanimated.

"You don't think this blood is like a clue or anything, do you?" Carmela asked. "That it should be tested for DNA?"

Ava continued to blot at Carmela's hands. "If it's Joubert's blood like you say it is, then they're bound to find splotches of it next door, too."

"I suppose you're right," said Carmela. She knew she wasn't thinking straight and fought to clear her mind. There was something she was missing. Something she should probably . . .

"Oh my gosh!" Carmela said, suddenly stiffening in her chair.

"What now?" said Ava.

"I should call Mavis."

"Who's that?"

"Mavis Sweet, the assistant."

"You mean that mousy little girl in stretch pants who works for Joubert?" said Ava. "Why bring her into this?"

"The thing is," said Carmela, "Joubert always introduced Mavis Sweet as his assistant, but I think the two of them had something going on—a little romance on the side. Well, maybe more than a little romance."

"Those two?" said Ava. "I never would have guessed. Well, I suppose it's only fair to give the poor girl a call."

"You mean do a notification?" The idea of telling Mavis that Joubert was dead terrified Carmela.

"Notification nothing," Ava advised. "Don't tell Mavis anything specific. Just make up some crazy excuse to get her down here."

"Then what?" said Carmela.

"Then," said Ava, "you let the cops do the heavy lifting."

WHILE CARMELA WAS ON THE PHONE WITH Mavis Sweet, asking her to please come down to Oddities without spelling out the exact reason why, Detective Edgar Babcock arrived.

"He's here," Ava called out. "Babcock." She was staring out Carmela's front window. "He just jumped out of . . . holy bejeebers, is that a BMW I see out there? What an awesome set of wheels. Oh yeah, and it looks like he brought a posse of uniformed officers with him. Though those poor peons arrived in a far more traditional black-and-white vehicle."

Carmela hung up the phone, feeling like a coward. She'd told Mavis Sweet that there was a dire emergency at Oddities, but she hadn't been at all truthful or specific. Still, the girl promised that she was on her way, so that was something.

Ava was still peering out the front window. "Did you hear what I said? Your love bunny arrived in a BMW. Do you think some crook finally bought him off? A drug dealer or a smuggler?"

"He bought it at a police auction," said Carmela. "Besides, Babcock's not like that. He's basically . . . well, he's straight."

"Well, hook me up at the next police auction, girlfriend," said Ava. "Because I could use a hot new set of wheels like that." She glanced out the window again. "Uh-oh, now he's waving at us. I suppose he wants us to come out there. Hmm, and he's got that serious tight-lipped look that means he's upset." She glanced back at Carmela. "Are you ready for this, sweetie?"

"No," said Carmela.

DUDED UP IN A CHALK-GRAY ZEGNA SUIT, DEtective Edgar Babcock was tall, thin, and attractive in an officer-of-the-law kind of way. The glow from the streetlamps gave his ginger-colored hair a slightly darker cast and made his pale skin look almost ethereal. His normally handsome face, usually lit with a warm, crooked smile, looked rather serious tonight with just a touch of grouch thrown in.

Still, to Carmela, Babcock looked wonderful. His pale blue shirt matched a tie of a slightly deeper tone that picked up the intensity and color of his eyes.

An Armani tie? Carmela wondered, as her heart did a small flip-flop. Had to be. Only the best for Babcock, always the most stylish duds. She knew that, someday, *GQ* magazine was going to do a feature on the ten best-dressed detectives in the country and Babcock was probably going to top the list. Then she wondered—how on earth could she be turned on by Babcock and completely repulsed by Joubert's murder at the same time? Those were two emotions that didn't seem to coexist, yet there they were. All intertwined and smooshed together in her slightly addled, hyperactive brain. Go figure.

"So," said Babcock. He rocked back on his heels when he caught sight of Carmela and Ava on the front sidewalk. "We seem to have a rather large problem here."

"I'll say," said Ava, who loved to be in on the action. Any kind. Even police action.

Babcock gestured toward the front door of Oddities. "Is it unlocked?"

"Yes," Carmela said in a small voice. "That's how I left it." *Especially since I came flying out of there like a crazed banshee.*

Carmela wished that Babcock would look at her, really *see* her, instead of holding her at arm's length, treating her like some sort of suspect or witness. On the other hand, that's probably what she was.

Babcock cocked a finger at one of the uniformed officers. "Lambert, you come inside with me. Wallace, stay by the door. Don't let anybody else in."

"Crime-scene guys are here," said Wallace, as a shiny black van pulled up tight to the curb.

"Send them in," said Babcock. "As soon as they unload their gear." He sighed as he led his little group into Oddities, and then stopped short when he saw the body. He held up a hand, indicating for them all to wait. Then he stepped forward, took a cursory look at the very dead Marcus Joubert, and said, "Carmela, you're going to have to walk us through this."

Chapter 3

"WHAT happened was . . ." Carmela began. She was ready to let it all come bubbling out. The terror, her jangled nerves, her fear that Joubert's dead body might come stumbling after her.

But Babcock held up a finger. "Let's wait a second for the crime-scene guys." He glanced around. "Aren't there any decent lights in this place? Where are the lights, anyway?"

"It's like a tomb in here," said Ava, which caused Carmela to flinch.

Officer Lambert scurried around, finally locating switches and flipping on several overhead lights.

"Oh man," said Ava, as Joubert's dead body was revealed in the now harsh light. "That's just . . . rude."

"You really shouldn't be in here," said Babcock. He shook his head. "Why is she in here?"

Nobody offered an answer until Carmela finally said, "I need Ava for moral support."

"Right," said Ava, giving a slow wink. "I gotta keep watch on her morals."

"Excuse me, excuse me," a youthful voice called out. "Coming through."

It was the crime-scene team, a flying wedge of three men all wearing dark blue jumpsuits and carrying black leather cases along with a clanking gurney.

"Charlie," said Babcock, nodding at the young man at the head of the group. Charlie Preston was the crime-scene team's young wunderkind. A smart, persistent technician who considered every case he handled a personal challenge.

"Hey, Charlie," said Ava. The two had met before and she was well aware of this young man's interest in her.

Charlie looked around, surprised, and then grinned impishly at her. "Ava. What are *you* doing here?"

"Another day, another murder," Ava quipped.

"Can we please just get down to business?" said Babcock. He raised an eyebrow and focused on Carmela. "Carmela?"

So Carmela led them hesitantly through her little adventure. As Charlie and his team snapped photos, bagged the hands, and poked at the body, she explained how she'd heard a couple of strange noises, had entered the shop, and then tripped and inadvertently opened the cabinet where Marcus Joubert's body had been stashed.

"Yowza," said Ava, when she'd finally finished. "That's quite a story."

"That's exactly how it happened?" said Babcock. "You didn't leave anything out?"

"I don't think so," said Carmela. *Just that I screamed my head off.*

"Sounds about right to me, Chief," said Charlie. "You look at how the body fell, where it landed and all. Her story pretty much tracks."

"Okay," said Babcock. He seemed to be chewing on something.

"There are spatter marks in the back of the shop," said Charlie. "So that's where the victim was stabbed. Then he was obviously dragged and stashed in that cabinet."

"Dead before they put him in there?" asked Babcock.

"Oh yeah," said Charlie. "This guy lost a lot of blood. It was all over pretty fast."

"But there's no sign of a weapon," said Babcock.

"The killer must have brought his own knife," said one of the crime-scene techs. "Then taken it with him."

"He would have been bloody after such a violent struggle," said Babcock. "It would be hard to stroll through the French Quarter covered in blood."

"Maybe not," said Ava. "Some guys party like rock stars down here."

"Maybe his car was parked in the back alley," said Carmela. "Or maybe the killer didn't have to walk far to duck out of sight and change."

Everyone was silent for a minute, and then Charlie said, "All right if we load him up now, Chief?"

"Yes," said Babcock. "But please don't call me Chief."

Charlie snapped off a blue latex glove and grinned up at him. "Isn't that where you're headed? The chief's office?"

This was news to Carmela. "Are you?" she blurted.

"Hardly," said Babcock. But he seemed embarrassed.

One of Charlie's team spread a black plastic body bag on the floor, then the three of them muscled Joubert's body into it and zipped it up. The bag was then rolled onto the gurney and the gurney was raised to waist height.

There was another collective moment of silence and then Officer Lambert glanced toward the front door and said, "Uh-oh."

"What now?" said Babcock.

But Carmela knew exactly what was going on. Mavis Sweet had just arrived at the front door and was struggling to push her way in. There was an exchange of heated words and then a high keening sound, like the screech of a dying hyena. And then Mavis cried, "Let me in! Let me in!" She seemed to be locked in a physical confrontation with Officer Wallace, who was pushing and grunting and trying to block her entrance to the shop.

"I'm sorry, ma'am," Wallace continued as he lowered a shoulder and tried an unsuccessful body block. "This is a crime scene. No one's allowed to pass."

"But I *work* here!" cried Mavis.

Carmela peered toward the front of the store. "That's Mavis Sweet," she told Babcock. "Marcus Joubert's assistant."

He cocked an eye at her. "Let me take a wild guess. You called her with a heads-up?"

Carmela nodded. "I thought Mavis had a right to know. And she's not just the assistant. I'm pretty sure she and Joubert were . . . romantically involved."

"Let her in," Babcock called to the officer at the front door. "It's okay."

"Although this whole scene is really *not* okay," Carmela mumbled.

"Oh my gosh, who's gonna tell that poor girl what happened?" Ava asked in a loud whisper. "Who's gonna break the bad news to her?"

Everyone in the room fell silent as they looked toward Babcock.

"I will," said Babcock, stepping past them to head off Mavis. "I suppose it's up to me."

But Mavis had already caught sight of the black plastic body bag lying atop the metal gurney. She flew through the shop, her frizzy brown hair flying out behind her, her face red, and her slightly plump form jiggling like crazy.

"Oh no!" Mavis cried. "Please no! Don't tell me . . ."

"I'm very sorry," Babcock said in a respectful tone of voice. "There appears to have been a break-in and possible robbery. In the ensuing struggle Mr. Joubert was stabbed." He said it straight out, with no wasted words.

Mavis was utterly stunned. "Stabbed, you say? Stabbed to death?" Words failed her for a few moments, and then she said, "You're saying he's . . . dead?" Her voice rose in a plaintive squeak.

"I'm afraid so," said Babcock.

"I need to see him," said Mavis, elbowing and fighting to push past everyone. "Please!"

This time Carmela, Babcock, Ava, and the entire crime-scene team tried to block her path.

"I wouldn't recommend it," said Babcock, trying to grab Mavis's arm and halt her progress. "Unfortunately Mr. Joubert sustained several rather severe injuries. Um, disfiguring injuries."

But Mavis remained firm. "No. I have to see him." Her eyes blazed and had grown to the size of saucers as she glanced from one person to another. Mavis seemed so freaked out that Carmela wasn't even sure if the woman recognized her.

"Maybe just a little peek?" said Ava.

Babcock looked unhappy.

Carmela, sensing a kind of standoff, put an arm around Mavis's shoulders and led her slowly toward the gurney. "Could you . . . ?" she said to Charlie. She motioned with her right hand. "Unzip it just . . . ?"

Charlie slid the zipper down six inches, allowing a partial view of Joubert's face.

Mavis's mouth opened and closed like a dying fish and tears streamed down her face. "Oh no, it's really him."

Charlie zipped the bag back up as Mavis fumbled in her pocket for a hanky.

"We need to ask you some questions," said Babcock.

"Really," said Carmela, who was still trying to comfort Mavis. "Can't they wait until tomorrow?"

"I suppose," said Babcock.

Mavis sniffled loudly and gazed at Carmela. "Carmela," she said.

"Yes," said Carmela.

"Who would do this?" Mavis cried. "You know that Marcus was . . . *everything* to me."

"I know that," said Carmela, trying to console her.

"He was kind and sweet and gentle," Mavis went on. "Such a dear, dear man!"

Ava, who was never comfortable with tears, said, "Well, he wasn't exactly Mr. Warmth." She thought for a minute. "Or even Mr. Personality."

"Miss Sweet," said Babcock. "Were you working here today?"

Mavis shook her head sadly. "No, Friday's my day off. Maybe if I had been here . . ." More tears leaked out. "This wouldn't . . ."

"We're going to need to know about next of kin," said Babcock.

"There really isn't anyone," Mavis sobbed. "Well, maybe a sister."

Babcock gave a nod to the crime-scene team and they slowly rolled the gurney through the store and out the front door. Carmela saw this tragic scene drawing to a close and felt terrible for Mavis. The woman lived by herself and she sensed that her job at Oddities, her relationship with Marcus Joubert, had been the only good things she had going on in her life.

As Babcock's keen eyes searched the shop, something seemed to register with him. He cleared his throat, then said, "This somewhat strange collection of, ah, merchandise . . . these items resurrected from the past, they might possibly attract a certain unsavory type of character."

"Strange things indeed," agreed Ava, glancing at the same stuffed monkey that had almost frightened Carmela to death.

But Mavis was suddenly defensive. "Some of these items are priceless. One of a kind! Marcus had all sorts of customers who thought the world of him and relied on his ability to seek out unique and unusual objects of art."

"Hence the chance that this started out as a robbery," said Babcock, trying to placate her. "Perhaps, since you are here, you could take a look around and see if anything is missing?"

"How could you even tell if something's missing?" Ava murmured. "This shop is like a cross between my Aunt Effie's attic and an episode of *Hoarders.*"

"Still," said Babcock, pointedly ignoring Ava's comment, "it would be a tremendous help if Miss Sweet was able to take a cursory look around right now. I wonder . . ." He focused his attention solely on Mavis. "Is there some sort of inventory list that you could consult? Maybe a stock status program on your computer?"

"Yes, we have that, but it was never completely up to date," said Mavis, sniffling loudly and wiping at her nose again. "Marcus was forever selling a piece here or there and then forgetting to delete it from our inventory list. It was the same thing when he purchased new items for the shop. Sometimes I'd notice something brand-new sitting on a shelf and not even know where it came from."

"What's the most valuable item in here?" Carmela asked suddenly. "If this was a robbery, and it certainly feels like it must have been, what would a thief be most likely to grab?"

Mavis suddenly looked really frightened. "Oh." She put a hand to her mouth and drew in a deep breath. "Oh no. It *couldn't* be . . . !"

"What couldn't be?" asked Babcock.

"The . . . the mask," Mavis stammered.

"You mean like a Mardi Gras mask?" said Ava.

Mavis gave a vigorous shake of her head. "No, it was . . ." She suddenly crossed the shop in three quick strides and placed her hands on a small tea-stained Tibetan cabinet. She paused. "You have no idea."

"No, we really don't," said Babcock. "Perhaps you could enlighten us?" Balanced on the balls of his feet, trying hard to follow the gist of Mavis's words, he seemed a little tense.

"Are you talking about some kind of tribal mask?" said Carmela. She knew Joubert often displayed carved African masks as well as Central and South American masks in his shop. She remembered a mask from Oaxaca in particular that had been carved from a cactus plant and threaded with honest-to-goodness horsehair.

But Mavis was suddenly in a tizzy. "It couldn't be . . ." she babbled. "Please tell me it's not . . ." She suddenly flung open the doors of the Tibetan cabinet and stared inside. Curious now, they all crowded around her and stared in, too.

The cabinet was completely empty. Just three empty shelves and a curious scent. Like a cross between cinnamon and eucalyptus.

"This can't be happening!" Mavis shrieked. She reeled backward and spun around, almost crashing into a tall, glass pyramid-shaped case filled with antique jewelry.

"Just calm down," said Babcock.

"Take a deep breath," Carmela urged. "Try to pull yourself together and tell us exactly what's missing." She helped Mavis limp over to a vintage horsehair chair and sit down heavily. "Really, it can't be that bad."

"Really, it can," Mavis moaned. She was bent forward now, her head in her hands, trying to pull herself together, struggling to get her words out.

Carmela knelt down beside her. "This mask that's gone missing," she pressed, "just what kind of mask was it?"

Mavis let her hands fall away from her face. Then she

lifted her head and gazed sorrowfully at Carmela. Her eye makeup had melted and run together and now she looked like a sad raccoon. "It was a piece that had been handed down through three centuries. It was priceless."

"You mean like a fancy *carnevale* mask from Venice?" said Ava.

"No," Mavis sobbed. "It was . . . Napoleon's death mask!"

Chapter 4

TIME seemed to stand still for Carmela. She felt like she'd suddenly been teleported to some weird art history mystery from the eighteenth century. Or back to the dark days of World War II, when all the art galleries, museums, and private collections of Europe had been outrageously plundered. "Wait a minute," she said to Mavis. "Could you repeat that please? Did you really say *death* mask?"

"Napoleon's death mask?" said Babcock. He straightened up and frowned. Rubbed the back of his hand against his cheek. "I've never heard of such a thing." He turned and gazed at Carmela. "*Is* there such a thing?"

Carmela shrugged. "I suppose. Or at least there was, once upon a time."

"No," Mavis said with firmness in her voice. "It's an acknowledged fact. There are four known Napoleon death masks in existence."

"Seriously?" said Ava. Then, "Come on, this is a joke, right?"

Mavis threw up her hands and stomped her foot like a petulant child. "No joke! At the time of Napoleon's death it was customary to cast a death mask of all great leaders. Special artisans would press a mold of wax against the dead man's face and then make copies cast in bronze."

"Where on earth would Joubert get such a mask?" Babcock asked. "I mean, it's not exactly your ordinary run-of-the-mill object."

"I don't know!" Mavis wailed.

"But you work here," said Babcock. "So you must know something about it."

"But I don't," said Mavis. "I only know that Marcus purchased it very recently and kept it in that small Tibetan cabinet under lock and key."

"So this isn't just a murder," Carmela said. "It's also a robbery."

"Homicide plus robbery," Babcock corrected as he ushered the ladies toward the front door. "Now . . . everybody needs to clear out. I have to get to work."

"I bet we could help," said Ava. She was clearly intrigued by the story about the death mask.

Babcock flashed her a stern look. "The only way you can help is by leaving me in peace."

Carmela raise her hand to her ear with her pinky and thumb extended in the universally recognized gesture for *Call me.*

Babcock gave Carmela a tight nod and then focused his attention on Mavis. "Miss Sweet, it's likely I'll be in touch with a few follow-up questions."

Mavis sniffled and managed to squeak out an, "All right."

Babcock closed the door to Oddities behind them and Officer Wallace hastily fastened a string of yellow crime-scene tape across the doorway.

Out on the sidewalk, Mavis pressed her fist to her mouth

and stifled a sob. All around them, darkness had settled upon the French Quarter like a cashmere blanket. Lights twinkled from old-fashioned brass lamps, palms swayed in the cool October breeze, tourists brushed past, talking excitedly and carrying geaux cups filled with daiquiris and hurricanes.

Carmela put her arm around Mavis's shoulders and walked her a few feet away from the store as Ava trailed behind them.

Mavis gulped, as if she was trying to form a sentence, then she reached down and grabbed Carmela's wrist tightly. "Please help me," she pleaded.

"Really," said Carmela. "There's not much I can do at this point. Or should do, now that you've got one of New Orleans's best detectives working the case."

Mavis aimed a plaintive gaze at Carmela. "I hope you know that Marcus thought the world of you."

This surprised Carmela. "He did?" She figured Joubert tolerated her only because they were neighboring shopkeepers.

"Absolutely he did," said Mavis. "Marcus was always telling me how smart you were. Not just about business strategies and coming up with smart marketing ideas, but that you were able to figure things out. Things like . . . mysteries and murders." Mavis delivered this last line with a pitiful, hopeful look on her face. "Like the one you figured out a couple of months ago . . . that fat-cat businessman who got killed in his Garden District home?"

Carmela and Ava exchanged quick glances. Ava raised a single brow, a dubious expression on her face.

Sensing their skepticism and hesitation, Mavis said, "This was kind of a secret, but did you know that Marcus and I were engaged to be married?"

"Seriously?" said Ava. She sounded just this side of disbelieving.

"Yes," said Mavis with a pained expression. "The minute Marcus and I locked eyes it was love at first sight."

"Okay, whatever," said Ava. Behind Mavis's back she made a face that clearly conveyed her distaste.

But Mavis seemed to sense the need to prove their love, because she suddenly shoved a pudgy hand right under Carmela's nose. "See?" she said, flashing a gold ring decorated with interlocked skulls and a Sanskrit inscription. "We hadn't announced our engagement yet." She paused to catch her breath, then her voice quavered as she added, "But we were going to be *married*."

Carmela rubbed Mavis's back as the girl broke down and sobbed. "There, there," she said, as her heart slowly warmed to Mavis. Carmela was a believer in love, a champion of love. After all, didn't everyone deserve to be happy? Of course they did.

"Could you *please* help me?" Mavis asked. "Help figure out who committed this terrible crime against my poor dear Marcus?"

"I think Detective Babcock is quite capable of doing that," said Carmela. "But I could probably do a little checking as well. Ask a few discreet questions."

"You would? You will? How can I *ever* thank you?" said Mavis. She seemed genuinely overcome with emotion.

"You don't have to," said Carmela. "But right now I want you to go home and take care of yourself."

"Fix yourself a good stiff drink," Ava suggested. "Or watch some trash TV."

"Just try to relax," said Carmela. "I know you're in terrible pain right now, but I promise you, your fiancé's killer will be found and brought to justice." She nodded, almost to herself, and added quietly, "Somehow he will. I'll see to it."

"Thank you," Mavis breathed.

"HO HO," SAID AVA, AS MAVIS SLOWLY SLUMPED away. "What's this?" A white van with a gray satellite dish on its roof was inching its way down Governor Nicholls Street.

"Holy crap," said Carmela. "It's KBEZ-TV. Good thing Mavis took off when she did. They'd probably have tried to interview her."

The passenger door was suddenly flung open and Zoe Carmichael, a young reporter for KBEZ-TV, popped out. Zoe was petite and cute as a button, with a pale complexion and a heap of reddish-blond hair. As she recognized Carmela and Ava, she let loose an enthusiastic wave and called out, "Hey there, ladies!"

Before Carmela could reply, Zoe's eagle eyes landed on the yellow crime-scene tape that was strung across the doorway of Oddities.

"What's going on?" Zoe asked, motioning for the driver to hop out of the van and join them.

Raleigh, the driver, was also Raleigh the cameraman, a middle-aged man dressed in khakis and a T-shirt. He pulled his camera out of the back, hoisted it onto his shoulder, and lumbered over to join them. He already had a battery pack strapped around his waist and was plugging in wires like crazy.

Ava frowned at Raleigh. "You okay there, big guy?"

Raleigh seemed to have a perpetual hunch from hauling camera gear around, and watching him negotiate a back-bend was like watching Quasimodo perform in Cirque du Soleil.

Raleigh angled the camera lens toward them and smiled. "Just a little stiffness, comes with the territory. We've been out cruising the French Quarter, looking for a story."

"I think we just found one," said Zoe. "What's with the crime-scene tape? What have we got? Robbery? Assault?"

Zoe seemed so anxious that Carmela was surprised she hadn't shoved a microphone in her face yet.

"Worse," said Ava.

Zoe looked suddenly eager. So did Raleigh.

"Murder," Ava said, drawing out the word in a breathy voice.

"I'm gonna need some details," Zoe burbled happily.

So Carmela and Ava brought Zoe and Raleigh up to speed on the gruesome murder of Marcus Joubert. The news team listened intently, nodding and frowning and gasping in all the appropriate places.

"Too bad we didn't get here sooner!" said Zoe. "To film the cops speeding to the scene and maybe talk to . . . what was her name again?"

"Mavis," said Ava. "Mavis Sweet."

Zoe turned to Raleigh. "We gotta talk to her."

"Of course," said Raleigh.

"And the body's still inside?" asked Zoe.

"Well . . . yes," said Carmela. Maybe she'd spilled the beans a little too much?

"This is a great story," Zoe chortled. "We'll hang out and catch the crime-scene guys wheeling the body out."

"Nothing like your dead-body shot," said Ava. "Film at eleven."

"This shop," said Zoe, gesturing toward Oddities, "also has a nice creep factor going."

Raleigh nodded. "Timing's good, too, since Halloween's only a week away."

"I can see this being almost episodic!" said Zoe. "We could do updates as the story unfolds."

"If it unfolds," said Carmela.

"Or unravels," added Ava.

"DOES MURDER MAKE YOU HUNGRY?" CARMELA asked Ava as they made their way across the courtyard that separated Carmela's garden apartment from Ava's small studio apartment above her Juju Voodoo shop. Water pattered in the fountain, a live oak tree swayed in the breeze, pots of pink bougainvilleas overflowed their terra-cotta containers.

"I'm not just hungry," said Ava. "I'm ravenous."

"Then come on in," said Carmela as she slipped her key into the lock.

No sooner had she cracked open her door than Boo and Poobah, her two dogs, flung themselves at her feet. Then Ava came inside, too, and the pandemonium increased.

Carmela grabbed Boo, her fawn-colored Shar-Pei, and stroked her triangle ears. "Did you miss me, Boo Boo?"

Boo's back end wiggled so enthusiastically it looked like she was dancing the cha-cha.

"And this little mongrel," said Ava, planting kisses on the top of Poobah's head. "If I didn't have my kitty, Isis, I'd probably dognap this sweetheart." Then she giggled and said, "Ooh, that tickles!" Poobah had discovered Ava's open-toed boots and was studiously licking her toes.

"First things first," said Carmela. She stepped over to her small galley kitchen and pulled open one of the cupboards. "We need a cocktail, right?" She surveyed her small collection of liquor bottles. "To take the edge off?"

Ava extricated herself from the muddle of swirling dogs and flopped down on the leather chaise. *Kersplat.* "Absolutely, I need a drink. I'm so edgy I could claw the wallpaper off your walls."

Carmela grabbed vodka, lemon juice, and sugar, added crushed ice, and mixed up two lemon drop cocktails in a silver shaker. Then she poured them into martini glasses. She took a quick sip, and pulled a casserole dish from the refrigerator.

"I have leftover chicken corn casserole, if anybody's interested," she called out.

"I'm interested," said Ava.

Carmela popped the dish into the oven, set the timer for thirty minutes, and carried the cocktails into her adjacent living room. Posh and elegant from dozens of forays through the scratch-and-dent rooms of Royal Street's finest antique shops, the place was furnished with a brocade fainting couch, marble coffee table, and the squishy leather sofa and matching ottoman that Ava now occupied. An ornate gilded mirror hung on one wall, lengths of handmade wrought iron that had once graced an antebellum mansion hung on the opposite redbrick wall. The wrought iron served as a perfect shelf for Carmela's collection of bronze dog statues and antique children's books.

Ava accepted her drink with a smile, tasted it, and said, "Ahhh. Doesn't that just tickle the old thirsty spot." She'd kicked off her shoes and Poobah had climbed up next to her and snuggled in tight. He seemed to be staring thoughtfully at Ava's feet.

"Poobah," Carmela said with a warning tone. Poobah sheepishly slipped off the leather sofa. The sofa was supposed to be off-limits.

Ava took another sip of her lemon drop and made a satisfied, puckered expression. "Tonight was awful, wasn't it?"

Carmela sighed heavily. "We sure don't need a murder right next door."

"Kind of rocks your world," Ava murmured.

"I know whose world it's really going to rock," said Carmela, reaching for her cell phone.

"Hmm?"

"Gabby."

"Oh," said Ava. "Yeah, I suppose. She is kind of your genteel type. Unlike us wild and crazy gals."

"I have to call her and let her know what happened. She can get awfully skittish about this stuff."

Gabby Mercer-Morris, Carmela's very capable assistant, answered on the first ring. "Hello?"

"Gabby," said Carmela. "I'm afraid I've got some, um, rather unsettling news."

"What happened now?" said Gabby.

Carmela almost smiled. Gabby, her conservative, preppy, twinset-wearing assistant, was used to seeing her pulled into crazy situations. And Carmela had definitely enjoyed her fair share, including a murder in a cathedral, a wild chase with the Honey Swamp monster, a foray into a haunted asylum . . . Oh well, the list did go on.

"Carmela," said Gabby, sounding concerned. "Tell me what happened."

And so, with more than a little hesitation, Carmela brought Gabby up to speed on Marcus Joubert's murder. She didn't mention him falling out of the cupboard at her—that would have been way too creepy. But she did tell her about the stolen mask and how upset poor Mavis Sweet had been.

"This is all so awful!" Gabby said, sounding frightened and a little breathless.

"The thing is," said Carmela, "I wanted you to hear about it from me first, and not some sensationalized report on TV."

"Even though it is sensational," said Ava.

But Gabby was clearly upset. "I can't believe Joubert was murdered. Mind you, I wasn't exactly his number one fan, but still . . ."

"I know," said Carmela. She thought about poor Marcus Joubert with his large pointed teeth, long jaw, and bushy gray eyebrows. He'd always given Gabby the willies, but now his memory would forever be embellished with the image of a blood-soaked body.

"Is Babcock . . . ?" Gabby began.

"Yes, he is," said Carmela.

"So there'll be an investigation going on next door," said Gabby. She paused for a moment, and then asked, "Were you thinking of closing the shop tomorrow?" She sounded a little hopeful, as if she didn't relish working so close to the scene of a grisly murder.

"We can't close," said Carmela. "We have a class scheduled. Plus, with Halloween right around the corner, customers will be flooding in for all sorts of craft supplies."

Gabby made a small noise into the phone, a cross between a sigh and a moan.

"Don't worry," said Carmela. "I know you're spooked, but this is New Orleans. Being spooked is normal."

AS SOON AS CARMELA HUNG UP THE PHONE, AVA pounced on her. "Please tell me you still plan to help out at Juju Voodoo this Sunday."

Carmela took a quick sip of her cocktail. Ava had already drunk hers down. Carmela decided she'd better get cracking. "Of course I will. I know this is your busy time."

Ava laughed. "Busy? We'll probably be slammed. This is basically my version of Christmas, when tons of tourists flock into town, eager to see the Halloween parades . . ."

The oven timer dinged and Carmela sprang to her feet. "And tramp through our aboveground cemeteries."

"And maybe get a peek at a real live vampire," Ava laughed.

Carmela chuckled as she made her way into the kitchen. "Or at least a peek at a real live vampire-story writer's house!"

Ava set her glass down. "Dang, that food smells good."

"Then meet me in the dining room," Carmela said as she slipped on a pair of oven mitts. "And bring those yellow place mats and that set of . . ." Her cell phone suddenly hummed inside her pocket. Carmela shucked off the mitts and looked at the display.

Babcock.

"Hey there, handsome" said Carmela, surprised to hear from him so soon. "Did you catch the killer already?"

"No," said Babcock. "But it turns out there's a small wrinkle to this crazy story."

"Really?"

"Actually, not so small."

"Tell me," said Carmela.

"What?" asked Ava. She strolled into the kitchen to stand next to Carmela. The better to listen in.

But Carmela held up a hand so she could listen to what Babcock was saying. "Go on."

"The death mask?" said Babcock. "The one that was stolen just a few hours ago from Joubert's shop?"

"Yes?"

"According to the National Art Fraud Registry, it appears to be the exact same death mask that was stolen from a private collector in Dallas just three weeks ago!"

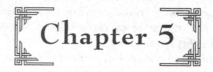

Chapter 5

"So here's the thing," Carmela said to Gabby. "Babcock found out that the death mask was actually stolen three weeks ago from the collection of a man by the name of Wallace Pitney who lives in Dallas."

"No," said Gabby. "Seriously?"

Carmela nodded. "I can't make this stuff up." She paused. "Well, I could, but then I'd probably be accused of writing a somewhat formulaic episode of *Castle*."

"That's totally bizarre," said Gabby, gazing at her with limpid brown eyes. "That means . . . well, doesn't it imply that Joubert stole the mask from this Pitney guy?"

"Bingo," said Carmela, jabbing an index finger in Gabby's direction. "You have just successfully connected the dots."

It was Saturday morning at Memory Mine and Carmela and Gabby were gearing up for what they figured would be a super busy Halloween week. Customers would be dropping in to frantically grab skeleton stencils, witch stamps, and ghost chalk. By next Tuesday they'd be completely out of orange cardstock. By Thursday they'd have spun their last spool of black cat ribbon. On Friday, which was Halloween, the store would be closed and they'd be partying their little hearts out.

Gabby shrugged and tucked a strand of her blond-brown hair behind her ear. "I suppose I can picture Joubert stealing the mask. Is that an awful, uncharitable thing to say?"

Carmela laughed. "It's terrible, just terrible."

Gabby smiled. "Now you sound like Stuart."

Stuart Mercer-Morris was Gabby's husband and the acknowledged Toyota King of New Orleans. He owned six dealerships, was negotiating for a seventh, and was trying for the land speed record on fleet leasing.

"What I meant to say," said Gabby, "is that even though I was never crazy about Joubert, never really felt comfortable around him, I still feel bad. In fact, I had nightmares last night just thinking about somebody sneaking in next door and stabbing him to death!" She adjusted the neckline of her cobalt blue cashmere sweater and folded her arms across her chest, as if she were protecting her heart.

Carmela sighed. She'd slept like a rock. Maybe that meant she was a horrible, uncaring person.

Either that or I drank one too many lemon drops.

"I still can't believe a gruesome murder happened this close to our cozy little store," said Gabby. "I always think of this as our private oasis. Nothing bad ever happens here."

"Except for a few questionable scrapbook page designs," said Carmela. She looked around at the inside of her shop and was overcome with a feeling of warmth. Deeper than it was wide, Memory Mine featured high ceilings, wood-planked floors, and arched front windows. It was no wonder that Gabby felt at home here—their scrapbook shop pretty much oozed Old World charm.

And then there was the crafty angle. The front counter was crowded with racks filled with buttons, brads, charms, beads, and other embellishments. Wire shelves that held almost a thousand varieties of paper were stacked floor to ceiling. Plus there were shelves filled with albums, rubber stamps, foils, and inks of all kinds. At the back of the store was an old wooden table that they'd dubbed Craft Central, where customers could sit and dip into the communal stencils, punches, paper cutters, and calligraphy pens to their hearts' content.

"You want me to brew a pot of chicory coffee?" Gabby asked, breaking into Carmela's reverie.

"Sure."

"Or we've got that chamomile and rose hips tea you ordered from the Indigo Tea Shop in Charleston."

"That might be better," said Carmela. Tea was always calming, right? It made you slow down, sip appreciatively, and breathe.

"You need any help pulling things together for this afternoon's class?"

"Maybe," said Carmela. "Probably." This afternoon she was teaching a class called Gossamer Threads and showing her crafters how to use simple pieces of cheesecloth to create Halloween crafts as well as a few other fun items.

"Okay," said Gabby. "Then I'll . . ."

The front door suddenly flew open with a loud thwack and the bell above it *da-dinged* as if struck by lightning. Then an exotic-looking woman with a swirl of long blond hair and a fox fur cape flew into the shop.

"May I help you?" Gabby asked in her most pleasant tone.

"I certainly hope so," said the woman. "I'm moving into the premises next door and I'm in a complete tizzy!" Her expansive gestures were accompanied by the clanking of heavy, chunky jewelry.

What? Carmela took a step forward. "Excuse me, did I

hear you correctly? You said you're moving in next door?"
How could that be? she wondered. Joubert hadn't even been
dead for twenty-four hours and his shop was still filled with
collectibles. What was going on?

The woman gave a perfunctory smile. "That's right, I'm
moving in. So I suppose that makes me your new neighbor?"
Her oval face was classically pretty, but seemed a little tight.
Carmela suspected the woman might have overindulged
with Botox or fillers.

"How it that even possible?" Carmela asked. "When Mr.
Joubert's shop is still occupying that space?"

When he just died last night.

The woman smiled again, but this time her friendly
factor dropped a few degrees. "Oh, but I haven't introduced
myself yet, have I? How terribly rude of me." She extended
a hand to Carmela. "I'm Countess Vanessa Saint-Marche."

"Nice to meet you," Carmela said, shaking her hand.

Was this woman for real?

But Gabby seemed to take her at face value. "Excuse me,
you're . . . you're an actual countess?"

The woman looked sublimely pleased at Gabby's reaction. "Yes, absolutely I am. But please don't let the title put
you off, dear." She waved a hand laden with sparkling rings.
"It really is a silly little thing. I simply married into it."

"How fortunate for you," said Carmela. She still wasn't
taking this woman seriously. Could she be a new French
Quarter crazy? A well-heeled bag lady?

But the so-called countess seemed to think a more detailed explanation was in order. "My dear husband, François
Saint-Marche, is the last in line of the Saint-Marches that
hail from Angoulême, France. Although the family lost
most of their money and property during the war, don't you
know? When hordes of those ruffian . . ." She threw up an
arm, then paused dramatically. "But that's all in the past.
Luckily, the title still remains intact." She threw a mirthless

smile at Carmela. "Look it up if you don't believe me. We're listed in Burke's Peerage."

"I believe you," said Gabby. She was impressed and seemed ready to curtsy or bow.

Carmela decided it was simply time to cut to the chase. "Do you know what just happened next door?"

The countess bobbed her head eagerly. "Murder."

"Just last night," said Gabby.

"So how is it you're already moving into that shop?" Carmela asked.

"Oh," the countess said in a pitch that was a little too shrill for Carmela's liking. "I've been in contact with the landlord for quite some time."

Carmela frowned. "Really?"

"Oh yes. I plan to open a shop filled with extremely high-end jewelry." The countess wiggled her fingers at Carmela as if to emphasize her point. "We'll feature all the new, important designers as well as beautiful estate pieces. Cushion cut diamonds, old mine sapphires, that type of thing."

"That sounds lovely," said Gabby. "I think some of the older gems and settings really are the best."

"I'm going to call my shop Lucrezia," continued the countess. "You know, after Lucrezia Borgia."

"The poisoner," said Carmela.

A sly smile spread across the countess's face. "Aren't you the smart one!" Then she seemed to practically glow as Carmela and Gabby stared at her.

"So what is it you want from us?" Carmela asked.

"Invitations!" said the countess. "I want to open my shop in no more than three weeks' time and I'm going to require some rather elegant invitations for my grand opening soiree. I'm thinking rich, creamy paper embossed with gold ink. And, of course, a logo of sorts." She glanced around. "I was told this was the place to come. I take it one of you is the designer?"

"That would be Carmela," said Gabby.

"Perfect then," said the countess, focusing on Carmela. She opened a leather folder and placed it on the front counter. "Here's what I'm going to need."

"Wait. Hold everything," said Carmela. This was all moving a little too fast for her. "The Oddities merchandise . . . well, it's still in place. And there's an ongoing police investigation."

The countess set her lips tight as Carmela continued.

"And I'm sure there's a lease that extends for at least a few months," said Carmela. "And maybe the estate has to go through probate?"

The countess prickled. "You needn't concern yourself with any of that. It's all being taken care of. Expedited, as they say."

"It is?" said Carmela. "By who?"

"Boyd Bellamy, the landlord," said the countess. "So you can see why I'm anxious to get started."

Carmela was incredulous. First, that the Oddities space had already been leased. Almost before Joubert's body was cold—certainly before he was even in the ground. And second, that this obnoxious woman was standing in her shop being so demanding. Still she tried to contain her temper. "Three weeks, that's an awfully fast turnaround."

"I have some amazing commercial space planners and interior designers," said the countess. "Of course, the first order of business will be to rid the store of all that atrocious merchandise. Have you been inside recently? Do you know what kind of bizarre items they were selling?"

Have I been inside? Carmela thought to herself. *I'm the poor klutz who discovered the body.*

"The shop *was* weird," agreed Gabby. "Tacky, even."

The countess waved a hand as if she possessed a magic wand that could instantly make all of Joubert's strange collectibles disappear in a pouf of smoke and a crackle of lightning. "We're going to clean the place from top to bottom, paint it a glowing cream color, and install elegant, plush carpeting. There'll be pinpoint spotlights in the ceiling, acres of smoked mirrors, and sparkling new display cases. My designers, painters, and carpenters are standing by, ready to rescue and refurbish the entire space."

"And this is all going to happen in three weeks' time?" said Carmela. "I can hardly believe it."

"Believe it," said the countess. "I plan to open the week before Thanksgiving, just in time to capitalize on the big holiday rush. Now, can we *please* talk about my logo?"

CARMELA SPENT THE NEXT TWENTY MINUTES poring over the countess's plans, showing her paper samples, and jotting down her likes and dislikes. It was no surprise that her list of likes was far shorter than her list of dislikes.

When the countess finally exited, after much fanfare and cries of "I'll be back," Carmela turned to Gabby and said, "Well, she's a handful."

"She might be fun to have in the neighborhood," said Gabby. She had just finished ringing up two customers who had, as Carmela predicted, loaded up on black and orange paper and ribbon.

"You think?" Carmela had the countess pegged as a real pill.

"Maybe better than Joubert, anyway," Gabby said, a tad defensively. She reached for a packet of silver brads and studied them carefully.

"I see your point. A shop with high-end jewelry could bring new customers into the neighborhood."

"That's a good way of looking at it," agreed Gabby.

Just as Carmela was studying a piece of unprimed canvas, figuring out how to make a batik-type painting, the door flew open again. This time it was James Stanger, their neighbor down the block and the proprietor of Gilded Pheasant Antiques. He had always struck Carmela as being a trifle brittle—James rather than Jim—with a clipped, rather reserved demeanor. Today, however, he was red-faced and in a tizzy, his blond hair ruffled and his tie completely askew.

"Was that crazy lady just in here?" Stanger demanded.

Gabby raised an eyebrow. "Do you mean the countess?"

"Is she telling you that she intends to lease the Oddities space?" Stanger asked.

"Do you know what happened at Oddities?" asked Carmela, stepping in.

"Yes, of course I do," Stanger snapped. "Joubert was killed last night. Probably during a robbery. Now, please, answer my question."

"About Oddities?" said Carmela.

"And the countess?" said Gabby.

"Yes!" said Stanger. "Is she going to lease it?"

"I think maybe she is," said Carmela.

"Maybe?" said Stanger.

"It seems like she has," said Carmela. *Boy, news sure travels fast around here.*

Stanger exhaled loudly and flapped a hand.

"The countess was pretty insistent," said Gabby. "I mean, she wants us to design announcement cards for her. Apparently she's planning a grand-opening party."

"That lying sack of crap!" exploded Stanger.

"Wait a minute," said Carmela, clearly confused. "Who are you referring to?"

"To Boyd Bellamy," said Stanger. "Our slum landlord. Correction, scum-of-the-earth slum landlord. I don't know if you realize this or not, but he promised that space to me." Stanger's antique shop was located a few doors down from Oddities.

"Were you planning to expand your shop?" said Gabby.

"Of course, I was," said Stanger. "No question about it. I've been waiting for Oddities to go out of business—I never thought they'd last as long as they did."

"Joubert did stick it out for almost two years," Gabby said.

Stanger waved a hand again, as if flicking away an annoying mosquito. "That's nothing in the scheme of things. The Gilded Pheasant has been a landmark on Governor Nicholls Street for more than twelve years. In fact, I'm one of the premier antiquities dealers in New Orleans. Really, ask anyone. They'll tell you I'm *the* top dealer between Miami and Los Angeles."

Carmela put her elbows on the front counter and leaned toward Stanger. "What exactly is the distinction between an antique dealer and an antiquities dealer?"

Stanger's face took on a bored expression, as if he'd answered this question a million times. "Antiques are mostly furniture, paintings, and household goods of at least eighty to a hundred years old. In my shop they're usually French or English, although for clean lines and minimal ornamentation, Biedermeier can't be beat." He held up a finger. "However, antiquities are from any period before the Middle Ages, usually coming from the ancient civilizations of Rome, Greece, Egypt, and China." Stanger continued in his somewhat lecturing tone. "To paraphrase Sir Francis Bacon, 'Antiquities are remnants of history which have escaped the shipwreck of time.'"

"Do you know anything about Napoleon's death mask?" asked Carmela. "That would count as an antiquity, right?"

Stanger stroked his chin. "Ah, you're referring to the death mask that was stolen from Joubert's shop last night."

"That's right," said Carmela. Gossip in the French Quarter really did spread like wildfire.

"A piece like that would be a spectacular find," said Stanger. "Especially if it was authentic."

"It certainly sounds as if it was," said Gabby. "I mean, if the death mask wasn't real, why would someone go to all the trouble of murdering Marcus Joubert and then stealing it?"

"I don't know," said Stanger. "The thing is . . ." His voice trailed off.

"What?" said Carmela.

"The thing is," said Stanger, "I wouldn't put it past Joubert to have stolen the mask himself."

"From that Texas collector," said Carmela.

"Yes," said Stanger. "You realize, Joubert wasn't the most *upstanding* dealer in our Crescent City. He's done his share of shady deals."

"But apparently he had quite a following of customers," said Carmela. She was recalling how Mavis Sweet had ranted on and on last night about all the prominent collectors who had relied on Joubert.

"There's no accounting for taste," snapped Stanger.

"I'm curious," said Carmela. "Would you have a customer for something like that? I mean, a death mask is quite a specialized piece."

"Oh, absolutely I would," said Stanger. "I have a list of customers, *international* collectors, in fact, who would be willing to pay a pretty penny for such a rare piece. No questions asked."

Carmela studied Stanger carefully. She'd always thought of him as sensitive but a bit pedantic. But now his persona was coming through as arrogant and caustic. Her eyes locked onto his and she said, "*Did* you have a customer for it?"

Stanger jerked convulsively as if he'd been poked with a hot wire.

"Why would you ask a question like that?" he demanded.

"Curiosity," said Carmela. She couldn't believe her words had elicited such a violent reaction.

"You know what they say about curiosity," said Stanger. He lurched for the door and jerked it open. "It killed the cat!" he flung at her over his shoulder.

"Wow," said Gabby, surprised at his violent response.

"Meow," said Carmela.

Chapter 6

CARMELA licked a drip of coleslaw off one finger as she took another bite of her po-boy sandwich. Gabby had run down to Pirate's Alley Deli and brought back lunch, a roast beef po-boy for herself, a fried oyster po-boy for Carmela.

"It's criminal how good these sandwiches are," Carmela said. She nibbled judiciously at the ten-inch-long hunk of French bread that threatened to squirt bits of its delicious mixture every time she took a bite.

Gabby laughed and wiped a glob of mayonnaise off the back craft table. "What's criminal is that bottomless pit of a stomach you have. Honestly, fried oysters, tomatoes, mayo, and . . ."

"What's for dessert?" Carmela asked with a wicked smile. When she wanted to, she could devour food with the best of them—Ava, Babcock, her restaurateur friend, Quigg.

Gabby smirked as she set out several spools of gossamer

ribbon for their upcoming class. "Dessert depends entirely on what Baby and Tandy bring with them."

"Hopefully something with chocolate," Carmela said as she hastily cleaned up her sandwich debris.

As if on cue, the doorbell *da-dinged* its high-pitched welcome and Baby and Tandy strolled in.

"Are you ready for us?" Baby Fontaine called out.

Gabby waggled a hand at them. "Come on back."

Baby Fontaine led the way, clutching her decadently expensive floral-print Dolce & Gabbana Miss Sicily Bag that she used as her craft keeper. In the other hand she held a platter covered with silver foil. Her pixie-cut blond hair bobbed up and down as she juggled the platter temptingly.

"Guess what I brought," Baby said as she placed the platter on the table.

Tandy reached forward and ripped off the foil in a grand gesture. *"Laissez les bons temps rouler!"* Which literally translated to "Let the good times roll."

"Wow!" said Gabby, feasting her eyes.

On display was a tantalizing collection of peanut butter and cornflake bars, as well as home-baked sugar cookies. The cookies had been cut into Halloween shapes and decorated as red devils, black cats, owls in pirate costumes, white ghosts, orange pumpkins, and even spiderweb cookies.

Carmela grinned. "They're almost too pretty to eat!"

Tandy Bliss, who was short, red-haired, and skinnier than a skeleton, shrieked, "Almost, but not quite!" And with that she grabbed a witch and chomped off its head. "See? Delicious. And melts in your mouth, too."

Baby set her bag on the table and focused on Carmela. "I saw you on the news last night."

"What?" said Carmela. This was news to her.

"Well, it was just a quick shot of you and Ava as you were walking away from Oddities," said Baby. "But I could tell it was you guys." Baby was fifty-something, with a patrician bearing and a very kind, sweet face. She still went by the moniker of Baby, which had been her sorority nickname way back when.

"Oh that," said Carmela. She made a face. "Yeah. We ran into Zoe and Raleigh from KBEZ-TV. I guess they stole a shot of us after all."

"And then I read in the *Times-Picayune* that you were the one who found poor Mr. Joubert," said Baby. "That must have been terrifying."

"Carmela's not afraid of a dead body," said Tandy, grabbing another cookie. "Are you, honey?"

"I'm more afraid of a person who turns someone *into* a dead body," Carmela admitted.

"So what on earth happened?" said Baby. "Was Napoleon's death mask really stolen?"

"Looks like," said Carmela.

"Do you know how preposterous that sounds in this day and age?" said Baby.

"It was like an art heist," said Tandy, her eyes glowing. "Those kind of things don't happen very often, do they?"

"Apparently they do," said Carmela. "Artwork and antiquities are selling for exorbitant prices these days, so I have to believe that museums, historical societies, and private collectors are constantly under siege." She glanced up and saw Gabby with her mouth set in a grim line.

"Wow," said Tandy. "But tell us about Joubert. So he was already dead when you found him?"

"I'm afraid so," said Carmela. "But maybe we shouldn't talk about this anymore. I'm afraid our dear Gabby is feeling a little spooked."

"I can understand why," said Baby.

There was a small commotion at the front of the shop and four more women pushed their way in.

One woman had a frightened expression on her face and her shoulders were scrunched up practically to her ears.

"Why is there crime-scene tape on the front of the shop next door?" she asked.

Gabby seemed to stiffen.

"That's got nothing to do with us," Carmela said in a soothing tone. "Come on back and make yourselves at home. Then we'll get started."

The ladies all seated themselves around the craft table as Carmela piled rolls of cheesecloth on the table.

"For our first project," said Carmela, "we're going to be making cheesecloth ghosts."

"'Tis the season," said Tandy.

Baby smiled. "Isn't it marvelous how, in New Orleans, Halloween enjoys its own season?"

"It really does," said one of the other women who'd just arrived. "Visitors pour in from all over the place to see our Halloween parades and venture out on cemetery tours."

"There's even one of those so-called haunted houses over on Rampart Street," said the woman who'd been spooked by the crime-scene tape. "My grandkids have been begging me to go."

Pleased that everything now seemed copasetic, Carmela grabbed one of the cheesecloth rolls and said, "This particular cheesecloth is one hundred percent bleached cotton. And, as you're about to find out, it's not just for making cheese or waxing furniture anymore."

Gabby reached in and set a large piece of fluffy, cotton batting on the table.

"First," said Carmela, "we're going to make gossamer ghosts."

"Oooh," said Tandy, getting into the spirit of things.

"Tear off a nice piece of cotton batting and shape it, more or less, into a ghost head," said Carmela.

They all did so, as Gabby snipped off pieces of cheesecloth for each of them.

"Now," said Carmela, "drape your cheesecloth over your

ghost head and arrange it however you want. Then take a snippet of thread and tie it fairly tightly around the neck of your ghost."

Six pairs of hands worked fastidiously away, shaping their ghost heads, ghost bodies, and then tying the thread.

"This is very cool," said one of the women.

"Now some of you might want to leave your ghost just as is," said Carmela. "All nice and flowy." She grabbed a can of spray starch, shook it, and said, with a mischievous grin, "But I always like to give my ghosts a little added dimension."

The women all chuckled.

"Show us," said Tandy.

Carmela spread a newspaper on the table, laid her ghost on top of it, and spread out the ghost's "skirt." "Once I've got my ghost arranged just so, I spritz a little spray starch onto it to give some heft and definition to its body."

"Body," said one of the women. "That's a good one."

"Ectoplasm, then." Carmela smiled. "But it works like a charm." She gave her ghost a couple of good spritzes, moving the spray can up and down and then across. "Then, once you let your ghost dry for a couple of minutes, you have a perfectly presentable member of the spirit world."

The women oohed and aahed as Carmela picked up her ghost and showed them. There was still some fluttering going on, but the ghost did look a lot more formed.

"I adore this," said Baby. "In fact, if it's okay with you, Carmela, I'm going to make a couple more ghosts and use them as decorations for my masquerade party!" Every Halloween, Baby held a huge masquerade ball at her Garden District mansion, complete with fortune-tellers, live music, great décor, and spectacular food. This year was no different, and Carmela, Gabby, Tandy, and Ava had been planning their costumes for months.

"Do you have a special theme this year?" asked Gabby. One year Baby had gone with a skeleton theme, and once she'd gone with actual games, like dunking for apples and pin the tail on the ghoul.

"This year's theme is just over-the-top deliciousness," said Baby. "I'm using those caterers I like so much, Alex & Athena Catering."

"Mmn," said Carmela. "You've used them before."

"I have and they're wonderful," said Baby. "They're this amazingly inventive couple that graduated from the Culinary Institute in Napa Valley. But it's not like they serve sprouts and wheat shooters. They're planning to serve Gulf shrimp in sherry sauce, crawfish and gouda cheese in puff pastry shells, crabmeat Charlene en croustades . . ."

"Stop!" said Carmela. "I just ate lunch and you're making me hungry all over again!"

Baby just chuckled as she applied starch to her cheese-cloth ghost.

"While we let our ghosts dry," said Carmela, "let's move on to making some nice sachets."

"Do we use the same type of cheesecloth?" asked one of the women.

"This will be a much finer cheesecloth," said Carmela, unfurling a bolt of fabric. "There are actually seven different grades of cheesecloth and this is one of the better grades, with a much tighter weave."

So Carmela showed them how to cut the cheesecloth into six-inch squares, fill them with small mounds of potpourri, and then tie them with a piece of pretty ribbon. "It's kind of like a reverse ghost," she said. "And smaller."

"Yum," said Baby, scooping potpourri. "This is a rose petal mixture?"

"And we've got lavender potpourri as well as orange citrus," said Gabby.

"These would work beautifully as gifts," said Baby.

"That's the general idea," said Carmela. "Once you've tied your ribbon, you can add little embellishments like silk flowers or beads or small charms. And remember, cheese-cloth can be dyed, too." She pulled out a square of lavender cheesecloth, added the lavender potpourri, and tied it with a piece of pink silk ribbon. Then she attached a small, brass butterfly charm.

"I want it," said Tandy. "Pleeease?"

Carmela smiled and handed the potpourri to Tandy.

"The other thing you can do with cheesecloth," said Carmela, "is make your own tea bags."

"You're kidding, right?" said one of the women.

"It works perfectly," said Carmela. "Especially since we're using food-grade cheesecloth."

They all stared at her, fascinated.

"What you want to do," said Carmela, "is cut your cheesecloth into a circle. You can freestyle it or use a template." She picked up her scissors and cut a freestyle circle. Then she placed it on the table for all to see, and dipped a spoon into a bag of loose tea. "This tea is chamomile," she said, dropping it into the center of the cheesecloth, "but you can use any type of loose tea that you like. Then you simply tie your homemade tea bag—very tightly, I might add— with a piece of string or thread."

"This has been eye-opening," said Baby. "And lots of fun, too."

"Wait," said Carmela, holding up a finger. "We're not done yet."

"Huh?" said Tandy. She voiced what everyone else was wondering. *What next?*

"Who doesn't love a long, relaxing soak in the tub?" said Carmela. "But for that you need a bath bomb."

"Kaboom," said Tandy. "You just said the magic words. I think I'm going to like this."

"We'll make our bath bombs using eight-inch squares of cheesecloth," said Carmela. She glanced up. "Gabby? You've got the herbs and things?"

"Right here," said Gabby. She set four medium-sized tins in the center of the table.

"Here's the thing," said Carmela. "You want to add a scoop of dried lavender to aid with relaxation, two scoops of oat flakes to soothe your skin, dried parsley for cleansing, and dried chamomile for that extra zap of relaxation."

"I can feel the z's coming on now," joked Tandy.

The room grew quiet then as all the women worked diligently, measuring, filling, and tying, seemingly pleased with the new crafts they'd learned.

Carmela was pleased, too. It was fun coming up with new craft ideas, and she especially loved the teaching part of it—watching the lightbulb come on as her crafters decided to add a silver tassel here, a blue and white Chinese bead there.

Tandy finished her bath bomb, plopped it down in front of her, and said, "Do you think my little ghost is dry yet?"

Gabby reached a hand out and her fingertips brushed the cheesecloth. "He's still a little damp. Give it another few minutes."

Baby passed around her cookies then, and they all chatted and munched and waited for their ghosts to dry.

"Look at this," said one of the ladies. "My ghost is almost dry and now I can kind of manipulate him. Make it look like his skirts are flying out to either side."

"You ghost is a he?" asked one of her friends.

"I think so," she said.

"Wait a minute," said Tandy. "What about faces?"

"I was getting to that," said Carmela. "If you want to give your ghost a little more personality, you simply take a black marker and draw on a pair of eyes and maybe a mouth."

Baby picked up a marker and drew two round ovals for eyes, then she filled them in. "Hmm," she said, studying him. "I'm pretty sure he's trying to moan or howl." She added a flat oval for a mouth.

"Teeth?" asked Tandy.

"No," said Baby. "I don't think so."

"Now it's like a mask," Tandy said in a low voice. "Kind of like that Napoleon death mask that was stolen."

"Well, not quite," said Carmela.

Tandy's brows knit together as she fingered her ghost. "How do they make those death masks, anyway?"

Carmela glanced at Gabby, who looked suddenly concerned.

"Basically, they take a mold of someone's face," said Carmela.

"How on earth would you do that?" asked one of the women.

"It's a fairly simple process," said Carmela. "Today, instead of messing with wax, you'd probably mold plaster bandages dipped in water."

"We should do that," said Tandy. "Have a class on making death masks."

"That sounds a little macabre," said Baby.

"Okay, so we'll call them life masks," said Tandy.

"It sure would be timely," said one of the women. "Because of Halloween, I mean."

"I suppose you're right," said Baby, slowly warming up to the idea. "If we made a few masks, I could use those as decorations for my party. I could even have my guests try to guess who it is. Kind of like pin the tail on the donkey, only creepier."

"Then it's settled," said Tandy. "We need to schedule an impromptu Death Mask class!"

"Can we, Carmela?" asked one of the women. "Will you show us how to make them?"

Carmela looked at her watch. "We don't have any time left today. But maybe next Tuesday?" She glanced at Gabby, who seemed to be busy sorting out packets of charms.

"Next Tuesday it is," said Baby.

Four of the women gathered up their ghosts and tea bags and bath bombs then, and toddled out the front door. They seemed delighted with their crafts and thinking ahead to next Tuesday.

Finally, only Carmela, Gabby, Baby, and Tandy were left in the shop.

"I think," said Tandy, "I'm gonna make one more of those bath bombs. A big super bomb."

"Sure," said Carmela. "And if you want, I can . . ."

The front door suddenly swung open and Mavis Sweet rushed in. Dressed head to toe in black, her outfit was vaguely reminiscent of some of the steampunk attire that Joubert had sold at Oddities—a Victorian corset laced in front and a long black skirt with netting over it.

As Mavis rushed headlong through the shop, sending papers flying, and slid to an ungraceful stop at the back table, the entire room went silent as a tomb.

Chapter 7

MAVIS'S darting eyes searched the table for Carmela. When she finally found her, Mavis's lower lip began to tremble and her eyes filled with tears.

Carmela dropped the bath bomb she was holding and rushed to comfort Mavis. She swept the girl into her arms and said, "What, honey? What's the matter now? What are you even doing in this neighborhood today?" She figured the police were still at Oddities, searching for clues.

Mavis's eyes were getting redder by the second and her eyeliner had begun to smudge. She swayed slightly as she clutched a small, leather notebook to her chest.

"Carmela!" Mavis sobbed. "The police . . . the police aren't investigating Marcus's death anymore!"

"Why would you say that?" said Carmela, although she had a prickly feeling for what might be coming.

"Now they're accusing him of *stealing* the death mask!" cried Mavis. "From some collector in Dallas."

Carmela nodded. "Yes, I did hear something about that."

"But Marcus didn't do that," said Mavis. "He *wouldn't* do that." She looked slightly crazed with makeup dripping and her frizzy hair standing on end. "Because . . . look!" She thrust a notebook forward. "On the exact date the mask disappeared in Dallas, Marcus was right *here*." She turned the book around so everyone could read the small, cramped handwriting. "See? Marcus had an appointment right here in New Orleans with Mr. Duval!"

"Titus Duval?" said Carmela. She knew him. Or knew of him, anyway. Titus Duval was the head of the CBD Orleans Bank, a chain that was a business rival to the Crescent City Bank, owned by her ex-husband Shamus's family. Titus Duval was also a bigwig in the arts community. He'd recently headed the capital fund drive for the New Orleans Art Institute. With his power and money he was not to be trifled with.

"Titus Duval," Mavis repeated. "That's right. So you see, it's perfectly clear that Marcus couldn't have stolen that mask. He couldn't have traveled to Dallas, grabbed the mask, and then made it back here in time for his meeting."

"I see what you're saying," said Carmela.

Maybe the meeting with Duval does clear Joubert?

"Did you show this book to Detective Babcock?" Carmela asked.

"Absolutely I did," said Mavis. "Only I could tell he didn't believe me. He hemmed and hawed and said he'd have to check his facts with Mr. Duval."

"I'm sure he'll do that," Carmela soothed.

"You poor thing," Baby murmured. They were all watching the conversation between Carmela and Mavis and they all looked concerned.

"What I'm wondering, though," said Carmela, "is where the mask—the mask that was stolen last night—actually came from?"

Mavis shook her head vigorously, her masses of hair shaking back and forth. "I don't know."

"Do you think Joubert had a certain customer in mind for it?" Carmela prodded.

Mavis looked pained. "I wish I knew. Oh dear Lord, I wish I knew. Maybe that would help us figure out who murdered my poor Marcus." She grasped Carmela's hand and held it firmly. "Carmela, you'll still help, won't you? You'll help figure out who killed Marcus?"

Carmela's chest felt heavy, as if she couldn't breathe. She could barely stand to see Mavis in such pain. "Of course I will, honey. Shhh." She wrapped her arms around Mavis again. "I promise I'll do whatever I can."

Mavis gazed up at her. "Can you talk to that detective?"

"To Babcock? Yes, I will."

"Can you call him now?" asked Mavis.

"Now?" said Carmela. She glanced over and saw collective pleading looks on Gabby's, Baby's, and Tandy's faces. That did it. "Okay, I'll call him right now."

Carmela ducked into her office and dialed Babcock's private number. He picked up immediately.

"Hello, hot stuff," said Babcock. He'd obviously glanced at his caller ID. And his baritone voice, ringing in Carmela's ears, sent a delicious tingle through her. "Are you calling to remind me about tonight?" he asked.

"There's that," she said. "And one other thing."

Babcock moaned. "Uh-oh."

"I've got Mavis Sweet here in my shop . . ."

"Yes?" His voice hardened slightly.

"Anyway, she has Joubert's calendar with her. Apparently he had a meeting with Titus Duval on the exact same day the death mask in Dallas was stolen . . ."

"Yes, yes," said Babcock. "We're still checking out this so-called alibi." He sounded like he'd uttered those words a million times. Probably had.

"I'm not so sure it's an alibi," said Carmela. She gazed at Mavis and gave what she thought was a hopeful nod. "I think it might be fact."

Babcock snorted loudly.

Carmela took a step back, not wanting Mavis to overhear Babcock's rather negative reaction.

"Here's the thing," said Carmela. "I think . . ."

"You know what? You don't have to concern yourself with this. We're covered. I'm checking it out. In fact I've got an entire team of detectives and uniformed officers who can check this out. So you don't have to."

"Tell me how you really feel," said Carmela, disappointed.

"Hey," said Babcock. "I'll see you tonight. I'm really looking forward to this theatre thing." And with that he hung up.

Carmela put the phone down and smiled at Mavis. "They're working on it," she said, with far more assurance in her voice than she really felt.

Mavis nodded and pressed a chubby hand to her heart. She fluttered her lashes, drew a deep breath, and said, "Thank you, Carmela, you're an absolute lifesaver."

ONCE MAVIS HAD LEFT THE SHOP, THE OTHER three women pounced mightily on Carmela.

"Is Babcock being an ass?" Tandy demanded.

"How's the investigation *really* going?" asked Baby.

"Babcock's working on it," said Carmela.

"Is he doing his best?" put in Gabby.

"I'm sure he is," said Carmela. Her mind was in a whirl and she was trying to figure out an angle or two. Then she looked at Baby and said, "Baby, do you know Titus Duval?"

"Oh sure," said Baby. "He lives right down the street from me."

"In that ginormous house with those two snooty-looking stone lions out front," said Tandy.

"*That's* his house?" said Carmela. "The one with turrets and stained glass windows?" The place wasn't just a landmark, it was a virtual castle.

"That's just one of his homes," said Tandy. "He's got another place up River Road near Destrehan. Supposedly he bought one of the old plantations and is working to restore it to its former grandeur."

"And he has a spiffy new condo in Aspen," said Baby.

"How'd he make so much money, anyhow?" asked Carmela.

"Business," said Tandy.

"Banking," said Baby. "And investing. He was big into technology stocks during the go-go '90s."

Tandy chuckled. "I was big into go-go during the '90s."

"If Duval is your neighbor," Carmela said to Baby, "then I'm guessing he's been invited to your Halloween party?"

"I invite all my neighbors," said Baby. "It's tradition."

"Just like your five city blocks lined with hundreds of carved, illuminated pumpkins," said Tandy.

"Absolutely," said Baby. "It's Halloween and we wouldn't have it any other way."

A FEW MINUTES LATER, SITTING ALONE IN HER office, Carmela put in a call to Ava.

"What's up, sweet cheeks?" said her friend.

"I feel all balled up. Like I stepped on a bunch of flypaper."

"Whoa," said Ava. "Rewind the tape and give me the sordid details, please."

"First I got roped into helping Mavis, and now some crazy countess lady dropped by this morning and wants a logo."

"A countess? For real? Does she have a crown and scepter?"

"I have no idea. She could have gotten her title from a Cracker Jack box. Still, she claims she's taking over the Oddities spot. Like immediately."

"I'm intrigued," said Ava. "Tell me more."

There was a crash and a loud bang and Carmela said, "Ava? What just happened? Are you okay?"

"Oops," said Ava. "A minor emergency with *Señor Muerte*, one of my Day of the Dead characters. Gotta go."

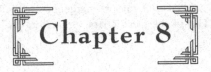

Chapter 8

THE Theatre du Marais was like something out of a novel by Flaubert. It was an impeccably restored Baroque theatre scrunched next to Beaufrain's Oyster House in the French Quarter. Constructed in the late 1800s, probably as a bawdy dance hall, it was left to languish as a movie theatre and then as a slightly unsavory nightclub. Finally, two years ago, the theatre was lovingly purchased, carefully sandblasted, and completely refurbished by the Friends of Preservation for Architecture.

Carmela squeezed Babcock's hand as they hurried down Royal Street, joining any number of other couples who were also headed for the theatre.

Babcock had come directly from work so he wore a camel hair jacket and dark slacks with a pair of John Lobb shoes that looked like heavy cop shoes but were really the same brand favored by British royalty.

Carmela had pulled out all the stops and borrowed a

flirty lace dress from Ava. The low-cut bodice was sleek and tight, the skirt a veritable cascade of ruffles. Every time a breeze came along and gently lifted her skirt, a peep show of breathtakingly hot pink lining was revealed.

"You like my dress?" Carmela asked as they stood in line at the box office, collecting the tickets that had been held for them. Babcock hadn't said anything, but his eyes had roved over her appreciatively.

"Yes, I do, and I particularly like your cape," said Babcock. "You don't see much of that these days—women wearing capes, I mean." He chuckled. "Only if you're into Daphne du Maurier novels."

"It's an opera cape," said Carmela, giving a kind of half twirl. "I thought it would be perfect for tonight."

Babcock tucked the tickets into his jacket pocket and pulled open the heavy gilded theatre door. "Refresh my memory," he said as he ushered her in. "Which comedy or drama are we here to see?"

"It's the Rue Morgue Theatre Company's production of *Frankenstein*."

"Ah, culture at its finest." He grimaced. "Seriously, Carmela? *Frankenstein*?"

"It's Halloween. Live a little."

"Interesting choice of words," said Babcock. "Considering the play is about dead body parts."

"Right up your alley," said Carmela, as she gripped his arm and they headed into the darkened theatre.

They found their seats, sat down, snuggled a little, and looked around.

"How many gallons of gold paint and freight cars of velvet do you think they used to refurbish this place?" asked Babcock.

Carmela had to admit it, Babcock was right on. The walls were gilded, the chairs were upholstered in plum-colored velvet, velvet drapes were slung across all the doorways, and the stage curtain itself was a gigantic waterfall of tufted velvet.

"Sure, it's a little over the top," Carmela agreed. "But it's atmospheric, right?"

"It is if you're Count Dracula," agreed Babcock. He pulled out his phone and started fiddling with it.

"And I think it's fun that some of the audience even came in costume." Sitting around them were other women wearing exotic dresses with capes and cloaks and high-laced boots. There were even a few men sporting Victorian-looking topcoats.

"I just hope they're all going to a Halloween party afterwards," Babcock muttered. "Not just playing dressup."

"Don't be an old poop," Carmela whispered as the lights began to dim. "Everybody's playing dressup this week. And by the way . . ."

"I'm just turning it off," he said.

Carmela smiled. "Good. I thought you might be calling for help."

THE FIRST ACT OF *FRANKENSTEIN* WAS A MASH-UP of moving scenery that included Gothic castles, a charming cottage, a graveyard, and a scary-looking laboratory. Music was heavy, ominous, and theatrical, dipping to barely audible levels, then soaring to a crescendo as stage lightning flashed and cymbals clashed. The character of Victor Frankenstein came across as wild-eyed and driven, while the Creature, played by a shirtless and fairly hunky-looking actor, was surprisingly sympathetic.

"Wow," said Carmela, as the curtain dropped dramatically for intermission. "That was great." She glanced at Babcock, who was scanning his phone again. "Excuse me?"

He gave her an apologetic smile and snapped the Off button. "Sorry. Just playing catch-up." He gripped her hand

and rubbed his thumb across it gently, communicating both his ardor and his apology. "Want to run out to the lobby and beat the rush? Grab a glass of wine or something?"

"You're on," she said as they threaded their way out of the theatre and into the lobby where a small bar had been set up.

"So, you're really enjoying the play?" Babcock asked her.

"That and your hand on my knee."

"Mnn," he said as they pushed up to the bar. "Two glasses of red wine, please," he told the bartender, and then turned with a questioning glance at Carmela. "That okay with you?"

Carmela nodded and went back to studying the amazing lobby décor. The walls had been rubbed with some sort of gilt paint that lent a warm glow, and a crystal chandelier dangled overhead, making the place sparkle like a small jewel box. A number of Baroque mirrors had also been hung, the better to give the impression of an opulent European theatre.

As Carmela gazed into one of those mirrors, her eyes bouncing across a sea of smiling, inquisitive faces—including her own—she realized with a jolt that she recognized the woman who was walking directly toward her. Then she spun around to find the Countess Saint-Marche, dimpling prettily and smiling a big pussycat grin.

"Carmela, darling!" squealed the countess, making a big to-do. "Is that really you?" The countess was wearing a long, black crepe dress with a buckle closure that managed to look both demure and provocative. And expensive-looking, too, Carmela thought. Maybe a piece from one of last year's Chanel collections? The Paris-Édimbourg collection?

"We meet again," said Carmela, just as Babcock handed her a glass of wine. And then, because it was the polite thing to do, Carmela made quick introductions.

"I had no idea your boyfriend would be so handsome," the countess gushed to Carmela. She said it in a way that implied she'd expected Carmela to be hanging on the arm of a troll.

"I take it you're a fan of live theatre?" Babcock asked the countess, if only to be polite.

"Not only do I adore the theatre," said the countess, "but I'm a *huge* supporter. You probably don't know this—well, of course you don't—but my husband and I provided some much-needed funding to this divine little theatre group. And we gave direct financial support for tonight's production as well."

"That's wonderful," Carmela murmured. She knew that a lot of well-meaning theatre patrons had also made donations. Including herself, Baby, and their friend Jekyl Hardy.

The countess tossed her head, the better to make her diamond earrings sparkle, and droned on. "If you look on the back page of your program you'll find our names listed under Platinum Donors."

"Kind of you," Carmela said with fading enthusiasm.

"Oh my," said the countess, fanning her arms wildly, almost clobbering a young artsy-looking man in a red beret. "Here comes my husband now. I can't *wait* for you to meet François."

An elderly gentleman with slicked-back white hair, a hawk nose, and piercing eyes handed a flute of champagne to the countess. Then he smiled absently and said, "Hello."

After the countess made elaborate introductions, the count lifted Carmela's hand to his lips and gave a dry kiss. *"Enchanté,"* he said.

"Nice to meet you, too," said Carmela, being purposefully casual. Who were these people anyway? Next thing she knew they'd be trying to worm their way into New Orleans society or onto one of the Mardi Gras krewes. Well good luck with that.

"What is it you do?" François asked Babcock as he rocked back on his heels, exuding a superior attitude.

"Law enforcement," said Babcock. He said it in a deliberately low-key manner, as if he were just a humble meter reader.

"Wonderful!" François proclaimed.

"And you, sir, are engaged in what line of business?" asked Babcock. He hadn't earned a gold shield for nothing. When his antenna perked up and began to blip red, he started asking questions.

"Ah," said François, looking thoughtful. "I find myself in the peculiar position of following in my wife's rather elegant footsteps. That is, assisting her in getting her jewelry shop up and running."

"You realize," the countess said to her husband, "Carmela is the owner of Memory Mine Scrapbook Shop right next door. She's my brand-new neighbor."

"That's wonderful," declared François. "And I can see that you're good friends already."

Carmela tried not to cringe.

"We certainly are," said the countess, studying Carmela over her glass of champagne.

Not ten feet away from them, a red-suited usher rang the intermission bell. Which sent the countess into a spasm of joy.

"Come along, François," said the countess. "We don't want to miss a single precious moment. Ta-ta." She waggled her fingers at Carmela and Babcock as she propelled François toward the theatre entrance.

"New neighbors," said Carmela. "My life and welcome to it."

"They are a little . . . theatrical," said Babcock.

"That's not the half of it," said Carmela. "The countess, if she really is a countess, is already prodding poor Mavis to pack up the merchandise in Joubert's shop so she can move right in. In fact, she's already hired store planners and decorators."

"It's going to be a jewelry shop?" Babcock was only half interested.

"High-end gems and estate jewelry."

"Don't we already have enough shops like that in New Orleans?" said Babcock.

"Apparently not," said Carmela, as they followed the slow-moving crowd.

Babcock tugged on her arm. "Hang on a minute."

"What?"

They waited at the door leading into the theatre, standing to the side while the audience filtered in.

"Do you really want to see the second act?" asked Babcock.

Carmela's brows lifted slightly. "I take it you don't."

He shrugged.

"And here I got all prettied up," she said, smiling at him but heaving a pro forma sigh of regret.

"Believe me," Babcock said in a low, sensual voice. "It hasn't been wasted. You have a most appreciative audience." And, as the lights dimmed, he leaned forward and kissed her.

A FEW MINUTES LATER, THE TWO OF THEM strolled along Bourbon Street, enjoying the Old World ambience of the French Quarter with a dash of hustle-bustle thrown in. Horses pulling colorful jitneys clip-clopped along on cobblestone streets, sweet notes of music mixed with riotous laughter floated out of darkly lit clubs and saloons.

In anticipation of all the French Quarter's Halloween activities, this party-hearty neighborhood was already decorated to the nines. Life-sized witches bent over cauldrons steaming with dry ice. Orange twinkle lights, like golden fireflies, were wrapped around wrought-iron fences and lampposts. Ghosts suspended from rooftops fluttered in the breeze. Two vampires with malevolent green eyes peered down from a wrought-iron balcony.

"Cheery," observed Babcock.

"You want to stop at Mumbo Gumbo for a drink?" Carmela asked.

"Sure. Or we could pop into Antoine's." Antoine's was much more high-end.

"Don't you need reservations on a Saturday night?"

"It's amazing how the word *detective* can make a maître d' so very accommodating."

"It's always worked on me," said Carmela, snuggling closer.

They stopped outside Perine's Antiques and gazed in the window. There was a coromandel screen that Carmela had long coveted. She thought it would make an elegant statement in her bedroom. That's if she could convince the dogs to let her move their overstuffed, overpriced dog beds to the opposite wall.

"Back there at the theatre," said Babcock, "when you were talking to your friend the countess, you didn't seem very happy about her moving into the space next to you."

"She's weird," said Carmela. "There's something off about her."

"Face it, somebody was bound to move in there sooner or later. She just happened to grab the space sooner. No landlord is going to let primo real estate like that sit vacant for very long. And it was fairly obvious that Joubert's young assistant didn't have the will or the wherewithal to keep that shop going."

"I hear you," said Carmela. "It just strikes me that the countess is a little too eager to move into Joubert's space." She hesitated. "And a little too thrilled about his untimely death."

Babcock grinned. "In other words, you see the countess as a suspect in Joubert's murder."

For some reason Carmela felt defensive. "Well, she *could* be."

"But probably not. The reality of the countess filleting him, fleeing the scene, and then trying to move in less than twenty-four hours later, is highly improbable." He took her hand again and they continued walking down the street.

"I don't know," said Carmela. She had a niggling feeling about the countess and intended to ride that horse until it dropped. "I still think you ought to put that phony countess on your list of suspects."

Babcock stopped and pulled her close. "Listen. I shouldn't be telling you this, but I'm going to anyway because you're so whipped up."

"What are you talking about?"

"I already have a suspect in Joubert's murder."

"What!" Carmela screeched. "Are you serious? Why on earth didn't you say something sooner? You made me sit through the entire first act of *Frankenstein* on pins and needles?" Then, "Who is it?"

Babcock cocked his head, as if considering something, then said, "Come on, better I should show you."

Two blocks away, in a less traveled part of the French Quarter, they stopped in front of Sparks Pawn Shop. Two enormous plate glass windows were brightly lit and surrounded by white chase lights. Stereo equipment, handguns, watches, and jewelry were all jumbled together on tacky red velvet in a semblance of a window display.

"It's a pawn shop," said Carmela, frowning. She'd been by here before and never given it a second look. Or even a first look. "What's the big deal?"

"Actually, it's a big deal because it's one of several pawn shops that are owned and operated by Johnny Sparks."

"Sounds like some kind of circus act. Johnny Sparks and his flaming . . . pants."

"Nothing quite that amusing," said Babcock. "Johnny

Sparks is a scumbag and probably the most notorious fence in New Orleans."

"Maybe I have heard of him. He's been written up in the *Times-Picayune,* I think."

"You probably saw his name in the 'Arrest' column. Unfortunately, NOPD has never been able to hang anything major on him. Not only does Sparks have a killer attorney, but he's insulated. Seriously buffered, as the more notorious crime bosses like to say."

"What makes Johnny Sparks your prime suspect?" Carmela asked. She was intrigued.

"Because, in the past, he's fenced certain choice items for Marcus Joubert."

"Fenced? You mean as in handled actual stolen goods?"

Carmela felt a chill run through her. While her neighbor Joubert had been extremely quirky, his business practices had always seemed fairly aboveboard. Now Babcock was telling her that the man was a thief? She suddenly felt both deceived and naïve. How could she not have known? So did this new information about Joubert mean that he probably had stolen the death mask? Was this an indictment of sorts?

"Wait a minute," Carmela said. "You know for a fact that Joubert and this Sparks guy, were, um, in collusion together?"

"They've done deals in the past," said Babcock. "So we're thinking they might have been in on this little caper as well." He hesitated. "The problem is, Robbery-Homicide Division's tried to set up any number of undercover sting operations over the years, but something has always gone wrong."

"How so?"

"Sparks is always tipped off," said Babcock.

Carmela let this percolate for a few moments. "So you're saying that Sparks has somebody inside the police department? An informant who watches out for him?"

"A skunk in the cellar," said Babcock.

"And this guy Sparks is a seriously bad guy?"

"We know for a fact that he's put several people in the hospital. And there are a couple of others who are unaccounted for."

Carmela's heart thumped a little harder. "You think he murdered them?"

"The possibility certainly exists that a couple of his enemies might have been deep-sixed in a bayou somewhere. On the other hand, lowlifes do have a penchant for skulking out of town."

Carmela looked up at Babcock as a blue light shone down on them. "Do you think this guy Sparks could fence something as important as Napoleon's death mask?"

"Are you serious?" said Babcock. "Given half a chance the man could probably fence the Brooklyn Bridge."

"Wow." Murder, antiquities, and a real-life fencing operation. It felt like a lethal combination. Carmela's mind was cranking with possibilities. Where to start? Who to talk to?

"Carmela?"

"Yes?"

As if he could read the blip in her brain waves, Babcock put a hand on her shoulder and gently spun her toward him. "I know you're particularly interested in this case."

She nodded. "I'm sure you can understand why."

"Yes, except I cannot impress upon you how dangerous it would be to get involved. This is a serious police matter."

"The thing is," said Carmela, trying to make her interest sound a lot more casual and low key than it really was, "Mavis asked for my help."

"Then you have to tell her no," Babcock said forcefully. "And do it very firmly. This is no time for amateur hour."

"Mmn," said Carmela.

"Carmela?"

She looked at him with guileless eyes. "I hear you."

"Good," said Babcock. "But I need you to more than just hear me. I need you to heed my warning." He paused. "Okay, why don't we just drop the subject and go grab ourselves an Abita beer and a tasty bowl of crab soup?"

"Sure." Carmela looked thoughtful as they strolled along together. According to her reckoning, she was already *in* the soup.

Chapter 9

JUJU Voodoo was New Orleans's premier voodoo shop. A mecca for tourists who were in the market for hard-to-find bat blood, saint candles, evil eye charms, love potions, Day of the Dead memorabilia, and, of course, genuine handmade voodoo dolls complete with red stick pins.

The welcoming exterior featured a high-gloss, lipstick red door with the words *Juju Voodoo* spelled out in bubbly black letters. There was also a glowing blue neon sign in the window that was in the shape of an open palm. Over the front door, the roofline dipped and curved, the rough wooden shingles giving the appearance of a thatched Hansel and Gretel cottage.

Inside, the atmosphere was cool and dark, with flickering candles and the scent of sandalwood wafting through the air. The store was jam-packed this Sunday afternoon, filled with folks who were eager to grab a few amusing Halloween items and maybe get a genuine tarot card reading to boot.

Walpurgisnacht, Mendelssohn's spooky, heavy-handed opus to witches and Druids, played softly over the speaker system.

With busloads of tourists roving through town, gaping at cemeteries and haunted hotels, then trooping into Juju Voodoo, Carmela was more than happy to help Ava out. Only problem was, she couldn't quite understand what this one particular customer was asking her in his heavily accented voice.

"Saint candle?" said Carmela, groping for an answer.

"Nix nacht," said the man, waving a hand. He had a long, black beard and was dressed in a long overcoat, the kind Uncle Fester of the Addams Family seemed to favor.

Carmela grabbed a little white voodoo doll with a down-turned expression and danced it in front of him. "How about this little guy? Kind of cute, huh? Make a fun present for the kiddies?"

The man only frowned and shook his head.

Carmela turned toward Ava, who had just rung up a full-sized plastic skeleton for a customer and was trying to figure out how to gift wrap the little darling. "Maybe Madame Blavatsky can do a psychic reading on this guy and tell me what he wants," she muttered under her breath.

Ava, dressed in her best Goth dress, with a tight leather bustier and jeweled cross necklace that probably out-glittered the local bishop, turned her attention to the man. "How can I help you, sir?" she asked.

He let go a rumble that sounded like "Acgh hit min tkt."

"Oh sure, honey," said Ava. "Coming right up. One ticket for our cemetery walk."

"That's" what he wanted?" said Carmela, as Ava accepted his American Express card and swiped it efficiently.

"Sure." Ava handed the man his ticket. "See you Thursday night." She gave a sultry wink. "Now don't be late!"

"Eik ein a meep," the man replied with a broad smile.

"What language was that?" Carmela asked.

"Who cares?" Ava shrugged as she rubbed her thumb

and index finger together. "The language of money. Remember, Halloween's my biggest season, *cher*. It's like back to school, Black Friday, and Christmas all rolled into one."

"And sales have been good?" asked Carmela. "Are good?"

"Honey," said Ava, "sales are through the roof right now and probably will continue to be." She grabbed Carmela's arm and gave a squeeze. "But I sure couldn't do it without you. Thanks for giving up your Sunday afternoon to come in and help."

Ava's two other employees, Miguel and Albert, were also there, scurrying back and forth, crawling up into the rafters to drag down furry bats and more dangling skeletons. It was, Carmela thought, a spectacle you'd see only in New Orleans.

They worked at a frantic pace for another hour or so, shepherding visitors back to Madame Blavatsky's reading room, selling more tickets to the cemetery walk, and giving fun explanations for Ava's various love trinkets and potions. When there was a break in the action, Ava hustled into her office and returned with two steaming mugs of coffee. She handed one to Carmela and leaned forward on her counter.

"So tell me more about this crazy death mask," said Ava.

"Twice stolen," said Carmela. "How weird is that?"

"But that's the gospel according to Babcock," said Ava.

"Right, he believes the mask was originally stolen from the collector in Dallas, and then, two nights ago, stolen again out of Oddities."

"The implication being," said Ava, "that Marcus Joubert stole the mask, and then it was stolen from him."

"Yes," said Carmela. "But Mavis is positive that Joubert was in town the entire·time. That there's no way he could have traveled to Dallas and swiped that mask."

"And you're saying Babcock doesn't believe her?"

"Of course he doesn't," said Carmela. "He's always got that cop instinct working for him. Or maybe against him, in this case."

"Because you believe Mavis."

"I want to," said Carmela. She reached over and straightened a display of ceramic evil eye charms on silver chains. "Mavis is a sweet girl and she swears that Joubert acquired it on his own, probably for a particular collector that he had in mind."

"So who's the collector?"

"That's where it all falls apart. She doesn't know. All Mavis keeps repeating is that the acquisition of the mask was a deep dark secret. Nobody knew that Joubert had it."

"Or where he got it from," said Ava.

"Mavis swears she doesn't know the source," said Carmela. "Though I've asked her to search through Joubert's records to try to find out."

"What if there never was a customer?" said Ava.

"I think there was. I think there pretty much had to be."

"So the plot thickens," said Ava. She dipped a hand into a half-empty box of candy. "Just like my waistline if I keep snacking on these incredibly yummy pralines."

"Not as thick as this coffee," said Carmela, wrinkling her nose. "What is this stuff, anyway?"

"The best part of waking up is Baileys in your cup," said Ava.

"No!" said Carmela. "No, you didn't!"

"Naw. Thought about it. But it's just plain old chicory coffee brewed nice and strong. Mostly to give you an extra kick after what was probably a late, late date last night."

"It's strong anyway."

"What is?" Ava grinned. "The coffee or your date?"

"Both."

"Yup, that's how I brew my cup of joe," said Ava, happily. "The same way I brew up trouble." She paused. "And, girl-friend, I can't believe you didn't stay for the second act last night."

Carmela smiled. "Babcock had food and a few other things on his mind."

"I guess."

They got busy again as more customers found their way in. They sold plastic skulls, strings of ghost-shaped lights, colorful amulets, and decks of tarot cards. Carmela even found herself digging through Ava's collection of books and selling a book titled *Candle Magic* to a self-proclaimed warlock.

Midafternoon, Jekyl Hardy came striding in. An art consultant and antique appraiser by trade, Jekyl was also one of New Orleans's premier Mardi Gras float designers. Whenever you spotted a fire-breathing dragon in the Rex krewe's parade or a purple, eight-tentacled octopus in the Pluvius krewe's parade, you knew it had been dreamed up by the perennially witty mind of Jekyl Hardy.

"Car-*mel*-a!" Jekyl sang out upon seeing her at the cash register.

Carmela looked up and smiled. Her dear friend Jekyl was a dead ringer for Anne Rice's vampire Lestat. With his pale oval face, long dark hair pulled into a tight ponytail, and taste for dressing completely in black, Jekyl not only looked the part, he was a force to be reckoned with. Though he lived in a rehabbed warehouse near the low-key Bywater District, he hobnobbed with the city's elite and often served as a plus-one for wealthy widows at Garden District dinner parties.

Naturally, the first question out of Jekyl's mouth was about the murder at Oddities.

"How'd you find out about that?" asked Ava.

"Are you for real?" said Jekyl. "I take it you two don't watch TV news or haven't seen the front page of today's *Times-Picayune*?"

Carmela and Ava exchanged startled glances.

"Jekyl, what?" Carmela asked, suddenly getting a queasy feeling in the pit of her stomach——as if she'd eaten too many pickled peppers.

"The murder of Marcus Joubert is hot, hot news in

today's paper," crowed Jekyl. "Your name is even mentioned."

"Rats," said Carmela. That wouldn't go over big with Babcock.

"But they probably don't have anything in there about the stolen death mask," said Ava. She jabbed Carmela with an elbow. "They probably don't even know about that."

"Au contraire!" said Jekyl. "They know all about the mask stolen from Joubert's shop and they've linked it to the one stolen three weeks ago from Wallace Pitney's collection in Dallas."

"That's not good," said Carmela. She knew it would sting Mavis that the media had drawn that type of connection.

Jekyl went on. "The newspaper even reported the fact that Pitney and his staff had tried to keep the theft on the down low because they figured they might get a phone call from the thief."

"Why would the thief call them?" asked Ava. "To taunt them and rub their noses in it?"

"Not at all," said Jekyl. "The Dallas collector thought perhaps the thief might call and demand a ransom."

"You mean Pitney would have to pay money to get it back?" Carmela asked.

"Not exactly," said Jekyl. "Most likely their *insurance* company would have been asked to pay. There's a big business in ransoming art and antiquities back to insurance companies."

"I never heard of that," said Ava. "That's a big thing? Insurance ransom?"

"Ransom and just plain old insurance fraud are getting to be popular schemes," said Jekyl. "You know, like boat owners who overinflate the value of their boat, then sink their own tubs just to collect the insurance money."

"You learn something new every day," said Ava.

"I've heard of people doing that with racehorses, too," said Carmela.

Jekyl's hands flew up and he waved them wildly. "Don't even go there," he begged. "It's way too sad."

Ava looked puzzled. "What do they . . . ? Oh."

"We're not going there, remember?" said Carmela.

Jekyl refocused his gaze on Carmela. "So what does the learned Detective Edgar Babcock think about this case?"

"He's of a mind that Joubert might have stolen the mask and then someone stole it from him," said Carmela.

"That sounds so convoluted," said Ava.

"I agree," said Carmela. "That's why I think there's a chance he didn't steal it."

"What are you saying?" said Jekyl. "That Joubert bought the mask at auction? Or from a private individual? And that he was just hanging on to the mask for safekeeping until he could resell it to some rich pigeon?" Jekyl let loose a derisive hoot. "A two-bit dealer like him? Never happen."

"He could have bought it on the up-and-up," said Carmela. "You never know."

"It's more likely that Joubert had coconspirators," said Jekyl. "That he didn't act alone."

"Maybe Joubert's accomplice turned on him and killed him!" said Ava.

"You watch too much TV," said Carmela.

Jekyl lifted an eyebrow. "Okay, how's this for a theory? What if Joubert had help on the inside? That's how art heists are often carried out these days. There's an inside man who has a spare key, or looks the other way, or knows a glitch in the security system."

"I suppose," said Carmela.

"Sure," said Jekyl. "Look at that big heist at the Gardner Museum in Boston, where they stole the Vermeer, a couple of Rembrandts, and a Manet right off the walls. The police still think there was an inside man, someone who gave the thieves the right kind of information."

"What's so special about that mask?" asked Ava.

Jekyl looked startled. "Are you serious? It's a magnificent, historical piece. It's Napoleon's death mask! It was created by skilled artisans just hours after he died. If you look at a depiction or photo of one of those masks, you can see that Napoleon's eyes are closed, his lips are parted, and his head is resting on a tasseled pillow. And that Gallic nose!" Jekyl thumped a hand excitedly against the counter. "All humped and bumped. Such a work of art."

"His nose?" said Ava.

"Yes," said Jekyl.

"What would a mask like that sell for?" Carmela asked.

Jekyl's eyes grew large. "On the open market, at a prestigious auction house like Sotheby's in New York, I think it could easily top one million dollars."

"Are you serious?" said Carmela. "For a death mask?"

"*Napoleon's* death mask," said Jekyl. "An emperor who was one of the greatest military minds in the history of Western civilization. A man who not only conquered Europe, but employed military tactics that were decades ahead of his time."

Carmela took all this in and was trying to process it. "Let's be serious here," she said. "Was Marcus Joubert really stupid enough to steal a mask from a private collector and then try to sell it for a million dollars? I mean, once rumors swirled that the mask was stolen, could he even *find* a willing buyer? I mean, have you seen the man's shop? He had *bug* collections, for gosh sakes. There are flea-bitten monkeys and weird medical devices on his shelves. I just don't see Joubert picking up the phone and talking to a primo crop of high-end customers. Most of his customers in the past have been tourists and a few fringe Goth types."

"Watch it," said Ava as she fingered her Goth-style necklace and skull earrings.

"Perhaps Joubert was desperate for cash," said Jekyl. "Or he had a buyer who tasked him with *finding* a death mask."

"There's another plausible scenario," said Ava. "Maybe his buyer set him up."

"How so?" asked Carmela. She was open to any theory at the moment. Anything that would hold water, that is.

"If Joubert was trying to fill an order," said Ava, "like Jekyl suggests, then maybe once he had the mask in his possession, the *buyer* killed him and stole the mask."

"I'm getting confused," said Jekyl.

"So am I," said Carmela. "I think we need to huddle with Mavis Sweet and pick her brain. See if she's remembered anything. Or else we'll have to come up with a new theory."

"Good idea," said Ava. "Let's call Mavis."

"I have a proposition for you ladies," said Jekyl, abruptly changing the subject.

"What's that?" said Ava.

"How would you two lovelies like to transform yourselves into a pair of ghosts this coming Friday night?"

"Why?" said Ava.

"You mean for Halloween night?" said Carmela. "Jekyl, what is it you're asking us?"

"The thing is," said Jekyl, trying to look self-important, "I'm in charge of theming, decorating, and staffing the Ghost Train."

Ava glanced at Carmela and said, "What's a Ghost Train?"

"Are you serious?" said Jekyl. "The Ghost Train is being touted as New Orleans's premier Halloween event and has been promoted up the wazoo!"

"I'm sure," Carmela said mildly. "Now tell us more about it."

Jekyl drew breath and gestured expansively. "Picture this if you will. A classic old passenger train consisting of six or seven plush Pullman cars, all glammed up with Halloween décor, and running on the New Orleans Public Belt Railroad between Audubon Park and the French Quarter."

"Wait a minute," said Ava. "You're asking us to *be* ghosts? And, like, ride on the train?"

"Yes, I am," said Jekyl. "Because I think you'd both make magnificent ghosts."

Carmela turned toward Ava. "Sounds like a sell job to me."

Jekyl held his index finger and thumb together. "It would be a tiny favor for *moi*."

"I hate to admit it," said Ava, "but it does sound kind of fun."

Jekyl fairly beamed. "I knew I could count on you two! Now, you're going to need costumes of course."

"What?" squawked Carmela. It wasn't enough just to show up?

"And not just the old bedsheet over the head with two eye holes cut into it," said Jekyl. "I'd love it if you ladies devised something really spectacular."

"You hear that, Carmela?" said Ava. "We're going to be ghosts."

"On the premier Ghost Train," said Carmela, playing along.

"Which means we're gonna need costumes that are really spooktacular!" said Ava.

"That's the spirit," said Jekyl, as he eased his way out of the shop.

"Honestly," said Carmela, "he does have a way of twisting your arm."

"But it might be fun. And Baby's party is Wednesday night, the Pumpkins and Bumpkins Ball is on Thursday, so we're home free on Friday, right?"

"That's what it looks like." Carmela dug in her bag and pulled out her cell phone. "I'm going to call Mavis. See if we can drop by her place before we head off for the Zombie Crawl tonight."

"Good idea," said Ava. "This whole Napoleon's mask thing has got my curiosity itching."

"You mean burning?"

"Yeah, that, too."

Carmela punched in digits, then waited a few moments. Mavis picked up on the third ring.

"Hello?" Mavis said in a shaky, tentative voice. It was obvious she'd been receiving calls from reporters, calls from police, and probably a few crank calls.

"Mavis, it's Carmela."

"Thank goodness," said Mavis, sounding hugely relieved. "I thought it might be another reporter."

"I was wondering," said Carmela, "if I could drop by and talk to you tonight? Maybe around seven?"

"Just you?"

"My friend Ava, too."

"This is about the investigation?" Mavis asked.

Carmela thought for a few moments. Babcock had warned her to stay out of it, but she was feeling more and more intrigued. "You might say that," she told Mavis.

"You have some new thoughts on the murder?"

Actually, Carmela had questions about the murder. But instead of blurting that out and scaring her off, she replied, "Yes, we do."

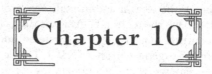

Chapter 10

"WE'LL have a quick bite," said Carmela, standing at her stove. "Then we'll hustle over to Mavis's place, ply her with a few questions, and head back down to the French Quarter so we can catch the Zombie Crawl."

"Sounds like a plan," said Ava. She was lounging on the leather chaise, rubbing Boo's little triangle-shaped ears. "And may I just say, whatever you're whipping up in there, it smells absolutely divine."

"More like heating it up," said Carmela, as she stirred her pan. She added another pat of butter to her sizzling shrimp, then dumped in the black beans. When everything was all savory and nice, she dished up steaming portions into yellow Fiesta ware bowls. "Come and get it." She carried the bowls to her dining table and placed them on rattan place mats.

Ava was at the table in mere moments.

"Whoa," said Carmela, "let me get you a . . ."

"Spoon," said Ava. She leapt for the sideboard like a

crazed ninja warrior, grabbed two spoons, and was back before you could say "Dinner is served."

Carmela sat down across from Ava and smiled. "Well, isn't this special. So elegant and formal. Too bad I let that British butler have the night off." Ava was digging in, fanning her mouth because the shrimp were so hot, but not letting up in her eagerness to stuff herself. The dogs danced beneath their elbows, whining and begging for handouts.

Carmela had to chuckle. She hadn't even had time to light a candle or put on music. Oh well, at least she'd made an effort in the kitchen. She hadn't just squirted ketchup on top of noodles and called it *sasgetti*.

When Ava finally came up for air, she said, "This is so delicious, *cher*."

"Wait till you see the dump cake I made for dessert," said Carmela. "With blueberry and pineapple."

Ava giggled. "What a great name. But, seriously, I'm gonna have to bite the bullet one of these days and go on a strict diet." She looked mournful as she patted her absolutely flat stomach. "At what point does a muffin top turn into a full-blown Bundt cake?"

"I think you look just fine."

"Maybe I should just eat tuna and Melba toast. Or down that gunky liquid protein drink. Dran-O or Food-O, whatever it is."

"I was planning to start my summer diet first thing tomorrow," said Carmela.

Ava snorted. "Don't make me laugh while I'm eating, *cher*. I could choke and die. Or shoot wine out my nose."

"Fat chance," said Carmela, which made Ava snort again.

TWENTY MINUTES LATER, DOGS WALKED AND dishes stacked in the sink, Carmela and Ava were out the door.

"You think I'm too dressed up for a Zombie Crawl?" Ava asked as they drove down Decatur Street, past the Café du Monde and the open-air French Market. Ava had changed into a leopard-print top, tight black leggings, and thigh-high black boots. She looked like Catwoman out on the prowl. Or a character in an old comedy sketch from the *Cher* show.

"In an outfit that prim and proper," said Carmela, "you could easily be mistaken for an Upper East Side Bergdorf Goodman shopper."

"You think?"

"Uh . . . no," said Carmela. "Face it, sweetie, you're dressed like your persona: fun, hip, and looking like you want to swan around the French Quarter and hit a few clubs." She hooked a right on North Peters Street, and added, "You for sure didn't want to dress like a zombie, did you?"

Ava shook her head and her mass of dark hair looked almost purple as they drove under a string of streetlamps that stretched down the dark street like glowing rosary beads. "Nope. Zombies are way too scuzzy for my taste." She shuddered. "All that hanging flesh, ripped clothes, and lank hair."

Carmela patted her own hair, which was due for a trim. "I know the feeling."

"But I like the idea of dressing up like a ghost for Jekyl's Ghost Train."

"I've got a couple ideas on that," said Carmela. "Costume-wise, I mean."

They cruised down Frenchmen Street and then into the heart of the Bywater District. It was an eclectic area, filled with longtime residents as well as a more recent influx of artists and musicians who'd been priced out of the French Quarter. Restaurants and pubs like Praline Patty's and Sugar Blue had recently popped up, but the area still retained its quaint, laid-back, tumbledown charm.

Mavis lived in a small, Caribbean-style cottage that had once been painted teal blue. Now, after wind, rain, humidity, and good old Louisiana heat had pounded away at it, the paint had been worn down to a fine patina and silvered wood shone through. In the small front yard, delineated by an ankle-high, white wire fence, a couple of scraggly palm trees and one orange tree made their brave stand.

From the looks of the run-down cottage, Carmela guessed that Mavis was probably one of the people who'd grown up here, instead of being a recent transplant with high hopes for a fixer-upper.

"Talk about dumpy," said Ava as they walked to the front door.

"I know," said Carmela. "But just . . . play nice, okay? She's really hurting."

Mavis answered the door on the third ring. It creaked open and she peered out tentatively, her complexion looking sallow and splotchy, eyes red-rimmed and sunken. Carmela couldn't help but feel they'd interrupted a serious crying jag.

"Hi," said Mavis. She opened the door almost fearfully. "Come in."

The living room, decorated in faded browns and purples, practically mirrored the way Mavis was dressed. *Drab* was hardly the word for it and Carmela felt her heart go out to the woman. In one fell swoop, Mavis had lost her fiancé, her livelihood, and probably her self-confidence.

Carmela and Ava plopped down on a sagging floral couch, while Mavis settled herself listlessly in a chair across from them.

"How are you holding up?" asked Carmela. Her eyes searched the room. Not much in the way of décor.

One of Mavis's shoulders hitched up a notch.

"Hang in there, honey," said Ava, trying to lend an encouraging note.

"I'm trying," said Mavis. "But it's been difficult." She gazed pointedly at Carmela. "The police were here again today. Asking questions, always these complicated questions that I don't have answers for."

"I'm so sorry about that," said Carmela. "I know this whole ordeal has been brutal."

Mavis pulled a tissue from the pocket of her lumpy sweater and dabbed at her eyes. "You have no idea."

"No, I'm sure I don't," said Carmela. She wanted to ask Mavis a few tough questions, but decided the woman was in a fragile, highly emotional state. She'd have to lead up to them gradually.

"It feels like . . ." Mavis began, then sniffled into a tissue.

"What, Mavis?" Carmela asked. She tried to keep her tone low and sympathetic. She wanted to create an even greater level of trust.

"It feels like the police don't want to believe my story," said Mavis.

"Typical," said Ava.

"I think the detectives are just trying to collect as much information as possible," said Carmela. "And then sort everything out." She wanted to sit on the fence, 50 percent Mavis, 50 percent Babcock. If that was even possible.

"I told them everything I know," said Mavis. She hunched her shoulders forward and pulled herself into a tight knot.

"I'm sure you did," said Carmela.

Mavis cleared her throat. "I sure do feel lucky having you on my side, though."

"That's right," said Carmela. "I *am* on your side. Ava is, too."

Ava nodded. "Believe it."

"You're both so kind," said Mavis.

"Girl power," said Ava, doing a quick fist pump. "We gotta stick together."

Carmela struggled to phrase her question delicately. "You're quite sure that Joubert was here in town the night the death mask was stolen in Dallas?"

"Oh yes," said Mavis, nodding fiercely. "I know it for a fact. You can even correlate that with Mr. Duval. They had a meeting together. Over dinner, I think."

"I'm going to check that out," said Carmela.

Mavis bobbed her head. "I wish you would."

Ava poked Carmela in the ribs. "Can't you talk to Babcock about this whole mess? Get him to ease off?"

"Is he your boyfriend, Carmela?" Mavis played with the ring on her finger. The silver ring with the skulls and Sanskrit inscription.

"Yes, he is," said Carmela. She felt awful. Poor Mavis was wearing her wedding ring . . . well, the ring that *would* have been her wedding ring had her fiancé not been murdered.

"So maybe you can reason with him," said Mavis. "Convince him that Marcus wasn't a thief."

"That's exactly what I'm trying to do," said Carmela. "I just need a little more . . . what would you call it? Evidence to the contrary."

Mavis oozed a few more tears.

"It was fairly obvious the other night," said Carmela, "that you knew all about the death mask. That you knew Marcus had the Napoleon death mask in his possession."

"Oh, absolutely," said Mavis. "He'd shown it to me just a few days earlier."

"Where did you think it came from?" Carmela asked.

Mavis shook her head slowly. "I don't know. Like I said before, I just assumed that he purchased it, like everything else in his inventory. Either at an auction or from a private dealer. You realize, Marcus had a very keen eye for unique pieces. And he knew there was always a huge market for the unusual."

"I'm sure there is," said Carmela. "But now, after talking to the police, after seeing the article in today's *Times-Picayune*, you must realize that the mask is being viewed as stolen property."

Mavis tensed up. "I know *a* mask was stolen. I don't know that it's the exact same mask."

"The thing is," said Carmela, feeling awful, "there are three other known Napoleon death masks out there and none of the museums or collectors who own them have reported those masks stolen. Or even recently sold."

"Just that collector in Dallas?" Mavis asked in a small voice.

"That's right," said Carmela. She remembered her conversation with the antique dealer James Stanger. He had told her that Marcus Joubert had been involved in several unsavory deals. Had this been one of them? For Mavis's sake, she hoped not.

Mavis's bottom lip began to quiver and her eyes sparkled. She began to shake and tears spilled down her cheeks. "Oh!" she wailed. "How did I get mixed up in all of this? Marcus showed me the mask and I thought it was beautiful, a real coup for him that might help turn his business around. But then everything went sour. Marcus was murdered, the mask stolen, and . . . and . . . then the landlord sent an eviction notice."

"I'm sorry," said Carmela. "I didn't mean to . . ."

"You know what the awful thing is?" Mavis continued. "There's barely enough money in the Oddities checking account to even rent a storage locker. And . . ." Her voice was shaking now. "We owe three months' back rent!"

Poor thing, thought Carmela. Her life really is falling apart.

"I'm so grateful, though," said Mavis, "that the two of you are listening to *my* side of the story."

"We'll do more than listen," said Ava. "Won't we, Carmela? We'll *do* something about it."

"We'll certainly try," said Carmela.

Mavis's voice was a high-pitched squeak. "Thank you."

"I was wondering," said Carmela, "when the mask first appeared at Oddities, did Marcus talk about it? Did he have a customer in mind?"

"I don't think so," said Mavis. "At least he didn't mention anyone by name."

"Maybe that guy Duval, that he had the meeting with?" said Ava.

"I just don't know," said Mavis.

Carmela decided to try another angle. "Mavis, do you have any idea what a genuine Napoleon's death mask might be worth?"

Mavis gazed at her and puckered her brows as if trying to dredge up a number. "No. Not really."

"The rumor," said Carmela, "is that it could be valued at close to a million dollars."

Mavis's face turned dead white. "That much?" She seemed utterly stunned. "Oh dear Lord, I had no idea. I thought it was more of a curiosity, like all the other items at Oddities."

"And you still have no idea where Joubert bought it?" said Carmela.

"If I knew, I'd tell you," said Mavis, blinking rapidly. "I really would. You *have* to believe me."

"We do, honey," said Ava. Even her heart had gone out to Mavis.

"I need you to dig through every scrap of paper you can find at the shop," said Carmela. "Go through his files, his notes, even his emails. Can you do that for me?"

"I'll do that," said Mavis. "I really will."

"Good," said Carmela. "Because if you really want to clear Marcus's name, we're going to have to figure out exactly *where* that doggone mask came from!"

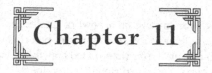

Chapter 11

TONIGHT'S Zombie Crawl was the first of its kind in New Orleans. Whether it was inspired by the old horror classic *Night of the Living Dead* or the more recent *World War Z*, the Zombie Crawl was being touted as the largest gathering of zombies ever seen.

Carmela doubted that it was the largest congregation of zombies. Heck, just look at any political convention, there were all sorts of dead heads in attendance. But this Zombie Crawl, and all that went with it, was enticing enough to draw her and Ava back to the French Quarter to take in the spectacle.

First of all, there was the Quarantine Zone over near Jackson Square. It was a roped-off area filled with food stands and food trucks. Never mind that they'd both eaten earlier, the fried shrimp, black beans and rice, and gumbo still beckoned.

"I've got to get me a sack of those fried clams," said Ava,

pointing at a red-and-white-striped tent strung with white twinkle lights. With full-on dark now, the food booths glittered like beacons. It was a regular *fais do do*, a kind of Cajun party.

"And I've got my eye on a bowl of mudbugs," said Carmela. "It's my reward for getting out of bed this morning." There was nothing better than boiled crawfish. Just twist off their little heads and slurp the juicy goodness.

They bought sacks of kettle corn, too, and got geaux cups filled with strawberry daiquiris. The thing about New Orleans was, the city prided itself on the fact that you could drink on the street and shoot from your car.

"Mnn," said Ava, as she crunched away. "The parade." She held up a deep-fried prawn to underscore her point. "We can't miss the big parade."

They hustled over to infamous Bourbon Street, where crowds had congregated outside the myriad bars and strip clubs. The countdown to Halloween had officially begun and the entire French Quarter looked as if it had been decorated by Bela Lugosi. Sunset had long retreated, while darkness crept in like a malevolent spirit. Victorian streetlights glowed and every nook and cranny seemed ready for a ghoul or goblin to take up residence.

Carmela and Ava jostled through the costumed crowd and found a spot practically right in front of Dr. Boogie's Music Bar.

"This is the life, huh?" said Ava. "Imagine if you lived in a one-horse town where bingo or bowling were the only big-time entertainment?"

"I'd for sure miss this brand of craziness," Carmela admitted. "I really would." She wished Babcock could be here with her, instead of out rubbing shoulders with lowlifes. Or chasing around with a magnifying glass and a Sherlock Holmes hat, or whatever he did when he was trying to solve a major crime. The whole spectacle tonight was over the top and fizzing with excitement. Typical fare for the Big Easy, where the livin' really was easy and nothing short of murder was considered a sin. Or if it was, confession and the ear of a forgiving priest were always a short hop away.

"Here come the bands and the funeral hearses!" cried Ava.

They could hear the high, tinny sound of a marching band tuning up. And pretty soon, the Crescent City High Steppers came into view. They clopped down the street in formation, playing a souped-up, swing version of Aaron Neville's "Tell It Like It Is." The brass trumpets blared and the bass drum boomed so loudly Carmela could feel it reverberate in the pit of her stomach.

And then, driving in a slow, stately manner, two abreast, came the hearses. There were shiny black hearses, bronze hearses, and ivory hearses. Hearses decorated with black crepe and bunches of lilies. There was even an antique hearse with a casket in back. In that one, the lid opened and closed while a real person (in gory makeup, of course) peeped out and waved as parade watchers cheered and roared.

"And now the doomsday vehicles," said Ava.

This was a whole different category. Some were Humvees that had been tricked out with fake guns and long protruding spikes, one was a VW bug that had been painted gunmetal gray, jacked up on enormous tires, and had plastic alligators glued all over it.

There was another snappy marching band, a couple of Halloween-themed floats from the Rex krewe, and then the long-awaited parade of zombies.

"This is what I've been waiting for," said Ava. She cupped a hand to one ear. "Listen to that."

A low moaning and groaning rose up to greet them as hundreds of zombies, all in full makeup and tattered regalia, trundled down the street. They limped, gimped, and lurched their way along, their moans getting louder and more plaintive. All wore garish gray and green makeup, tattered clothes, and gobs of red paint that had been haphazardly spattered on. Most of them had fake blood dripping out of their mouths. One enterprising zombie even had fake entrails strung around his neck, and another carried his pet rat and kept holding it up as if to take a chomp out of it.

"The animal rights folks are gonna be all over him," said Ava.

"Do you recognize anyone?" Carmela asked. All the zombies were friends and locals that had been improbably raised from their fitful slumber.

"Miguel should be somewhere in this horde," said Ava. "Jeez, it just occurred to me. I probably should have sponsored him."

"You can sponsor a zombie?" said Carmela.

"Yeah. For fifty bucks you can hang a cardboard sign on your zombie's back. You know, to advertise your charity or business."

"Good to know," said Carmela. She was already wondering who she could cajole into wearing green makeup and super gross clothing next year. Babcock? No way. Gabby? Hardly.

"Maybe *we* should dress up as zombies next year," Carmela said as they watched the parade hobble by. When you got past the moaning and groaning and fake bloody entrails, they did seem like a fairly congenial bunch.

"I don't know," said Ava. "Some things are often better in theory. Case in point, joining a gym or doing actual physical activity."

"I hear you there."

When the zombie parade had pretty much petered out, Ava said, "You want to go watch the 'Thriller' dance-off contest?"

"Why not?" said Carmela.

But the dance-off, held near the French Market, turned out to be just a couple dozen or so costumed zombies herking and jerking to Michael Jackson's "Thriller." And the dancers weren't even that good.

"Aw, they're not even as good as *Lord of the Dance*," Ava observed.

They wandered back toward Jackson Square. Near the Pontalba Apartments they encountered a troupe of six zombies who were putting on a street performance. They tumbled and jumped, juggled, and one guy was even a fire-eater.

"If downing buckets of Cajun food doesn't give you heartburn," said Ava, "then watching that guy swallow his flame burger surely will."

Fascinated by the act, they moved closer.

"There's their sign," said Carmela, squinting. "The Post-Mortem Street Performers." There was also a brown felt hat, turned upside down in front of their sign. Naturally, Carmela and Ava both tossed in a couple of dollar bills.

"They're not bad," said Ava. "In fact, that one guy, the fire-eater, is kind of cute."

"If you don't mind a certain crispy aesthetic," said Carmela.

"What I'm thinking," said Ava, twirling of lock of hair, "is that we should go to the Zom Prom after all." The Zom Prom was a late-night dance party being held in the ballroom at the Hotel Tremont. The Hotel Tremont was purported to be haunted and guests had been known to run screaming from their rooms in the middle of the night. Definitely Ava's kind of place.

"The Zom Prom's not exactly in my plans," said Carmela. "After all, this is a school night. We both have to get up tomorrow and work and . . . oh crap." She took a step sideways, as if she wanted to disappear. And then hesitated. Caught like a rat in a trap!

"What?" said Ava, seeing Carmela's distress.

Carmela sighed, knowing it was too late to duck into a bar or dash across the street.

"I can't believe this!" the countess trilled as she rushed

up to greet her. "We meet again!" She wore a camel jacket with a black cashmere shawl thrown over it. The aroma that came off her was a mingle of Joy, once touted as the world's most expensive perfume, and good old bourbon.

"Hi," said Carmela, showing a bare minimum of enthusiasm.

"Excuse me, did you really just say *countess?*" Ava's head spun in Carmela's direction. She seemed just this side of intrigued.

Carmela made hasty, albeit reluctant introductions. Then she turned to Ava and, enunciating carefully to send a clear message, said, "The countess is moving into the Oddities space next door to me."

"Ohhh," said Ava. Smart girl that she was, she'd immediately figured out Carmela's subtext. In other words, this lady standing in front of them was the cuckoo new neighbor. "And what sort of shop are you opening?" Ava asked, just to be polite.

"Gems and jewels," gushed the countess. "A mix of premier pieces handcrafted by contemporary designers, as well as a nice selection of estate jewelry." She pointed to the silver bat-wing earrings that dangled from Ava's ears. "You know, we'll be offering a tasty collection of Victorian funeral jewelry, too. If that happens to be your cup of tea."

"I'll have to check it out," Ava said. "Nothing like fine design that's been ripped from the crypt."

"Maybe you could come to my grand opening," purred the countess.

"Is your husband here tonight?" Carmela asked. She was curious as to why the countess was wandering the streets of the French Quarter all by her lonesome. After all, she was new in town and supposedly didn't know very many people. On the other hand, that's the reason why lots of people *did* wander the streets of the French Quarter. New in town and . . . well, you get the idea.

The countess waved a hand dismissively. "Oh, François is around here somewhere." She peered intently at Carmela. "It was so interesting meeting your boyfriend last night. The dedicated and rather intense Detective Babcock."

"The boy's a real charmer," said Ava. "A cross between Kojak and George Clooney."

"I was wondering," continued the countess. "Has your handsome detective made any progress in solving the Joubert murder? Or the related case of that stolen death mask?"

"I haven't spoken with him today," said Carmela. "But I'm confident Detective Babcock is working diligently on both investigations. He always does." Why was she suddenly droning on like Jack Webb in *Dragnet*? And why was she getting that continued weird vibe from the countess? Was it just because the woman was incredibly obnoxious . . . or was something else going on?

"I have a small tip I'd like to offer your Detective Babcock," said the countess. "And I'd appreciate your passing it on."

"What's that?" said Carmela.

"That antique dealer that's located just down the block?" said the countess. She gazed at Carmela with wide eyes and swinging earrings. "I'm afraid that person is *highly* unethical in his business dealings."

"You mean James Stanger?" Carmela was taken aback. She didn't really think Stanger had anything to hide. He might act all prim and proper, but deep down he was an Iowa farm boy who'd spent six months in England, and come back with a fake accent and a hoity-toity sales shtick. The important thing, however, was that Stanger had never struck her as being unethical.

The countess waggled a finger at Carmela. "I'll have you know James Stanger has skirted the law *multiple* times."

Was this just a wild accusation, Carmela wondered, or did Countess Crazy really know something? There was only one way to find out, and that was to call her bluff. "Skirted the law. In what way?"

The countess brightened, obviously eager to spill the beans as well as a little pent-up vitriol. "Stanger has been accused multiple times of bringing in *illegal* antiquities. Why, you probably don't even know this, but your friend Stanger was involved in a *huge* flap with the Chinese government!"

"And how would you know that?" Carmela didn't put much stock in these blanket accusations. They amounted to nothing more than character assassination.

"Oh, my dear," said the countess, practically chortling now. "I may have just moved here from Palm Beach, but I *do* keep up with all the latest news in the world of art and antiquities."

"And you're saying that Stanger made news?" said Carmela.

"Absolutely, he did," said the countess. "Which is why I wouldn't put it past him to murder your friend Joubert. Stanger is unethical and highly dangerous. And you realize he desperately wanted that little piece of real estate for himself."

It was interesting, thought Carmela. The countess was furiously bad-mouthing Stanger, while just yesterday Stanger had pointed his finger at Joubert, accusing *him* of illegal and unsavory deals. What a round robin of wild accusations. Who should she believe? Everyone or no one?

"I'm just putting the facts out there as best I can," said the countess as she started to turn away. "Make of them what you will." She hesitated and frowned. "But, seriously, Carmela, I'm convinced Stanger was willing to do just about *anything* to get his hands on that property."

"That may be true," said Carmela. "But it's your property now. So it sounds like *you're* the one who'd better be careful."

"IS SHE AS CRAZY AS SHE SEEMS?" ASKED AVA AS they strolled down Governor Nicholls Street.

"Worse," said Carmela. "I think she's delusional." On the other hand, maybe the countess was dumb like a fox. Who knew? Who could tell behind her façade of bravura and brashness?

"She strikes me as the worst kind of Eurotrash."

"I hear you," said Carmela. "But I'm not even sure she's from Europe. There's something unpleasant and inherently phony about her and her husband and their goofball titles."

"But she must have some money, right? After all, she is opening a high-end jewelry boutique. I'm guessing that requires some serious cash and inventory."

As Carmela was about to answer, the white KBEZ-TV van slid to a stop directly in front of them and a door popped open.

"Hey there," said Zoe. She sprang out of the passenger seat to greet Carmela and Ava.

"What are you guys up to?" Ava asked with a broad smile and a toss of her head. She was never opposed to having her lovely face appear on TV. In fact, she could photo bomb with the best of them.

"Raleigh and I are just cruising the Quarter," Zoe explained. "Shooting zombies and the parade." She shrugged. "Human interest stuff."

"Not human." Ava chuckled. "*In*human."

Zoe pointed a finger at her. "Ha, good one. Mind if I use that in my report?"

"Be my guest."

Zoe switched her focus to Carmela. "What I'd really like is an update on that Marcus Joubert murder."

"I haven't heard much," said Carmela. She was reluctant to let too much slip for fear she'd end up a crazy sound bite.

"You're trying to turn KBEZ into a regular disaster channel," said Ava.

"How about that Napoleon death mask thing?" Zoe pressed.

"Nope." Carmela decided the safest route was to play innocent.

Zoe studied Carmela with a look of cool appraisal. "Are you sure about that? Because it seems to me you're a fairly skilled investigator in your own right. And being so close to Detective Babcock, you might even pick up some inside information."

"Who me?" said Carmela. "No, no way. You really think Babcock's going to let me elbow my way into his homicide investigation?"

"Eh," said Zoe as she flipped a hand. "Whatever. But let me know if you hear anything, okay?" She gestured to Raleigh, who nodded and shouldered his heavy camera with a sigh. "C'mon. Let's go shoot that gang of zombies across the street."

Ava tugged at Carmela's sleeve as the TV team headed out. "*Cher*, please don't go home just yet. Let's just peek in on the Zom Prom. After all, it's the official kickoff for Halloween week!"

"That's funny," said Carmela. "And here I thought the murder of Marcus Joubert was the kickoff."

Ava considered Carmela's words for a moment. "Hmm, I guess it kind of was."

"You go and have fun," Carmela urged. "Grab yourself a good-looking zombie dance partner and lurch your little heart out."

"You sure you don't want to come along?"

"I'm going to run home and grab the dogs. Take them for a quick walk."

"Okay," said Ava, spinning on her heels. "See ya later!"

BOO AND POOBAH WERE DELIGHTED TO SEE Carmela. They were even more thrilled when she clipped leashes to their collars and led them outside. The night air was cool and lush, with moonlight shining down through the live oak tree in the courtyard and creating interesting spatter patterns on the bricks. The small fountain burbled noisily as Boo stopped to take a drink.

Then they walked through the porte cochere and out onto the street.

It was quiet and fairly subdued in this part of the French Quarter. Most of the festivities were going on in the more touristy parts like Jackson Square, Pirate's Alley, and all along Bourbon Street.

Carmela and the dogs loped along, passing Buisson's Deli, a tiny map shop, and Strutt's Bakery. On impulse, she cut over to Conti Street, where she and Babcock had strolled just last night, when he'd taken her to Sparks Pawn Shop.

Johnny Sparks, she thought. She should Google him and see what comes up. See how bad a guy he really . . .

Carmela caught a hint of movement just ahead of her and stopped dead in her tracks. Boo and Poobah stopped, too, realizing in their doggy brains that something was up. She watched as, half a block away, a tall, lean figure loitered outside Sparks Pawn Shop, peering in the window.

Ducking into a doorway, the doorway that led into a camera shop, Carmela yanked the dogs in after her. All the time wondering if the person on the sidewalk might be Johnny Sparks himself.

Of course, she didn't know what Sparks looked like. She'd never even seen a picture of him. Or, if she had, she didn't remember.

So . . . maybe she should try to catch a glimpse of him right now? What could it hurt?

Slowly, methodically, moving in what could only be called extreme slow motion, Carmela stuck her head out. It was dark and the figure had his shoulders hunched forward and was glancing about almost furtively. Then, as the man turned, a sliver of light from the window fell across his face.

Carmela was stunned by the flash of recognition that rocketed through her brain!

That's James Stanger. What on earth is he doing here?

Stanger was fidgeting outside Sparks Pawn Shop, hands shoved deep inside his jacket pockets, peering anxiously through the front window.

What was going on? Was Stanger waiting for some sort of meet-up? Did Johnny Sparks and James Stanger *know* each other?

She turned this notion over and over in her head and decided that Stanger had to be waiting for Sparks. They must be hooking up for some sort of meeting. So . . . was it a *business* meeting?

Carmela's first inclination was to immediately rush home and call Babcock. Tell him exactly what she'd seen and what she thought might be going on.

Then she stepped back into the shadows and considered her actions a little more carefully. Maybe she shouldn't call Babcock. Maybe not just yet. Because she really didn't know *what* was going on.

There was certainly no law against loitering. So maybe, just maybe, she should stand her ground and see if she could figure out if there was a meeting after all?

Carmela stood in the gloom of the doorway as five minutes ticked by, then ten minutes. Meanwhile, Stanger bounced nervously on the balls of his feet, gyrating this way and that. It looked as if he was waiting for something big to happen.

But what? Carmela wondered.

Boo and Poobah tugged at their leashes, restless and bored. The night was growing colder and the lateness of the hour meant this part of the French Quarter was getting more and more deserted.

Finally, when Stanger's back was turned to her, Carmela slipped out of the doorway and hurried away. As she walked along, she came to what she thought were a couple of logical conclusions.

Stanger had something weird going on.

No one seemed to be in any immediate danger.

So . . . she would definitely keep this sighting of him under her hat. That way, she'd be free to follow up on the Stanger-Sparks connection all on her own.

Chapter 12

"I thought you were going to wear a costume today," said Carmela. It was Monday morning and she and Gabby were at Memory Mine, sipping cups of coffee that Gabby had thoughtfully picked up at the Café du Monde. She'd also grabbed an order of beignets, those legendary little New Orleans pastries that were deep fried, smothered in powdered sugar, and came three to an order. Carmela had eaten one, Gabby had eaten one, and now the third beignet sat between them like a ticking, sugar-coated time bomb.

"Carmela, I *am* wearing a costume." Gabby smirked. "I'm dressed as a volunteer for the Junior League."

Carmela pretended to study her assistant carefully. "Let's see. Cashmere twinset, check. Tasteful gold and pearl earrings, check. Pencil skirt and loafers from Talbots . . ."

"Oh you!" Gabby grabbed a package of black crepe paper and pretended to give Carmela a whack.

"Ouch!" said Carmela, jumping up and almost spilling her coffee. "No harassment, please."

Gabby snorted. "Why? Because you're the boss?"

"Because we don't have time for this stuff," said Carmela. "We're going to be busy today. Head-spinning busy, in fact, like that poor kid in *The Exorcist*."

Gabby had to agree. "Just four more days until Halloween means we'll be inundated."

"Did our shipment of paper and charms arrive?"

"Yes, and you were right, Frisky Creations did release some wonderful new stuff. In fact . . ." Gabby ducked down and pulled a cardboard box out from below the front desk. "You should take a look at some of the charms and paper. Very cool."

"Let's start unpacking and get everything on display then," said Carmela.

Gabby pulled out a plastic bag filled with smaller cellophane bags. "These are the Halloween brads and charms. What do you think?"

"Cute. And what about the paper?"

Gabby dug a shrink-wrapped stack of paper out of the box, grabbed a cutting tool, and slit the package open. "Refills on the Halloween stuff we ran out of and then packages of rice paper and some other fibers, all pretty neat stuff."

"Perfect."

Gabby narrowed her eyes and peered at Carmela. "Did you know that Mavis is next door packing things up?"

"She is? Already?"

"I think she got to her shop real early. I noticed that the lights were on and that she was working away when I arrived here. And you know I'm kind of an early bird."

"Ava and I paid a visit to Mavis last night," said Carmela. "To kind of, you know . . ."

"Pump her with questions?"

"We tried to be a little more polite than that."

"Did you find out anything new?"

"Not really. Just that Mavis is heartbroken, suffers from low self-esteem, and received an eviction notice from the landlord."

Gabby made a face. "Every single bit of that is just awful and downright unfair. But all three problems piled one on top of another . . ."

"You can thank Boyd Bellamy for issuing that eviction notice."

"I hate that he's our landlord, too," said Gabby.

"I hear you. And he's apparently salivating until he can dump the Oddities merchandise and rent the newly improved space to that crazy countess lady."

"The whole situation is abhorrent," said Gabby. "It's always about the money, isn't it? Remember when business used to be conducted in a far more genteel fashion?"

"Not really," said Carmela. "Ever since I've been in business it's always been dog-eat-dog." When Gabby gave her a reproachful look, she added, "Well, maybe not for us. We're not driven mad in our scramble for the almighty dollar. Memory Mine keeps humming along because we love scrapping and crafting and helping our customers find a creative outlet."

Gabby's expression was just this side of dubious. "That sounds awfully altruistic, Carmela."

"Okay, and we make a buck or two while we're at it."

"There's the Carmela I know and love."

Carmela picked up a spool of ribbon and hung it on a display rack. "I think I'm going to run next door before things get too crazy and see how Mavis is doing. See if I can be of any help."

"Blessings on your head," said Gabby. "That's very thoughtful of you."

But as Carmela flew out the front door, she knew she wasn't doing this because she was thoughtful. She was checking on Mavis because this whole murder and death mask situation had stirred an insatiable curiosity within her. Yes, she felt terrible for Mavis Sweet. But, at the same time, she was intrigued. By the murder, by the mask, by pretty much everything that was going on.

Carmela rattled the knob on the front door and found it locked. She knocked on the window and peered in. Through a wavering pane of blue-green glass, she saw Mavis glance up from where she was working at the rolltop desk. Then a flash of recognition registered on the girl's face and she hustled forward to unlock the door.

"Carmela," said Mavis as she let her into the shop. "I was going to come over and say hello, but I . . ." She gestured at dozens of brown cardboard boxes that were tumbled everywhere. "I have so much packing to do."

"It all has to be packed up?"

"Lock, stock, and barrel, and as soon as possible. The landlord isn't giving me any grace period at all."

Carmela followed Mavis to the back of the shop, where a radio played faintly and the faux Tiffany lamp cast a puddle of brightness in the dimly lit shop.

"This is so sad, so awful," said Carmela. Merchandise that had been painstakingly displayed was scattered haphazardly, and she could literally feel Mavis's pain.

"Closing this shop is like a dagger to my heart," said Mavis. "But what can I do? I have zero options. And, in the long run, it's probably what Marcus would want. Just pack it all up and dispatch it to . . . wherever."

Carmela looked around at the cardboard boxes and strapping tape and rolls of bubble wrap. "What *will* happen to all this stuff?" she asked.

Mavis made a grimace so painful it had to be involuntary. "First it'll be packed and stored in a warehouse. And then, when Marcus's estate is finally settled, it will all probably go to an auction house. He has a sister who lives in Pomona, California, who I talked to late last night. It appears she'll be making all the decisions from here on. She'll keep me as an employee until I'm able to empty out the shop. And then, like I said, she'll probably sell everything at auction or to some dealer."

"You can't carry on with the shop?"

"I *thought* about trying to keep Oddities going," said Mavis. She grabbed a bronze goblet and a piece of bubble wrap and began wrapping. "In fact, I sort of pitched the idea to his sister. But the more I noodled it around, the idea of carrying on without Marcus was just emotionally crushing. This place wouldn't be the same without him. I'd always feel sad. Like there was a piece missing."

"You realize," said Carmela, "there's a chance you have a claim to this shop. I mean, you were formally engaged to Marcus, right?"

Mavis stopped her packing. She balanced a crystal globe in her hand and now she stroked it gently. "I hadn't thought about that angle."

"There might be a will or some sort of directive."

"I really don't know," said Mavis.

"Did Joubert have an attorney? Someone who helped him with business contracts and such?"

"Yes."

"Then you have to huddle with that attorney and see if you somehow figure into the estate. In fact, you need to go through all the papers that are stashed here in the shop. See if there's some kind of will." Carmela paused. "You told me you were going to look around and see if you could locate a sales receipt on the death mask. Have you done that yet?"

"No." Mavis cleared her throat. "What happened was . . . I came in here, felt depressed, and got kind of muddled down. But I'll look, I promise I will."

"Do it for your own sake," said Carmela. "For your own peace of mind. Because there's a possibility you really could have some sort of claim."

"That would be . . . interesting," said Mavis. "Though I'd still probably have to strike a deal with the sister."

"Sure," said Carmela. "But maybe you could try to swing a bridge loan. To buy out her share of the shop and its contents." She looked around at the beetle collection, stuffed monkey, and old jewelry. "It couldn't be worth that much."

"But the lease is gone."

"Relocate," said Carmela. "There are other spaces for lease around the neighborhood. Or close by in the Faubourg Marigny."

"Gosh, you're smart," said Mavis. "How did you learn so much about business?"

"Trial and error," Carmela told her. "Mostly error." She shifted uncomfortably from one foot to the other. "I don't suppose . . . well, is there going to be a funeral?"

"Not a funeral per se," said Mavis. "But I talked to a few of his friends and we're putting together a simple memorial service for this Wednesday in St. Louis Cemetery No. 1. I hope you'll come."

"Of course I will."

Looking relieved, Mavis put a hand to her chest. "Thank you. Because I think it's going to be a pretty small group of mourners."

"Let me ask you something," said Carmela. "What do you know about James Stanger?"

"You mean . . . ?"

"The man down the block who owns Gilded Pheasant Antiques."

"Mnn . . . I don't know much of anything," said Mavis. But the pained expression on her face gave it away. Mavis wasn't a very good liar.

"You know *some*thing," said Carmela.

Mavis bit her lip. "Okay, I know for a fact that Marcus and James Stanger never got along."

"Lots of people don't get along," said Carmela. Case in

point, she and her ex-husband, Shamus. The sex had been great, but the "everything else" had been ghastly. Then again, Shamus was a liar, a cheat, and a braggart. A trust fund baby who'd been born with a silver foot in his mouth. Carmela turned her attention back to Mavis.

"Something about the mention of Stanger's name made you feel . . . mmn, uncomfortable."

"Okay, how about this? You might say that he and Marcus *hated* each other."

"You mean like sworn enemies?" This was news to Carmela. "Why do you say that? Better yet, do you know what caused this rift?"

"Apparently, they got caught up in some horrible dispute. Way back when."

"What was it about?" Carmela asked.

"Marcus never did tell me. He just always said that Stanger was a miserable cheat." She hesitated and her eyes went big. "Wait a minute, why are you asking about Stanger?"

"Just something I'm following up on. A kind of . . . thread."

But Mavis was no dummy. "Carmela," she said, practically breathless. "Is that who you think might have come in and stabbed Marcus? I mean, he might have let Stanger in the back door. Might have dropped his guard for a minute."

"No, no," Carmela said hastily. "I was really just asking an innocent question."

"I'll tell you something." Mavis looked thoughtful. "I never cared for James Stanger. I never trusted the man."

"Based on a feeling?" Carmela asked. "Or actual working knowledge of something?"

"Let's call it past performance," said Mavis. "Stanger kind of prided himself on trying to outbid Marcus at the various auctions they found themselves together at. Plus I heard that Stanger had imported some Chinese antiquities and was in big trouble with the Chinese government."

"Interesting," said Carmela. "I heard that exact same thing from another source."

"Which means it must be true," said Mavis.

"Do you know a guy named Johnny Sparks?" Carmela asked.

Mavis's brows pinched together as if she was thinking hard. "I don't think so."

"You're sure?"

"Wait a minute, is he the sleazy guy who owns all those pawn shops? And he sometimes does obnoxious TV commercials? There's, like, a jingle."

Carmela nodded. She'd had that stupid jingle stuck in her head once for an entire day and it had driven her crazy. Made her want to bash her head against a brick wall. Something about *You think it's trash, but it could mean cash.* "That's the guy," she told Mavis. "The Pawn Shop Czar of New Orleans."

"I can't say that I really *know* Sparks."

"The thing is, did Joubert know him? Do you know if he ever did business with him?"

Mavis looked doubtful. "That I wouldn't know." Then she rethought her statement. "Well, *maybe* they did know each other. It's kind of a stretch, but they were basically in the same business."

"Sparks was into antiques? I though he just handled stolen Rolex watches, car stereos, and wedding rings pawned by unhappy divorcées."

"I think he might have handled a few paintings and bronze statues, too." Mavis shrugged. "But everybody in the French Quarter does that. Antiques, estate jewelry . . . it's basically our bread and butter."

Carmela nodded. She had an inkling that there might be a connection there. "Go through your records, will you?" she urged. "See what you can come up with on the origin of the mask. And try to figure out if Marcus had any business dealings with Stanger."

"Now you've got me wondering," said Mavis. "So I'll for sure take a look."

Carmela glanced around. "Just out of curiosity," she said, "now that you've had a chance to look through the inventory—is there anything missing from the shop?"

Mavis threw her a nervous glance. "I wouldn't exactly call it inventory, Carmela. But there is one thing."

"What's that?"

"I kind of hate to mention this, because I think it might be illegal."

"Mavis, tell me," said Carmela. "What else is missing?"

Mavis practically cringed. "A gun."

"What!"

She waved her hands in a nervous arc. "Marcus always kept a gun here, a small revolver. Or maybe it was a pistol. I don't know the difference." She shivered. "I don't really know anything about handguns at all."

"Where did Marcus keep this gun?"

Mavis pointed at the rolltop desk. "In the bottom left drawer of his desk."

"And now it's gone. You're sure it's gone?"

"Yes."

"Did you tell Detective Babcock about this?"

"No, I just discovered it was missing. Like . . . twenty minutes ago. Just before you came in."

"Well, call him, will you?"

Mavis shuffled a foot and looked reluctant.

"You have to call him," said Carmela.

"Okay," said Mavis. "Okay."

"Do you want me to talk to him, too?"

"Would you?" said Mavis.

"HOW GOES IT OVER THERE?" ASKED GABBY, AS Carmela sailed through the front door.

"Sad. Depressing." Carmela had gone over to give a pep talk and had returned with the wind knocked out of her sails.

"Well, hang on to your hat," said Gabby as she rang up a customer. "Because it's like old home week here. If you could maybe . . ." She nodded toward the back of the shop where four women were busily loading paper, rubber stamps, and ribbon into their shopping baskets.

"No problem."

Carmela hustled over to her customers. "Help you?" she said, a friendly chirp that was meant for all four of them. "With anything?"

One of the customers, a woman with a bouncy brown ponytail, said, "Me. Please." She wore a neat caramel-colored leather jacket with matching boots and blue jeans.

"What do you need?" Carmela asked.

"I have a ten-year-old son who's crazy over pirates," said the woman. "And for Halloween, I wanted to make him something special. Like . . . a pirate scrapbook. Except I don't quite know what that is."

"You have photos of him dressed as a pirate?" Carmela asked.

"About a dozen." She tore open an envelope. "See?"

Carmela smiled at the photos. The boy wore a tricornered black hat, eye patch, quasi-military jacket, and black buckle boots. In some poses he brandished a saber, in others he held up a Jolly Roger flag. "Cute," said Carmela. "So maybe . . ." She was already looking at her stack of albums, wondering which one would work best. "Okay, this one." She pulled out an eight-by-ten-inch album that had a black embossed cover and about a dozen black pages inside.

"Cool," said the woman. "But what do we do with it?"

"This cover already looks like it's been aged," said Carmela. "So let's go with that theme and attach a ribbon and brass button to it . . . something that looks like it was stolen from the royal treasury." She grabbed a plastic packet and showed it to the woman. "This button's got a nice crown motif."

"I like it," said the woman.

"Then we take the inside pages and kind of rough up the edges."

"Make it look used."

"That's right," said Carmela. "Now over here where we have our rubber stamps . . ."

"You can stamp on black paper?" asked the woman.

"Sure, especially if you're using gold, silver, or even bronze-colored inks. Ah, here's a rubber stamp of an old sailing ship and here's one of an old-fashioned compass. And over here . . ." They moved over toward the floor-to-ceiling racks of paper.

"Map paper?" asked the woman.

"Exactly," said Carmela. She pulled out a sheet of paper that depicted an old sepia-colored map. "And here's some paper with sailing ships—galleons, really—and another map. Oh, and sea monsters. We can't forget them."

"This is all absolutely perfect," said the woman.

"I've got a couple more items to suggest," said Carmela. "How about a small Jolly Roger decal and a bronze treasure chest key."

"Perfect. I would never have dreamt this up on my own," said the woman. "How can I thank you?"

"Just have fun making your scrapbook," said Carmela. "And come back and see us again real soon."

"I will," said the woman as she carried her loot up to the front desk.

Carmela helped another woman pick out some water-based metallic markers. Then she showed her how to apply the markers to a piece of glossy black cardstock, spritz on some distilled water, and then swirl the colors around to create a marbleized metallic effect.

When things finally settled down to a dull roar, when Carmela finally got a break, she went into her office, fully intending to do work on a commercial scrapbook for her friend Jade Germaine. Jade was starting her own tea party business called Tea Party in a Box, and she planned to cater tea parties for bridal showers, book clubs, and garden clubs in her customers' homes. She'd given Carmela several photos of three-tiered trays that displayed the most delicious-looking tea sandwiches, as well as photos of teacups, teapots, and elegant tea tables that she had decorated. Her album would be her calling card to show customers her work and convince them to hire her.

Carmela was thinking about doing a pink and green theme, and using a cream-colored album that would have ribbon ties in those same colors.

On the other hand . . .

Carmela spun around in her chair, barely noticing the swatches of paper, snips of ribbon, and scribbled page sketches she had tacked to her office walls.

There was the question of Johnny Sparks.

She'd vowed to do a little research on the man. And now was as good a time as any. In fact, time was probably of the essence. With a hasty glance over her shoulder, Carmela scrunched down in front of her computer and Googled Johnny Sparks.

What she found didn't really surprise her.

Sparks had been in trouble any number of times. He'd been accused of handling stolen merchandise, he was constantly in arrears on his property taxes, and had even been in trouble with the state of Louisiana for failing to pay proper withholding taxes on his employees. Nice guy.

It was also interesting that, even though Sparks had been arrested numerous times, nothing had ever really stuck.

Carmela decided that Sparks was either a tricky guy or a smart guy. Trouble seemed to slide off his back like he was

Teflon-coated. Maybe he had excellent lawyers, maybe he was masterful at covering or obliterating his tracks, or maybe he was just plain lucky and always caught a break. Or perhaps, as Babcock had hinted, he had somebody on the inside, watching out for him. She'd have to quiz Babcock about this. If he deigned to share the teensiest bit of information with her, that is.

On a wild impulse, Carmela also ran a Google search on James Stanger. She didn't find much. Mostly his website, Facebook page, a few articles where he was mentioned, and a nice article about a charity event at the New Orleans Museum of Art where Stanger had donated an antique French clock to their silent auction. Just as she was about to quit her search, she stumbled upon some sort of document from an organization called the USITC.

The what?

The USITC turned out to be the United States International Trade Commission. What Carmela found was a wordy document, heavy with legalese and lots of heretofors and heretowiths. But the gist of it seemed to imply that James Stanger had purportedly violated a number of import-export laws. She continued to search through the document, but never did find anything specific. No glaring accusation that stated "James Stanger single-handedly ransacked a Ming tomb and stole eight thousand life-sized carved figures."

So maybe his dealings had just caused a misunderstanding? Carmela knew that doing business with China could be fraught with problems. There were rules, regulations, taxes, and tariffs on both sides of the Pacific. There was the matter of *guanxi*, or tea money. Which was basically a bribe or tribute. Depending, of course, on whether you were the briber or the bribee.

Carmela chuckled to herself. What had Gabby said earlier? That business used to be more genteel? Perhaps it had, but not anymore, baby. This new leaner, scarier economy carried a whole new set of non-rules. It was the Wild West out there and you'd better watch out.

Reaching for her phone, Carmela dialed Babcock's cell number. She got him on the fourth ring, just before she was dumped to voice mail.

"What, Carmela?" Babcock said.

"And a deliciously good morning to you, too," she replied.

"Sweetheart, I am so swamped," said Babcock. He sounded swamped. And a little perplexed. "Please tell me this is super important."

"It is," said Carmela. "Did Mavis call you about the gun?"

There was stunned silence and then Babcock said, "Gun? What gun?"

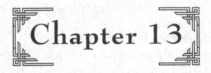

Chapter 13

CARMELA hastened to explain. "Apparently, along with Napoleon's death mask, a gun was stolen from Odd-ities."

"First I've heard," said Babcock. Now he sounded ticked off. "Nice that your friend Mavis didn't bother to report that crucial fact."

"I think she's in such a dither over Joubert's murder and the stolen death mask controversy that she didn't realize the gun was missing until just this morning."

"You were over there?"

"I was," said Carmela. "Just to peek in on Mavis and see how things were going. She's packing everything up *tout de suite*. Our Snidely Whiplash of a landlord handed her an eviction notice."

Babcock made a sound like air moving through his front teeth. "That's tough."

"No, it's heartbreaking," said Carmela. "The poor girl has enough to deal with."

"You've taken quite an interest in her," said Babcock. "Or, should I say, you've taken her under your wing."

"I didn't set out to, but Mavis doesn't seem to have anyone else."

"My sweet Carmela. You're always the champion of stray cats and dogs, aren't you? And turtles that wander across the road."

"Well . . . yes. Is there something wrong with that?" Of course she helped turtles. Who *wouldn't* rescue a turtle?

"Not a thing. It's just that you tend to get emotionally involved in these little mini-dramas."

"Not dramas, more like real life."

"Same thing," said Babcock. "At least from a police perspective."

"By the way," said Carmela. "I think James Stanger might have had a meeting with Johnny Sparks last night."

Babcock practically exploded. "What are you talking about?" Then, "Carmela, have you been investigating? When I specifically warned you *not* to?"

"No, it's nothing like that," she lied. "I just happened to make an innocent observation. I was walking my dogs last night and saw Stanger sort of lingering in front of Johnny Sparks's place. You know, the one we walked past the other night." She paused. "I'm thinking they might have had a meeting planned."

"That's your take? Just from catching a glimpse of Stanger on the sidewalk in an area where he lives and works?"

"A meeting is not outside the realm of possibility," said Carmela. She was a little stung by Babcock's dismissiveness. "I also just learned from Mavis that Joubert and Stanger didn't get along. That they pretty much hated each other."

"A tiff between two antique dealers is hardly major news

or a serious motive for murder. If that's where you're going with this."

"Don't be so sure about that," said Carmela. "I think Stanger could be up to no good. Or *was* up to no good. Could you run some sort of check on him?" She thought about the Chinese importation allegations she'd just read about. "Or put a tail on him?"

"We don't actually do things like that. That's only in cop movies. And only old movies starring Mel Gibson."

"Okay, I'll just come right out and ask my question then. Is there any way that Sparks and Stanger could be in collusion?"

"I sincerely doubt it."

"Why not?"

"Because that would be too nice and neat," said Babcock. "In my line of work, nice and neat rarely happens. I'm used to nasty and messy."

"Even if there's a lot of money involved? Jekyl seems to think a true Napoleon's death mask would be worth almost a million dollars."

"Tell me about it. The mayor, two city council members, and a curator at the museum have all called to rag on me about this stolen death mask. Everybody's up in arms and wants a quick resolution."

"Then we're all on the same page," said Carmela.

"No, we're not. At least *you* aren't. Listen to me, Carmela. Whoever murdered Joubert and then snatched that death mask is a criminal of the worst kind."

"Is there any other kind?"

"Be serious for a moment," said Babcock. "Besides the obvious penalty for murder, the Justice Department's guidelines for a major art theft are rather harsh."

"Oh?"

"It's a federal crime to, and I quote, 'steal, receive, or dispose of any cultural object that's worth more than one hundred thousand dollars.' "

"What's the net-net on that penalty?" Carmela asked. "Like, life in some kind of federal penitentiary?"

"I'm not familiar with sentencing guidelines," said Babcock. "But I can guarantee you it's a lot more than just a slap on the wrist." He paused. "So stay out of this, okay?"

"Okay," said Carmela. "I'll talk to you later." She hung up, knowing that her tacit okay was not really an agreement to back off. Rather, it was just an *okay* okay. If that made any sense at all.

Feeling oddly unsettled, Carmela picked up a black marker and flipped open her sketch pad. She'd promised the countess that she'd work on a logo design for her new shop. Of course, she'd agreed to do the design work way before she knew what a crazy, uncharitable shrew the countess was. Now, just the *thought* of designing her logo felt like drudge work.

But a promise was a promise. And Carmela was a woman who kept her word. If she promised Jekyl she'd volunteer her time at the Children's Art Association, then doggone it, she'd be there. Or if a local charity needed a poster, she'd for sure design one. That's just who she was. A cross between a savvy entrepreneur and a do-gooder Girl Scout.

As Carmela doodled idly on her drawing pad, the creative juices started to flow and a few ideas popped into her head.

First Carmela sketched a logo that gave a quick nod to French heraldry. Her design, after a few hasty sketches, was a noble-looking lion set against a rampart of fleur-de-lis. With maybe a color combination of blue and gold?

On the other hand, the shop's name was Lucrezia. So maybe she should try to work something around that?

Let's see now, Lucrezia had been a femme fatale who lived in and around Rome during the Renaissance. That theme seemed ripe with symbols and metaphors. So what would work for an image of the Eternal City? The seven hills of

Rome? Perhaps the Spanish Steps or some Roman architecture?

Carmela sketched a Roman column. It was interesting in a classical sort of way, but not all that compelling. In fact, she'd seen that sort of image many times before, especially on boxes of pasta. She needed something better, something that would tie in thematically.

Well . . . she knew that Lucrezia had been married several times and was reputedly a murderess and a Jezebel. And legend held that Lucrezia wore a hollow ring filled with poison that she would waft over someone's goblet if they fell out of favor with her. Carmela smiled to herself. Now *that* made for an interesting story as well as a provocative image.

Since this was a logo for a high-end jewelry store, wouldn't an ornate, medieval-looking ring be almost perfect?

Carmela continued to sketch, tightening up her designs, adding a few refinements. She grabbed a typeface book for inspiration, then sketched a ring, and scanned it into her computer.

She gazed at the image on her screen, made a few minor adjustments, then hit Print. When her page was spit out of the computer, she snatched it up and took it out to show Gabby.

"I like this," Gabby said immediately. "It's edgy, but still right on the mark."

Carmela smiled. From her years working in graphic design, designing labels for Bayou Bob products, she knew that first impressions were usually the best and most honest. You always went with your gut. Or, in this case, Gabby's well-toned gut.

"Yes," Gabby said again. "A ring." She tapped an index finger against the sketch. "It's elegant and jewel-encrusted, and feels very Renaissance."

"That's exactly what I was going for," said Carmela.

"I'd say you hit the nail right on the head."

"I'm still going to work up a couple other ideas. Then,

once we get an image that flies with the countess, it can be translated into signage, marketing materials, even business cards. Once that's all done, we can be done with *her*."

"Not quite," said Gabby. "Not if she's settling in as our next-door neighbor."

"Let's hope the countess is the kind of neighbor who keeps to herself. Who doesn't want to get involved in block promotions or the exchange of customer lists. Or . . ." Carmela stopped abruptly. She looked over to see Boyd Bellamy fumbling at the front door. He fiddled with the doorknob, shook the glass until it rattled noisily, and then stomped his way in.

"Mr. Bellamy," said Gabby, giving her best effort to present a friendly face to their notoriously cranky landlord. "How are you today?"

But Bellamy wasn't buying it. True to form, he was rude and ungracious to a fault. He ignored Gabby's friendly greeting and, instead, pointed a chubby finger directly at Carmela. "How many months have you got left on your lease?" he demanded.

Carmela rushed to confront him, waving an index finger back in Bellamy's face. "Not months, *years*. I have three years left on my current lease." No way was she going to let herself be intimidated by this loudmouth boor.

"That's too bad," Bellamy grunted. "Especially with space going for such a premium right now." Bellamy was short and portly with watery blue eyes, vague wisps of reddish hair, and a nasty temper that was in perfect sync with his pugnacious-looking face. Carmela had always joked that Bellamy reminded her of a cross between a bulldog and a cottonmouth snake. Today, he was proving that it was a doable combination.

"You look upset," Carmela needled him. "That can't be good for your blood pressure." Bellamy was always complaining about his high blood pressure and all the pills he had to swallow to keep it in check. Small wonder when the man spent his days stalking the French Quarter, working himself into a frenzy as he terrorized tenants. Though for Bellamy, Carmela figured it was more sport than actual work.

Bellamy glanced around the interior of Memory Mine. "If I were to lease this space to an upscale boutique or wine bar, I could get top dollar. Maybe even three times what I'm currently charging you."

Carmela crossed her arms in front of her. "Is that so." One thing she had to admit about Bellamy, he always thought big. Big ideas, big money. And the man did have an uncanny knack for spotting trends.

"You wouldn't be interested in a sublease, would you?" Bellamy asked. "I could put you into a similar space, maybe even a little *more* space, over on Carondelet Street."

"No," said Carmela. "Absolutely not."

"We're happy here," said Gabby, finally finding the courage to speak up.

Bellamy sighed heavily as he stared out the front window. "Thank goodness I'm finally rid of that awful neighbor of yours," he mumbled.

"You're referring to Marcus Joubert?" said Carmela.

Bellamy glanced back at her and nodded. "Biggest mistake of my life was leasing to that man. Terrible blight on the neighborhood."

"Are you referring to Joubert's recent murder, or to his shop?" said Carmela.

Bellamy's faded eyes focused more tightly on her. "Both," he snapped. "Good riddance to him, I say."

Bellamy's nasty attitude toward Joubert raised Carmela's hackles even more. She wanted to walk up to him and give his chubby pink cheek a good smack with the back of her hand. Instead, fighting to hold her temper in check, she gritted her teeth and said, "It sounds like you're happy he's gone."

"Not happy, overjoyed," said Bellamy. He flashed a mirthless grin that revealed small, pointed teeth.

"That's not a very charitable attitude," said Gabby.

"You're looking for charity?" barked Bellamy. "Go to church." And with that last bit of venom dangling in the air, he dashed out the door. As fast as his chubby legs could carry him.

"That man is just horrible," said Gabby. She shuddered and pulled her sweater around herself protectively, as if she could ward off the bad karma he spewed. "He's . . . he's not even Christian."

"I think he's barely human," said Carmela. This wasn't her first run-in with Boyd Bellamy and she knew it wouldn't be her last. Sooner or later he'd be back, trying to wheedle her with a sweet offer, or maybe threaten her with eviction. Whatever deal du jour struck him as opportune that day. On the plus side, that's why she kept a good, tough attorney on retainer. To keep the Big Bad Wolf away from the door.

But Gabby remained upset. "We're not going to move, are we? We're not going to be forced out?"

"Absolutely not," said Carmela. "In fact, I'm going to call our attorney and have her eyeball our lease agreement, just in case Bellamy decides to try some kind of end run."

BY MIDAFTERNOON, CARMELA HAD COME UP with so many ideas for trick-or-treat bags, party favors, and place cards that her head was spinning. Finally, she was able to escape to her office for a little personal time and major snooping via the Internet.

Concerning Napoleon's death mask.

Mavis had been quite correct, there were supposedly four authentic death masks, with a few that were considered copies, or copies of copies.

Interesting, she thought. *But a little creepy, too.*

Carmela wondered if the one that had been stolen from Oddities was even still in New Orleans. Right now it could easily be winging its way to a private collector in Europe or the Far East.

She also wondered if any of the masks had been sold recently. Or had been put up at auction?

There was only one way to find out.

"Jekyl?" she said, once she had her friend on the line. "Didn't you once tell me there was some kind of art website where you can see what pieces have been on the market recently and what they sold for?"

"Yes, of course," said Jekyl. "The Art Resource Bureau."

"How would I access them?"

"I have a membership."

"Ooh, could I use it? I mean, use your password?"

"For you, darling, anything."

The minute Carmela hung up the phone, it rang again. Ava.

"Are we still going dress shopping tonight?" she asked.

"More like ghost gown shopping," said Carmela.

"As long as it's shopping I'm all for it." Ava laughed. "My Visa card was getting dusty, just laying around like that. See you sevenish?"

"You got it."

Carmela hung up the phone and began clicking away, logging into the Art Resource Bureau's website using Jekyl's password. She entered the words *death mask* in the search engine and immediately discovered that a death mask of President Woodrow Wilson had been sold to someone just last year.

How weird. Who on earth would want something like that?

As Carmela contemplated this strangeness, Gabby tiptoed in and peeked over her shoulder.

"Death masks," she said. "How creepy."

"And look at what it sold for," said Carmela, pointing at the screen. "Two hundred and fifty thousand dollars."

"I can think of much better ways to spend that kind of money," said Gabby.

An image of a sky blue Dior handbag danced in Carmela's head and she nodded. "So can I."

Chapter 14

MAGAZINE Street was New Orleans's own version of L.A.'s Melrose Avenue or New York's SoHo. Newly energized in a post-Katrina era, the bustling street twinkled with lights this Monday evening, and fairly sparkled with upscale restaurants, gift shops, boutiques, music clubs, and one exquisite hole-in-the-wall shop that Carmela and Ava truly treasured—The Latest Wrinkle.

This was the hidden gem that sold Joe's jeans, knuckle-dusting statement rings, fluttery scarves, and Cosabella lingerie. Besides carrying all the latest trends, The Latest Wrinkle also featured rack after rack of carefully curated vintage clothes as well as some fairly recent designer duds that were there on consignment.

"I'm lovin' it, I'm lovin' it," said Ava as she danced her way through the shop. She grabbed a felt hat, stuck it on her head, and then shrugged into a tweed blazer with a crest on the lapel. "Look at me," she said, thrusting out a hip and doing her own brand of voguing. "Do I look veddy veddy British? Do I look like Kate Middleton?"

"Not quite," laughed Carmela. "And FYI, that jacket is *way* too sedate for you."

"You think?" said Ava. She skipped to another rack and grabbed a long black gown with a plunging neckline. She held it up and asked, "Is this more my speed? Sex kitten with a touch of Cruella De Vil thrown in for good measure?"

"Yes," said Carmela. "But I know how kindhearted you are, so you could never be cruel to a bunch of Dalmatians."

"Ya got that right," said Ava. She sauntered past a round table stacked with cashmere shawls, slinky gloves, and opera-length strands of pearls. She looked around and smiled. "Gosh I love this place."

The shop was decorated in lush tones of pink and mauve. Oriental carpets whispered underfoot, crystal chandeliers twinkled in the rafters, and, should one be in the mood to sit and relax, there were plush velvet love seats set against antique, '30s-era three-fold screens.

"Oh my," said Ava. "Look at this." She held up a black St. John Knits jacket. It was sleekly tailored with a black silk oyster collar and sparkly crystal buttons down the front. *"Très chic*, yes?"

"Très chic, yes. *Très* Ava, no."

Ava cocked her head. "Whadya mean?"

"Isn't that a trifle conservative for you? Isn't a St. John Knits jacket more appropriate for ladies who lunch?"

"I lunch," said Ava.

"I meant at Antoine's or Galatoire's."

"Oh." Ava frowned. *"That* kind of lunch. A fancy lady-with-hat-and-gloves lunch. Garden District ladies. *Rich* ladies."

Carmela didn't want to offend Ava. "Well . . . yes."

"Okaaay," said Ava. She grabbed another jacket off the resale rack. "What do you think about this one?"

"Mmn, I definitely see Mademoiselle Chanel's deft touch," said Carmela. Then she gazed at the price tag. "But used clothing that costs *this* much isn't just resale. Then it carries the cachet of vintage."

Ava looked at the price tag and whistled. "You're so right."

"I see you found one of our Chanel jackets," said the clerk, strolling over to greet them. She had long dark hair and wore an elegant white blouse and tapered black pants. "That Chanel piece is extremely special, from the early '90s. You see the round collar and exquisitely braided trim? It's what's known as a legacy jacket."

"Because you need to be born into old money to afford it?" asked Ava.

"Funny," said the clerk. She smiled at Carmela. "Your friend has a wry sense of humor."

Carmela decided to jump right to the main subject. "We're the ones who called this afternoon about the vintage wedding gowns," she said. "I'm Carmela?"

The clerk's face lit up. "Oh sure, I remember talking to you. In fact, you seemed so enthusiastic that I went ahead and grabbed a bunch of gowns for you. Pulled them out of storage." She motioned excitedly with her hands. "Follow me, I've got everything set up in back."

Carmela and Ava followed the clerk to a corner of the shop where a rolling metal rack was hung with at least a dozen wedding gowns.

"Wow," said Ava. "And these are all . . . used?"

"Some are vintage, some are quite contemporary," said the clerk. "Probably about half of the gowns we sell here were never even worn."

"Ouch," said Ava. "Brides just changing their minds, huh?"

"Grooms, too," said the clerk. "Unfortunately for the poor brides." She put a smile back on her face. "Now, what exactly did you have in mind?"

"We basically want to find a couple of gowns that we can

turn into ghost costumes," said Carmela. She'd had what she loosely termed one of her "creative visions" and was eager to start snipping and painting.

"That's a new one on me," said the clerk. "But it sounds like fun. Obviously a costume for an upcoming Halloween event?"

"The Ghost Train," said Ava. "Carmela and I are going to be guest ghosts."

"Ghostesses," Carmela added.

The clerk chuckled. "Well, I'll let you ladies look through the merchandise. If you have any questions, just holler."

"Will do," said Carmela. She was already perusing the rack of wedding gowns. Flipping past a ball gown, scrutinizing a fishtail gown.

"So what exactly are we looking for?" asked Ava. She grabbed one of the wedding gowns off the rack, held it up to herself, and said, "Yikes, what bride in her right mind wore this monstrosity?" The gown had a ruffled neckline, balloon sleeves, and a three-tiered skirt. "This is supposed to be *vintage*?"

"Vintage doesn't always mean tasteful," Carmela laughed. "That gown looks like it's probably from the '80s, which would explain the big poufy shoulders and tiers of ruffles. It's . . . what would you call it? The Joan Collins *Dynasty* look."

"Either that or a bow factory vomited all over it," said Ava. "So . . . we're supposed to somehow salvage a couple of these weird old dresses?"

"Remember," said Carmela, "I'm going to turn them into ghost costumes. Here, why don't you try this one on and I'll show you." Carmela pulled a more modern-looking dress from the rack, one with a scoop neckline and long, fishtail skirt.

Ava looked worried. "I don't know if that one's really me . . ."

"Just scoot into the dressing room and slip it on," Carmela urged.

Two minutes later, after several loud snorts, an impatient guffaw, and three "I don't *think* so"s, an unhappy-looking Ava emerged from the dressing room.

"This is awful," said Ava, studying herself in the three-way mirror. "I look like a human cream puff." She smoothed at the skirt nervously. "This sure ain't my dream dress."

"But we're going to work on it," Carmela soothed. "Make it into something ghostly."

"How we gonna do that?" Ava lifted a sleeve, gave a sniff, and wrinkled her nose. "Ugh, smells like mothballs."

"First of all," said Carmela, "we'll air it out. Then we're going to shred the heck out of it. We'll slit the skirt in a couple dozen places so it literally hangs like rags on you. Then we're going to beat the living crap out of it until it's tattered and ratty and dirty."

That drew a smile from Ava. "Kind of like the bride who wore this dress had some real wild fun at her reception, huh? Like she partied her brains out and then got kidnapped by a pack of wild groomsmen?"

"See?" said Carmela. "Now you're getting the hang of it. Now you can see the wicked possibilities. Anyway, what we'll do is rip off all the extraneous poufs and swirls and seriously distress the dress."

"That sounds like a new reality show."

Carmela chuckled. "We're going to make our wedding gowns look like they were once worn by the brides of Dracula."

"Now you're talkin'," said Ava. She wandered over to another rack and picked through it. When she came to a short, flouncy Pepto-pink dress, she said, "Ack, look at this bridesmaid's dress." She turned to Carmela. "You know what's worse than buying a bridesmaid's dress? Buying a nearly identical one for yet *another* wedding."

"Always a wedding guest, never a bridesmaid," said Carmela. "That's me."

"Me, too," said Ava. "Though I do want to get married

someday if Mr. Right comes along. Instead of just Mr. Right Now." She looked a little wistful. "On the other hand, I worry about giving up my freedom. And my closet space."

"You're definitely in the free spirit category."

"I'm a sprite," said Ava. "But then, when I think about all the gorgeous presents that brides are showered with, I say to myself, *Yeah, that could be me, rackin' up all that swell stuff.* Plus you get to star in a big fancy ceremony at a church or in some gorgeous garden, and you get to drink champagne and enjoy an amazing wedding cake to boot. So my thought process starts to go a little wonky and I think—maybe I'll get married just for the cake."

"I can understand that," said Carmela. "Especially if buttercream frosting is involved."

Ava studied herself in the mirror again. "Okay, so I'm starting to seriously buy into your vision. Now what?"

"A dress for me, too," said Carmela. She sorted through the rack again and picked out a wedding dress with an enormous ball gown skirt.

"Love it," said Ava.

"I thought we'd also wear dingy long gloves and cover our heads and shoulders with shrouds."

"Mmn, I like the creepy shroud part."

"We have to look the part," said Carmela. Then, much to Ava's amusement, she slipped into her dress.

"That's one big-ass skirt," said Ava. "Makes you look like you jammed about fifty Hefty bags under there."

After they'd laughed themselves silly and changed back into their street clothes, they carried their wedding gowns up to the front register.

"Oh good, you both found something nice," cooed the clerk. "I had a feeling you might."

"These dresses should work great," said Ava. "But are they expensive?"

"How does thirty dollars each sound?" said the clerk. She

dropped her voice to an almost-whisper. "We've had them sitting around in storage for a *long* time. I'm just happy to see them go out the door."

"Sold," said Carmela.

AVA WAS ABOUT TO CAREFULLY FOLD THE TWO dresses into the backseat of Carmela's sports car, when Carmela held up her hand and said, "Wait. While we're at it, we may as well kill two birds with one stone."

Ava crooked an eyebrow. "Meaning?"

Carmela flipped open her trunk and pulled out two red bungee cords. "Here," she said, handing one to Ava. "Thread this cord through the armholes of your dress and then hook it to my back bumper."

"You're serious?"

"Sure," said Carmela, as she worked on her own dress. "The way I see it, if we drag these dresses behind us, they'll crash and bang and twist against the pavement and start shredding like crazy."

"Takes a licking and keeps on ticking," said Ava. "Works for me."

They tied their dressed on to the bumper and hopped in the car. As Carmela gunned the engine she said, "Just keep an eye out, we don't want another car to get too close and run up onto our dresses. We don't need any"—she chuckled—"skid marks."

"I'll wave 'em back," said Ava, as she stuck her head out the passenger-side window. "Or fire a warning shot across their bow. Whichever comes first."

Ava was as good as her word. As they spun down St. Charles Avenue, the dresses bouncing and spinning behind them like a couple of deflated parachutes dragging across open ground, they heard shouting and honking from the cars that zoomed past.

"Hey!" Ava yelled, waving back at a couple of guys in a blue pickup truck who hooted and pointed at their dresses. "Want to meet me at the altar?"

"You're really having fun with this, aren't you?" said Carmela. She'd cranked up the radio and WKBU was blasting out Mitch Ryder's classic tune "Devil with a Blue Dress On."

"This is crazy," screamed Ava. "It's like a new recipe for stone-washed jeans. Only we're doing cobblestone-washed dresses."

"And the attention's not bad, either."

"I haven't enjoyed this many catcalls since I wore my red leather mini and fishnet stockings into St. Louis Cathedral."

"Dear Lord," said Carmela.

"Well, not quite," said Ava. She pulled her head in and said, "Maybe you should tell me about the shrouds."

"I'm going to cut big hunks of cheesecloth and then stiffen and dye them."

"This all sounds terrific," said Ava. "Even better than the vampire costume I cooked up for my haunted cemetery tour."

"When is that anyway?"

"Thursday night. Hey, you wanna come along?" She reached over and plucked excitedly at Carmela's sleeve, causing her to swerve dangerously toward the sidewalk and Big Bubba's Rib Joint, almost knocking over a homemade sign that said, *Ribs Come and Git Em. Grits too.* "You have to come with me, *cher*, it's going to be quite the spectacle. I've got a group of almost twenty people who've signed up, and I just hired a professional werewolf to pop out and terrify everyone!"

"How could I possibly resist a werewolf?"

"A big hairy guy with flashing eyes and gnashing teeth. What's not to love?"

Carmela glanced in her rearview mirror. "Are those dresses still okay?"

"Hanging in there."

"There sure is an awful lot going on this week," said

Carmela. "I mean, the Pumpkins and Bumpkins Ball is the same night as your cemetery tour."

Ava nodded. "It is. But you've got your tickets, right? And Babcock's coming, too?"

"That's the plan," said Carmela, knowing he would try to back out of it. "For now anyway."

DRAGGING THE DRESSES BEHIND HER, CARMELA burst into her apartment just as the phone started to ring. Vaulting over a leather ottoman, she fended off Boo's and Poobah's excited advances and plucked up the receiver just as her caller was about to be kicked over to voice mail.

"Hello?" She hoped it was her hottie patottie boyfriend.

It was.

"Hey," he said.

Carmela, who was still in a playful, upbeat mood, said, "Is this a booty call or do you have something really important to tell me?"

"Carmela, please. Don't we mean more to each other than that?"

"I don't know," said Carmela. "You roar up in your big shiny car, don't come in to meet the folks . . . you tell me what your motives really are."

"The only time I'm in a hurry is when I'm in a squad car, lights and siren."

"Is that so?"

"All kidding aside," said Babcock, "I did stumble across an interesting little nugget of information today. Your buddy Stanger . . ."

"Hold it right there," said Carmela. "Stanger is not my buddy."

"Well, good, because it would appear that James Stanger has been in some deep doo-doo with the Commies. You know, the guys in the little blue Mao suits with the red books?"

"You're referring to the Chinese government? The People's Republic of China?"

"Oh, you want to be politically correct?" said Babcock. "Yes, with the PRC."

"Let me guess . . . does this have to do with the importation of Chinese antiquities?"

"What?" Babcock sounded surprised. "How did you know about that?"

"I ran into that phony countess again last night," said Carmela. "And, like, five seconds into our meeting she started railing about Stanger. About how he was some kind of smuggler." She paused and thought about all the Chinese artwork in Stanger's shop. "So tell me about this importation law."

"I'm no expert," said Babcock, "but it turns out the Chinese passed a law several years ago that prohibits exportation of any Chinese antiques after 1972. In other words, no more art treasures are supposed to leave their country."

"But the art still is. Leaving, I mean." Carmela knew that, besides French and English antiques, the French Quarter was stuffed to the rafters with Chinese art. There were probably more crates full of it in dozens of dealers' back rooms, too.

"Like everything else," said Babcock, "there are a few sneaky ways to skirt that law."

"Such as?"

"If your merchandise comes from a government-approved dealer and carries an official government export stamp you're apparently in the clear."

"That's interesting," said Carmela, "because I see Chinese antiques all over the place. Carved screens, blue and white vases, jade statues, you name it. And I've yet to hear anything about an official export stamp."

"Well, there you go," said Babcock. "I guess there are scofflaws in China, too. Lord knows, we have enough of them in New Orleans."

"So what exactly are you saying?" said Carmela. "That Stanger has no scruples in dealing with stolen artwork?"

"I'm guessing he doesn't have any scruples about anything."

"Which means he's sitting squarely on your hit list?"

"He's on my *possibles* list."

"Your list is getting longer and longer," said Carmela.

"Only because you keep making suggestions," said Babcock. "*You're* the one who keeps adding to it."

"Face it, you need my help."

"No, I really don't."

"Then why exactly did you call?"

"To try to get out of going to that stupid Halloween ball?"

"No way," said Carmela. "You promised to take me to the Pumpkins and Bumpkins Ball and I'm holding you to it." She hadn't been all that excited about going, but now it somehow seemed important to her. "You're going and that's the end of it."

"Even if I have official business?"

"Sweetie," said Carmela, "this *is* official business."

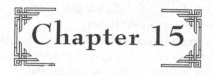

Chapter 15

HALLOWEEN in New Orleans was not relegated to one saccharine night of miniature Kit Kats and Snickers dominated by pint-sized superheroes and tiny princesses. In fact, this Tuesday morning at Memory Mine, Carmela and Gabby were proving that the grown-ups could party with the best of them.

"Reach for the sky, Bonnie Parker. This town ain't big enough for the both of us," Gabby joked. She pulled a silver six-gun from the holster that was slung around her gingham cowgirl dress and aimed it at Carmela.

Carmela, dressed in a camel-colored beret, canary sweater, and black pencil skirt, played along. "With the size of this crowd, I'm thinking this *store* isn't big enough."

Gabby reached for a packet of silver beads, then did a pirouette and grabbed a roll of silk ribbon. Even though it was midmorning, Memory Mine was crowded and nearly filled to its designated fire-code limit. Customers jostled for

albums, colored markers, paper, ink, and cardstock while
Carmela and Gabby worked hard to accommodate them.

As Gabby rang up a stack of embossed paper, she turned
to Carmela and said, "Is Babcock going to play the handsome Clyde Barrow to your Bonnie?"

Carmela looked thoughtful. "Maybe, maybe not. He
claims he's beaucoup busy and is already trying to beg his
way out of the Pumpkins and Bumpkins Ball."

"He's out there fighting the good fight," said Gabby. "So
I'd kind of have to agree with him."

"I know, but . . ." Carmela sighed.

Gabby dropped her voice. "Are there any breaks in the
investigation? Any new clues?"

Carmela debated her words for about one second. "Our
friend down the street . . ."

Gabby shook her head, not quite understanding.

"You know," said Carmela. Then, under her breath, she
said, *"Antiques? Stanger?"*

Gabby bobbed her head, catching on. "Oh, *him.*"

"Turns out he's broken a few laws on the importation of
Asian antiquities."

Gabby's brows lifted in surprise. "So Babcock's looking
into that?"

"Says he is."

"But Stanger could never have . . . well, you know." She
was referring to the murder of Joubert.

"That's right," said Carmela. "I don't know. But I intend
to find out." She hustled over to a paper bin where three
women seemed to be in an argument over the last few sheets
of orange foil paper.

"Can I offer any help?" Carmela asked.

While all three women jabbered at once, Carmela
reached into a storage bin and pulled out fat stacks of paper
that featured skull motifs, bats, and witches' hats. Problem
settled via inventory.

"Everything okay?" Gabby asked, as Carmela scooted back to the front counter.

"It is now."

"So how goes the hunt for your vintage wedding gowns?"

"Oh, I meant to tell you," said Carmela. "We found them. Last night. Horrible gowns, really, but they're going to be perfect once we distress them and turn them into ghost costumes."

Gabby practically giggled. "How on earth are you going to manage that? Wave your magic wand?"

"For one thing, we already dragged the gowns behind my car."

"That must have been quite a sight."

"Yeah," said Carmela. "As you might expect, Ava was in her element, laughing and screaming and hanging out the window, waving to folks like she was grand marshal of the Bacchus Parade. She could have filled up her entire social calendar, what with all the men hollering back at her."

"You two," said Gabby.

"I'm still not sure what was so interesting about a couple of gals dragging ugly wedding gowns down the street, but men were practically hanging in the trees to get a look."

"I think it was the ripped angle," said Gabby. "A torn dress bodice to men is like blood in the water to sharks. They can smell it for miles."

"You seem to have a real feel for this." Carmela chuckled. "Maybe I should be making a ghost dress for you, too."

"Pass," said Gabby.

More customers came bounding into the shop. One was a woman named Samantha who was one of their regulars. She pushed her way directly to the counter and said, "Carmela, I am in *desperate* need of your help."

"Of course," said Carmela. She stepped smartly around the counter. "What can I show you?"

"It's more your creative ideas that I need," said Samantha.

"I'm having a Halloween party and I want to serve vampire wine."

"Okay," said Carmela. It wasn't the strangest request she'd ever heard.

"Let me rephrase that," said Samantha. "I want *labels* that say *Vampire Wine*."

"Gotcha. I'm guessing this is red wine in standard wine bottles?"

"Sure."

"Here's what I'm thinking," said Carmela. "Let's grab a couple of rubber stamps . . ." Her fingers danced along the shelves. "This one of a spooky castle and this one depicting a caped vampire."

"Ooh, I like it already."

Carmela snatched up a sheet of purple cardstock and a sheet of Gothic transfer letters. "First we'll spell out *Vampire Wine* on the cardstock, then use our rubber stamps to make a vampire montage. And maybe shade it judiciously with a red pen. Then you just cut your label to size and have it color copied. You need, what? Maybe ten labels?"

"Six would do it," said Samantha.

"In that case, just sit right down at the back table. And once you have your label figured out, I'll scan it into my computer and print out your six colored sheets."

"Just like that?"

Carmela smiled. "I could make it trickier if you want."

"No," said Samantha. "This sounds just fine."

CARMELA DECIDED TO TAKE ADVANTAGE OF A small lull to retreat to her office and work a bit more on designs for the countess's logo. As she sat down at her desk, she felt a little shudder run through her. There was something about the countess that made her uneasy. She wasn't sure if it was the woman's pretentiousness or if she sensed real danger, but the sooner she was done with this project the better.

She doodled a few ideas, playing with the notion of using the yellow and red colors of the Borgia family crest. The colors worked beautifully together and a crest motif was always classy and upscale. She sketched dutifully for ten minutes until she had a design she liked.

Okay. So I've got the earlier ring logo and now the crest logo. What else?

Carmela set to drawing again, this time sketching a Roman skyline with the word *Lucrezia* written in sinister-looking calligraphy. With the name wrapping around the dome of St. Peter's Basilica, it looked as if the entire expanse of Rome was Lucrezia's property. And maybe, a long time ago, in Renaissance times, that wasn't so far from the truth.

Carmela worked up the two designs, printed out wine labels for Samantha, and managed to wolf down a chicken salad sandwich that Gabby set on her desk. Finally, just after noon, Carmela ducked out of Memory Mine with a quick reconnaissance mission in mind.

CARMELA HAD NEVER VISITED A PAWN SHOP BEfore and she was finding it fairly fascinating. Sparks Pawn Shop had a scuffed hardwood floor, buzzing fluorescent lights, and rows of heavy-duty metal shelves running down the length of the rectangular room. Each shelf was piled high with a mishmash of stuff: lawn mowers, shiny purple electric guitars, chain saws, battery starters, golf clubs, and musical instruments. On the floor in back was a stack of ocean-going kayaks. Another two rows of shelving were dominated by enormous towers of stereo equipment—speakers, receivers, and equalizers, everything piled to the ceiling.

Probably, she decided, when iPods and iPhones and MP3

players came into existence, these massive black stereo components were rendered virtually useless.

So who would buy them now? Maybe a garage band? Although didn't today's music-obsessed youth know how to record and even edit music tracks right on their computers? Or even on their mobile phones? Sure they did.

A woman with a beehive hairdo glanced up from the glossy pages of *Star Whacker* magazine. "Help you?" she asked. She was wearing gold glitter eye shadow and fake eyelashes that made her look like she had tarantulas perched about her eyes. At first glance, Carmela thought the woman might be in costume. But no, this was how she normally looked. Well, not *really* normal, but there you have it.

"I'm just looking around," Carmela told her.

"Suit yourself." Tarantula Lady stuck her nose back in her gossip magazine.

Carmela wandered around some more and found herself gazing at a stack of oil paintings, a few lamps, and some candelabras.

So Johnny Sparks does carry some quasi art and antiques.

The next aisle over was sporting goods. Piles of water skis, baseball bats, fishing rods, and croquet sets were stacked on shelves next to . . .

What is this?

Carmela reached to the back of the shelf and shoved a mound of bicycle helmets out of the way. And smiled when she found a long blue and white fiberglass board with a large shark fin. A paddleboard.

Carmela had seen people using them on Cane River Lake up in Natchitoches. It looked like fun and was supposed to be terrific exercise, especially for your core muscles. And the trim ladies in their skimpy bikinis always looked so tan and athletic as they glided along on their paddleboards. At least they did on TV.

Then again, where would she actually go paddleboarding? Lake Pontchartrain was filled with hotdoggers in speedboats and if she ventured out onto the Mississippi, she'd probably get mowed down by a barge.

So . . . paddleboarding in the bayou? Somehow, the idea of a big old alligator swimming silently up behind her was enough to make her rethink the merits of a nice safe hot-yoga class. She pushed the board back and moved on.

As she perused a pile of camera gear, Carmela caught a glimpse of a thin, round-shouldered man emerging from the back of the shop. Was this Johnny Sparks? She tried to steal a few nonchalant glances at him. She vaguely remembered his face from a grainy picture she'd found on the Internet.

Yes, it had to be him. He was the epitome of an unsavory character—bad teeth, bad skin, bad comb-over. His narrow face was pulled into a twisted grimace that made him look like he'd just discarded a hunk of Limburger cheese.

Carmela moved over to a glass case filled with surprisingly upscale jewelry and watches, figuring this might attract his attention. She set her phone down on the counter, bent her head, and studied a glittering tray of watches.

Sparks came charging at her like a lunker after a piece of bait. A crocodile smile crept across his face as he said, "See something you like?"

"That silver Cartier is awfully nice."

His smile widened, though it wasn't the least bit warm or endearing.

"Excellent choice," said Sparks. He slid open a panel behind the case, reached in, and brought out the watch. His fingernails were spotlessly clean, but the nail on his little finger was at least an inch longer than the others and ended in a sharp point.

Setting the watch down on a black velvet display pad, Sparks launched into his sales pitch. "This watch is actually white gold, which has a far richer glow than sterling silver."

"It's nice," said Carmela, slipping the tank watch onto her wrist.

"Now, if you like analog, I've also got a ladies Rolex."
Sparks removed a glittering Rolex from the display case and
dangled it enticingly. "Very gently used. This beauty is a
mix of eighteen karat gold and stainless steel with a pavé
diamond bezel. Far superior to the Cartier."

"It's beautiful," Carmela said, because it was. She handed
him back the Cartier.

"If you're in the market for a top-of-the-line timepiece,"
said Sparks, "nothing's gonna beat a Rolex. Holds its value
like nothing else."

"How much is it?"

Sparks frowned. "Ohhh . . . I could probably let you have
it for around six. Thousand."

Dollars? Is this guy crazy?

"It's a gorgeous watch," said Carmela.

"If it's not exactly what you have in mind," said Sparks,
"just tell me what model you're interested in. I've got lots of
connections and can put my hands on pretty much anything
you want."

I'll bet you can.

"What about artwork? Or antiques?" said Carmela. She
tried to keep her voice low key. "You ever handle things like
that?"

"Art, huh? I could tell you were a high-class broad just
by looking at you," Sparks said. "Yeah, you never know, I
get some of this, some of that. What exactly are you in the
market for? That way I can kinda keep an eye out."

"I collect antique dog statues, mostly bronze," said
Carmela.

Sparks was nodding. "Yeah, I come across those once in
a while."

"Old etchings are always interesting. Particularly if they
depict scenes around New Orleans. And I'm partial to—"

Carmela's phone shrilled loudly, interrupting their conversation. Sparks glanced at her phone, a look of sheer

annoyance on his face, then his eyes suddenly widened in surprise.

"Excuse me a min—" Carmela started to say.

Quick as a whip, Sparks's hand shot out and swooped the phone up off the counter.

But not before Carmela saw the caller ID light up. It said *NOPD Babcock*.

Sparks's eyes narrowed and his mouth pulled into a wolfish snarl. "Say now," he hissed. "Just what the heck is going on here?"

Carmela reached out and grabbed her phone away from him. "What are you talking about?"

"You can't fool me, girlie," said Sparks. "I saw the caller ID on your phone."

"So what?" said Carmela.

"You with the cops?" said Sparks. "Are you guys trying to run a sting on me? If you are, you better believe I'm gonna phone my lawyer!"

His loud voice had roused Tarantula Lady from her magazine. "What's wrong, Johnny?" she called out. "Want me to call the cops?"

"Go ahead and call the cops," said Carmela.

"Johnny?" Tarantula Lady sang out again. "Everything okay?"

"Johnny's just fine," said Carmela as she eased herself away from the counter. "I was just leaving."

"You got that right," said Sparks. "And don't come back!"

Chapter 16

GABBY fussed about at the back table, laying out plaster bandages, a box of plastic straws, and several small plastic spray bottles filled with water.

"Where did you run off to?" she asked Carmela.

"Um . . . Sparks Pawn Shop."

"Sounds awful."

"It was," said Carmela. She was trying to shake the queasy feeling that lingered from her encounter with Johnny Sparks. He was scummy all right. The question was, could the man also be a killer?

"I'm still kind of spooked about this whole thing," Gabby said as she unwrapped a second box of plaster bandages.

"You mean about our Death Mask class?" Carmela measured out a piece of pink gossamer ribbon she was going to add to a cylindrical gift box she'd made using purple cardstock and some tricky origami techniques.

"Well . . . yes. Somehow it seems in poor taste."

"Probably because it is," Carmela chuckled. She thought for a moment, then said, "You know what, Gabby? It's really just good fun. We're coming up on Halloween, for gosh sakes. We've endured Zom Proms and vampire cams, and Ava's Haunted Cemetery Walk is coming up in a couple of days. Heck, I'm even going to ride the Ghost Train on Friday night."

"I suppose," said Gabby. Her nose twitched as she considered Carmela's words. "The Ghost Train actually sounds like the *least* bizarre of all this week's activities."

"Let's hope it is."

Carmela finished her gift box, carried it to the front window, and did a little rearranging of her display. She decided to group the memory boxes together, put the tags up front and, oh, she had two velvet clutch bags that she'd decorated with gold rubber-stamped images. So they should enjoy a prominent place, too.

Just as she was moving a miniature Halloween triptych, her would-be mask makers came tripping through the front door. Baby, Tandy, and Tandy's daughter-in-law.

"Car-*mel*-a!" Tandy called out. "You remember Julie Bergeron, don't you? My dear, sweet daughter-in-law."

"Don't be fooled, that's what Tandy says about all her daughters-in-law," said Julie, grinning at Carmela. She was tall, blond, and athletic, with ice blue eyes. She looked, Carmela decided, like she should be competing in the Winter Olympics, riding a luge downhill at breakneck speed, instead of being a stay-at-home mom who homeschooled her three little ones.

Then Gabby came rushing up to greet everyone and there was a brief flurry of children's photos being passed around and a cacophony of "ooh"s and "isn't she sweet."

When the niceties had been taken care of, Carmela led her group back to the craft table.

"How's the party coming along?" Carmela asked Baby.

Her blowout of a Halloween party was happening tomorrow night.

"Everything's pretty much ready," said Baby. "Catering, décor, and music." She eyed the table where all the supplies were laid out. "Except we could still use a couple of masks."

"Then let's get to it," said Carmela. "Who wants to be our first guinea pig?"

Tandy immediately raised a hand. "Me."

"Okay, sweetie," said Carmela. She pulled out a chair for her. "Sit down right here and we'll get started. "I hope you're not wearing too much makeup."

"Why?" said Tandy, as Carmela slipped a shower cap over her red hair.

"Because I'm going to smear your face with Vaseline, that's why," said Carmela. She dipped a finger into the jar and smoothed a gob of the clear jelly across Tandy's forehead. Then she smeared Tandy's nose, cheeks, and jaw.

"That's not so bad," said Tandy. "Just feels a little gooey."

"Close your eyes," said Carmela.

"Uh-oh," said Julie, as Tandy obliged. "Here comes the tough stuff."

"I gotta *keep* 'em closed?" asked Tandy.

'That's right," said Carmela. She took a plastic straw, snipped off a couple of two-inch lengths, and carefully inserted them into Tandy's nose.

"Arggh!" said Tandy, giving a snort. "That feels weird. Tickles."

Carmela patted her shoulder. "Try not to talk."

"Or move," said Baby, who was enjoying this spectacle immensely.

Carmela took her plaster bandages, dipped them into a bowl of water, squeezed them out gently, and started in earnest. "I'm going to make an X across Tandy's nose," she said, laying two smaller bandages down, "and then build from there." She proceeded to add layer after layer of plaster bandages, then spritz them with water. "Notice, you have to pay special attention to all the facial features. The nose and eyebrows especially, gently pinching them into ridges as you go along."

There was another muffled exhalation from Tandy and the heels of her loafers drummed against the wooden floor.

"Easy now," said Carmela. She smoothed the bandages around the sides of Tandy's face, adding another layer here and there, wherever it was needed.

"This is fascinating," said Baby, picking up one of the spray bottles and giving Tandy's face a spritz. "And once you're done . . . well, how long does the plaster have to set?"

"About fifteen minutes," said Carmela.

"You hear that?" Baby asked Tandy.

There was a muffled reply that was either "Yes" or "Help."

When fifteen minutes had passed, Carmela tapped the mask with a fingertip. It felt good. Maybe a trifle damp still, but it wouldn't take more than a few minutes longer for the mask to be completely set. "Tandy, what I need you to do now is wiggle your face a little. Smile, frown, even twitch your nose if you can."

Tandy nodded and, five seconds later, with some gentle guidance from Carmela, the mask popped free.

"I'm never doing *that* again," Tandy declared. She was wild-eyed and pink-faced.

"Yes, you are," said Julie. "Because I want to do one of you, too."

Tandy wiped a hand across her forehead. "Whew. That was downright claustrophobic. I'm shaking like crazy, I think my nerve and my blood sugar plummeted at the exact same moment."

"How about an ice cream sandwich?" Gabby offered. "To help make things better."

"Really?" said Tandy, her good humor flooding back. "What kind?"

"The best kind," said Gabby. "Homemade. Carmela made 'em. She layered butterscotch ice cream between pieces of fresh-baked shortbread."

"Sounds delish," said Tandy, brushing at her cheek to dislodge a remnant of plaster.

Gabby dug into their tiny freezer and distributed the ice cream sandwiches. As the women munched happily, Baby said, "Now what? I mean, what do you do with the mask now that it's practically dry?"

"That's the fun part," Carmela told her. "The creative part. First you refine your mask by rubbing it with fine-grain sandpaper, getting rid of any extraneous lumps or bumps. Then you decorate it, paint it, or do a kind of decoupage by adding strips of colored paper or even gold tissue paper."

"Neat," said Baby.

"Ooh," said Tandy. Her eyes went wide as she suddenly put a hand to her forehead.

"What's going on?" asked Baby. "You trying to read our minds?"

"No," said Tandy. "This ice cream is so cold I think I'm having a brain seizure."

"A Mr. Misty headache," said Carmela.

Gabby handed Tandy a bottle of water. "Here, drink this. A sip of water makes it all go away."

Tandy took a glug. Then she stopped, burped, and smiled. "You're right."

Baby was still nibbling daintily at the last of her ice cream sandwich. "You know all the brouhaha that's been going on over that missing death mask?"

"Yeeees?" said Carmela.

"Guess which one of my neighbors has a couple of death masks hanging in his home?" said Baby.

All eyes were suddenly focused on her, especially Carmela's.

"Who?" Gabby asked.

"Titus Duval," said Baby. She looked pleased with her announcement.

"Seriously?" said Carmela. It felt like her world had just tilted on its axis. Titus Duval was the wealthy collector that Marcus Joubert had been meeting with that same fateful night the Napoleon death mask had been stolen from the Dallas collector. And if Duval was also a collector of masks, could he have been part of that robbery? Obviously, she had lots more probing and digging to do.

"The masks are hung in his house?" asked Carmela.

"They're part of his so-called art collection," said Baby.

"What kind of death masks are they?" Gabby asked. She glanced nervously at Carmela. "Or should I say who are they?"

"I've never seen them firsthand," said Baby, "but I understand that one is a former U.S. president."

"Now there's a definite creep factor," said Gabby.

"And I heard another mask was of a famous Hollywood director," put in Tandy. She tried to grin but her face was still so stiff her expression was more of a grimace.

Which was exactly how Carmela suddenly felt.

"CARMELA?" A SMALL VOICE SUDDENLY BROKE their stunned silence.

Carmela turned in her chair to find Mavis Sweet standing a few feet away and smiling tentatively at her.

"Mavis," Carmela said. "How are you?" She hadn't heard Mavis creep in. On the other hand, she'd just been knocked for a loop by the revelation of Duval's death masks.

Mavis gave a halfhearted shrug. "I'm okay." She gestured with her thumb. "I was just next door, packing up the last of the boxes. I thought I'd pop in and say hello."

Carmela stood up from her chair. "Mavis, you know

everyone here, don't you? Gabby and Tandy and Baby. Oh, and this is Julie, Tandy's daughter-in-law."

Mavis gave a nervous wave. "Hi, everybody."

"I'm so sorry about all your troubles," said Baby. "The death of your employer . . . the closing of your shop."

"Thank you." Mavis reached up and twisted a hank of her hair. She looked nervous, as if she wished the earth would open up and swallow her for good. "Carmela, I just wanted to remind you about the memorial service tomorrow?" It came out as a question. Obviously she was still hoping that Carmela would attend.

"What time is it going to be?" Carmela asked. She had every intention of showing up. How could she not? This poor girl was beside herself.

"Ten o'clock," said Mavis. She started to back away from the group.

"Mavis," said Baby, "if there's anything I can do to help . . ." Baby wasn't just a New Orleans socialite, she was kindhearted and charitable, too. And not just the check-writing kind of charity.

"That's very kind of you," Mavis murmured.

"In fact," Baby continued, "I'd love it if you came to my Halloween party tomorrow night." She smiled kindly. "It might help take your mind off things and do you a world of good to get out for a while." Baby fully subscribed to the good-to-get-out-of-the-house school of thinking.

Carmela imagined Mavis sitting all alone in that awful, tacky house of hers and her heart swelled at Baby's kindness.

At the same time, Mavis's eyes lit up and her demeanor shifted to one of interest and happiness. "Oh, my goodness. I'd *love* to come. That's so kind of you."

Carmela put an arm around Mavis's shoulders and led her back through the shop.

"She's so nice," Mavis whispered. "Did she really mean it?"

Carmela smiled. "Of course she did. And it's a costume

party, a masquerade, so we'll all expect you to wear a grand costume and be front and center tomorrow night."

"Wow." Mavis seemed suddenly energized.

"So the packing's almost done?" Carmela asked.

"Almost."

"Is Boyd Bellamy still pressuring you?"

Mavis made a face. "He dropped by a while ago. I think he enjoys making me cry."

"He enjoys making grown men cry," said Carmela. She stopped and faced Mavis. "Listen, have you found any paperwork yet that relates to that death mask?"

Mavis shook her head. "No."

"And you looked through all of Joubert's records?"

"I've been through everything," said Mavis. She hesitated. "Why do you think it's so important?"

"Because it's still critical to work out the provenance of that death mask," said Carmela. "I don't know what the ramifications are if it turns out the mask *was* stolen from that Dallas collector . . ."

"I'm sure it wasn't," said Mavis.

Carmela held up a finger. "Hear me out, please. If it was, that collector could launch a claim against Oddities. Against what remains of the estate."

Mavis worked her upper front teeth against her lower lip. "That doesn't sound good."

"It's not good. Especially if you still have faint hopes of opening a shop of your own. Depending, of course, on whatever agreement you work out with the sister."

"Okay," said Mavis. "I see where you're going with this. I'll go through everything again."

"Good girl," said Carmela. She saw that the reality of her words had caused Mavis to go a little numb. She hated to push Mavis any harder, but knew it was necessary. "The other thing I wanted to ask about—did you find any sort of connection between Joubert and Johnny Sparks?"

Mavis's eyes slid away and Carmela realized she'd hit a nerve.

"What?" said Carmela. "What did you find?"

"There was a necklace."

"What kind of necklace? What about it?"

Now Mavis seemed reticent. "Apparently, Marcus bought some kind of diamond necklace at auction and then had Joubert sell it for him. On commission, I think."

"Do you know the value of the necklace?"

Mavis hunched her shoulders. "I found a note that said three thousand dollars less nine hundred dollars' commission."

Carmela made a quick calculation. Sparks had helped himself to a 30 percent commission. "So you're telling me that Joubert had Johnny Sparks sell a necklace for him?" *Or fence it.*

"I guess so," said Mavis.

"Why would he do that?"

"I don't know. Maybe Sparks had better connections?"

"This is all getting a little strange," said Carmela. "Don't you agree?"

Mavis furrowed her brow. "It's all I think about," she moaned. "How is this connected, how is that connected? Why was Marcus doing business with Johnny Sparks?"

Carmela was just as confused. There were too many strings all balled up into one unhappy package. Only problem was, if you pulled one string a couple of others seemed to unravel, too. And then there was the problem with the mask . . . or masks.

"Mavis," said Carmela, "I'm still wondering how that death mask was stolen from your cabinet. It seemed like it had been fairly well hidden. Are you sure nobody else knew about it except you and Joubert?"

Mavis stared at her. "Actually . . ."

"Actually what?" said Carmela, pouncing on her words.

"Now that I've had time to think about it, I guess maybe I did show it to one person."

"You're kidding."

"Last Tuesday, I think it was. A week ago."

"Who was it?" Carmela felt excitement fizzing up inside of her. If somebody else had seen the mask and suddenly gotten greedy, this could crack the case. If someone else knew about it, *they* could be the thief and killer! "Who was it you showed the mask to, Mavis? A potential buyer?"

"No, not a buyer." Mavis made an unhappy face. "It was actually the landlord. Boyd Bellamy."

Chapter 17

CARMELA did a double take that would have been comical if she hadn't been so stunned. "You showed Boyd Bellamy the death mask?" she sputtered out. "Why on earth would you do something like that?"

"Because I was trying to get him off our case," said Mavis. She was suddenly defensive, her voice growing a little strident.

Carmela grabbed Mavis's sleeve and pulled her outside onto the sidewalk. "Go on. Keep talking." A woman with a small collie dog walked by and they both hesitated.

When the woman and dog had passed, Mavis said, "You have to understand. We were way behind in our rent and Bellamy was literally breathing down our necks, threatening us with eviction. Marcus and I were planning a wedding and I saw our life just . . . well, evaporating. Anyway, I figured if I could convince Bellamy that the mask was going to sell for a lot of money, then maybe he'd back off and give us some leeway."

Carmela was listening intently. "So . . . did he? I mean, was Bellamy impressed enough with the mask that he was willing to give you more time on the rent? Did he understand the mask's historical significance or . . . uh, monetary value?"

"He just sort of looked at it and nodded," said Mavis. "Like he didn't really care." Her eyes swam with tears and she brushed at them with her fingers. "You don't think Bellamy was the one who broke in, do you? That he came back and killed Marcus?"

"I don't know what to believe anymore," said Carmela. "I supposed he could have, though it doesn't feel quite right." Bellamy struck her as more of a cash-up-front type of guy.

Mavis hung her head. "You must think I'm really stupid. A stupid, trusting cow."

"Not at all," said Carmela, feeling a tinge of regret at giving Mavis's feelings a glancing ding. "I think you're a sweet, caring girl who's found herself smack-dab in the middle of a nasty situation she can't figure out."

"The thing is, can *you* figure it out?" asked Mavis.

Carmela shook her head. "I don't know, honey, but I'm sure going to try."

CARMELA LEFT MAVIS ON THE STREET, LOOKING sad and troubled, and hurried back inside Memory Mine. When she checked her crafters, it was Baby's turn to be swaddled in plaster bandages while Tandy squirted water at her. Their peals of raucous laughter were a welcome sound after Mavis's strange revelations and quiet pleadings.

Slipping behind the front counter, Carmela let her thoughts flash back to Boyd Bellamy. Had he seen the mask and, quick as a wink, made up his mind to swipe it? Had he come back, gotten into a nasty confrontation with Marcus Joubert, and then murdered him during an ensuing struggle?

Or had it been someone else entirely? Someone who knew about the mask or had stumbled upon it. Like the uber-wealthy Titus Duval? Or the strange Countess Saint-Marche? Or the scheming Johnny Sparks?

Carmela's meditation on murder was interrupted by the ringing of the phone.

She snatched it up, trying to shift into chipper mode. "Memory Mine."

"*Cher*, we're still going to the Witches' Run tonight, right?" It was Ava. And just hearing her upbeat voice caused Carmela to grin and her shoulders to unknot.

"Don't you ever just want to stay home? Crawl into your jammies and watch something on Netflix?"

"Nuts," said Ava. "I can rest when I'm dead and stuck away in some spooky mausoleum that's hopefully kitty-corner from Commander's Palace so I can order in when I feel like it. But for right now, I want to party my brains out."

"Ava . . ."

"Please, please, please, Carm. I'll even buy you dinner at Mumbo Gumbo."

"Hmm . . . bribery will get you everywhere," said Carmela. She knew Mumbo Gumbo would be jumping tonight and they did dish up some wicked gumbo and jambalaya.

"Hah," said Ava. "I thought so. And *cher* . . . ?"

"Yes, dear?"

"Wear something fun tonight, something a little kinky. Enough with that conservative Republican beige. Maybe try . . . a rubber dress?"

"You're incorrigible."

"Yes, and I'm very corruptible, too."

AS SOON AT THE MASKS WERE DECORATED— Tandy's with red zigzags that were almost tribal, and Baby's image with gold leaf—Carmela hastily straightened up the back table. There were lots of snips and snippets scattered around, what she like to call craftermath.

"Are you coming back to the French Quarter tonight?" Gabby called to her. "For the 5K and the parade?" Baby, Tandy, and Julie had just tumbled out the front door, giggling and waving their good-byes.

"I think so. You?"

Gabby shook her head. "No, Stewart's receiving some kind of award tonight from the local Rotary Club. For being a model citizen and selling, like, eight million Toyotas."

"Eight million. Very impressive."

"Well, maybe not *that* many." She paused, a piece of peach-colored rice paper in her hands. "I feel sorry for Mavis. She seems like one of those poor misguided souls who never really finds their way in life."

"You may be right."

"So . . . perhaps we should help her?"

"I think," said Carmela, "that we already are."

CARMELA WAS THE LAST ONE OUT THAT NIGHT. As she turned her key in the lock, always mindful to latch the door carefully, she realized that she still felt haunted by the specter of murder next door. She walked a few steps down the sidewalk to Oddities and peered in the window. Where jade statues, antique weapons, and taxidermy animals had been displayed just days ago, now there were just dust balls. It felt like an entire year had passed since she'd peered in the window and noticed a faint light. Had heard that awful telltale thump.

Oh my, kind of like Poe's "Tell-Tale Heart"!

But it had been only four days.

Babcock was working his fingers to the bone, trying to solve Joubert's murder, but he didn't seem to be getting any closer. She'd been snooping around herself. And while she'd sniffed out a few rotten eggs—suspects, really—she hadn't drilled down to the heart of the matter. Who was the killer? Someone who freely walked the French Quarter? Someone who all the unsuspecting players were rubbing shoulders with?

The thought made her shiver.

So what to do? Go home, flake out for a while, and then go out with Ava again tonight? Well . . . she had promised her friend. And Babcock, that squirrel, was still complaining about how busy he was.

Which he really was, but that didn't mean she wasn't craving a little snuggle-bunny time with him.

Carmela looked through the darkened window again and sighed. Then she spun on her heels and fought to get her head clear. It was a lovely, late-October afternoon, crisp and cool, just a faint residual shimmer of sun off to the west in the darkening pinkish-purple sky. She strolled along slowly, thinking about Joubert's untimely death, thinking about possible suspects. Flickering gaslights were coming on in their old-fashioned wrought-iron stanchions, musicians were tuning up in nearby jazz clubs, neon lights were starting to buzz and blaze.

As an idea slowly took root in Carmela's brain, she picked up her pace and marched down the block to the Gilded Pheasant.

Unlike the desolation that hung over Oddities, James Stanger's front window glowed warmly and was chock-full of choice merchandise. Carmela gazed at an ornate French mantel clock, a painted Limoges vase, and a string of pistachio-colored Baroque pearls. There was a landscape oil painting, too, probably Northern European, that had to date to the seventeenth century. Everything looked very tasteful and elegant. And expensive.

When did Stanger start carrying such upscale pieces? Carmela wondered. She'd had always thought of him as more of a second-tier art and antique dealer, but it looked like he'd seriously upgraded his merchandise of late.

Acting on impulse, Carmela climbed the two steps to his shop and pushed open the door. The lights were low and music played over the speakers, a light, frothy piece, harpsichord only. Several large, ornate library tables held a wide mix of pieces. There were bronze sculptures of horses and dogs, a stone Buddha, snuff bottles, gilded French candelabras, and what looked like a piece of Tiffany glass. The dark red walls were hung with original oil paintings, crowded so close together they looked like a mosaic.

Her hand outstretched, Carmela walked a few more steps and touched a cloisonné vase. The enamel, done in colors of rose and green, felt cool and pure and looked expensive. She checked the price tag. It was expensive. $1,200.

Crooking her head to the side, Carmela looked around for Stanger and saw that he was sitting in his small office. He was behind his desk, talking urgently to a customer who was seated directly opposite him. The two were speaking in low, hushed tones, as if their discussion was very much in earnest. A negotiation of some sort? Maybe.

Her curiosity piqued, Carmela moved a little closer, trying to keep her body language nonchalant, but, at the same time, angling to see who Stanger's customer might be.

No dice.

Carmela gave up and busied herself with a collection of snuff bottles on a rosewood stand. They were cunning little bottles carved from jade and some other highly polished, bronze-colored stone. Then she heard the back door click open and felt a whoosh of cool air. Stanger's mysterious customer had left by the back alley. Interesting.

Two seconds later, James Stanger rushed out to greet her.

"Carmela," said Stanger, "I had no idea you were going to drop by." He was cordial but cool at the same time, his brittle manner reinforced by his staid black suit.

"I had no idea, either," said Carmela. "This is just . . . impromptu."

They smiled at each other. Not much of a joke but there it was, hanging in the air between them.

"I didn't meant to interrupt your meeting," said Carmela, glancing back at his office. She was still wondering about the visitor who'd beat a hasty retreat into the alley, wondering if Stanger would offer an explanation. He did not.

"Not a problem." Stanger clapped his hands together then spread his arms out wide. "What can I show you? What lovely treasure can I tempt you with today?"

Carmela, who was really on a fact-finding mission, decided to play along with his largesse.

"I'm on the hunt—actually I've been looking for a while—for something to punch up my living room. A piece that's Old World and a little special."

"Do you live around here? I mean, I assume you do, since your shop is right here, too."

"Yes, I'm fairly close." Something inside Carmela told her not to reveal her exact location. She pointed to a pair of Chinese ceramic dogs. They were fierce-looking creatures with bulging eyes and oversized muzzles. "Those are gorgeous creatures. Just the kind of thing I was looking for."

Stanger immediately launched into dealer mode. "Those are foo dogs, sometimes called lion dogs, dating from the Qing Dynasty. Done in blue and white porcelain as you can see."

"So they're old, they've got some age on them."

"Absolutely. More than three hundred years."

"Isn't it difficult to get pieces like that out of China?" Carmela glanced around, suddenly noticing dozens of different Chinese art objects. The snuff bottles, various jades, Chinese porcelain plates on rosewood stands.

Stanger basically ignored her question and continued on with his sales patois.

"I don't know if you realize this, Carmela, but Chinese foo dogs are quite significant. These regal beasts were the traditional guardians of temples and palaces. And they always come in pairs—a yin and yang." He paused. "Quite lovely, wouldn't you say?"

"They're beautiful. What is the price?"

"Those particular dogs are priced at twenty-two hundred for the pair." He eyed her cautiously, as if knowing the price might be a stretch for her. "I really don't want to split them up."

Carmela smiled. "I think the dogs would be upset if you did."

"I know it's a pretty penny," said Stanger. "But think about it. The dogs are not only unique, they're an amazing investment as well."

"I will think about it."

Stanger offered up a smile with very little warmth. "I understand you've been doing some investigating into Marcus Joubert's murder."

She remained impassive. "Why would you think that?"

"Because that's what you do. At least, that's what I've *heard* you do."

"No, not really."

Stanger upped the wattage in his smile. "Come on, Carmela, you can level with me." He dropped his voice to a conspiratorial tone. "The Countess Saint-Marche seems to think you're the second coming of Nancy Drew."

"In that case," said Carmela, "maybe you won't mind me asking you a couple of questions."

"What are you talking about?"

"I happened to see you lingering outside Johnny Sparks's pawn shop the other night."

"What?" He suddenly looked on edge.

"Did you not hear what I said?"

"I heard you just fine," snapped Stanger. "I just don't know where you're going with this."

"I was wondering why you were meeting up with Sparks?"

Stanger's brows pinched together. "That's really none of your business. But in the interest of quelling any wild and crazy rumors on your part, I'm going to tell you." He paused. "Johnny Sparks had some sort of Chinese bronze that he wanted me to look at. An archaic piece."

"Archaic," said Carmela.

"From the Bronze Age. A vessel called a *yu*."

"He was trying to sell it to you?" asked Carmela.

"That was his pretext," said Stanger. "But I think he really just wanted to pump me for information and try to get an idea of what it was worth."

"So did you ever connect with him?" asked Carmela.

"No," said Stanger. "And considering he was a no-show, I don't intend to ever deal with him again!"

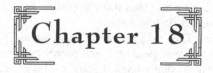

Chapter 18

SITTING at a table in Glissande's Courtyard Restaurant, Carmela enjoyed the people-watching as she sipped her glass of red wine. After sunset was when all the partiers, carousers, and phantoms came out, while legends of ghosts and specters were whispered in every dark alley of the French Quarter. Covering just seventy-eight square blocks, the Vieux Carré, or Old Quarter, had almost three hundred years of history in its rearview mirror. So it was no surprise that the city proper flocked here to enjoy the music clubs, absinthe bars, strip clubs, haunted hotels, and gumbo shacks, not necessarily in that order. And, of course, the 5K Witches' Run was the main attraction tonight.

As the caped and costumed crowd swirled and shifted, Carmela caught sight of Ava shouldering her way toward her. Then again, Ava always stood out in a crowd. Her high cheekbones, snapping eyes, and raven hair turned heads and generally caused grown men to stumble and gape in her wake.

Tonight, however, there was something different about Ava.

"What did you *do*?" Carmela squealed.

Ava batted her lashes and smiled a radiant smile as she scraped back a metal chair and plopped down at Carmela's table. "Whatever do you mean?"

"Your lips. They're, like, totally blimped out!"

"I *told* you I was getting Botox above my brows," said Ava. "Anyway, it went so well, I opted for lip plumper, too."

"You sure did."

"The place I went to . . ."

"Place," said Carmela. "Was it a clinic? Cosmetologist? Plastic surgeon?"

"My manicurist," said Ava. "Remember Bambi, the girl with the hot pink extensions and the boyfriend doing three to five in Dixon Corrections? Well, she was offering a special."

"Three syringes of blowfish-my-lips for the price of one? I mean, for that kind of volume, she can't have used just one vial."

Ava giggled. "No, no, we're talking multiples."

"So you want a drink? Maybe some wine? That's if you can get those lips around a wineglass."

Ava nodded. "I'll work it out. But why don't we wander around the Quarter and grab us a couple of geaux cups? Check out the action and watch the race."

"Sure," said Carmela. She tossed down a few dollars and they skittered off on their adventure.

THE VERY COOL THING ABOUT THE WITCHES' Run was that most of the runners were in costume.

"Lookie," said Ava, as they paused in front of Deek's Oyster Bar. "Here come some of the runners."

There were witches, fairies, a Red Riding Hood, a football player, and a cowboy. They loped along, looking almost professional, obviously the front-runners in the pack.

After these more serious runners—those who'd probably finish the 5K at around twenty minutes—came the amateurs. Glinda the Good Witch, as well as her counterpart, the chartreuse-faced Wicked Witch, were both zooming along on roller skates. Then there was a monk, a guy in a bear suit, and any number of fluttering ghosts.

There was also a man running with two bulldogs, the three of them chugging along as best they could.

Luckily, a local running club was manning a nearby stand of cauldrons, all of them stocked with bottles of water and cups of Gatorade that were handed out to runners as they streamed by.

Carmela and Ava bought strawberry daiquiris and wandered up Bourbon Street. Around eight o'clock there was a loud burst from a cannon.

"What's that?" asked Ava, startled. "The redcoats are coming? There's going to be a redux of the Battle of New Orleans?"

"I think that's to announce the winner," said Carmela. "Somebody must have crossed the finish line."

"Oh, sure. I knew that."

"Yeah," said Carmela. "The race is over for sure. Look, here comes the parade."

Two black-and-white police cars, lights flashing, led the way as a marching band high-stepped its way up the street. Instead of traditional band uniforms, the band members were dressed completely in black ninja outfits with outlines of neon skeletons affixed to the front. They played a jazzy version of "When the Saints Go Marching In" as they passed by.

Following close behind were a trio of flambeaus twirling their flaming torches. And behind them was a troupe of acrobats, flipping and bounding along.

As the first parade float rolled into sight, Carmela immediately recognized a familiar face. It was her ex-husband,

Shamus Meechum, riding proudly at the helm, standing next to a red and purple octopus. Glowing red eyes moved from side to side in the behemoth's head, while four scantily clad mermaids writhed and struggled in the octopus's tentacles. Shamus and his friends waved and played to the crowds as they tossed out candy and glow sticks.

"Shamus! Hey, Shamus!" Ava hooted. They waved and hollered at him until he looked down and grinned in recognition. He gave a wave, and then dashed toward the back of the float. Two seconds later, the float slowed down to a crawl and Shamus hopped off.

"Uh-oh," said Carmela. "He's coming over to talk to us. I didn't think he'd do *that*."

"Just play nice," said Ava.

Carmela's grin stretched uneasily across her face as Shamus approached. He was dressed in a jaunty black leather jacket, gray slacks, and black boots, with not a hair out of place. And he was still devastatingly handsome with his easy smile and languid, confident way of moving. Still, she decided, it was a strained relationship. Especially since they shared joint custody of the dogs.

Shamus wrapped Carmela up in an uncomfortable hug. "You look amazing," he purred, his lips lightly brushing her throat.

"You look great, too," said Carmela. Then, "How come you didn't run in the 5K tonight?"

"Yeah," Ava piped up. "I thought you were a real jock. Didn't you letter in track at Tulane?"

"He did," said Carmela. She took a step back. "At least he *said* he did."

"So you should have been out there leading the pack," said Ava.

Shamus offered a pained expression. "Me? Heck no, ladies. I've got myself a really bad knee." He reached down and made a big production out of massaging his left knee. "My patella's all screwed up. Old football injury, you know."

Carmela frowned. "That's funny. I thought it was your ankle that gave you trouble."

"And that you played soccer instead of football," said Ava.

"Yeah," Shamus said, suddenly switching over and favoring his right leg. "That, too."

Carmela peered at him. "Have you been drinking?"

"What if I have?" said Shamus. "You've got no reason to tell me not to. Not anymore."

"He probably crossed over the legal limit at one o'clock this afternoon," said Ava. She said it lightly, but there was a touch of venom in her voice. Ava still liked to needle Shamus for bugging out on Carmela.

"So what?" said Shamus. "We're coming up on Halloween, after all." He offered them his trademark shit-eating grin. "A major holiday."

"Which explains why you also drink on Flag Day and Arbor Day," said Carmela. "And pretty much every . . ."

"I hear you finally sold the house," said Shamus, hastening to change the subject. Carmela had received Shamus's Garden District home as part of their divorce settlement. "Get a real sweet price on it?"

"We're supposed to close next week," said Carmela. The selling price wasn't any of his business.

"It's the end of an era," Shamus lamented as he clapped a hand to his chest. "The last nail in the coffin of our relationship, and our family manse . . . gone."

"But you didn't want to live there," Carmela pointed out. "You never wanted to live there. Face it, Shamus, you're happier than a nerd at a *Star Trek* convention living in your high-rise condo. That way you can date lingerie models and bottle hostesses to your heart's content and never have to hide or shred another hotel receipt again."

"Ooh," said Ava. "Bottle hostesses. That's your seriously sleazy type of gal."

"Doesn't matter where I live now, babe," said Shamus. "But I got to say it, that house was in the Meechum family for almost a hundred years. It has a serious history."

"Look on the bright side," said Ava. "Now it can be in some other dysfunctional family for the next hundred years."

Shamus's float was about to turn the corner and disappear into the night, when Shamus suddenly yelled out, "Hey, Darlene," to a lithe blonde who was driving a bright red convertible in the parade.

She squealed and waved back at him.

"Put your tongue back in your mouth, Shamus," said Ava.

Shamus was suddenly hot to move on. "Gotta go! Maybe I'll catch you gals later."

"Sure," said Carmela, knowing he'd be off trying to charm Darlene.

"What a poser," said Ava. "Talk about dodging a bullet, *cher.* Your divorce was the best thing that clown ever gave you."

"That and the house."

"And the house," agreed Ava. "Now let's go get us a big bowl of gumbo."

MUMBO GUMBO WAS A COZY RESTAURANT LOcated in a former art gallery that had gone belly-up three years ago. Crumbling brickwork crept halfway up the interior walls, giving it a rustic, European feel. From there the smooth walls were painted in a gold and cream harlequin pattern. A large bar, high gloss and the color of a ripe eggplant, dominated a side wall. Above the bar, glass shelves displayed hundreds of sparkling bottles. Heavy wooden tables with black leather club chairs were snugged next to antique oak barrels that held glass and brass lamps. Large bumper-car booths were arranged in the back. Potted palms and slowly spinning wicker ceiling fans added to the slightly exotic atmosphere of the place.

The music tonight was zydeco interspersed with haunting Cajun ballads, while about three dozen people jostled at the hostess stand, hoping for a table.

Quigg Brevard, the owner, spotted Carmela immediately and hustled over to greet her. All broad shoulders in a sleekly tailored sharkskin suit, Quigg was slightly dangerous-looking with his dark eyes, olive complexion, and full, sensuous mouth.

"Carmela." Quigg uttered her name in his trademark big-cat growl. They had dated a couple of times, though nothing had seemed to spark. Still, whenever Quigg saw her he was more than accommodating. "Can I get you ladies a table?"

"If you can fit us in," said Carmela.

"Not a problem," Quigg said smoothly. He had just the right amount of stubble to effect the look of a devil-may-care restaurateur. Leaning forward, he gave Carmela a quick, tickling peck on the cheek, landing barely a half inch from her mouth.

"Hey, hot dog," said Ava. *She* wouldn't mind dating this guy.

Quigg focused a smile on Ava. "Those are some bee-stung lips you've got there."

"I keep a trained honeybee back at my apartment," said Ava.

Quigg smiled appreciatively. "I'll bet you do." He turned to his hostess, a frantic-looking woman in a tight red dress, and said, "Stacey, take them to booth eight, please."

"Judge Hardwick and his party have been waiting for that booth for*ever*," warned Stacey. She gave a sideways nod. "They're still at the bar."

Quigg's right eyebrow hitched up a notch. "Send the judge a bottle of my Ruby Revelry wine along with my sincere apologies for the wait."

"You're the boss." Stacey grabbed two oversized menus and beckoned for Carmela and Ava to follow.

Not two minutes after Carmela and Ava were cozily ensconced in a booth that could easily hold six, Quigg was there with a bottle of champagne and two champagne flutes.

"You have to try this champagne," he told them.

"From your own St. Tammany Vineyard?" asked Carmela.

Quigg nodded. "I call it *Blanc d'argent*." He filled their glasses and then hovered there, waiting for them to taste the wine. Quigg was your basic obsessive-compulsive vintner, dying to get their opinion.

"Fantastic," said Ava, who loved anything with bubbles.

"Lush," said Carmela. "But with a dry finish."

Quigg grinned broadly. "You see, that's exactly what I was aiming for. Something with sparkle and fullness, but refined." He spun around to the booth next to them. "Who wants to taste my new champagne?" he asked in a magnanimous voice.

Everyone at the next booth smiled and held up a glass.

So, of course, several more bottles had to be brought out and more corks popped. Carmela and Ava chatted with their fellow champagne drinkers and eagerly accepted a second pour in their own glasses.

It wasn't until Quigg began his belated introductions that the party came to a screeching halt.

"Carmela, Ava," said Quigg, "I'll have you know you've been clinking glasses with one of my most prominent customers."

"Who's that?" asked Ava, looking interested.

Quigg pointed to the distinguished-looking gentleman at the head of the table. "This is Titus Duval, one of New Orleans's major bankers and a collector of fine art."

"Oh crap," Carmela muttered under her breath as Quigg continued to rhapsodize.

"What?" whispered Ava.

"That's the guy who supposedly already owns two death masks," Carmela told her.

"Oops," said Ava. "Now what do we do?"

"I don't know," she said slowly. "Talk to him? Maybe try to figure out if he was in the market for a third death mask?"

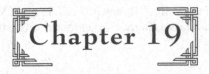

Chapter 19

QUIGG waved a hand in Carmela's direction. He was ebullient and had no doubt been nipping at his own wine. "If you like my menu design, folks, Carmela here is the super talented lady who did all the graphics. She's also the owner of Memory Mine Scrapbook Shop over on Governor Nicholls Street." There were smiles and a spatter of applause, and then he added, "Right next to the shop where that very strange man was murdered a few nights ago. The one who stole the death mask."

"Allegedly stole," said Carmela.

Duval peered at Carmela, suddenly looking interested. "Your shop is adjacent to Marcus Joubert's?" he asked.

Carmela nodded across the booth at him. "I take it you knew him?" She was stammering a bit, knowing full well that Mavis Sweet had sworn on a stack of dusty books that Joubert had an appointment with Duval the very same day the mask was stolen.

"I was a sometime customer," replied Duval.

"Interesting," said Carmela, smiling faintly. She figured that, with the kind of money Duval had, he would be frequenting New York art galleries, buying first-class paintings by David Hockney or Damien Hirst. Not poking through dusty odd-lot merchandise at Oddities.

Duval turned his attention back to his table, while Carmela continued to gaze at him. He was tall and slim, white-haired, and carried himself with a cool, patrician attitude. And he looked rich. Fat and sassy rich. From his manicured nails and hundred-dollar haircut, right down to the cut of his suit and the silk tie he wore.

Silk tie, thought Carmela, her eyes going to it. *And look at the pattern. It's a bee motif. But not just any type of bee.*

Carmela recognized this design as the Napoleonic bee, the one the great French general had elevated to his own personal symbol and had artisans emblazon on everything from his dinnerware to his horse blankets.

"You favor the Napoleonic bee," Carmela called to Duval.

He turned sharply. "Excuse me?"

"Your tie," she said. "It's the Napoleonic bee."

He gave her a steady gaze and then said, "Clever girl."

Ava punched Carmela. "Did I just miss something?" she hissed. "What's going on?"

Carmela dropped her voice and hastily explained the bee symbol to Ava as Duval focused on his dinner guests.

"Oh jeez," said Ava. "You don't think . . ."

"I don't know what to think," said Carmela. "But I do know that man is so rich, he could buy and sell us a few thousand times."

"What's he . . . wait, is he one of those tech billionaires?"

"Duval heads CBD Orleans Bank."

"Ah," said Ava. "So he's a competitor of Shamus's bank."

"Yes, and Duval recently led the fund-raising campaign for the New Orleans Art Institute."

"Sounds like he's got money to burn," said Ava, glancing over at him. "Oh yeah, he must have. Look. Now he's pouring Cristal champagne for his entire table. Very impressive."

"Uh-uh," said Carmela, sensing Ava's interest. "Look but do not touch."

"Killjoy," murmured Ava.

They ordered steaming bowls of gumbo—crab gumbo for Carmela, oyster gumbo for Ava—and when dinner arrived, they tucked into it with gusto.

"Hot," said Ava, waving her spoon. "But good." She dabbed gently at her forehead with her napkin. "I gotta go easy, I almost beaded up."

"Must be all those secret Cajun spices," said Carmela. She reached for the champagne bottle. "More wine?"

Ava nodded. "I don't care if my glass is half empty or half full, as long as it's got champagne."

"I hear you."

Ava took a sip and gazed around the restaurant. "You know what's weird?"

"What's *not* weird?" said Carmela.

"Look around. Everybody's paired up. It's mostly couples here tonight."

"Okay."

"Why is that?" said Ava.

"Because all these people enjoy being unhappy?" Carmela snorted. "Just kidding. Bad joke."

"No, really," said Ava. "What *is* the deal with relationships? My single friends complain that all the good men are taken. But then all the married women complain about their husbands! What's a girl supposed to do?"

"Look who you're asking. I have no idea."

"I guess you're not rushing to get married again?" asked Ava.

Carmela tilted her head. "I wouldn't rule it out, but I can't say I'm anxious to tie the knot anytime soon."

"That's because you've got Babcock. A good, steady guy."

"You make him sound like a pack mule."

"Sorry," said Ava. "But for me . . . I mean, I *like* male attention. And lots of it."

"And you could use more?"

Ava nodded. "Even the bag boy at Broussard's Deli is starting to look good."

"Eeyuuu. The one who looks like Joe Pesci?"

"Does he? I always thought he looked more like Matt Damon."

"I guess you have to catch him in just the right light," said Carmela.

"Or the produce section," said Ava.

"You do need to find a man. And fast."

"What I'm thinking," said Ava, "is that I'm going to put in an application to Millionaire Matchmaker."

Carmela opened her mouth to tell her what a terrible idea that was, but Ava's phone suddenly shrilled.

Ava raised a finger, snatched her phone off the table, and said, in dulcet tones, "Hello?" She listened for a few seconds and then giggled. "It's Charlie, my sweet little pupu platter."

"Charlie . . ." said Carmela. She couldn't remember Ava mentioning anyone named Charlie. On the other hand, Ava was a serial dater, so she couldn't be expected to amass a database on each and every eligible (or not-so-eligible) man.

"Just a minute," Ava said into the phone. She turned toward Carmela and rolled her eyes. "You know who . . . *Charlie*."

"I really don't. Give me a hint."

"That cute crime-scene guy?"

"The tech?" said Carmela. "The one Babcock refers to as a wunderkind, because he's basically twelve years old, wears his cap backward, and probably still tears around town on a skateboard?"

"Charlie's endearing," said Ava. "And he's maybe two years younger than I am at most."

"How old are you?"

Ava spoke into the phone. "Hang on a minute, sugar." Then she turned her attention on Carmela. "You mean this year? Or next year?"

"Right now, at this very moment in time and space."

"Okay, okay, you got me. So Charlie's maybe three or four years younger than I am. Whatever. The only time I really quibble about numbers is when it comes to my weight. Anyway, my little cupcake wants me to meet him for a drink at Dr. Boogie's."

"He's going to need a fake ID to get in there."

Ava mimed *Ha, ha, ha.*

"In fact, your invitation sounds more like a booty call," said Carmela.

"It's not," said Ava, trying to sound prim. "It's a last-minute date."

"Booty call," said Carmela.

"It's not *technically* a booty call unless someone calls after midnight."

"That's your cutoff time?"

"It's as good a marker as anything else."

"Okay," said Carmela, glancing at her watch. "Have it your way. Who am I to stand in the way of true romance?"

"I'll see you there in a couple of shakes," Ava said into her phone. She hung up and said, "Walk me over there?"

"Sure, then maybe Charlie's dad can give me a ride home. Of course, he'll have to move Charlie's car seat." Carmela raised a hand. "Check please."

Their waitress hastened over. "It's all been taken care of."

"Neat," said Ava as she grabbed Carmela's hand and pulled her out of the booth.

Quigg accosted them as they passed the hostess stand. "Ladies, I hope you enjoyed your dinner."

"You can't keep doing this, you know," Carmela told him.

"What?" said Quigg. He was eyeing her as if she were a tasty hors d'oeuvre. "Being hospitable, showing my appreciation for good customers?"

"No," said Carmela. "I mean feeding us for free and constantly flirting with me."

Quigg laughed soundlessly. "Who's flirting?"

"You are," said Carmela. "Anytime I come within twenty feet of you."

Quigg leaned forward and whispered in her ear, "Maybe because I'm fascinated by you."

"You're not."

"I could be."

"Quigg, you're a rogue and a womanizer," said Carmela.

Quigg raised an eyebrow and smiled at her. "Just like your ex-husband?"

"Ouch," said Ava, grabbing Carmela's arm and swiftly propelling her toward the front door. "We're outta here!"

"He's impossible!" Carmela sputtered, glancing over her shoulder at Quigg, who was still laughing softly.

"He's adorable." said Ava. "Tall, dark, handsome, owns a fancy restaurant and a winery. If he wasn't so madly in love with you I'd go after him myself."

"Quigg's not in love with me."

"Oh, *cher*," said Ava. "What you don't know about men sometimes."

THE CROWDS WERE STILL THICK IN THE FRENCH Quarter as Carmela and Ava strolled along. When they got to Dr. Boogie's, a large group of people stood outside, drinking and smoking below the hot pink neon sign. Inside, music twanged, men bellowed, and women shrieked.

"You gonna be okay?" Carmela asked as she peered in the door. "It looks awfully raucous in there." A garbled high-pitched scream pierced the night. "Out here, too."

"Raucous is my middle name," said Ava. She fluffed her hair, tugged her T-shirt lower in front, and basically chomped at the bit.

"Just remember, honey, you know you're in big trouble when the bartender knows your first and last name."

"And friends you on Facebook," said Ava, giggling.

"Yeah, well, all I'm saying is be careful, okay?" Carmela hugged Ava and started down the street.

"It's not a booty call," Ava called behind her.

CARMELA CONTINUED DOWN THE STREET, GLAN-cing occasionally into the front windows of various galleries and antique shops. She was happy from the champagne, sated by the food, and delighted to be heading home. Pushing her hand into the pocket of her tweed jacket, Carmela decided she just might give Babcock a call. See what was new in the wonderful world of crime fighting. Especially since she wasn't exactly making any huge advances herself.

Glancing into the window of Barnard's Booksellers, she noticed a clock and was surprised to see how late it was. Eleven o'clock already? Where had the evening gone? No wonder the crowds had thinned out considerably.

Crossing in front of an alleyway, Carmela quickened her pace. Maybe she should have grabbed a cab for safety's sake, even though she was enjoying the quiet and the cool wind that whooshed like a jet stream off the nearby Mississippi.

A car crunched behind her and headlights splashed across her, illuminating her in the glare. Then it swept past and she was alone again.

Scruff, scruff.

Carmela frowned. What was that? It almost sounded like . . . footsteps? Footsteps behind her? She spun around, hoping to see who it was. But no one was there.

I heard something.

She hurried across the street against the red light. She had her phone with her, so she could definitely call for a cab. But that would mean waiting here. In the dark. Not such a good option.

Scruff. Scrick. Scrape.

There it was again. Spinning fast on her heels, Carmela turned around, half expecting to be faked out again.

Half a block behind her was a lone zombie, walking steadily in her direction.

She froze for a moment, then tried to relax. Of course there's someone in a costume, she told herself. It's the week before Halloween. This poor guy probably ran the race tonight, which would even account for the slight limp. Still, the way the zombie had looked at her was slightly disconcerting. His eyes had drilled into her as if he knew her. She certainly didn't recognize the zombie. Then again, he was wearing green makeup and tattered clothes.

Carmela's heels beat a rapid tap-tap-tap against the sidewalk. But as her pace increased, so did the zombie's! She felt her heart flipping madly, like a trout out of water. What was going on? And why had she found herself in this more deserted part of the French Quarter where the shops were closed and the orange gaslights seemed to fade and falter?

The zombie continued to draw closer to her.

What was he thinking? No matter, Carmela was angry at what she perceived as harassment, and decided to handle it right then and there.

Spinning around, Carmela stood her ground and said, "Do you mind? It's really not very amusing to pull this creepy routine of yours."

The zombie just stared at her, an arrogant hint of a smile on its gray-green face.

Carmela's heart hammered inside her chest. She hadn't expected to be met with this confrontational, almost passive-aggressive attitude. And a smile that seemed to convey, "You're a tasty little morsel and I'd like to eat you up."

Reaching down, she quickly pulled off her heels. Then, clutching her purse to her side like a running back grasping a football, she broke into a fast trot. Her bare feet pounded hard against the pavement as she raced for home, the zombie right behind her.

Adrenaline coursed through her veins as her legs pumped faster and faster. She covered two blocks before she managed a quick backward glance. The zombie was still pursuing her, but he had fallen behind. Thank goodness. Because even if he wasn't a real teeth-gnashing, flesh-eating zombie, he was certainly a very real person. Who seemed intent on doing her harm!

Feeling real terror now, her heart bumpity-bumping, Carmela dashed past the front door of Juju Voodoo and skidded around the corner. Her foot shot out from beneath her and she slipped on a cobblestone. One knee slammed hard against the pavement and she felt a hot trickle of blood. Then she was up and running, through the porte cochere and into her courtyard.

Dropping her shoes on her front step, she rifled frantically through her purse.

Keys! Dear Lord, where are my keys?

Her fingertips finally touched metal and she ripped them out of the bottom of her purse. She was fighting to stave off a full-blown panic attack as she fumbled her key in the lock.

Carmela heard pounding footsteps closing in. She glanced back, didn't see anything, but promptly lost her focus and dropped her keys.

No!

The keys bounced once against a cobblestone and flew into the flowerbed. Carmela knelt down, her fingers hastily raking damp dirt. There they were. Vaulting back onto her front step, she jammed the key into the lock, heard a satisfying click, and burst through the door into the safety of her apartment.

Breathing so hard she sounded like an overwrought teakettle, Carmela slammed the door and locked it. She paused, glanced around wildly, and saw two inquisitive doggy faces staring at her. Their gaze seemed to say, "What the heck happened to you?"

"Am I ever glad to see you guys," Carmela told them. Then she quickly stepped to the window and peered out. Dry leaves blew across the courtyard, tick-ticking against cobblestones. The trees were bathed in moonlight. But no zombie came lurching out of the darkness toward her front door.

What to do now? Dial 911 and try to explain what she'd thought to be a dire situation? Call Babcock and babble for help? She put a hand to her still-thumping chest and forced herself to think straight.

No, calling Babcock would be like detonating a nuclear warhead. He'd freak out and send the SWAT team over. Then he'd stake out her apartment and scrapbook shop night and day. Or, worse yet, he'd keep her sequestered somewhere. Probably in his bedroom.

No, what she had to do was try to get past this nasty little episode. Tell herself, in a keep-calm-carry-on kind of voice, that she was fine, that she'd somehow *handled* the situation. She needed to reassure herself that Boo and Poobah, her faithful fur babies, would stand guard over her all through the night.

That's it. That's what I have to do.

She glanced at the door as if, any minute, a crazed zombie might come crashing through it.

No. That's not going to happen. I dare not let my imagination run wild like this.

She glanced at the door again. Still, it would be nice to drop a drawbridge over a moat teeming with vicious, zombie-snarfing alligators.

Chapter 20

CARMELA wasn't all that thrilled to find herself rambling through a cemetery this Wednesday morning. Especially not after last night and especially since this was spooky old St. Louis Cemetery No. 1, just off Basin Street.

But she'd promised poor Mavis that she'd for sure attend Marcus Joubert's memorial service, so here she was. Banged-up knee and all.

This place was a strange choice, really, because there wasn't even a chapel in this particular cemetery. It was just a parking lot of tombstones as far as the eye could see. Row upon row of ancient stone and brick tombs, a few more upscale mausoleums, and various chipped and dinged statues that depicted lambs, angels, and random people who had long since passed.

This was the cemetery where the famous LSD scene from *Easy Rider* had been filmed. And, even now, Carmela could picture the long, lean Peter Fonda curled up in the lap of one of the marble statues, the impassive stone eyes of the statue staring down at him.

Crunching down a gravel passageway edged with a black wrought-iron fence, Carmela found herself in the heart of the cemetery—if that's what you could call it. To her right was a long row of tombs that looked almost like miniature white marble condominiums. They were the famed oven tombs. Once a body had been entombed in them for a year and a day, and the heat and humidity had battered away, the bones were eligible for removal. That is, they could be shoved down a slot to a *lower* level so another body was free to take its place.

Just ahead, Carmela could see a small gathering of people, all dressed in black like a passel of restless crows. Hopefully, this was Mavis's group, not just a gaggle of camera-toting tourists.

Yes, it was. There was Mavis, passing out fluttering sheets of music or prayers or maybe it was an auction notice. Who knew?

As Carmela drew closer, Mavis caught sight of her and waved an enthusiastic arm. "Yoo-hoo," she whooped. "Over here!"

Carmela started toward the group, what appeared to be a half dozen uninterested-looking people, as Mavis rushed to greet her.

"Oh, Carmela," said Mavis. She threw her arms around Carmela and gave her a tight squeeze. "I am soooo glad you came." Mavis was dressed in a shapeless black dress and leather boots. A spill of black lace covered her hair and hung over her eyes. At first glance, Mavis looked like she'd just stepped out of an episode of *American Horror Story*.

Carmela, who was wearing a jaunty red leather moto jacket over a white T-shirt and khaki slacks, suddenly felt a trifle gaudy. But Mavis didn't seem to notice or care.

"You're such a good friend," Mavis sobbed. "I was hoping

to get a full house today for Marcus. He deserved better, but this is all . . ." Her lower lip quivered and fat tears coursed down her face.

Carmela's heart went out to her. "Oh, Mavis, you did your best. And Marcus loved you. So I'm sure he'd understand. That's all that matters."

Mavis nodded and sniffed deeply, then grabbed Carmela's hand and pulled her toward the small group of men and women who were gathered nearby. They were shifting about nervously, unhappily, glancing at their watches, no doubt counting the seconds until they could make their escape.

Probably, Carmela decided, Mavis had begged and cajoled these few mourners into coming. Probably she had . . .

As Carmela composed herself and gazed directly at the small entourage, her smile literally froze on her face. Excuse me? What on earth was James Stanger, he of Gilded Pheasant Antiques, doing here? And Boyd Bellamy, the nasty landlord that Mavis had complained so bitterly about?

Carmela turned to Mavis, searching her face, looking for some kind of explanation.

"I know," said Mavis, patting Carmela's hand. "But these are all the people who were the closest to Marcus in the last days of his life."

Indeed they were, Carmela thought. Not only that, two of them occupied a prominent place on her suspect list!

But Mavis seemed to have her own agenda. She held up her arms and urged everyone to gather around a bronze plaque that commemorated the Battle of New Orleans. How this was apropos, Carmela had no idea. She only hoped that Jekyl would appear. He'd promised to meet her here— be her plus-one, if that's what you even called it at a funeral. Really, she just wanted him for moral support.

"Thank you so much for coming," said Mavis, addressing the group. "I want you all to know that our dear Marcus was cremated yesterday and that I have his precious ashes here with me." At that, Mavis bent down and pulled a bronze urn from a black leather tote bag. She held it up, like a prize recently won, and continued. "He would have been in favor of a simple, humble memorial service, it would certainly be in keeping with . . ."

Carmela felt warm fingers press against her arm and turned slightly to see who had just slid in next to her. It was Jekyl. He hadn't let her down. Dressed in a black three-piece suit that was tailored expertly to his slim figure, he beamed a smile her way. Though a pair of John Varvatos sunglasses masked his eyes, she knew they crinkled warmly.

"You made it," Carmela whispered as Mavis droned on.

"Sorry I'm late," said Jekyl. "You having fun yet?"

"This is so sad," she whispered back.

Jekyl looked around. "Not exactly a record turnout."

"That's what makes it sad," said Carmela.

But Jekyl wasn't the only latecomer. Just as Mavis was recounting some of the highlights in Joubert's career, a familiar face from last night suddenly appeared—Titus Duval. He glanced her way, gave no hint of recognition, and settled a few feet from Mavis.

Interesting, Carmela thought. But what did it mean? That Duval was here out of duty or guilt? Or that Mavis had strong-armed him?

Mavis continued rattling off the highlights of Joubert's life, finally finishing with the opening of Oddities. Then she smiled at Titus Duval and crooked a finger.

Duval stepped forward and cleared his throat.

Oh my gosh, thought Carmela. *He's going to speak.*

Duval turned out to be a rather eloquent speaker. He talked about how Marcus Joubert had been a man with a burning curiosity for art and antiquities. He praised his quest for knowledge, his courage for opening his shop, all the while conveniently leaving out any and all references to the stolen death mask or to Joubert's untimely murder.

It was, Carmela thought, a nicely sanitized memorial speech.

When Duval finally finished, he accepted a gracious hug from Mavis and then stepped away.

Mavis drew a deep breath and suddenly broke into a shaky a cappella rendition of "Amazing Grace." She waved her hands like a manic choir director, encouraging everyone to please sing along. Everyone glanced about nervously and then reluctantly joined in.

When the service, what there was of it, was finally over, Jekyl gave Carmela a nudge. "Whatcha been up to?" he asked.

"This and that, hanging out at Mumbo Gumbo last night, then getting chased by a crazed zombie."

"A zombie," said Jekyl. "Did he catch you?"

"Obviously not. I'm still here, aren't I?" Then she gave him the long-story-short version of last night.

"Who do you think it was?" Jekyl asked. "An old boyfriend, somebody who knows you've been investigating, or just some random creep?"

"Not sure," Carmela said slowly. "But now that you bring up random creep . . ." She inclined her head toward Titus Duval, who was speaking quietly with Mavis.

Jekyl gave a snort. "You think *he* was the zombie? Come on, he's as fat a cat as they come. You don't believe for a minute that Duval would put on full stage makeup and take a sprint through the French Quarter, do you?"

"Maybe not him, but he could certainly *hire* someone to do that."

"Hmm," said Jekyl. "You might be right." Then he cocked his head and said, "Oh rats, will you look at that."

Carmela followed his gaze and saw Zoe and Raleigh from KBEZ-TV pushing their way toward them. Zoe's face was set in a determined journalistic smile, her microphone was out, and she moved at a fast jog. Raleigh was paddling behind her, struggling to keep up under his heavy equipment.

When the group of mourners saw the reporters bearing down on them, they scattered like zebras in the path of a hungry lion. It was all of two seconds and they were gone, dodging gravestones and disappearing behind crypts.

"Looks like they're camera shy," Jekyl remarked with a wry smile.

"Who do you think called Zoe and Raleigh?" Carmela asked. "Who would tip them off?"

Jekyl lifted a shoulder. "Your friend Mavis looking for publicity?"

"Doesn't feel right."

Zoe skidded to a breathless stop directly in front of Carmela and said, "Did we miss it? Is it over?" Her face was pinched and pink and she seemed a little breathless.

"It's over," said Carmela.

"Where are all the people?" Zoe looked confused.

"Gone," said Carmela. She snapped her fingers. "Just like that."

Zoe dropped her microphone as Raleigh chugged up behind her. "Crap, they didn't want to talk to me, did they?"

"Perhaps not," said Jekyl. "At least that's the feeling I got."

Zoe fought to recover. She wanted to get something . . . anything. "So was the service at least interesting?"

"Routine," said Carmela.

"Any surprise guests show up?" Zoe asked.

"Nope." Carmela was amazed she could give monosyllabic answers with such a straight face.

"Do you know . . . are the cops any closer to solving Joubert's murder?" said Zoe.

"I'm afraid you'll have to ask them," said Carmela.

Zoe pursed her lips in frustration. "Okay, Carmela. Let me put it this way, are *you* any closer?"

Carmela just shook her head. "Please." The less said the better.

"I'm gonna keeping coming around," Zoe warned. "I'm not gonna let this go."

"ARE YOU LOOKING FORWARD TO TONIGHT?" Jekyl asked. They were driving, rag top down, in his bottle-green classic Jaguar, headed for Carmela's shop.

"Oh, absolutely," said Carmela. "I always love Baby's parties. Especially her Halloween parties. Good food, good people."

"Rich people," Jekyl murmured. "The cream of the crop. And so many of them are in need of a knowledgeable art connoisseur." His car was filled with dozens of half-empty water bottles, a painted coconut that kept rattling around on the floor, and a white clown mask. Carmela didn't ask.

They spun through the French Quarter, crossing Rampart Street and running past the Old Absinthe House. A quick turn onto Royal took them past Court of Two Sisters.

"When are you and I going to do brunch there?" asked Jekyl. "Eggs Benedict, waffles, and hot-boiled shrimp."

"Anytime you want," said Carmela. With the sun lasering down and a cool breeze lifting her hair and her spirits, she was starting to lose herself. The sights and smells of the French Quarter were seducing her into a daytime dream state. She smiled to herself as Jekyl zipped around a horse-drawn jitney, then spun past the Click! Gallery, and hooked a left onto Governor Nicholls Street. A few moments later they lurched to a stop in front of Memory Mine.

"Door-to-door service," said Carmela, smiling. "Thank you."

But Jekyl turned suddenly serious. "Carmela, as one of your bestest and dearest friends, I have to warn you about getting too involved in this thing with Mavis."

Carmela was suddenly jerked back to reality. "What are you talking about? You do know I promised to help her."

"I realize that, and I commend you for your sweet nature and loyalty. But there's a lot of money involved, Carmela."

Carmela shook her head. "Involved . . . how? What do you mean?"

Jekyl leaned back in his seat, steepled his fingers together, and thought for a few moments. "I don't know how to explain this exactly, but anytime you've got old-line New Orleanians involved in something to do with Napoleon, you're sitting on a powder keg."

Now Carmela really was puzzled. "Explain please."

Jekyl smiled. "You don't know about the plot?"

Carmela rolled her eyes. Jekyl loved nothing better than doling out little mysteries, secrets, and innuendos. "Okay, I'll bite. What plot are you referring to?"

"Here's the thing . . . I'm talking about Napoleon. How he had long talked about a *new* French empire."

"Okay." Had he really? Carmela had no idea. Her recollection of history, which to her was basically anything before Kennedy and the Beatles, was a little fuzzy.

"And guess where that new *empire* was going to be launched?" Jekyl pronounced the word as *ahm-peer*.

"I'll bite. Where?"

"Right here in New Orleans."

"This is for real?" Carmela thought this sounded very romantic and swashbuckling, but awfully far-fetched.

Jekyl held up a finger. "Remember, New Orleans was home to a bevy of French loyalists—many of whom had been battle tested with Andrew Jackson at the Battle of New Orleans. So this same group made up their minds to rescue Napoleon from his exile on the island of Elba."

Carmela leaned in, suddenly fascinated by Jekyl's tall tale.

"The French loyalists even enlisted the help of Jean Laffite to take a garrison of ships and rescue Napoleon."

"Are you serious?" *Jean Laffite, the infamous pirate?*

"I'm as serious as a heart attack. Carmela, baby, there are people here with French ancestries that stretch back two hundred and fifty years. There's history here, a proud heritage." He paused. "You know about the Napoleon Club?"

"I've heard of it."

"That fellow who showed up late at the cemetery? Titus Duval? He happens to be a charter member. Not only that, he's the great-great-great-grandson of former New Orleans mayor Nicholas Girod, one of the men who led the charge to rescue Napoleon and bring him to New Orleans."

"So why didn't they?" Carmela was caught up in the romance of the story. "Rescue Napoleon, I mean."

"That's just the point—they did! Only poor Napoleon died of stomach cancer while they were en route to grab him." Jekyl suddenly looked nervous. "So please, never underestimate the interest that some of these old families still have in Napoleon." He paused. "And Napoleon's death mask."

Carmela licked her lips and nodded. In offering to help Mavis, she wondered just what kind of hornet's nest she'd managed to kick open.

Chapter 21

"As far as handmade paper goes," said Carmela, "this is what we've got in stock right now. Mulberry, creamy Nepalese lokta, Japanese rice paper, Florentine linen, and some gorgeous Thai paper that contains pineapple, kozo, and salago fibers."

"I love them all," said Amy. Amy Defler was a Memory Mine regular. She'd just dropped by to grab a handful of twelve-by-twelve-inch scrapbook sheets. "But that mulberry paper really knocks me out. I mean the *colors*. Look at that bright raspberry. And the intense green."

"Sounds like you just made your choice," said Carmela. She was finding it infinitely comforting to be back at Memory Mine, pulling out paper, test-driving new rubber stamps, and sorting through die cuts. In fact, this type of normalcy felt wonderful, considering this morning's rather strange memorial service compounded with Jekyl's equally bizarre warning.

"Ooh," said Amy, pointing at a roller stamp wheel. "What's that all about?"

"You'd like this," said Carmela. "You click on one of our mini roller wheels, ink it up, and run it across your paper for a continuous design. It's especially terrific for creating borders."

"What designs do you have?"

"Let's see," said Carmela. "Stars, ferns, frogs, curlicues, angels, and lots of graphic patterns. Oh, and here's a daisy motif."

"I think I need one of the graphic patterns. That squiggly one."

"Excellent," said Carmela. She popped everything into a brown paper bag, grabbed one of her colorful crack-and-peel labels, and stuck it on the side of the bag. "There you go. That'll be nineteen ninety-five."

JUST AS AMY WAS LEAVING AND CARMELA WAS about to break out in song, her good mood skidded to a screeching halt. Because the Countess Saint-Marche suddenly tapped on the front window and mouthed an elaborate *Hello.*

"Oh no," Carmela said to Gabby. "Looks who's just arrived to darken our doorstep."

Gabby looked up from a wire embellishment she was working on. "What?" Then she caught sight of the countess. "Oh . . . yeah."

"Hell-*o*!" the countess called out loudly as she pushed through the front door. Her strident voice not only turned heads it seemed to reverberate off the walls like a bullhorn. "How are all my busy little chickadees?"

Carmela straightened up. "Busy," she said, vowing to hang on to her good humor. Grasp it tightly with her fingernails if need be.

"I understand you have some logo designs to show me?" sang out the countess.

Carmela gazed at Gabby.

"She called here this morning," Gabby hastily explained. "I mentioned that you had come up with some great ideas."

"So I did," said Carmela. She reached under the counter and pulled out her stack of sketches, mentally girding herself for a clash of creative differences, maybe even a prolonged battle.

But when Carmela spread out all three Lucrezia logos, the countess studied them briefly, and then tapped the ring design decisively with her index finger. "That's the one."

Just like that? Carmela thought. *It's that easy?*

"You didn't even let me launch into my patented sales-and-marketing pitch," Carmela said. Truth be told, she was secretly pleased that the countess was a good decision maker. So many people weren't.

"Oh, this is it," said the countess. "The ring design is absolutely perfect. You don't have to waste time selling me, because I *love* it."

"It's my favorite, too," said Gabby.

"That was way too easy," Carmela said.

"I'm easier than I look," smiled the countess.

Carmela chuckled. "I wouldn't touch that line with a ten-foot pole."

"Now what about paper stock?" asked the countess. "I want paper that's rich and elegant, something that will reflect the upscale interior and artistry of my shop."

"All along I've been thinking a cream-colored stock," said Carmela. "Perhaps a nice linen finish." She pulled out a book of paper samples and flipped through a couple of pages. "Something like this."

As the countess studied the samples of paper stock, her brows pinched together. It was a pinch that Carmela recognized as the first warning sign that this might not be so easy after all.

"Now I'm thinking the color should be more fawn or mushroom," said the countess.

Gabby looked up. "You mean beige?"

The countess tilted her head. "Actually, more biscuit. Or bone."

"Sure," said Carmela. She wasn't about to argue the merits of one beige-colored paper stock over another. "So you're going to want invitations, business cards, and letterhead?"

"And envelopes," said the countess. "Smaller square ones as well as business-sized."

"Let me work up a bid on that," said Carmela. "I'm thinking a quantity of . . . what? Maybe two thousand each?"

But the countess had mentally moved on. In fact, she bent down, lifted a small piece of Louis Vuitton luggage off the floor, and placed it gingerly on the counter. "I want to show you ladies something," she said in a conspiratorial tone.

"What have you got there?" asked Gabby. She was a Vuitton fanatic.

In reply, the countess smiled broadly and clicked the brass latch on the small, elegant case. She lifted the lid to reveal three stunning pieces of jewelry nestled atop a red velvet cushion.

"Oh my goodness!" said Gabby. "If that doesn't blow your socks off."

"Aren't they lovely?" cooed the countess.

Carmela peered in. "What are you doing walking around the French Quarter with all that loot?" she asked. There was a diamond pendant on a braided gold chain, a silver necklace with a half dozen brilliant blue stones, and a gold necklace with pear-shaped cabochon rubies surrounded by pavé diamonds.

"These pieces are just a few of my recent acquisitions,"

said the countess. "Jewelry that will be offered for sale in my new shop."

"Are the necklaces all vintage?" Gabby asked. She was completely agog.

The countess nodded with the faintest of smiles. "The oldest and really the most pricey is the Cartier. She lifted it out of the case and held it up. The rubies glinted enticingly, the diamonds were like shards of pure light.

"It's absolutely gorgeous," said Carmela. She had to admit, she did have an affinity for vintage jewelry. Then again, what woman could resist a piece like this? Especially since it was Cartier.

"Wouldn't it be something to actually *wear* one of these pieces?" said Gabby.

"They're killer pieces," Carmela agreed.

The countess handed the Cartier piece over to Carmela. "It suits you," she said.

"Oh yeah," Carmela agreed. "But not my bank account."

"Why not try it on?" suggested the countess.

Carmela gazed at the countess. "You mean wear it?"

"Wear it tonight if you'd like. I assume you're going out."

"Do it, Carmela!" said Gabby. "It would look stunning with your Scarlett O'Hara dress." She turned to the countess and explained, "We're going to a fancy masquerade ball tonight. In the Garden District, no less."

"Then it's settled," said the countess. "You *must* wear it."

"I don't know," said Carmela as she fastened the necklace around her neck.

Gabby dug into a drawer and whipped out a hand mirror. "Take a look," she said, pushing it forward.

Upon seeing the necklace sparkling brightly around her neck, some of Carmela's unkind feelings toward the countess seemed to evaporate. In fact, she felt like she was suddenly in a dream sequence, magically transported to a beautiful

kingdom and made an honorary princess for a day—complete
with crown jewels.

Then Carmela thudded back down to earth.

"Are you sure you want me to wear this?"

"Oh, absolutely!" said the countess. "It would be my
pleasure."

Gabby, who was still goggle-eyed, murmured, "If something like that was offered to me, I'd certainly wear it."

"Then it's settled," smiled the countess.

CARMELA MADE SURE THE NECKLACE WAS
securely locked in a file drawer before she went back to
work. She loved the idea of wearing it tonight (who
wouldn't!), but in the back of her mind hung the knowledge
that a death mask had disappeared from right next door.

*What if there's a cat burglar prowling the French Quarter and
he's targeting this block? What if he staked out Oddities and now
has his eye on the countess? And me?*

Still, all the what-ifs in the world weren't going to help
solve the murder of Marcus Joubert, and they certainly
weren't going to help Carmela's customers get more creative
with their scrapbooks. So she flitted about the shop, cutting
lengths of ribbon, digging out memory boxes, giving tips
on tag art, collages, and card making.

Gabby brought in lunch, but Carmela only managed a
few bites of her blueberry muffin and citrus salad before she
was called upon to help a customer create an altered book.

"Here's the thing," said the woman, whose name was Jill.
"I want to do an altered book for my daughter, Kristen. You
know, for the upcoming holidays."

"A Christmas book," said Carmela. It would be fun to
work on a project that wasn't Halloween.

"That's right," said Jill. "I have this lovely book of poetry and my husband's already carved out a niche inside using an X-Acto knife."

"Very carefully I hope?"

"No fingers lost," said Jill. She flipped open the cover to reveal the inside. "And I've already glued all the pages together."

"You're halfway there," said Carmela. "Did you have a theme in mind?"

"Angels?" said Jill.

Carmela thought for a moment, then darted about her shop, grabbing paper, ribbon, and a few miscellaneous packets. "Here's an idea," she said as they both settled down at the back table. She slid a piece of paper toward Jill. "This scrapbook paper is printed to look like sheet music."

Jill studied it. "'Angels We Have Heard on High.' That's one of my favorite Christmas hymns."

"Perhaps that could be the background design in your niche," said Carmela. "Then you add this small ceramic angel." She handed Jill a white, cherubic angel. "The angel could be set off with some white velvet ribbon, silver aspen leaves, a ruffle of white lace, and anything else you'd like."

Jill nodded, a smile on her face. "A miniature still life. I like it."

"You could cover the outside of your book with blush-colored faux velvet paper and accent it with a small gilded vintage frame inset with an image of a Botticelli angel. And then . . . maybe wrap the book with a string of pearls?"

"Perfect," said Jill.

CARMELA ALSO HELPED A WOMAN CREATE trick-or-treat bags by stamping witch images with orange embossing ink. Then she took small black fuzzy balls, inserted wings and eyes so they resembled flying bats, and glued them on the bags.

But as Carmela worked, her mind continued to hum. She thought about Joubert's murder, her various suspects, and what else she could possibly do to move the investigation along. She was pawing through a box of vintage jewelry findings when she suddenly looked up and said, "I know what I can do."

"Hmm?" said Gabby absently.

She could call Wallace Pitney, the wealthy Dallas collector whose Napoleon death mask had been stolen.

Of course, she didn't have his number, and she couldn't exactly pry it out of Babcock (heaven forbid!), so she spent five minutes at her computer and Googled Mr. Pitney. That produced a phone number that might or might not be his.

Fingers crossed, Carmela made the call. Bingo. She was in luck. After pleading her case to a secretary, who was a fairly tough gatekeeper, she was finally put through to Mr. Pitney.

"You're calling from New Orleans?" Pitney asked in a slightly quavering voice. "Did you recover my mask?"

"I'm afraid not," Carmela told him. "I just wanted to ask you a few follow-up questions." She held her breath, wondering what his reaction would be.

"You're with the police?"

It was exactly what she thought he would ask.

"I've been working with them, yes." Okay, a little white lie. *Just one, okay?*

"I've been through this already," said Pitney. He sounded cranky, like he wanted to go lie down. Or have a cocktail. Or lie down and have a cocktail.

"I just wanted to know a little more about the circumstances of your break-in."

"What's to know?" complained Pitney. "Some crackpot

threw a brick through my window, came in, grabbed the mask from its case, and took off before my idiot security company arrived." He made a sound in the back of his throat. "Lot of good they were."

"I hear your frustration," said Carmela. She was warming up to Mr. Pitney. He had the feisty gene. "I know you've been asked this before, sir, but now that a few more days have passed, do you have any idea, any suspicion as to who the burglar might have been?"

"That's all I've thought about," said Pitney. "And the only thing I can come up with is that Marilyn and I—that's my wife, Marilyn, she was Miss Texas back in '59. But that's another story."

"I'd like to hear it sometime," said Carmela.

"Anyhoo," said Pitney, "we hosted a big charity event at our home a month or so ago and there were several hundred guests."

"And you think one of them was the thief?"

"*Might* have been," said Pitney. "Hard to know for sure until we catch the bugger."

"Was your event covered by the newspapers or any magazines?"

"A couple, yes. Do you think that's how I was targeted?"

"Maybe," said Carmela. "Mr. Pitney, are you familiar with the name Marcus Joubert?"

"You know, a New Orleans police detective asked me the same thing—a Detective Babcock, I believe."

"Yes, I'm know him well." Carmela smiled. Did she ever.

"I can't say I'm familiar with the name Joubert. Sounds French. Like the surnames you folks over in New Orleans have." He pronounced it *New Or-leens*, not *Nawlins*, like the natives did.

"So you've never met Joubert?"

"Not that I can recall."

"How about a James Stanger?"

"No, sorry," said Pitney.

"Mr. Pitney, thank you so much for your help."

"I don't know what help I've been," he said, sounding quarrelsome again. "I really just want my mask back."

Carmela hung up the phone and gazed at the wall next to her desk. It was papered with photos, sketches, ideas she'd ripped out of magazines, and layouts she'd cadged from graphic design publications. Time was ticking away and she hadn't made any real progress. Sure, she'd managed a few weak speculations, but nothing seemed to pan out. Mavis had begged for her help and so far she'd come up with a big fat zero.

Carmela grabbed her phone again and called Juju Voodoo.

"Juju Voodoo," came Ava's voice. "Candles and spells and charms that foretell."

"Ava, it's me."

"Good," said Ava, "I can talk normal."

"How's business?"

"Busy. I'm running my hind end off, though that may be a good thing. We're precariously low on saint candles and practically sold out of Day of the Dead items. I mean, *any* Day of the Dead item, even the crappy key chains."

"How's your inventory of voodoo dolls holding up?" She was thinking of getting one and naming it Shamus. Let the dogs drag it around, slime it up, and maybe chew a leg off.

"Sheesh," said Ava. "We sold out of those last week. This week has been like . . . what do retailers call that day after Thanksgiving again?"

"Black Friday," said Carmela.

"Yeah," said Ava. "Only we're having ours on Wednesday." She seemed to drift away, talking to someone in the shop, then she came back. "But tonight we relax and have fun, right? Which means I'm gonna head home in about twenty minutes, have a simple little wine-tasting party on my couch, put on a Frank Sinatra album, and dance around in my underwear."

"Frank's always worked for me," said Carmela.

"Then I'm gonna get all glammed up for Baby's Halloween hoedown. Smear some Crisco on and slither into my costume."

"Be at my place at seven, okay?" said Carmela. "Don't be late."

"Don't worry. I won't!"

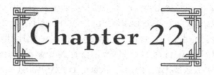

Chapter 22

CARMELA pulled her car to the curb, glanced in the rearview mirror, and, without meaning to, nervously fingered her necklace. She probably shouldn't have worn it, but the countess had been so insistent, and it did go gorgeously with her costume.

"*Cher,*" said Ava. There was a distinct *tone* in her voice. "You have to stop obsessing."

"I know," said Carmela as her fingers once against crept toward the necklace.

"You said yourself what a big deal the countess made about wanting you to wear that necklace. Besides, people are going to go gaga and ask where you scored such a killer piece. And when you tell them . . . well, the way you look, you're going to be a walking advertisement for the countess's new shop."

Ava was right, Carmela decided. She had to quit worrying. Had to Nike up and just do it.

"C'mon," said Ava, climbing out of the car. "Time's a wastin'. I think I hear the enticing pop of champagne corks."

Carmela and Ava headed down the street. Darkness had settled in a good hour ago and the night had swept in cool and clear. Immense live oak trees, many still clutching the last vestiges of leaves, cut etchings into a full moon. The street was filled with strolling people. A few elegant couples were headed for Baby's masquerade party, while most were out to enjoy the Halloween spectacle. As per tradition, all the streets in Baby's neighborhood, block after elegant block, were lined with glowing jack-o'-lanterns. Some scowled malevolently, others offered benign toothy grins, and all were lit by flickering candles.

"This is so cool," Ava shivered. "Every Halloween I feel like a kid again."

"You don't *look* like a kid," said Carmela. "Not in that costume." Ava wore a figure-hugging black latex dress, metallic stockings, and black thigh-high boots. Her pointed hat and black mask completed her witchy ensemble.

"You should talk," joked Ava. "You look like a walking wedding cake with all those hoops and flounces."

"Wearing this skirt is like being trapped in a barrel," Carmela complained as they headed up the front walk to Baby's brightly lit Victorian manor.

"Not sure what you expected, sweetums. Scarlett O'Hara's life was anything but easy."

Dozens of glowing lanterns lined Baby's ornate portico. White, filmy spiderwebs stretched across three jelly palm trees, and the ivy that curled up the side of the manse had hands, arms, and legs sticking out of it, giving it the appearance of a carnivorous plant that had just enjoyed a few tasty snacks. Austin Powers, a member of KISS, and Charlie Chaplin were gathered on the front porch, taking in the night air and smoking cigars.

Baby and her husband, Del, stood front and center in the

elegant entryway, smiling and greeting guests. When Baby saw Carmela and Ava, she fairly beamed. Then she hitched up her long diaphanous skirt, poked her knight in shining armor in the ribs, and said, "Carmela . . . Ava!" Breathlessly administering multiple air kisses, she added, "We're so glad you could make it."

Del Fontaine, Baby's attorney husband, clasped a hand to his chain mail and knelt down on one knee. "M'ladies, welcome to our humble castle."

"Del and I always dress as one of history's most romantic couples," Baby explained. "This year we're Guinevere and King Arthur."

"That's cool," said Ava. "Just watch out for Sir Lancelot. I hear he's a real home wrecker."

"Oh you," Baby giggled. Then to Carmela she cocked her head and said, "No Babcock?"

"He'll probably turn up sooner or later," said Carmela.

"More likely later," said Ava. "Her guy's a workaholic."

"But it's all for a good cause," said Baby. "I mean, he's still investigating that murder, isn't he? Marcus . . ."

"Joubert," supplied Carmela. "Yes, yes he is."

"So he . . ." Baby's eyes went suddenly wide. "Carmela, my dear. What *are* you wearing around your neck?"

"That necklace happens to be vintage Cartier," said Ava, sounding a little jealous.

"I should say so," said Baby. "Wow, that is some incredible bauble. Please tell me it's a gift from your absentee boyfriend."

"I wish," said Carmela. "No, I'm afraid the necklace is just on loan. From Countess Saint-Marche, the lady who's opening the high-end jewelry store in Marcus Joubert's old . . ."

"Right, right," said Baby, nodding. "I remember."

"Speaking of which," said Carmela, "has Mavis Sweet showed up yet?"

Baby frowned. "I'm not sure. People keep piling in and I *try* to greet everyone, but . . . well, things have been a little crazy." Her eyes flicked to the front door where a new group of guests was spilling through.

"No problem," said Ava. "We'll wander around and see what kind of trouble we can get in." She grabbed Carmela's arm and pulled her into the fray of the party.

And it really was a fray. Tuxedoed waiters carried silver trays of champagne flutes, a rock band played in the library, and, everywhere, costumed revelers drank, danced, kissed, and caroused. Baby's enormous home, with its Aubusson carpets, ginormous white S-curved sofa, and fireplace so big you could roast a pig in it, was more than conducive to a raucous party.

"Car-*mel*-a!" came an eager voice.

Carmela and Ava spun, only to find Gabby rushing toward them. She had her husband, a disgruntled-looking Stuart, in tow.

"Oh my gosh," marveled Carmela, "you really are getting some mileage out of that cute Annie Oakley costume."

"And such cool six-guns," said Ava.

"I'm sure you all remember Stuart," said Gabby, showing him off like a prize heifer. "Masquerading tonight as Buffalo Bill."

"Howdy, pardner," said Ava. She gave him a slow wink.

"Hi." Stuart, stone-faced and some thirty pounds over-weight, looked supremely uncomfortable in his outfit of buckskin and fringe.

"How's business?" Carmela asked. She felt obliged to say *something* to him.

"Sales have been a little flat," said Stuart, grabbing hold of her question like a rabid jackal. "But extended warranties and fluid flushes have been a real bright spot, thank goodness."

"That's terrific," said Carmela. She'd just run the table on conversation starters with Stuart.

Fortunately, Gabby pushed Stuart toward the buffet line and Ava aimed Carmela at another tray of drinks.

"Don't you just love champagne, *cher*? All those tiny bubbles dancing happily across your tongue." She raised her glass in a salute, gazed across the room, and said, "Uh-oh."

"What?" said Carmela.

Ava inclined her head. "Look what somebody's black cat just dragged in."

Carmela turned around, thinking it must be Babcock. Instead her eyes fell upon Shamus. She grimaced. "I was afraid he'd show up here," she told Ava.

"I know, Baby's so sweet she can't bring herself to drop Shamus from her guest list."

"And look who else," said Carmela, her tone suddenly wary.

"Carmela," came a grating voice. Glory Meechum, Shamus's big sister and bona fide crazy lady, had just closed in on her like a great white shark going after chum. Glory was a parsimonious meanie who controlled the purse strings for the Meechum family and their chain of banks. When Glory told Shamus to jump, he generally inquired, "How high?"

"Hello, Glory," said Carmela, fighting to keep her voice neutral, vowing not to get drawn in to one of their typical verbal slugfests. "You remember Ava?"

"Hey there," said Ava. She smirked at the blue scrubs Glory was wearing and said, "I take it the doctors at Summer Hill gave you an overnight pass?" Summer Hill was a nearby mental institution.

"This is a *nurse's* costume," Glory hissed.

Shamus, dressed as a vampire, complete with fangs, was suddenly at Glory's side. "Are you two having a nice conversation?" he asked hopefully. Only, because of the fangs, it came out conver-*thashun*.

"No, Shamus," said Carmela. "We are not."

"C'mon," Shamus wheedled. "Can't we all just be *friendsth*?"

"I think we tried that once and it went rather badly," said Carmela.

But one of Glory's wandering eyes had suddenly landed on Carmela's necklace. "Goodness be," she said in a slightly condescending tone. "Will you look at that necklace?" She turned to Shamus. "Carmela must have snagged a rich new boyfriend, though I can't imagine how she ever managed that." Her grin darkened. "It's more likely a sugar daddy."

"Okay," said Carmela, spinning on her heel so fast her skirt practically became a deadly weapon. "We're going to help ourselves to the buffet."

Carmela and Ava left Shamus and Glory behind in their dust.

"Talk about the Croods," said Ava.

"If I never saw that woman again . . ." said Carmela. They caromed into the dining room where a sixteen-foot-long table, festooned in white linen, held an imposing array of silver chafing dishes.

"Holy fried oysters," said Ava. "Will you look at this food? There's andouille sausage, and trout meunière and shrimp in remoulade sauce."

"And pork chops with bing cherries," said Carmela, grabbing a plate.

"I'm loading up as we speak," said Ava. "Ooh, and chocolate cake, too."

The dark chocolate cake had been cut into squares to replicate clods of earth. Peaks of green frosting formed the grass and red and yellow gummy worms crawled through each piece.

"Nothing like sugar-rich cake," said Carmela, helping herself to a large piece.

"Right," said Ava, grabbing an even bigger piece. "If I'm gonna push my body to adult-onset diabetes anyway, I may as well enjoy this."

"Calories, calories," came a taunting male voice.

Carmela and Ava both looked up at the same time to find Boyd Bellamy, Carmela's landlord, shaking a finger at them.

"Excuse me?" said Ava.

"If you gals want to keep your girlish figures," he leered, "you'd better lay off those rich desserts."

Ava looked at Carmela. "Did he just chastise us?"

"It sure sounded like it," said Carmela.

"Let's get one thing straight," said Ava. "We're not *gals* and we sure don't need a Porky Pig look-alike telling us how to fill our plates."

Bellamy fairly bristled. "It was simply an observation. Heh heh. A joke."

"Go peddle your jokes somewhere else," said Ava, as she and Carmela headed out with their plates.

"Imagine that," said Carmela, as they settled into wicker chairs on Baby's sunporch. "That overweight slug criticizing us."

"No wonder some poor women develop body dysmorphia," said Ava. "When they should just relax and enjoy their food."

"Agreed," said Carmela. Then she paused, as a recurring thought suddenly bounced into her brain.

"What?" said Ava. "You're not stroking out are you?"

"That guy Bellamy."

"Yeah?"

"You don't think he'd murder Joubert just to get rid of him, do you? Just so he could lease the space to someone else?"

Ava stared back at her. "It never occurred to me. But from the sourpuss face you're making, it's obviously rattled around in your brain."

"Yes, just now."

"Doggone," said Ava. "Here we are at an A-list party and we're talking about that stupid murder again."

"Sorry," said Carmela. And she meant it. "I really am sorry."

Ava waved a hand. "Ah, it's okay. It's only natural for you to . . . oh hey!" She waved a hand and a half dozen plastic skull bracelets clanked. "Mavis. Get out here, girl. Come sit with the cool kids."

Carmela pasted a neutral smile on her face as Mavis Sweet hurried toward them, carrying a plate of food and a glass of champagne. "Don't say anything about . . ."

"I won't," Ava whispered.

"You made it," said Carmela, as Mavis sat down to join them. "I'm so glad you decided to come."

"I am, too," said Mavis. She glanced around as if in shock. "This party is so . . . elegant. With real champagne, not just Cold Duck. And all these important people . . . it's like something out of a movie." She seemed pathetically grateful to be included in such a tony guest list.

Carmela smiled with encouragement. Mavis's words seemed so innocent . . . so heartfelt.

"I really like your costume," Ava told Mavis. Mavis wore a Cleopatra headpiece and a long gold tunic. She'd rimmed her eyes with kohl and the added makeup gave her a startling, bug-eyed appearance. "You look . . . interesting."

"Thank you," said Mavis. "And you—your dress—it's so glamorous."

Ava waved a hand. "Aw, it's just something I threw on. I always try to be a little fly."

THIRTY MINUTES LATER, THE PARTY GOT EVEN crazier. The band was blasting out a toe-tapping rendition of "Clarinet Marmalade," couples were dancing and singing at the top of their lungs, champagne was being consumed directly from the bottle, and Babcock finally showed up.

"I was wondering when you were going to get here," said Carmela. For some reason, he'd brought Charlie the tech along with him. Carmela didn't know if they'd just come from a nasty crime scene or if they were both here to party. No matter, the minute Ava spotted Charlie she swept him up in a quick embrace and took him to a corner where they could enjoy a quick canoodle.

That left Carmela facing Babcock, who seemed a little tired.

"Excuse me," said Carmela, who was feeling no pain. "But you're supposed to be wearing a costume." Babcock was dressed impeccably in an Armani suit.

He smiled tolerantly at her. "This is my costume."

"Say what?"

"I came as a hedge-fund billionaire. Note the bespoke suit and Church's shoes?"

"Tricky," said Carmela. "And here I thought you were just a well-dressed cop."

"That, too," said Babcock. His arms encircled her and he pulled her close. When she was pressed up against him, feeling his warmth and smelling his yummy aftershave, he bent down and kissed her tenderly.

Carmela felt her heart race (it couldn't just be the champagne!) and her entire body begin to melt. "Want to leave?" she whispered in his ear. "Go back to my place?"

Babcock shook his head regretfully. "I can't. I'm still on the clock and still smoothing out details for that Zombie Chase on Friday."

"Hmm," said Carmela, pulling away slightly. "A Zombie Chase." Hadn't she experienced that already?

Babcock saw her look of apprehension and grinned. "Oh, you're going to like this. It's basically a rousing game of paintball where you tag zombies for charity. I told you about this event, remember? We're trying to raise money to buy new computers for all the units. You have to come. Ava, too."

"It doesn't sound all that fun," said Carmela, hedging.

"I'll make a deal with you," said Babcock. "I'll put on a tux for the Pumpkins and Bumpkins Ball tomorrow night if you come to the Zombie Chase on Friday. Is it a deal?"

"Deal," she said, but not without a certain amount of trepidation.

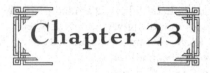

Chapter 23

So of course Ava wanted to make a second run at the buffet table.

"Have you tried the oysters Rockefeller yet?" she asked. Scooping up three cream-and-bread-crumb-filled oysters with a silver slotted spoon, she deposited them on her plate. "Because these tasty little mollusks are to *die* for. Or at least worth plunging into a food-induced coma for. Oh, and pray tell, why did Babcock just up and leave this party and take my adorable little stud muffin along with him?"

Carmela scooped up a helping of shrimp *étouffée*. "He claimed they were still working."

"You believe him?"

Carmela shrugged. "Sure."

"Working," said Ava. "That blows."

"You know what, I bet there are five dozen men right here at this party who would love to meet you. Who would *kill* to meet you."

Ava brightened. "Ya think?"

"Rich, Garden District guys," said Carmela, really piling it on now.

Ava fluffed her hair and gazed around. "When you put it that way it does sound slightly . . . irresistible."

"Ladies!" Jekyl exclaimed as he hurried over to join them. "Where have you been all night?"

"Right here eating," said Ava.

"What's up, killer?" asked Carmela.

But Jekyl's eyes were suddenly fixed on Carmela's necklace, which, interestingly enough, Babcock hadn't commented on or even noticed.

"What *is* that priceless bauble that's encircling your lovely swan-like neck?" Jekyl demanded. "Dare I ask, have you cultivated a new admirer?"

"Same old, same old," said Carmela. She touched the necklace with an index finger. "This gaudy little piece happens to be borrowed."

"As in something borrowed, something blue?" he asked.

"Noooo," said Carmela. "It's actually on loan from the Countess Saint-Marche."

"Countess Cuckoo," said Jekyl. "The jewelry lady you told me was moving into the Oddities space."

"That's right."

"Looks like the two of you are already best buddies."

Carmela suddenly felt uncomfortable, almost regretting her decision to wear the necklace. "We aren't. It's just that she . . ."

"She twisted Carmela's arm," said Ava, jumping in.

And maybe my head, Carmela thought. *After all, I was even considering her as one of my suspects.*

Thankfully, Jekyl let the whole matter drop. "So what mischief have you two gotten into so far?"

"Not nearly enough," said Ava.

"But the night is still young," said Carmela. "Or at least we are."

"Wait," said Jekyl. He pulled out his iPhone and held it up. "Scrunch together, ladies, so I can record this moment for posterity. That's right, bend forward, show a touch of décolleté, and say *soufflé*."

"Soufflé," Carmela and Ava said together as Jekyl's flash popped.

Pleased with his snapshot, Jekyl went barreling off to find Baby, while Carmela and Ava wandered into one of the salons. This room carried a more masculine theme with leather sofas, dark green wallpaper, and fox and hound paintings.

Ava nudged Carmela. "That guy over there."

"What guy?"

"Perched on the end of the sofa. He's the one who was dining at Mumbo Gumbo last night."

Carmela followed Ava's gaze and saw that it was Titus Duval. He was drinking amber liquid from a cut glass tumbler and carrying on a rather intense conversation with two other men. "Titus Duval," she said. From the look of his costume, his broad-brimmed hat and brocade vest, he was either dressed as a riverboat gambler or a pimp from the '70s.

"He's the rich guy," said Ava. "The one who's on your suspect list. The one you think could have stolen that death mask."

"I feel like everybody and his brother is on my suspect list."

"That would also make him a murderer." Ava was watching him intently.

"Point taken."

"What do you think he's discussing so intently with those other two fat cats?" asked Ava.

"Kicking puppies, foreclosing widows' mortgages, and the optimum wax for grooming one's handlebar mustache," Carmela joked.

"I do kind of like that silver fox look," said Ava.

"And I'd like to ask him a question or two."

Ava nudged her. "He's getting up, better go get 'em, tiger."

Carmela trailed Duval to the bar. He ordered another whiskey while Carmela asked for a glass of champagne. She glanced sideways at him with what she hoped was an ingratiating smile.

"We meet again," said Carmela.

Duval glanced at her. "Hello." He couldn't have been more bored.

"At Mumbo Gumbo last night?" Carmela prompted. "And you spoke at the service this morning."

That brought a ghost of a smile to his face. "Of course. *Hello.*"

Carmela decided to dive right in. "There's something I'd like to ask you."

Duval looked suddenly wary. "What's that?"

"Did you have a meeting with Marcus Joubert the night the death mask was stolen from that Dallas collector?"

Duval blinked. "Excuse me. *Who* are you again?"

"Carmela Bertrand. I . . ."

"Never mind," said Duval. "I'm actually not that interested. And I'm certainly not interested in answering any of your questions." And with that he picked up his drink and walked away.

"NO WAY WAS HE GOING TO ANSWER MY QUEStions," Carmela told Ava.

"Then he's a jerk. A rude jerk."

Carmela shrugged. "He either doesn't want to get involved or he's extremely involved."

"Huh," said Ava. She looked thoughtful for a moment. "Didn't you tell me Duval lived right here in the Garden District?"

Carmela nodded. "You know that enormous home two

blocks from here, the one with the mansard roof and pair of stone lions out front?"

"That's where he lives?" said Ava. "That place is big-time, like one of those old dinosaur mansions in Beverly Hills or Bel Air. Pickfair or something like that, places where the stars lived."

"Stands to reason he'd have a big place, since Duval's got big money."

Ava narrowed her eyes. "My overactive brain has just hatched the most intriguing plan."

Carmela took one look at Ava and said, "Uh-oh, you've got that sneaky, snarky look on your face. What are you thinking?"

"I think we should go creepy-crawl Duval's house and see if that Napoleon mask is there."

Carmela was horrified. "You mean break in? We can't do that!"

"But you'd like to."

"Well . . . sure. I mean, I suppose I would."

Ava set her glass down with a loud *clink*. "Then let's do it. Let's throw caution to the wind and live every week like it's Shark Week."

"Oh dear Lord," Carmela muttered. But she followed Ava outside just the same.

THE NIGHT WAS STILL AS DEATH, THE ALMOST-full moon hiding behind a wall of dark clouds. Most of the jack-o'-lanterns had sputtered out by now, the melted candle wax dribbling down the curbs and sidewalk. The sidewalks were practically devoid of people.

"I can't believe we're doing this," Carmela said as they hurried along. She was having second and even third thoughts about their breaking and entering. What if they got caught? What was the penalty? And what if they went to all the trouble of sneaking inside Duval's home and found absolutely nothing? If something really went awry, she'd have only herself to blame. Sure, Ava may have hatched this crazy scheme, but she was a willing participant. Unless, of course, she called a halt to the plan this very minute. She opened her mouth just as Ava said . . .

"Isn't this exciting? We're just like Cagney and Lacey."

"I was thinking Lucy and Ethel," said Carmela. *Go? No go?*

"Here we are," said Ava, as they crept up on Duval's monster-sized mansion. It was Second Empire style, a look that was derived from many of Paris's monumental buildings. The home featured a mansard roof pierced with multiple dormers. Narrow arched windows seemed to gaze down at them with haughty disapproval.

Carmela trailed a hand along the wrought-iron fence that surrounded the entire property. "Are we sure about this?"

But Ava only put a finger to her mouth. "Shhhh," she whispered. "This way."

They snuck past the stone lions, stepped onto a cobblestone path, and followed it through almost total darkness. Hanging tendrils of Spanish moss brushed their shoulders like so many spidery fingers. A few more steps brought them into the backyard.

"I figure we've got a better chance back here," said Ava.

"Better chance of getting caught?"

"Silly girl. Of prying open a window and slipping in."

"How are we going to manage that?" said Carmela. "Do you think Duval has one of those plastic key holders that looks like a rock?" She gazed around the lush backyard. Between the sweep of arborvitae and clumps of banana palms, it was like being in a jungle. A kidney-shaped pool, lights glowing to reveal azure blue water, added to the tropical feel. Carmela saw something shimmer at the bottom of the pool and wondered if it was a snake.

"We just have to find some little nook or cranny," said Ava. "Something opportune." She slipped through the shrubbery and up to a pair of French doors. Unfortunately, when she rattled the handle gently, the doors were clearly locked.

"What'd I tell you?" said Carmela.

But Ava was not to be deterred. She snuck along the side of the house, one hip pressed against the damp stone foundation, her fingers crawling along, searching out every nook, cranny, and window ledge.

"Here," said Ava.

"Where?" said Carmela. Ava had practically disappeared into the darkness. The only clue was the faint rustling of leaves.

Ava let loose a low whistle and said, *"Here."*

Carmela took a deep breath, stepped into a flowerbed, brushed past a palm tree, and found herself in the secluded alcove where her friend was hiding.

"This window is open," Ava whispered. "I think we can ease it up a notch and then shimmy in."

Carmela's heart hammered inside her chest. Should she? Shouldn't she? The "good girl" inside her said no, but it was too late. She heard a creak as the window slid up. Then, quick and stealthy as a ninja, Ava climbed through.

"Come on!" said Ava. She held out a hand.

Carmela grabbed on to her, stepped up onto some kind of mechanical watering apparatus that was hidden among the plants, and suddenly found herself tumbling through the proverbial rabbit hole and into Titus Duval's darkened house. She blinked, smoothed her dress, and glanced around nervously. "Where are we?"

"Some kind of sunroom," said Ava. "Come on, let's go."

Together, they tiptoed across a tiled floor, bumping toes into overstuffed chairs and knocking a lampshade askew. When they reached a dimly lit hallway, they were able to see a little better. Small brass sconces, set just above eye level, lit the way.

Clutching each other, they headed into what had to be the interior of Duval's house. They passed two closed doors, heading for the main living area.

"Wait a minute," said Carmela.

Ava stopped.

"Back here," said Carmela. She took two steps backward and gently pushed open one of the doors they'd just passed. The door creaked open slowly, revealing a small brass lamp set on a massive oak desk. But it was enough to illuminate most of the room. "I think," she said, "that this is Duval's study."

The room smelled of incense and gun grease. One wall held a mahogany bookcase packed with expensive-looking leather-bound books. Another wall was covered with a jumble of interesting art pieces—African masks, curved pieces of carved jade, several small oil paintings.

"C'mon," said Carmela. "We need to take a closer look."

Carefully, quietly, they shuffled in.

"He likes guns," said Ava, pointing to an antique der-ringer that was encased in a glass shadow box. "And look at this . . . some kind of framed document."

Carmela moved closer. "It's a letter signed by Jean Laffite. Wow. This piece has got some history on it."

"And must have cost him a pretty penny," said Ava.

When they moved to the next case, their breath came faster and their mouths literally dropped open.

Staring out at them was a face. But not really a face—because it was a marble death mask. Eyes closed, lips pursed delicately, cheekbones smooth and rounded, it appeared to be a woman's face.

"Jackpot," whispered Carmela.

"This is sooo creepy," said Ava. "Imagine having that

thing staring at you while you're perusing the evening paper? Or during a storm, when the lights are flickering and . . ."

"Keep looking," said Carmela. "There's supposed to be a second mask."

Ava's footsteps whispered across the silk carpet. "Maybe over . . . oh yeah, Carm. Here it is."

Carmela was at her side in an instant. "Who is it? Is it Napoleon?" She stared fixedly at the second death mask. It was an image of what had once been a rather large man with a heavy nose and pronounced, bony cheekbones.

"I don't know," said Ava, sounding flustered.

Carmela studied the mask. "It's not him." She'd Googled Napoleon's death mask and studied several different images. This mask didn't resemble any of the masks she'd seen. "The Napoleon mask isn't here." She didn't know if she felt relief or disappointment.

Unfortunately, Carmela didn't have time to savor either emotion, because a sudden creaking noise sounded at the front of the house. A door opening. Then the sound of heavy footsteps shuffling into the portico.

"Crap on a cracker!" said Ava. "The dude left Baby's party early."

"We have to get out of here," Carmela whispered.

"How?"

"Same way we came in. All quiet and sneaky."

"Where do you think he is now?" asked Ava.

Carmela tensed as footsteps started down the hallway.

Please no, Carmela prayed.

The footsteps hesitated, then another door creaked open and a faint light spilled into the hallway. There was a noise that sounded like ice cubes tumbling into a glass.

Wasting no time, Carmela grabbed Ava and pulled her into the hallway. Soundlessly, they snuck through the darkness and into the relative safety of the sunroom.

When they got to their entry point, they jumped into overdrive. Ava stuck a long leg over the windowsill, pulled the other leg across, and hopped down, landing soundlessly in the foliage below. Carmela gave a quick look back over her shoulder and hoisted herself up. She was sitting on the window ledge, poised to scramble out, when she felt a hard jerk.

What the . . . ?

She was stuck, unable to move, unable to escape! Panic fizzed in her brain as she looked back and saw that her dog-gone skirt had hooked on part of the window fixture!

"I'm stuck," Carmela whispered to Ava.

Ava reached a hand up and waggled her fingers. "Hurry up."

"I'm *trying*," said Carmela. She managed to slide forward maybe an inch or two before she was hung up again.

"It's your skirt," said Ava.

"I *know* it's my skirt, but I can't exactly take it off."

"Just give yourself a good hard push and let 'er rip," said Ava.

Carmela slithered forward as her skirt slid up above her knees.

"That's it," Ava coaxed. "Give me your hands and I'll give you a good tug."

"Okay."

Ava, who had both height and heft on Carmela, grasped her friend. "You ready?"

Carmela nodded as Ava gave such a heroic jerk she thought her arms would be yanked from their sockets.

Riiiiip!

Carmela popped through the window like a champagne cork exploding from a bottle. She toppled onto Ava with such force they both tumbled to the damp ground.

"Eeyuh," said Ava, wiggling nervously, "I hope there aren't worms."

"Forget the stupid worms. We've got to get out of here!"

Helping each other up, they dashed around the side of the house and headed for the street. Gasping for air, nervously looking back over their shoulders, they beat feet down the dark, deserted street. It wasn't until Carmela's car was in plain sight that they finally felt safe.

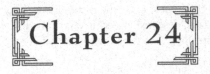

Chapter 24

GABBY spun out a length of cream-colored velvet ribbon and gazed at Carmela. "Where did you and Ava disappear to last night?"

"You don't want to know," said Carmela. It was Thursday morning at Memory Mine and Carmela was regretting her sneaky little foray into Titus Duval's home. They'd barely escaped discovery and she'd had fitful, nightmarish dreams about death masks all night long.

"You two ducked out with a couple of guys?" she asked.

"Nooo," said Carmela.

"Went home early?"

But Carmela had made up her mind to remain mum on the subject. It wouldn't do any good to give Gabby a blow-by-blow account of their little creepy-crawl. She'd just fret about it. Or somehow manage to spill the beans to Babcock. And Carmela really didn't need that right now. Babcock was already on her case about freelance investigating.

"Okay, so you're not going to tell me. Then how about explaining those weird wedding gowns that are hanging in your office. Is there some secret ceremony I don't know about?"

Carmela smiled. "Those are our ghost dresses. For when Ava and I ride the Ghost Train tomorrow night."

"I do remember you mentioning that. So you guys bought tickets?"

"We're actually *characters* on the Ghost Train," said Carmela.

"Yeah?"

"Jekyl asked us to help out. He's been hired to do all the spooky, moody decorations and Ava and I were recruited to be part of that décor."

"That sounds pretty cool. I wish I could get Stuart to attend an event like that."

"It would do him good," Carmela agreed. "Loosen him up."

"He's always so focused on business."

"Unlike us?"

"Oh, we're focused on business, too," Gabby smiled. "It's just that our business happens to be lots more fun."

"You got that right," Carmela agreed.

CARMELA HELPED TWO WOMEN PICK OUT PAPER for trick-or-treat bags, then showed them how to fashion the paper into tubes, add pieces of candy, and then secure the ends so the whole thing looked like a big, gorgeous Tootsie Roll. Then, when she had a few moments, she ducked into her office to work on her ghost dresses.

Since the dresses were already nicely tattered, Carmela set about adding some extra pieces of gossamer, using pieces of fabric to lengthen sleeves, drape the skirts, and add shroud-like details about the waist.

Then came the really fun part—painting the gowns. First Carmela brushed on long zigzags of white tempera paint. Then she mixed together equal amounts of gray and green powdered paint. She spattered the dry paint onto the still-wet paint, creating a subtle hint of mold.

Perfect.

Sewing on a few carefully placed sequins gave the dresses some sparkle, and then she dabbed on spatters of silver.

Carmela remained caught up in her ghostly couture project until there was a soft knock at her door.

She glanced over. "Yes?"

It was Mavis, looking as tentative and apologetic as ever.

"I don't want to interrupt," said Mavis.

"You're not," said Carmela. "I'm practically finished here." She dipped her brush in a puddle of gray paint and spattered on a little more paint, freestyle.

"I wanted to thank you for the invitation last night," said Mavis.

"You should really be thanking Baby, since she was the gracious hostess."

"I know that and I already did. But you're her good friend. If it wasn't for you I wouldn't have been invited to the party at all."

Carmela smiled. "I take it you enjoyed yourself?"

"I had a blast!" said Mavis. "Really, the whole event was amazing. The food, the guests . . . everything." She stood there in a brown dress, looking a little like Cinderella after the ball. Back in her ratty old clothes.

"Have you got everything at Oddities all packed up?"

"I'm just working on the last few bits," said Mavis. Then she brightened. "But I received an interesting call some twenty minutes ago. From a friend of yours—Jekyl Hardy. I met him at the party last night."

"Jekyl? What on earth did he want?"

Mavis grinned. "He wanted to borrow a few pieces from Oddities to decorate his Ghost Train."

"I thought everything from Oddities was packed and ready to go into storage."

"It is," said Mavis. "Or was. But then he offered me money to rent a few items, so I decided to pull out a few choice pieces for him. Apparently, he wants to decorate one of his train cars in a kind of Victorian Sherlock Holmes theme."

"That actually sounds pretty neat," said Carmela.

"That's what I thought, too," said Mavis. "Anyway, I dug out a Sherlock Holmes–style cap, an old-fashioned pipe rack, leather steamer trunk, a watch, a few old books, and some more cool stuff."

"So Jekyl asked you to come and set it all up, too?"

"Oh no, Mr. Hardy said he'd personally take care of arranging things. In fact, he seemed very intent on that. But he did invite me to come aboard the Ghost Train and kind of keep watch over things. So I'm thinking I might do just that."

"That's a great idea. You know"—Carmela pointed at her handiwork—"that's what these gowns are for. Ava and I are going to be wearing them—posing as ghosts."

"Ghosts?" Mavis giggled and Carmela was pleased to see her suddenly light up with enthusiasm. "That's wonderful! It'll all be one big happy family."

"Carmela." Gabby was suddenly at the door. "Telephone."

"I've got to take this," said Carmela.

Mavis gave a quick wave and ducked out. "And I've got to get going."

Carmela picked up the phone, expecting to hear Ava's soft drawl. Instead it was the countess.

"How was your big blowout last night?" cried the countess. "Did you wear the necklace? Did you look terribly haute couture and stunning?"

"I think I did," Carmela laughed. "I certainly received multiple compliments." *And a nasty jab from Glory.*

"I knew you would. Oh, Carmela, I'm thrilled you wore the necklace. I hope you told absolutely everyone where it came from."

"I sure did." *Sort of.*

"You are so sweet," the countess gushed.

"I want to get the necklace back to you as soon as possible, though."

"Do you have it with you? At Memory Mine?"

"It's here," said Carmela. She glanced at the red leather box sitting on her desk.

"Perfect. I'll be dropping by my new shop later today with my decorator to finalize some measurements. You can give it to me then. I'll just pop in and grab it."

"Perfect," said Carmela.

"Au revoir," said the countess.

Carmela hung up the phone and glanced at the jewelry box. The necklace had been a stunner and she'd definitely enjoyed wearing it. Probably, if the countess had more such pieces in her inventory, her business was going to flourish here in New Orleans.

Or was it?

Carmela suddenly wondered why the countess had moved from Palm Beach, a noted enclave of the super wealthy, to New Orleans. Yes, New Orleans had upscale pockets, like the Garden District and Lake Terrace. But weren't there a ton *more* rich ladies in Palm Beach? And nearby Boca Raton and Miami? Wouldn't the chances of selling high-ticket estate jewelry be even greater there?

It sure seemed like it would.

So why, Carmela wondered, was the countess switching cities? Or was she? Maybe she was keeping her Palm Beach store. Maybe this shop was supposed to be Lucrezia west.

Curious now, Carmela sat down and Googled "Lucrezia." She came up with a nail salon, a candle shop, and a modern dance troupe.

She typed in "Lucrezia Palm Beach." Still nothing.

Hmm. Well, let's try "estate jewelry Palm Beach."

That spawned a number of hits. Mostly for high-end jewelry stores, but none with the name Lucrezia.

And then, as she scrolled down, something caught her attention. A headline from the *Palm Beach Daily News* that read, *Cat Burglar Strikes Again on Cocoanut Row!*

Curious now, Carmela clicked and read the entire article. Which, basically, had been written some six months ago and detailed how a very skillful thief had broken into the home of a wealthy Palm Beach resident on Cocoanut Row and stolen an entire cache of precious jewelry.

Carmela blinked hard as her mind raced, jumping to conclusions. Conclusions that were probably quite illogical. Unless . . .

No. It couldn't be, could it? Could the countess and her husband, who had been vaguely introduced as an entrepreneur, have engineered this particular jewel theft? Could the strange vibes she'd been getting from the countess be based on the fact that the woman was possibly a notorious thief?

Could be. Then again, maybe not.

Good thing Carmela had Jekyl on speed dial.

"Hello, buttercup," was Jekyl's greeting when he answered the phone.

"Do you have caller ID or do you greet everyone that way?" Carmela asked.

"Everyone," Jekyl laughed. "What's up?"

"You know that photo you snapped of Ava and me last night?"

"Sure."

"Does it show my necklace fairly well?"

"Give me a moment and I'll check." There was silence for a few moments, and then Jekyl came back on the line and said, "Pretty well. Why?"

"Do you have a way to run that necklace through the National Art Fraud Registry and see if it's stolen goods?"

"Are you serious?"

"Yes, I think I am."

"I can do it but . . . well, who do you think stole it?"

"Mmn . . . maybe the woman who lent it to me."

"You mean the Countess Saint-Marche? With the phony-baloney title?"

"That's right, and I'm thinking her story might be phony, too. I don't know that she ever did own a high-end jewelry store in Palm Beach."

"And you arrived at this conclusion . . . how?"

"I just found an article from the *Palm Beach Daily News* . . ."

"Ah, the Shiny Sheet."

"That's right," said Carmela. She quickly related the article to Jekyl, and then told him about her Internet investigation and how she'd been unable to find any record or mention of a jewelry shop in Palm Beach owned by a countess.

"So now you think your countess and this pussycat thief are one and the same?"

"I don't know that at all, but I'm just curious enough that I'd like to check her out. She and her merchandise. And you, my dear, are my resident antiques guru and art expert. And now, I guess, jewelry expert."

"Okay," said Jekyl, "I'll get back to you."

The minute Carmela hung up the phone she immediately regretted her suspicions. Probably, she decided, she was just being super paranoid. Probably, the countess really was on the up-and-up and she shouldn't be so inquisitive. Shouldn't go looking for problems.

Then again . . .

Just to make sure, just to ease her addled mind, Carmela ran a quick Google search to see if any jewelry heists had taken place in Dallas around the time the Napoleon death mask had been stolen from Wallace Pitney.

Much to her disappointment, she didn't find a thing.

LATE AFTERNOON FOUND CARMELA WITH bunches of cheesecloth spread out on the craft table.

"Now what's going on?" asked Gabby. "More ghosts?"

"I'm making a couple of shrouds to compliment our gowns," said Carmela.

"Shrouds," exclaimed Gabby. "You don't miss a trick, do you? Who would think of shrouds?" She shivered. "The whole notion is so . . . so . . ."

"Ghostly?"

"Ghastly. Still, I can see where you're going with this."

Carmela glanced at her watch and pursed her lips. "You know what? I'm gonna have to come in and finish these tomorrow."

"Even though we're going to be closed for Halloween?" said Gabby.

"Has to be done. Plus, I've got to take off now because I promised to help Ava with her Cemetery Crawl. After that, it's off to the Pumpkins and Bumpkins Ball with Babcock."

"Wow," said Gabby. "Big night." Then she added, almost wistfully, "Well, have fun."

"Oh!" said Carmela. She dashed into her office and returned with the jewelry case. "The countess is going to drop by later. Can you give this to her?"

"Sure, no problem."

Let's hope there isn't, Carmela thought to herself.

BY THE TIME CARMELA ARRIVED AT JUJU VOO-doo, Ava was frantic.

"Look at this place!" she screamed. "We're hip-deep in customers!"

"Calm down," Carmela told her. "That's a good thing."

"I know, I know," she jabbered back.

Carmela did a quick check of the shop. Madame Blavatsky was doing a tarot reading in back, Miguel was helping two customers at the counter, and there were another half dozen customers wandering around, looking at shrunken heads, love potions, and saint candles. So she did what came naturally to her, she plunged in to help.

Carmela checked Ava's patron saint chart, found out that Saint Andrew was the patron saint of singers, and promptly sold a half dozen candles. Then she climbed a rickety step-ladder to snag a wooden skeleton that was dangling from the rafters and ended up selling a Day of the Dead sugar skull, too. Two giggling teenagers wanted a love potion, so Carmela searched a shelf of purple bottles until she found Lady Amore's Sure Fire Love Potion.

As she was ringing the potions up, a familiar face seemed to ghost past her.

Huh?

A man circled a shelf containing magic kits, voodoo charms, and skull jewelry, and then cruised back in the direction of the cash register.

Oh shoot, it's that awful Johnny Sparks. What on earth is he doing here?

When Sparks recognized her, he sputtered out, "What are *you* doing here?" in a none-too-friendly tone of voice.

"I work here," said Carmela.

"Yeah?" said a disbelieving Sparks as he furowed his brow. Then, "You got any tarot cards?"

"Of course," said Carmela. "Would you like Rider-Waite or our new vampire wisdom cards?"

Sparks scowled at her. "Just give me the cards and make it snappy."

AN HOUR LATER, MOST OF THEIR CUSTOMERS taken care of, Ava's werewolf came loping in.

"Bert," said Ava, looking flustered. "You're early."

Bert, who wasn't dressed in his werewolf costume yet, just jeans and a leather jacket, looked at his watch and said, "You told me five. It's five."

"Already?" said Ava. She threw a pleading look at Carmela. "Can you get Bert zipped into his werewolf suit? It's hanging in my office."

"Come on, Bert," said Carmela, taking his soon-to-be paw. "Let's pretend there's a full moon and change you into a loup-garou."

The suit wasn't the best werewolf suit Carmela had ever seen. First of all, it was cheesy brown polyester that looked more grungy than furry. Still, in the darkness of a cemetery, with candles flickering and imaginations running wild, it would probably be just dandy. Carmela reasoned that most people signed up for a Cemetery Crawl because they *wanted* to be scared. Hence, once Bert was zipped into his suit and let loose a few maniacal howls and grunts, he should fill the fright bill nicely.

But the zipping up of the suit proved to be a huge problem.

"This suit is a size medium," complained Bert. "And I'm a large."

"Try to suck in a little," Carmela coaxed. Bert was a good old boy with long hair, whiskers, and an ample tummy.

"I'm *try*ing."

"Try harder. There, now it's . . . oops!"

"What?"

"The zipper's caught," said Carmela. "Brace yourself, I'm going to give it a good . . . shoot, now it's really stuck."

"Oh man," said Bert. "I don't wanna lose this gig."

"Relax, I'll just sew you into your costume," said Carmela. She scrounged through Ava's desk drawer, finally coming up with a needle and thread. Two dozen good whipstitches later and the suit was a permanent part of Bert.

"Feels good," he said, patting his tummy. "Nice and tight."

"Just don't try to bend over," Carmela warned. "Or take a deep breath."

Bert grabbed the werewolf head and plopped it on his shoulders. "Grrrrr!"

"Perfect," said Carmela. "You're gonna kill 'em."

Bert took the head off and gave her a puzzled expression.

"Well, not *literally* kill," said Carmela. She grabbed the head and stuck it back on. "Go out there and show Ava. Let her see how professional you look." She steered Bert out the door.

"Oh my gosh, that's great!" Ava exclaimed when she caught sight of him. "Really perfect."

"Thanks," came Bert's muffled reply.

"You know where to meet us?" said Ava.

The werewolf head bobbled an affirmative.

"Perfect. We'll see you there."

Bert waved a paw, turned, and promptly banged into a cabinet. There was a muffled, "Ouch."

"Oh dear," said Ava, scrambling to help. "This is kind of like playing blind man's bluff, isn't it? Maybe you should take that big old head off."

Bert pulled the head off. His face was already bright pink from being encased in all that fur. "But I want to wear it when I'm driving."

"Sure," said Ava as he bumbled out the door. "Whatever." She turned to Carmela and chuckled. "How'd you like to be the guy who pulls up next to him at a red light?"

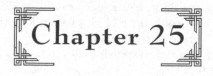

Chapter 25

LAFAYETTE Cemetery No. 1 was the perfect setting for Ava's Cemetery Crawl. Crumbling and sublime, it was located on the edge of the Garden District and boasted black wrought-iron gates, tumbledown tombs, ancient mausoleums, and several hair-raising legends that involved ghost sightings and hovering orbs.

Carmela and Ava both wore black velvet vampire dresses that Ava had pulled from her closet. They'd clipped in long hair extensions and applied black lipstick. Now Ava stood just inside the gates that were kitty-corner from Commander's Palace, consulting her clipboard and efficiently checking off names as her Cemetery Crawl guests showed up.

As Carmela adjusted the bloodred sash on her dress, she had to marvel at Ava's amazing wardrobe. Her large walk-in closet rivaled that of a Vegas showgirl who moonlighted as a Halloween-loving stripper. Except when it was Mardi Gras, and then Ava seemed to have ball gowns galore.

"Names?" said Ava, as two giggling women hurried toward her.

"Beth Crowley and Barb Higgins," said one of the women. She was dressed in a black tunic and shiny black leggings. Her friend wore a black sweater, long skirt, and boots. "Are we almost ready to go?"

"Almost," Ava replied sweetly. "All you have to do now is go over to where Carmela is standing and pick up your official Crawl candle."

Carmela had been designated Keeper of the Candles tonight. As such, she passed out white candles with black paper ruffles at the bottom to all the guests who arrived. And plastic glow-in-the-dark skull rings, too. That had been Ava's last-minute brainstorm.

As more guests arrived and nervous giggles ran through the crowd, Carmela lit all the candles and then made her way over to Ava. "Are you about ready to get started? I think the crowd is growing restless."

"We're still missing two of our guests," said Ava. "I hate to take off and just . . . oh, wait, I see a couple of stragglers coming now."

"Wait!" screeched a familiar voice as two women dashed through the rather foreboding gates. "Don't leave without us."

"Oh my," Carmela said under her breath. "It's the countess."

"But without her count," said Ava. "Does that make her countless?"

"Don't let her hear you say that."

Instead, Ava beamed happily at her late arrivals. "You're just in time, ladies, not a second to spare."

The countess left her friend with Ava and made a beeline for Carmela. "I had a feeling you'd be here tonight," she gushed.

"And here I am," said Carmela. "Did you get a chance to stop by Memory Mine and pick up your necklace?"

"Yes, indeed. Gabby gave it to me. So not to worry, it's safe and sound, back where it belongs."

"Thank you again for letting me wear it—that necklace was a real showstopper. A conversation starter, too." *Was it ever.*

"Really, Carmela, anytime you'd like to borrow a piece of jewelry just let me know. I'm more than happy to oblige and I do have some *marrrrvelous* pieces."

"That's very kind of you." Carmela suddenly felt a twinge of guilt for thinking that the countess might be a garden-variety crook. After all, here she was, being generous to a fault. Or was it some kind of act? Only time would tell. Or maybe a little more investigating.

Ava held her candle high and waggled it back and forth, like she was out on the tarmac, guiding in a celestial 747.

"This way, everybody come this way," she cried. When her guests had gathered around, she said, "Now stick close to me. We're in one of New Orleans's oldest cemeteries. And since it harbors many restless souls, I can assure you there have been numerous spirit sightings reported here."

That brought on a round of giggles.

"The first tomb I want to show you in this City of the Dead is right this way." They crunched along a narrow pathway, threading their way through rows of tombs. Bits of moonlight shone through bare trees, lending a ghostly quality to the white gravel underfoot.

Ava stopped near a large marble mausoleum with an engraved plaque and bars on the double doors. "If you've ever seen the movie *Double Jeopardy*, a few of those scenes were filmed right here."

There were nods and murmurs. The strange guest that Carmela had sold the ticket to nodded and exclaimed, *"Nish au vlek!"*

"And over here is a very unusual cast iron tomb." They all gaped as Ava gestured to a rusty metal tomb that looked half-melted and pitted with age. "You might also find this factoid a bit unusual," she continued, "but almost seven thousand people are buried right here in a single city block."

"How is that even possible?" asked one of the guests.

Ava bit her lower lip. "Heat, humidity, and the hands of time. And the fact that many of these old family tombs have what you might call *cellars* underneath them."

"Gulp," said one woman, realizing exactly what this implied.

Ava continued her tour, keeping up her running commentary as she guided her group through the dark cemetery. Candlelight flickered and bounced off the whitewashed tombs as she pointed out the most interesting graves and shared spooky legends and lore that served to prickle the hair on the back of their necks.

One woman raised her hand tentatively. "Is this the graveyard Anne Rice always wrote about?"

"Yes, it is," said Ava. "Her house is just a few blocks from here, and I happen to know that she based the Vampire Lestat's tomb on one of the tombs right in this area."

"Do you know which one?" asked the woman. "Do you have any idea?"

"That's still up for speculation," replied Ava. She gazed at her group, a twinkle showing in her eye. "But if it were up to me . . ." She threw out an arm. "I'd select *that* one!"

All eyes jumped to the tomb Ava had just pointed at. Which was the opportune moment for the werewolf to suddenly leap out!

"Arrh!" growled the werewolf, scrambling on top of the tomb, then sinking down into a menacing crouch.

"Eeeek!" cried the guests. Those who were thoroughly startled by the werewolf's surprise appearance backpedaled quickly, while a few brave and curious souls moved closer. All in all, they were perfectly delighted to be scared out of their wits.

* * *

'THAT SURE WENT WELL,' SAID AVA, AS CARMELA wove her car down St. Charles Avenue. They were scurrying home so they could change into formal attire for tonight's big ball.

"It did, but now I feel like Cinderella, rushing home to change," said Carmela.

"Oh yeah?" said Ava. "Then who am I supposed to be, the ugly stepsister?"

Carmela chuckled. "If the glass slipper fits. After all, it *is* called Pumpkins and Bumpkins Ball."

"Jeez," said Ava. "The last thing I want is to turn into a pumpkin."

"Or end up with a bumpkin," said Carmela.

"How are we gettin' there?" asked Ava. "Since we're supposed to meet our sweeties at the hotel."

"Hang on to your garters, Babcock is sending a limo for us."

"For us? That sounds extremely glam."

"Oh, I don't know," said Carmela. "I think some guy . . . um, owed him a favor."

THEIR WHITE STRETCH LIMOUSINE GLIDED UP to the circular drive in front of the Hotel Barnabas.

"Holy gumbo and grits," said Ava, peering out the window at the red carpet and all the lights. "I feel like I'm hangin' with P. Diddy. Or like I'm one of those celebs you see on E! Entertainment."

"Just make sure everything's strategically covered when you step out."

"Don't worry. I don't plan to end up on some crazy Internet peep show."

The driver pulled open the door and Ava, in her full-length black and purple gown, stepped out carefully. She lifted her chin, posed carefully, and gave a big smile to three very bored-looking photographers who'd probably been sent out by their very bored editors. "Please," she called out as she dramatically threw up an arm, "no photos." Which only served to capture their attention and make them rush forward to snap copious photos of Ava.

"You minx," said Carmela. She gathered up the skirt of her strapless black gown as the two of them hurried up the steps and into the ornate hotel lobby.

Ava arched an eyebrow. "Ain't I just? But isn't this fun?"

"You know," said Carmela. "It kind of is."

THE HOTEL'S MILLENNIUM BALLROOM WAS AL-ready crowded with men in tuxedos and women wearing hybrid costumes that combined ball gowns with masks, outlandish headgear, and other fun trinkets.

The band, the New Improved Headbangers, was dressed in bright orange jackets and black slacks and were already blasting the roof off the place. Their horn section was just capping off a rousing version of "Down to New Orleans," then the whole band jumped in to play "Apache Rose Peacock." Gilded pumpkins, silvered cobwebs, and tree branches hung with fluttering ghosts lent an air of Halloween elegance as guest swirled on the dance floor.

"The bar," said Ava, glancing around. "I'm supposed to meet Charlie at the bar."

"Let's do it," said Carmela. "I think we could both benefit from a cool, refreshing drink."

They threaded their way through the revelers, dodging a man in a black sequined dinner jacket and a woman in a gold ball gown with a boa of brown, furry rats strung around her neck.

"Lots of cool costumes," said Ava as they bellied up to a bar that was swathed in orange and gold.

"Take a look at that bondage couple dancing over there," said Carmela.

"Mmn, studded leather, chains, and a little skin peeping out. Be still my heart."

"Ava!" said Carmela.

"Just looking," she said primly.

They ordered Witches' Cauldron cocktails, which were basically a lethal concoction of rum and fruit juices.

Ava took a sip from her giant goblet. "Tasty."

Carmela took a sip and made a face. "Strong."

"Too strong?"

"I can live with it."

"Look," said Ava. "There's Baby and Del over there."

"And Tandy and Darwin."

"*Cher,*" said Ava. "Who's that guy staring at you?"

Carmela frowned as she glanced around. "What guy?" Was Babcock hanging back somewhere, watching her, and doing his undercover cop impression?

"That guy over there in the weird green slacks and shiny black jacket."

Carmela's eyes continued to search the crowd. She saw a lady in an ermine cape, a man in a black velvet tux, a woman in a medieval-looking gown, and . . .

"Boyd Bellamy," Carmela murmured.

"Who?" said Ava.

Bellamy gave a knee-jerk reaction when Carmela spotted him, and quickly turned away. Started jabbering, in fact, to a woman in a poufy red dress.

"Boyd Bellamy, my landlord," Carmela explained. "You remember . . . the guy who drop-kicked Mavis out of her space so he could lease it to the countess. The one who insulted us at the buffet table last night."

"Oh, *that* jerk. So why do you think he was watching you?"

Carmela shrugged. "I don't know. Maybe he wants to kick me out of my space, too. He came tromping into Memory Mine a couple of days ago chortling about how he'd love to relocate me."

"Don't do it."

"I have no intention of moving. I've got an ironclad lease, or so my attorney insists."

"Good girl," said Ava. "Smart girl."

"Ava. Oh, Ava." Charlie Preston was creeping toward them, grinning like a lovesick puppy. He was dressed in a T-shirt and tux, and wore a blue baseball cap that bore a yellow *CSI* logo.

Ava took one look at him and snatched the cap from his head. "Take that silly thing off."

"What?" said Charlie, looking a little hurt. "You don't like it?"

"Nope." Ava snuggled up next to him and rubbed a bare shoulder against his chest. "But I'm glad *you* showed up."

Charlie suddenly looked like he'd died and gone to heaven. "I thought about you all day long."

"Just the day?" teased Ava. Which made Charlie blush even more furiously.

"I don't suppose you know the whereabouts of Detective Babcock, do you?" Carmela asked.

"Oh, he's here," said Charlie. "Somewhere."

Carmela cast her eyes into the crowd again. When she still didn't see Babcock anywhere, she took a step closer to Charlie. "Charlie, sweetie, do you know if there's anything new in the Marcus Joubert investigation?"

Charlie swallowed hard. "You know I'm not supposed to talk about ongoing cases."

"But it's just us," Ava cooed.

"We were *there*," Carmela reminded him. "We're already part of the inner circle." They weren't really, but, hey, it was a shot.

"What . . . what do you want to know?" Charlie stammered.

Carmela came at him like a snapping turtle. "Anything you can tell us!"

"Well," said Charlie. "It appears there might have been more of a struggle than we initially thought."

"How so?" asked Carmela.

"The vic's clothing was extremely ripped and disheveled."

"Interesting," said Carmela. So Joubert had struggled mightily to fight off his assassin. "What else?"

"Trading secrets?" a familiar male voice teased.

Carmela jumped like a scalded cat. Then she whirled around as Babcock's arm encircled her waist.

"We wouldn't do that," Carmela told him.

Babcock flashed her an easy grin. "Sure you would."

Ava came to Carmela's rescue. She poked an index finger into Babcock's starched white shirt. "You. Are late."

He gave her a wink. "But I'm here now. All dressed up with no . . . wait, I *do* have someplace to go." He took Carmela gently by the arm. "Namely the dance floor." He spun her out into a crowd of slow-dancing partiers.

Carmela nestled close to him as they danced. "I was afraid you weren't going to show up."

He smiled down at her. "Really? Even after I sent a bigtime limo to pick you up?"

"That was nice," Carmela admitted. She relaxed in his arms, enjoying the music, the closeness, the background chatter and party atmosphere. There were plenty of fancy balls held in New Orleans all year round. But this one, the Pumpkins and Bumpkins Ball, was one of her favorites. It was dressy but not as seriously dressy or high society as some of the Mardi Gras balls or major charity balls. In other words, the pressure was off.

When the music ended, Babcock kissed the tip of her nose, then his lips traveled downward.

So nice, Carmela thought as he kissed her full on the lips. *So lovely.*

And then, out of nowhere, "I've got someone I need to talk to," Babcock told her.

"Here? Now?" She couldn't quite believe it.

Babcock smiled his crooked grin.

"You're serious?" said Carmela. "You're still on the job?"

"I'm always on the job." He was leading her to one of the hors d'oeuvres stations where fancy cheeses and smoked oysters beckoned.

"No," said Carmela.

"Ten minutes," said Babcock. He hesitated, his blue eyes staring at her with great intensity.

"Okay," Carmela relented. She had just spotted Jekyl scooping up an inordinately huge amount of shrimp dip onto his cracker. "I'll go talk to Jekyl over there. Maybe lure him out onto the dance floor, too."

"Ten minutes," Babcock said as he slipped away.

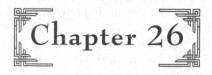

Chapter 26

JEKYL was dressed in a purple velvet jacket with shiny black lapels that may or may not have been genuine stingray. His slacks were a pale gray and his shoes high-gloss Gucci loafers.

"You're like Babcock," Carmela told him, pointing to his shoes. "Always with the spendy footwear."

"That's because I have terrible feet," said Jekyl. "So I'm forced to buy expensive Italian or British shoes." As if to explain, he lifted one foot off the floor. "I have extraordinarily high arches. Do you know how difficult it is to walk around with high arches?"

Carmela smiled tolerantly. She knew Jekyl enjoyed his upper-crust tastes. "Do you know how difficult it is to walk around in four-inch-high stilettos?"

Jekyl just smiled and popped another cracker into his mouth. "So what's up? You look fab as always, sweetums. Is that gown new?"

"Old. But thanks anyway. Did you have a chance to check on that necklace?"

Jekyl dusted his hands together. "I did. And I didn't find a goldarned thing that would indicate your precious borrowed necklace was stolen goods."

"So that's good." *Good goods.*

Jekyl held up a finger. "That doesn't necessarily mean that it's not stolen."

"Then it's not good news. So where does that leave us?"

"First thing tomorrow I'm going to check a couple of other resources."

"Thank you," said Carmela. She touched his shoulder just as her cell phone chimed. "And Jekyl, please don't breathe a word of this to anyone, okay? This is just a silly little hunch that I'm following up. It'll probably turn out to be a wild-goose chase."

Jekyl just smiled benignly at her.

She pulled out her phone. "Jekyl . . . are you listening? I don't want the countess to know a thing about this."

"Mum's the word," he finally said.

Carmela turned away from him and said, "Yes?" The screen on her phone had indicated *Unidentified Caller* and she wondered briefly if there had been some sort of trouble at her shop. Or something else?

"Hello?" said a soft voice.

"Yes?" Carmela said again.

"Miss Bertrand?" Now the voice was so low it could barely be heard above a loud crackling noise.

Bad connection.

Carmela was only steps from a doorway, so she stepped out into a dimly lit hallway, hoping to find a quieter spot.

"Hello?" she said as she walked down the long, carpeted hallway. It was practically deserted here. And quite a bit cooler, too. "Hello?" she said again. Now she stepped through a puddle of light into a dim area that led to an outdoor patio. When she passed a door marked *Utility Closet*, she said, "I can hear you a little better now. Are you still there?"

"This is very important," said the voice. Whoever it was sounded nervous and very upset. "Can you hear me?" Unfortunately, there was still a loud crackling on the line.

"I'm trying," said Carmela. "Just give me a minute." She walked farther down the hallway and stood next to a large linen cart. "Hello? Do we have a connection now?"

She heard nothing but dead air.

Carmela sighed heavily. *Just my luck.*

Just as she was about to hang up, a shadow seemed to materialize from the doorway across from her.

"Oh!" she said, surprised that someone was even there. Then she had a fleeting impression of something scary and green lunging at her, and then a dimly lit figure put a hand at the base of her throat and shoved her up against the wall. Hard enough to shake her up and make her teeth rattle.

Stunned beyond belief, feeling like a terrified butterfly held in place with a stick pin, Carmela stared wide-eyed at her attacker.

Green bug eyes glared back at her!

A mask? Has to be a mask. A costume!

"Who are you?" Carmela cried out. "What do you want?" But the bug-eyed man wearing a scaly-looking green alien suit just shook his head.

"Quiet," he growled. "Shut up and listen."

She fought hard to push his hand away, her fingertips flailing against his rubber suit. "Get away from me, you jerk, before I scream my head off! Do you know who my . . . ?"

This time her attacker clamped his rubber-clad hand directly over her mouth, cutting off her words.

Carmela fought back with renewed fervor, chewing at his hand, clawing at him desperately, trying to bang him in the head with the phone that was still clutched in her hand. But the green alien was too strong for her; he towered above her and outweighed her by easily seventy pounds.

Not a fair match, Carmela thought as she seethed inwardly.

The horrible green mask and bug-like body leaned even closer, smashing against her, practically choking off her breathing.

"Leave it alone," the green alien hissed.

Carmela could see the edges of his rubber mask vibrating as he spewed out his threat. His breath was a lethal combination of beer, cheeseburgers, and garlic.

"What are you talking about?" Carmela managed to stammer. Her mind was an angry blur. "Leave *what* alone?"

"All your investigating. Stop being so nosy. Otherwise you and your cop friend are going to get hurt!"

"What?" she cried. "What are you . . . ?" But he'd pressed his hand tight against her lips once again.

"Listen to me," he snarled. "Now you are going to stand here like a good little girl and slowly count to one hundred. You are not going to scream or run. You are not going to *move*." With that, the green alien gave her a final shove and dashed down the hallway.

Carmela, shaking with anger, quivering from too much adrenaline juicing through her veins, was too stunned to do anything at all.

Except use her phone. In a split second, she aimed it, one-handedly, toward the green alien's back as he streaked down the corridor. And snapped his picture.

Now what? Gotta think.

Carmela knew she was experiencing a mild form of shock, but realized she had to do something to jump-start her brain. She had to think hard and take something away from this hideous encounter. Something she could use later. Something she could use to catch this horrible person!

Who had he been? Carmela wondered. And what exactly had he said to her?

Back off. He told me to back off.

Had the green alien been warning her to back off on the Oddities investigation? Or did his words have something to do with the countess and her jewelry?

Carmela touched a hand to her throat where the horrible green alien had touched her. Inches below she could feel her heart beating frantically like the wings of a dove.

Could the green alien have been one of Titus Duval's minions? Had he figured out that she and Ava had snuck into his home last night?

Or was he one of Johnny Sparks's henchmen? Had her visit to the pawn shop the other day set off some kind of trip wire?

Carmela's first instinct was to run screaming to Babcock. Rush into the safety of his arms and plead and beg him to put out an all-points bulletin on this crazy person who had just accosted her.

No, I can't do that.

Once again, she knew that if Babcock had any inkling that she was in physical danger, he'd put her in lockdown. Station armed guards all around her shop and apartment.

No, she had to tough this out by herself. She had to go back into the ballroom, find Babcock, and try to pretend this never happened. For now.

Later she would try to figure this out.

Because in one part of her mind—the part Carmela kept secret, the part where she harbored her talent for investigating and for exacting revenge—she knew she had just gazed upon a huge, hulking clue.

An actual physical threat, like the one she'd just experienced, surely meant that someone—probably Joubert's killer—was worried and very, very desperate!

Carmela walked slowly down the corridor, struggling to

mentally and physically pull herself back together. The music was coming to her loud and clear now, and she could hear the jubilant voices of hundreds of revelers.

Then she drew a deep breath, as everything snapped back into focus for her, and she walked into the ballroom.

IT WAS AFTER 1:00 A.M. WHEN CARMELA FINALLY tumbled into her apartment. Babcock had taken her to Antoine's for a late dinner of grilled pompano, and then they'd hooked up with some friends and gone to Bombay Club to listen to music. She'd kept up a good front, laughing and joking with the group. But, all the while, her mind had darkly ruminated over her various suspects and the possible meaning of her earlier encounter.

Now she was tired and dragging, ready to hit the sack.

Carmela tossed her beaded bag onto the counter, kicked off her shoes, and let the dogs out into the courtyard.

Just as she pulled a bottle of spring water from the refrigerator, the dogs started barking wildly and the phone shrilled.

Now what?

Carmela grabbed up the phone even as she rushed to the door to try and shush the dogs. "Hello?"

It was Ava and she was hysterical.

"*Cher*, I've been trying to call you! I need you to get over here right away!"

The dogs came thundering in past Carmela, practically clipping her knees. "Ava, what's wrong?"

There was a loud hiccup and a half sob, and then Ava said, "Somebody broke into my shop!"

Carmela felt the breath being sucked out of her. "Is it bad?" *What am I thinking? Of course it's bad.* "Has the place been trashed?"

"Better you should come and see." Ava's voice sounded thready and choked. "Can you? Come, I mean?"

"On my way."

Thirty seconds later, Carmela dove through the back door into Ava's shop.

It wasn't good. In fact, Juju Voodoo was a mess. Broken candles were strewn across the floor, skeletons had been pulled down from their perches, shattered bottles lay everywhere.

"Look at this," Ava cried. "My skull candles are smashed to smithereens, all my jewelry has been knocked down, and there are perfumed oils and incense spilled all over the place! My sandalwood, my patchouli, even my sage clusters."

Carmela took a tentative sniff and sneezed loudly. "You're right, this place smells like a cross between a requiem mass and a hippie colony."

Ava almost laughed, but instead let out a sob. "The thing is . . ."

Carmela interrupted. "Who would do this? What's the motive? Was it a robbery? Was all your cash stolen?" She machine-gunned questions at Ava.

"Maybe around thirty bucks from the register," said Ava. "The rest is still locked in the safe. But the mess and the money aren't the worst of it!" She pointed to a scrawl of red paint on top of the wooden counter. "Look at that!"

Carmela tiptoed forward and cocked her head to one side. Someone had dipped their finger in red paint and printed out the words *Back off.*

The words chilled her. It was exactly what the green alien had said to her a few hours ago. Doggone it.

"Back off from what?" Carmela muttered to herself. *Could it be the same person? Had the green alien put in an unwelcome appearance here, too?*

Ava stared at her with dark, tear-filled eyes. "*Cher*, I think this warning was meant for you."

Carmela's thoughts were definitely focused on the green alien. And on Johnny Sparks, who'd been here just this afternoon. As her thoughts congealed, her eyes turned to ice chips and her jaw hardened.

Ava continued to stare at her. "Because you're the one who's been, like, investigating." She paused and frowned. "Carmela, is something wrong?"

Carmela gazed at Ava, who looked beyond traumatized. She gripped her hand and said, "Honey, I think you might be right about this."

"Really?"

Carmela quickly told Ava about the big green alien who'd cornered her in the hallway at the Pumpkins and Bumpkins Ball. And about his harsh, no-holds-barred warning.

"Dear Lord," said Ava, quickly making the sign of the cross. "So somebody really *is* serious about stopping this investigation. Did you tell Babcock?"

"No, because then he'd up and have a coronary."

"Did you get an inkling as to who this green alien might be?"

"I don't have a clue." Actually Carmela *did* have a tiny clue. She'd remembered that Boyd Bellamy had been dressed in green slacks this evening. Could he have been the green alien? It was possible. Then again, anything was possible.

A few more tears spilled down Ava's cheeks as she gazed about her shop. "And I was supposed to be open tomorrow morning. And stay open until at least one o'clock. Oh man, now I won't be able to go to the Zombie Chase with you. And I was really looking forward to that!"

"Please, don't worry," Carmela assured her. "I'll help you clean up this mess. We'll get Juju Voodoo shipshape in no time at all."

"You think?"

I hope. "Of course."

"So I shouldn't call Miguel and beg him to come in immediately?"

"Not at all," Carmela told her. "We'll get this sorted out

so you can be open tomorrow at nine on the dot." Carmela wiggled her nose and sneezed again. "In the meantime, prop open the doors, will you?" She waved a hand in front of her face. "And a couple of windows?"

"What a friend you are!" exclaimed Ava.

"Tell you what," said Carmela, kneeling down. "I'll gather up all the broken stuff while you dig in your stock-room for replacement candles and things."

"You're really going to help?" Ava was deeply touched.

"Sure," said Carmela. "I bet we can knock this off in an hour." She sneezed again. "Or two or three at the most."

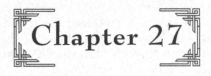

Chapter 27

CARMELA yawned as she gazed bleary-eyed around Memory Mine this Friday morning. Halloween morning.

The shop was officially closed, but Carmela was there anyway. She had to finish the shrouds to go with her and Ava's ghost dresses. Only problem was, she'd only had about six hours' sleep.

The cleanup at Ava's shop hadn't been that bad. Mostly things had been overturned, spilled, and smashed. Still, Carmela's brain had been up late, working overtime. Trying to puzzle out who was behind all these nasty warnings.

Someone obviously thought she was getting too close to solving Joubert's murder. But who? And just how close was she? She'd shown her cell-phone photo to Ava—the one of the green alien's backside—but Ava hadn't recognized him. Then again, the creep had been in costume.

Carmela shook her head as she patted the fabric that she'd dampened and sprayed with a stiffening agent. It was half dry, on its way to crisp. Now all she had to do was crumple it up a bit and form it into a shawl that would drape nicely around their shoulders.

She pinched and tucked, forming both shawls into a distinct U shape. When they were dry and really quite hard, she hit them with a couple coats of gray paint. There. Almost good to go.

Just as Carmela was wiping her hands on a damp towel, the phone rang. It was Ava.

"How are things at your shop?" Carmela asked her.

"Things are hoppin'," said Ava. She sounded in high spirits. "We've got at least a dozen customers wandering around. Buying stuff, too!"

"See?"

"You were right. Last night was only a small burp in the scheme of things. Or more like a stinky belch."

"But we got it done," said Carmela. "And now you're open for business."

"Thanks to you. How are the shrouds coming?"

"Great. I'm gonna dab on some more paint and be done with them."

"So I should pick you up around one? We're still going to the Zombie Chase, right?"

"How could we not?" said Carmela. "Oh, Ava, and when you come by? Bring some food, okay?"

"Gotcha."

Carmela was just sewing tiny, tinkling beads on the hems of their ghost dresses when she heard a pounding at the front door.

Can't they read? Don't they see the sign that says Closed?

Carmela set her needle and thread down and hurried to the front door. The words, *Sorry we're closed*, were forming on her lips when she skidded to a halt and gaped at the face that peered in through the glass.

Boyd Bellamy.

Oh no.

But Bellamy was attacking the door with his fist, demanding to be let in.

Against her good judgment, Carmela unlocked the door.

"Hi," she said, sounding brittle and overly chirpy. "What's up?"

Bellamy flashed a cheesy smile and said, "I see your neighbor finally moved out."

"Not because she wanted to," said Carmela. "Really, Mr. Bellamy, you could have given Mavis a longer grace period than just one week."

Bellamy beetled his brows. "I got a real estate company to run. Time is money and the sooner I get a paying tenant in there the better off I am."

"You think the Countess Saint-Marche is going to be a good tenant?"

"I got no reason to think otherwise," said Bellamy. He glanced around, pretending to look interested.

"That's great," said Carmela. "That you're such a keen judge of people, I mean."

Bellamy moved a step closer to her. "What are you getting at?"

Carmela moved a step backward. "Nothing." Carmela was listening to the inflections in Bellamy's voice, trying to decide if he was the one who'd threatened her last night. Wondering if he was the green alien. Or could he have been the one who broke into Ava's shop? Maybe he was trying to take over that space, too!

But Bellamy wasn't all that interested in her or her shop. He rocked back on his heels and said, "You've been a good tenant, Carmela. Always pay your rent on time. I like that."

"I imagine you would."

He sucked air through his front teeth. "Commercial real estate is a crazy business. You have no idea."

"I suppose not." Actually, she did, since Shamus's division at the bank managed several commercial properties.

"Ah well, have yourself a good day. Be sure to lock up tight. There's going to be Halloween mischief afoot for sure tonight."

"I'll be careful," she said, as she let Bellamy out the door. He turned around and gave a perfunctory smile as she made a big show of turning the dead bolt.

When he was gone, Carmela let loose a shudder.

What was that all about? Was Bellamy trying to scare her into moving? Or was he just a lousy conversationalist? Who knew? But somehow, she had an inkling that, sooner or later, she was going to get to the bottom of this whole entire mess.

Carmela had just finished spraying a final hit of gray paint on her shrouds when there was another knock at the door. But this one was totally expected. Ava. And she'd brought along sandwiches. Po-boys, to be exact.

"I got you the fried oysters that you like," Ava bubbled. "And meatballs for me."

"Perfect," said Carmela as she led Ava to the back table. "Oh, and take a look at our dresses. And shrouds." She lifted a shroud up and draped it around a dress.

"Just fabulous," Ava proclaimed. "And I like that you really stiffened them up."

They cleared off the table and snarfed down their sandwiches. Ava had brought bottles of Diet Coke, too, and they drank those, suppressing burps as best they could.

"I love those little tinkling beads you sewed around the hems," said Ava, leaning back and relaxing. "And the gray and green paint you spattered on the dresses and shrouds is fabulous. Very Jackson Pollock." She chuckled. "We're going to make quite a pair."

"Doppelgangers," agreed Carmela.

THE ZOMBIE CHASE WAS A CHARITY EVENT sponsored by the New Orleans Police Department. Held at

City Park, it was basically a paintball game where contestants attempted to run through an enormous field filled with lurching zombies. Contestants were given a paintball gun, and, if they tagged a zombie, that zombie was considered dead. On the other hand, if a zombie tagged a contestant with a paint stick, you were dead. Or infected. Or undead, as the case may be.

"What are Babcock and his brothers in blue trying to raise money for?" Ava asked. She and Carmela were waiting in line, waiting to sign releases and get their guns.

"I think they want to buy new computers or something," said Carmela. She was standing on tiptoes, trying to get Babcock's attention, but he was busy with other things.

"We're gonna have to kill a lot of zombies, then," said Ava. She craned her neck around. A circus atmosphere prevailed throughout the entire park, with food booths, games for the kids, face painting, and musicians.

"Isn't this interesting," said a man as he bumped up against Carmela. "We meet again."

Carmela turned her head and stared into the wary eyes of Johnny Sparks.

"What are you doing here?" were the first words that flew from her mouth.

Sparks smirked. "You might say I'm keeping a watchful eye on the police."

"That's funny," said Carmela, "I figured you were here trying to buy one off."

"That's some sense of humor you got, girlie," snarled Sparks as he shambled off.

"Who was that?" asked Ava. "The guy with the constipated look on his face."

"That was that pawn shop guy again," Carmela told Ava. What she didn't tell her was that Sparks could very well have been the jerk who broke into Juju Voodoo last night. But why spoil the day when Ava was just beginning to regain her good humor?

Carmela and Ava shuffled ahead with the crowd and were finally herded into a paddock with twenty other gamers. There they signed releases and were issued protective vests and paint guns.

"How does this work?" Ava asked as she aimed her gun at the face of one of the police officers.

The officer touched the barrel and pushed it aside, away from his face. "You pull the trigger," he told her.

"Sounds easy enough," said Ava. "And how many zombies are out in that field?"

"About a hundred."

"That doesn't seem fair," said Ava. "Aren't the odds stacked against us?"

"Remember," said the officer. "They're zombies. They can only shuffle along slowly and moan. And they have to physically touch you with their paint stick to tag you out."

Carmela leaned forward. "What do we win if we make it through the field without getting zombified?"

The officer smiled. "You get a gift certificate for dinner at Dufresne's Oyster House."

"Okay," said Ava. "Let's do it!"

The officer got on his walkie-talkie and called to another officer across the field. There was loud static and an exchange of 10-4s. Then their gate swung open and Carmela and Ava and the rest of their group were released into the park.

Ava, with her longer legs, led the charge, striking out into the field of zombies. "Take that," she cried, firing right and left.

Ava's gun exploded to Carmela's right just as she caught up. *Boom!*

A burst of yellow paint spattered dead center on one of the stumbling zombies.

Splat!

"I got him!" Ava chortled. "Dead center."

"Nice shot," said Carmela, as a group of six zombies started to close in on them.

"You take the three on our right flank, I'll handle the ones on our left," ordered Ava. She was totally into it.

Boom, boom, splat, splat splat!

More zombies were forced to take a knee.

"We're doin' it!" Ava yelled. "Gettin' it done!"

They ran along, giggling like crazy as they shot at zombies, their guns making rapid-fire *pop-pop-pops*.

Ava spun and fired. "That one's mine. And that one, too. Man, this is my kind of game." She lifted her paintball gun and blew at the barrel. "Nailed another two of those suckers. Just like Maggie on *The Walking Dead*!"

As more zombies shuffled and moaned toward them, Carmela cranked her gun, dropped in more paint pellets, and took aim. This time red paint spattered across her zombie's chest. "Another one bites the dust," she crowed.

"Come on," said Ava, plucking at her sleeve. "Let's split up, take out a whole bunch more, and meet up at the finish line."

"You got it," said Carmela.

They sprinted off in high spirits.

But as Carmela was closing in on the finish line, the zombie just ahead of her turned around, stared straight at her, and raised his right arm.

A warning blip in her brain told her something was wrong.

A zombie shooting at me? What's wrong with this picture?

Zombies weren't supposed to have guns; they carried paint sticks. But this zombie suddenly knelt down, laid his gun across one arm, combat style, and fired at her.

Holy crap! That zombie is shooting at me!

Carmela felt something zing by her head! A bullet? Whatever it was, it smashed into a nearby tree, causing splinters to fly everywhere.

Kicking it into high gear, Carmela zigged and zagged her way across the field, heading for the safety of the exit. She looked over her shoulder once, expecting the killer zombie to be in hot pursuit, but he was nowhere to be seen.

Panting, gasping for breath, Carmela pulled up short at the finish line. Ava was just coming in, too, face animated, her cheeks high with color, tousled hair flying everywhere.

"Ava, get over here," Carmela called.

"Did you see . . . ?" Ava cried as she rushed up. Then she stopped abruptly. "What's wrong?"

"I think a zombie shot at me!"

Ava gazed at her. "No, Carmela, *we* shoot. The zombies have these . . ." Her words trailed off. "Oh my gosh, you're serious, aren't you?"

Carmela nodded.

"Tell me," breathed Ava.

Carmela told her, and, halfway through her story, started to get hopping mad.

"We've got to find Babcock," said Ava. "This is major."

But when they found him—and Carmela told him her story—he was incredulous.

"Are you serious?" said Babcock. "There no *way* that could have happened." Then, when he saw Carmela's face darken, he put his arms around her and pulled her close. "Are you sure you didn't get into the spirit of the game a little too much?" he asked.

"She said he had a gun," Ava said in a very deliberate tone. "She said he *shot* at her."

"But it was probably a paint gun," said Babcock. "Or, at the very least, a beanbag gun, don't you see?"

"It *looked* like a real gun," said Carmela.

"Carmela," said Babcock, "you've been under a lot of pressure lately. You've taken your promise to Mavis—to investigate Joubert's death—way too seriously. I mean, your kindness is all very noble and good, but . . . don't you think you might have been *imagining* things?"

Carmela thought about his words for one full second. Then she nodded slowly. "You're probably right," she said. "Maybe I imagined it."

"But *cher*!" said Ava.

Carmela shook her head silently as Babcock hugged her again. "Good girl," he said.

But Carmela knew she hadn't imagined that bullet. She knew it had been for real. Just as she knew the green alien's warning last night had been for real.

"Okay, crisis averted," said Babcock. He held up a hand and gestured to a nearby uniformed officer. "Frankie, have you got two of those gift certificates?"

The officer hastened over with the certificates. "Yes, sir."

"Here you go," said Babcock. He smiled at them. "Everything okay now?"

Carmela nodded. "Sure, no problem."

"Sweetheart," said Babcock, "I worry about you."

"That makes two of us," said Ava.

Babcock hesitated, as if a fleeting thought had crossed his mind. A thought that perhaps Carmela hadn't imagined it? "You two are going to be okay?" he asked.

"We're just going to head home now," said Carmela. "Get ready for the Ghost Train."

"Have fun then," said Babcock. He watched them go, waved, then turned and shook his head, a concerned look on his face.

"I believe you," said Ava, as they headed for the car. "Even if Babcock doesn't."

"Thank you," said Carmela.

"But you changed your . . ."

"Story," said Carmela. "Yeah, I did. To make things simpatico and to keep Babcock from flipping out." She hesitated. "Still . . . why would someone *shoot* at me?" She wondered if it was connected to last night, to the green alien.

"Maybe for the same reason somebody ransacked my shop last night, broke all my bottles, and scribbled that warning?"

Carmela just shook her head. She was feeling disheartened. She hadn't figured anything out and had seemingly put the two of them in serious danger.

As they settled in the car together, Ava scrunched up her face. "If you ask me, you must be dang close to figuring out who Joubert's killer was! In fact, you have to be getting way too close for comfort."

"Even if I'm close, I don't *know* I'm close."

"It doesn't matter," said Ava. "You have to look at this logically. If somebody *thinks* you're close to solving the murder, if they're worried you're going to break open the whole case, then their perception is really their reality. You see what I'm saying?"

Carmela shook her head. "No, I don't. In fact, now I'm more confused than ever."

Chapter 28

CARMELA stood at her stove, stirring a pot of seafood bisque while Ava lounged at the dining room table, pawing through her makeup case. Boo and Poobah danced around the table, toenails clicking, tails wagging, as they grinned up at their beloved aunt Ava.

"This is so sweet of you. To cook actual food."

"Hard to live on virtual food," said Carmela as she lifted a spoon to her lips and tasted. "Mmn, we're ready. I think dinner is a go."

"Hot diggity, want me to set out bowls?"

"Just clear your makeup case off the table."

"Done." Ava swept up her eyeliners and shadows, dropped the case on the floor, and immediately started punching buttons on her phone.

Carmela carried two bowls of bisque to the table and then plopped down blue-checked napkins and spoons. "We're informal tonight. I hope you don't mind."

But Ava was hot and heavy into her Facebook page. "Dang, no new friend requests."

"Which probably means you haven't been out and about much."

"Every night this week," protested Ava. "The problem is, the men I meet don't want to be just friends."

"I could have told you that," said Carmela.

Ava laughed. "Come on. You know what I mean."

"You're big into social media, aren't you? Facebook and Twitter."

"And I'm plugged into all those celebrity sites, too," said Ava as she continued to scan her screen. "I love it all." She frowned. "Unfortunately not much is happening right now." She set her phone down and picked up her spoon.

"No?"

"What we need is a good celebrity death," said Ava. "Nothing brings out the worst in people like a good celebrity death."

"SO HOW DO YOU WANT TO WORK THIS?" ASKED Ava. With dinner finished and dishes cleared, she was sipping a glass of wine as she emptied the entire contents of her train case onto the table. Besides bottles of foundation, pots of lip gloss, eye shadows, tweezers, blushers, and eye pencils, there were also firecrackers, baby doll contact lenses, and a vial of fake blood.

Carmela looked nervous. "You're positive we need this kind of heavy-duty makeup?"

Ava nodded. "We gotta look like *ghosts*, not all fresh and flowery like Cindy Crawford."

"You're scaring me."

Ava gave a wicked grin. "Good."

"We should probably get dressed first," said Carmela.

"Yeah, that way if we spill puke-green eye shadow on our dresses it'll blend right in."

"I love your logic," said Carmela as they both shucked out of their clothes and pulled on their ghost gowns.

"Yowza," said Ava, as she preened in the full-length mirror. "I love it. You really worked wonders with this crazy '80s dress."

"Ah, but there's more," said Carmela. She pinned an overskirt to Ava's costume, one she'd fashioned from some old sheer curtains, then wrapped a sash around her waist. "And we've got our shrouds, too."

"It just gets better and better," said Ava as Carmela tied on her own overskirt and sash. "But now we do makeup." She tapped a chair. "Sit down and let me make with the magic."

Carmela sat stiffly as Ava applied a sticky makeup base and then fluffed on a heavy layer of white powder. Gray and green eye shadow was brushed above and below her eyes to give her a hollow, haunted look.

"Are we done yet?" Carmela asked. She was antsy, ready to go.

"Nope." Ava outlined Carmela's lips with red lipstick and filled them in with purple lipstick.

"Now?"

"Not quite," said Ava. She took a kohl pencil and heavied up Carmela's eyeliner on both the top and bottom rims, extending the edges into a modified cat eye. "How's that feel?" she asked.

"Weird. Sticky. But the important thing is how it looks."

"Here," said Ava. She handed Carmela a hand mirror. "Take a look."

"Eek!" Carmela could hardly believe how awful she looked!

"You like it?"

"It's . . . uh . . . unusual, to say the least."

"The white powder lends a nice ghostly look, don't you think?"

Carmela frowned. "I look like that French mime, Marcel

Marceau. I feel like I should be pantomiming riding a bike or sewing my fingers together."

"Enough with the kvetching," Ava said as she daubed a touch of pink blusher under Carmela's eyes.

Carmela stared in the mirror again. "Now I look like I've either aged sixty years or been perpetually hung over for six months."

"That's the whole idea. To get rid of that all-American peaches-and-cream glow you always seem to exude. And impart a nasty death-like pallor."

"But nobody's going to recognize me."

"That's a good thing, *cher*. Think how free you'll feel. You can throw off the bounds of normal constraints and just be a . . ."

"Free spirit," Carmela laughed. She glanced down at Boo, who stared up at her with a worried expression. "What do you think, baby girl?"

In answer, Boo spun around, ran into Carmela's bedroom, and dove under the bed.

"She's a little afraid of you," said Ava.

"You think?" said Carmela.

But Ava was busy applying her own makeup, doing the white-powder thing but using a lighter touch (or so Carmela thought) on the purple and green eye shadow. She smiled at herself in the mirror. "You think I should black out a tooth?"

"Couldn't hurt," said Carmela. She glanced at her watch. "Okay, go time. We gotta throw on our shrouds and head for Audubon Park."

Ava popped up. "Do mine?"

Carmela draped Ava's shroud around her shoulders, pulled it up in back until it formed a sort of collar, then wrapped it around her a second time.

"Now you got me wrapped up like a hard-shell taco."

"Sounds about right."

They exchanged stares for a long moment and then broke into a fit of uncontrollable laughter.

"We look totally weird," said Ava.

"Which is why Jekyl is gonna love us," said Carmela. "Come on, let's go."

"Hang on a minute." Ava pawed around on the table, then grabbed her purple lipstick and vial of fake blood. She slipped them into her tiny silver shoulder bag.

"Is that for luck?" asked Carmela. "Or in case we need a touch-up?"

Ava winked as they hustled out the door. "You never know."

AUDUBON PARK WAS THRONGED WITH PEOPLE as they pulled into the parking lot.

"Good thing we got here early," said Carmela.

"What a crowd," said Ava.

Almost a hundred people milled around the grassy park, waiting to climb on the Ghost Train. All wore costumes, most were guzzling drinks.

"Look at that," said Carmela, pointing to an elaborate setup of coolers and lights. "They've even got a portable bar set up."

"And velvet ropes just like Studio 54," said Ava.

Then, as they pushed their way through the crowd, they caught sight of the train. Seven vintage Pullman cars had been strung together behind a magnificent-looking steam-powered locomotive. The whole thing looked glamorous, extravagant, and extremely fun.

"There's Jekyl," said Carmela. "Over by the ticket booth."

So of course they hustled over to greet him.

"Ladies," said Jekyl when he caught sight of them. "Welcome to the Ghost Train." Jekyl was all tricked out in a fabulous vampire costume. His black cape was lined with purple velvet, he wore fake fangs, and his slicked-back hair was pulled into a low ponytail.

"You look very Transylvanian!" Ava gushed.

"And you're right off a ghostly runway," said Jekyl. "Let me take a gander at those fabulous gowns."

Carmela and Ava both struck a pose.

"Delightful," said Jekyl. He touched Ava's arm. "Do a twirl, darlin'. So I can get the full effect."

Giggling like crazy, Ava happily obliged.

"Really fantastic," said Jekyl. "You'll both fit right in."

"We were wondering about that," said Carmela. "How exactly *do* we fit in?"

"Come on aboard and we'll talk about that," said Jekyl.

The three of them climbed aboard the train.

"This is amazing," Ava marveled as she gazed at the interior of the antique car. "I feel like I just took a giant step back into the 1890s."

"It's very glamorous," agreed Carmela. The restored passenger car had plush plum-colored seats, mahogany woodwork, and smoked mirrors. Besides the cobwebs and sparkly ghost decor, the car was lit with a soft pinkish glow from old-fashioned frosted lamps.

"I created seven themed cars in all," Jekyl explained. "All highly atmospheric." He ticked them off on his fingers. "There's *Murder on the Orient Express*, a ghost car, undertaker's coach, jazz car, two haunted club cars, and my Sherlock Holmes car."

"And this is the ghost car?" Carmela asked.

Jekyl beamed. "That's right."

"How many players will be working on your Ghost Train tonight?" Carmela asked.

Jekyl touched an index finger to his lips. "Let's see. There are about thirty of us, all told. Bartenders and waiters, plus musicians, actors, dancers, and jugglers. You know . . .

278 of LAURA CHILDS

performers. The kind of folks you see working the crowd in Jackson Square or at a Renaissance fair."

"And then there's us," said Ava. "Just floating around to lend a little ethereal loveliness."

"Oh no," said Jekyl, "you need to work up a slick little act, too."

"What?" said Carmela, suddenly taken aback by Jekyl's words.

"Huh?" said Ava. "We have to *work*?" She said the word *work* like she was referring to manure.

Carmela just winced. She'd been under the impression that this gig would be a push. That they'd swan around, contribute to the overall atmosphere, and enjoy a few drinks. Now Jekyl was telling them they had to . . . gulp . . . work?

"You're telling us there's no free lunch?" Carmela said to Jekyl.

"How about free drinks?" asked Ava.

"Listen," said Jekyl, suddenly looking serious. "Each and every one of our passengers shelled out one hundred dollars per ticket for the pleasure of this ghostly experience. So they're expecting over-the-top excitement."

"Can't they just wander down to the bar car?" said Ava. "Wait a minute, *is* there a bar car?"

Jekyl chuckled. "Basically, this train is one enormous bar." He nodded to a group of men who were just getting on. "You see those guys in the green jackets and orange fedoras?"

"They're the waiters?" said Carmela. "And bartenders?"

"Right," said Jekyl, "They'll be serving Hurricanes, Bloody Marys, and champagne for the entire ride."

"So we're not just dealing with passengers who are expecting a rip-roaring good time," said Carmela, "we're talking about passengers who might be rip-roaring drunk."

"And want to have a high old time," finished Ava.

Jekyl shrugged. "What do you expect, my lovelies? It's Halloween in New Orleans." He paused. "Any questions?"

Carmela sighed. "Did you find anything out about the necklace?"

"Not a thing," said Jekyl as he turned to go. "And, Carmela, I really think you might be barking up the wrong tree."

"JEEPERS," SAID AVA, LOOKING A LITTLE LOST. "What did we get ourselves into?"

"A lot more than we thought," said Carmela. She was leaning over one of the seats, peering out the window. "Do you know who's about to get on this train?"

"No, who?"

"Titus Duval," said Carmela.

"Uh-oh, that's one dude we better try to avoid," said Ava.

But he wasn't the only one.

As soon as the conductor swung down from the steps and sang out, "All aboard!" a veritable who's who came pouring onto the train. The Countess Saint-Marche and her husband scrambled aboard, wearing his and hers goblin costumes.

"Carmela! Fancy seeing you here," cried the countess. "And Ava, too!"

Carmela and Ava smiled weakly, then hastily squeezed down the aisle, edging past witches, Robin Hood, Spiderman, and two skeletons, finally taking refuge in one of the bar cars.

"Safe at last," breathed Carmela.

"I'm not so sure," said Ava. "You'll never guess who I saw as we squeezed through the jazz car."

"Who?"

"Your buddy James Stanger."

Carmela was about ready to throw up her hands. "This is

just terrific. Every stupid suspect we thought might've had a hand in Marcus Joubert's murder is here tonight."

Ava suddenly clutched Carmela's arm tightly. "It's a sign from above. It's like a *real* murder on the Orient Express!"

"Don't say that," said Carmela. "Quick, knock on wood."

But just as they did, the Ghost Train gave a hard jerk and lurched out of the station.

"Too late to get off," said Carmela.

"Stuck like rats on a sinking ship," said Ava. "Or, in this case, a chugging train."

As the Ghost Train rumbled along, picking up speed, the action among the passengers started to get a little frenzied. Lubricated from several drinks in the park, they shifted from pleasantly happy to incredibly raucous in about five seconds flat. A werewolf made a grab for Carmela's skirt, a warlock tried to steal a kiss from Ava.

"This is awful," said Ava. "Maybe if we grabbed a tray of drinks or something. Used it as a weapon."

"Good idea," said Carmela. "Put some fortification between them and us." They picked up silver trays filled with Bloody Marys and threaded their way back through the bar car and the undertaker's coach.

"Care for a drink?" said Carmela, tilting her tray slightly toward a passenger.

"Get your Bloodys here," Ava called out.

They slipped down the crowded aisles, serving drinks, trying to studiously avoid Duval as well as the countess.

Ava brushed up against Carmela. "The last thing these folks need are more drinks," she murmured.

Carmela nodded. "What they really need is some black coffee."

"Oh right, then we'd have wide-awake drunks."

"Is that what happens?" said Carmela. But just then, the

train rounded a curve, and the swaying car lifted her off her feet and dumped her unceremoniously into a passenger's lap.

"Excuse me!" said Carmela, fighting to regain her footing and keep her tray stable.

"Carmela?"

Carmela stared into the startled face of Boyd Bellamy!

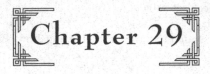

Chapter 29

"UM, Mr. Bellamy," Carmela blurted out. "I didn't see you there."

Buoyed by more than a few drinks, Bellamy grabbed her arm, smiled a scuzzy smile, and said, "Sit with me, sweetie. Have a drink."

"Uh, no thanks," said Carmela. She managed to get back on her feet fast, avoiding his lecherous clutches.

"What's wrong?" said Bellamy. Only it came out *"Whachs shrong?"*

"Gotta refill my tray," said Carmela, backpedalling like crazy, searching for Ava and (hopefully!) a rescue.

She found Ava three rows down, flirting with a good-looking passenger.

"Come on," said Carmela, "we have to get out of here."

Ava followed her back to the jazz car.

"This isn't going well," said Carmela.

"No? I thought the evening was starting to perk up."

"I'm seriously thinking of jumping off this train."

"Just relax, *cher*, chill out."

Carmela was about to launch an all-out protest when Jekyl tapped her on the shoulder.

"Excuse me," said Jekyl. "Have you worked up your act yet?"

Carmela stared mutely.

"We're all set," Ava said, without missing a beat. "No problem."

"That's a relief," said Jekyl. He lifted the tray out of Carmela's hands. "Since you two are all geared up, you can go on right after the Jiggling Jugglers."

"You mean right away?" said Carmela. "Like now?" The jugglers in the next car were tossing hot pink Indian clubs back and forth like crazy, looking like they were working up to a big finish.

Ava set her tray down and grabbed Carmela. She whispered in her ear for a few moments until Carmela nodded and said, "Okay. I got it. I hope."

Then Ava made her way to the jazz trio and whispered some more quick directions. They nodded back.

"All right," Ava said to Carmela. "Get ready to put your game face on."

"I'll try."

As soon as the last club flew through the air, the upbeat strains of "Me and My Shadow" swelled to fill the train car.

Heads up, smiles flashing, projecting far more confidence than they really felt, Carmela and Ava shuffled down the aisle, singing along to the music:

> *Me and my shadow*
> *Strolling down Napoleon Avenue.*
> *Yeah, me and my shadow,*
> *Lookin' for a rendezvous.*

They spun around, stood back-to-back, and negotiated a quick soft-shoe dance with some energetic jazz hands thrown in for good measure. Then they continued their song:

> *And when it's twelve o'clock,*
> *We climb the stair*
> *We never knock,*
> *'Cause the party's there*
> *Just me and my shadow . . .*

It wasn't that they were so good, it's just that the passengers were so drunk. But when they wrapped up their number, they were met with a huge round of applause as well as numerous shouts of "Bravo!"

Carmela and Ava took a bow, then a second bow. They held hands as they backed down the aisle, smiling, feeling enormously relieved.

"We did it," Carmela quipped out of the corner of her mouth.

"We sure did," said Ava, still smiling maniacally at the applause.

Carmela was about to take another step backward, when a hand snaked out and gripped her wrist. She flinched, instinctively trying to pull away as her eyes fell upon her unwelcome admirer.

Titus Duval glared up at her.

"Let go, you're hurting me!" Carmela cried. She was stunned to see him, and even more shocked when he wrenched her closer. Gritting her teeth, she said, "If you don't let me go I'm going to . . ."

Duval suddenly thrust a piece of ripped green fabric in Carmela's face.

She gulped, realizing immediately that it was a hunk out of her Scarlett O'Hara dress.

"Your buddy Jekyl Hardy told me you'd be on the train

tonight," Duval snarled. "But he didn't know that I had this! Recognize it?"

"Uh . . . no," said Carmela, still trying to wrest herself away from him.

"You should. It's from the green dress you wore to the Fontaines' party." Duval let her go and tapped an index finger against the side of his head. "You can't fool me, I have a photographic memory."

"Is that so?" said Carmela as panic bubbled up inside her. She'd been found out!

Duval had worked himself into a first-class snit. "Want to know where I found it?"

"Not particularly," said Carmela.

"In my house!"

Carmela backed away from him. Then her panic turned to fear as she suddenly realized what Duval was wearing. He had on some sort of scaly green suit! She didn't know if he was supposed to be an alligator or the Jolly Green Giant, but she was so stunned that she cried out, "You! You're the one who grabbed me at the Pumpkins and Bumpkins Ball last night! You're the one who broke into Ava's shop!"

Duval looked as if he'd been slapped. "What are you talking about?" he demanded.

But Carmela's brain was working overtime, trying to stitch together her few paltry clues. "I can't prove it yet," she cried, "but I'm ninety-nine percent sure that you broke into Marcus Joubert's shop and stabbed him to death!"

"You're utterly insane," Duval shouted back at her.

"And you're a killer!" Carmela screamed. She spun away from Duval and grabbed for Ava. "We've got to get out of here!" she pleaded.

Ava turned, startled. "What's wrong?"

"I'll explain everything once we're safe and sound," Carmela hissed from between clenched teeth. So Ava followed her, no questions asked, as they tore down the aisle, sprinting from the club car to the jazz car.

As they raced through the jazz car, guests began to clap and cheer all over again.

"They think this is still part of the act," Ava cried. She sounded almost happy.

"Never mind that," said Carmela. "Is he following us?"

"I don't know," panted Ava. "I don't know who you're talking about."

"Never mind. Just keep running!"

"I am," said Ava. "But I don't see anybody coming after us. Carmela, tell me what's going on!"

But Carmela was in full-on flight mode and determined to find a safe spot for them to hole up in. "We've got to get help. We've got to call Babcock!"

"What's going on? Who are you so afraid of?"

"It's Duval," Carmela told her as they dashed toward the back of the train. "He knows we were in his house that night. And I'm pretty sure he's the killer!"

"Holy rat poop!" said Ava.

They dashed into the Sherlock Holmes car only to find it empty.

"Where is everybody?" said Carmela, momentarily stunned.

"I think they're all in the club car sucking down drinks."

"That's good then," Carmela jabbered. "That's perfect. Come on, hurry up and shut the door. Lock it, too!"

Ava slammed the door. "I don't think there *is* a lock . . . ooh, hurry up and make the call, Carmela." Ava had gotten a shot of nervous energy off Carmela.

Carmela fumbled with her cell phone. "I have to get help before Duval comes after us and . . ."

A sudden pounding caused the flimsy door to rattle and shake.

"Oh no," said Carmela. She rushed for the door, her phone call momentarily forgotten. "We've got to barricade ourselves in." Her eyes frantically searched the train car and landed on an overstuffed chair. "Help me push that chair in front of the door."

Ava panted and shoved as the pounding continued. "It's not moving so well. It doesn't want to slide on this old carpet."

"Try harder," Carmela cried.

"Carmela!" Now a woman's voice sounded from the other side of the door.

Startled, Carmela put an ear to the rattling door and called out, "Who's there?"

"It's me, Mavis," came a muffled cry.

"Mavis is here?" said Ava.

"That's right," said Carmela, suddenly remembering. "Because of all the Sherlock Holmes stuff."

"It's not a trick? That's really you?" Ava called through the door.

"Yes," Mavis's voice came again. "Are you guys okay? I saw you blitz past like a couple of crazed sprinters and got worried."

Carmela put a hand to her heart. "Thank goodness it's her!" she whispered to Ava. Then she made a hurry-up gesture with her hand. "Let her in here."

Ava muscled the chair back out of the way and the narrow door creaked open.

Carmela grabbed Mavis's wrist and hastily pulled her into the Sherlock Holmes car, then slammed the door again.

Mavis looked puzzled. "Carmela, what's wrong? You've got the strangest look on your face. As if . . ."

Carmela dropped her voice to a hoarse, urgent whisper. "I don't want to scare you, or upset you. But I'm pretty sure I just figured out who Marcus's killer is!"

Mavis's mouth dropped open and she gasped in horror. "Oh no. Oh . . . Carmela, are you serious?"

"Yes!" Carmela cried.

Mavis looked like she was ready to cry. "Tell me how . . . well, just *tell* me."

"Tell her!" said Ava. "Tell *me*!"

"Here's the thing," said Carmela. "Ava and I were just . . ." She felt a tickle in her nose and sneezed abruptly.

"Bless you," said Ava.

"Wait a minute," Mavis said to Carmela. "From the look on your face, the way you're acting . . . are you saying the killer is on this very train?" She looked utterly terrified. As if she wanted to escape at any cost, even if it meant jumping from the train.

Carmela bobbed her head and sniffled again. "Yes, he is!" But something was beginning to bother her. Something else had seeped through her fear and worry. Some sort of odor suddenly seemed strangely familiar. She pushed it aside—revealing the killer to Mavis was far too important. "He's on this train!" she cried. "It's Titus—"

Carmela stopped abruptly, suddenly cognizant of the scent that had her nose all tickly and stuffed up. It was the scent of the spilled oils from Ava's shop!

"Duval," finished Ava. But she was looking at Carmela, who was suddenly gazing in horror at the gun that was clutched in Mavis's hand. The gun that was pointed directly at Carmela, then at her, then back at Carmela again!

"Wait a minute," Ava said in a small voice. "Don't tell me . . ."

Mavis clicked her teeth together and shook her head in disgust. "You two couldn't leave well enough alone, could you? You couldn't just send your cop friends after all the phony suspects I threw at you."

Carmela's mind may have been in a whirl, but the blinders had suddenly been lifted. Mavis was pointing a gun at her. Mavis! Did that mean she'd killed Joubert herself? All the while pretending to be in love with him?

"Figure it out yet?" snarled Mavis. "Are you putting two and two together?"

"But you asked for my help," said Carmela. "*Begged* me for help."

"Of course I did," Mavis snapped. "Because you're an incredibly snoopy person and amazingly astute. By pulling you into my confidence, by getting you on my side, I figured it was the only way I could keep an eye on you." She gritted her teeth and sneered. "And now look what's happened . . . now everything's completely blown!"

"You were trying to set Duval up," said Carmela.

"You slimy skank," Ava threw in.

"You stole the mask," Carmela said in a low voice that was a cross between a whisper and a snarl. "You were the one who stole the Napoleon death mask from Wallace Pitney."

Mavis just stared at her, a nasty, knowing smile on her face.

"You've had the death mask all along," said Carmela. "But were trying to hang the theft on poor Joubert!"

"And cast suspicion on a few other people who happened to be convenient," put in Ava.

"Here's what we're going to do," said Mavis. She shifted her gun so it pointed directly at Carmela's heart. "We're going to ride this stupid train to the very end of the line." Her voice never wavered and neither did her gun. "And then we're all going to get off, all nice and orderly like. And we'll take a quiet stroll over to your little scrapbook shop."

"I've got an even better idea," a menacing male voice growled from behind them.

All three women swiveled their heads to see who on earth was speaking.

"We're going to have an accident," said the green alien, stepping out of a closet. "A train accident."

"You!" Carmela screeched.

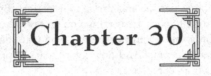

Chapter 30

MAVIS smiled up at the green alien. "An accident. What a perfectly marvelous idea."

"Who the heck are *you*?" Ava shrieked at the green alien. Even with someone pointing a loaded gun at her, Ava's bravado hadn't faltered.

"He's not a nice guy," Carmela murmured. "Unfortunately, I've encountered him before."

The green alien slid closer to Mavis. Then, in the manner of a lover, he put an arm around her waist and pulled her close. "I thought you might be needing some help," he said.

Mavis turned her face up and let him kiss her.

"Yuck," said Ava.

"Shut up," said Mavis.

Carmela wanted to fly at both of them. To kick, scratch, and claw them to death. Unfortunately, there was a gun pointed at her chest.

"Who are you?" she demanded of the green alien.

"Just a friend," smirked the green alien.

"A very good friend," said Mavis. "My Ricky." Her eyes had taken on a strange glint and, for the first time, Carmela believed she was truly dangerous.

"Ricky," said Carmela. "Were you the zombie who chased me the other night? Did you shoot at me today?"

"Look at her," Mavis crowed. "The hotshot investigator wants some answers."

"We don't have time for that," said Ricky. "We need to get rid of them."

"You're going to *shoot* us?" said Carmela. "You'll never get away with it. Your shots will echo all the way through the train and bring . . ."

Ricky stepped swiftly over to the back door and pulled it open. A whoosh of cool air immediately filled the car. The rattle of the train as it thundered down the tracks was almost deafening.

"I've got a better way," said Ricky. "A more *final* way."

"No, no, no," said Ava, her courage finally faltering. "We can be reasonable about this, can't we? Find another solution?"

"No," said Ricky.

Mavis waved her gun again. "Get outside," she commanded.

Both Carmela and Ava were herded out onto the rear platform. It bounced and swayed dangerously as the train hammered along. They had to grab hold of the flimsy metal railing just to remain on their feet.

"You first," Mavis said to Carmela as pure malevolence shone in her eyes.

"Yeah, you," said Ricky. He shoved Carmela closer to the open edge of the back platform.

Still, Carmela hung on for dear life. And as warehouses, boat slips, and views of the Mississippi flew by, Carmela felt like she was seeing her life flash by, too.

Dear Lord! If ever there was a time for prayer . . .

Mavis prodded Carmela in the ribs with her pistol. "Time to say good-bye."

Carmela gazed sorrowfully at Ava, who seemed to be sneaking a hand into the shoulder bag that was slung across her body.

"Ava," Carmela choked out. Her mouth was dry, devoid of any moisture whatsoever. In fact, she was so frightened she could barely draw breath.

"Come on, come on," Mavis snarled. She shot a knowing look at Ricky. "We need to take care of her while the train's still running along the river."

"You heard her," said Ricky. "Time to get off." He shoved Carmela all the way over to the very edge of the platform where there was no protective railing at all.

Carmela looked straight down through the metal grill and saw tracks spinning by. The thought of landing on those metal tracks and crushed cinders made her dizzy and sick to her stomach.

Mavis moved over and poked her gun into the small of Ava's back. She would be the next victim.

"You don't want to do this," Carmela babbled. She knew it was a pathetic, made-for-TV-movie line, but it was all she could dredge up at the moment.

"Sure we do," Mavis cackled. She prodded Ava again and said, "Just do it, Ricky. Give Carmela one hard shove!"

Just as Ricky was about to give Carmela a fatal, final shove, Ava ripped the vial of fake blood from her purse. In one fluid motion she popped the top off and spattered gobs of red liquid directly into Mavis's eyes.

"Owww!" Mavis howled. Her wild-animal scream rang out loudly as she pawed frantically at her injured eyes. As she struggled to wipe them, she fumbled the gun completely and it dropped hard and loud onto the train tracks.

Fast as a snapping turtle, Carmela whipped around, tore off her stiff white shroud and snapped it at Ricky. The stiff, hardened material caught him across the forehead and, as he batted it, like an unsuspecting bug suddenly trapped in a spider's web, Carmela spun sideways and quickly wound it around him. Then Ava got into the act, too, hastily ripping off her shroud and wrapping Ricky up completely, as if they were circling a maypole.

Then, as the train slowed slightly to round a curve, Carmela planted her foot directly against Ricky's backside and gave a mighty shove. Flailing and helpless, Ricky went tumbling onto the tracks as Mavis continued to shriek at the top of her lungs.

"Waaaah!" was all they heard from Ricky as the train chugged away.

"Ouch!" said Ava, scrunching up her face. "That looks like it might have hurt."

"I sincerely hope so," said Carmela. She spun Mavis around and shoved her back inside the train. "You shut up," she ordered. And to Ava, "Better hang on tight. This isn't going to be pretty." Then Carmela reached up and yanked the emergency cord as hard as she could. The smile hardened on her face as she braced herself with all her might. Beneath them, the train shuddered dangerously. The antique cars rocked and careened from side to side as their wheels locked tight and the entire Ghost Train ground to a screeching halt.

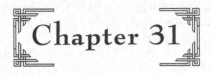

Chapter 31

"JUST think," Ava beamed at Carmela. "You have the power to stop a train."

"Excuse me," said Jekyl. He was standing nose to nose with Carmela, wildly flailing his arms. "Did you *really* need to rip on that emergency brake? Was it necessary to bring the entire train to a *screeching* halt?"

They were standing in a narrow patch of weeds next to the waiting, belching train. Carmela had made her call to Babcock, while Ava was happily pointing the gun at a cowed and greatly subdued Mavis Sweet.

A terrible situation had been defused and a pair of killers had finally been apprehended. But Jekyl remained upset.

"You couldn't have resolved this problem any other way?" Jekyl asked. "I mean, stopping the Ghost Train is a disaster of epic proportions! What if all our customers demand refunds?"

"Are you insane?" Carmela shouted back at him, but there

was a hint of a smile on her face. "For the great show we just put on? Turn around and take a look, Jekyl. And while you're at it, wave to all the nice people on the train who are hanging out the windows—because they're waving at *us*!"

Carmela gestured toward the halted train, where everyone really was hanging out the windows. Smiling faces looked on with laughter and encouragement, and there were shouts of "More, more!" and plenty of applause. Clearly, all the passengers had enjoyed the rather unorthodox "show" that they'd just witnessed.

Then Babcock arrived in a blast of sirens and blaze of red and blue lights.

"Uh-oh," said Ava, "you're gonna have some 'splaining to do, Lucy."

But Mavis, still smeared with fake blood, was promptly put into handcuffs. And Babcock kept his words and temper in check as Carmela laid out the entire story for him. At one point he even held up a hand and demanded that Titus Duval be brought out to join them.

When everything was explained and unraveled—and Carmela had made a formal apology to Duval—the episode appeared to be over.

Except for one thing.

"Who *is* that jackhole, anyway?" Carmela asked as a uniformed officer marched a limping, trembling Ricky toward them. She was happy to note that his green alien costume was shredded beyond repair and he sported a couple of enormous red welts on his forehead.

"That sorry sight is Ricky Bumgard," said Babcock, recognizing him immediately. "He's a known thief and sometime arsonist. Needless to say, he's got quite a record." Babcock threw Ricky a nasty smile. "From everything I've heard tonight, it looks like we can add murder, too. Am I right, Ricky? Did you overstep your smarts and get a little too greedy, Ricky?"

Thankfully, Ricky was still too shaken to muster an answer.

"Ricky, the green alien," Ava said in a challenging voice. "Now he'll have to trade his green costume for an orange jumpsuit. Then he'll be Ricky the jailbird."

"Uhrrhmm," said Ricky, shaking his head.

"So where *is* the death mask?" asked Titus Duval.

"I'm guessing it's probably stashed at Mavis's house," said Carmela. "She probably tucked it away all nice and neat until she had a chance to sell it."

"You'd have to sell it on the black market," said Jekyl. He pursed his lips. "Although underground art sales seem to be flourishing these days."

"That's why I was so suspicious of James Stanger," said Carmela. "And Johnny Sparks."

"They may be clear of this," said Babcock. "But if they are guilty of art fraud we'll get them eventually."

"And I'm still not sure if the countess is on the up-and-up," said Carmela.

"She'll be right next door to you," Babcock smiled. "So you can keep an eye on her."

"If you ask me," said Ava, "that death mask is bad luck. Bad juju."

Babcock gazed mildly at Ava. "You're imagining things. A simple object can't possess the powers of good or evil."

"Sure it can," said Ava. "Look at the curse of King Tut's tomb. Or the Hope Diamond. Those things carry well-known curses!"

"Excuse me," said Titus Duval. He looked thoughtful and very interested in their conversation. "Is there any possibility that stolen mask might be for sale?"

"No!" Carmela and Ava cried together.

"We need to return the mask to its rightful owner," said Carmela. She gazed at Babcock. "And the sooner the better—don't you think?"

"Absolutely," said Babcock. "It's the law." He pulled Carmela closer to him and beamed at her. Then, throwing caution to the wind, Babcock leaned forward, dipped Carmela over backward, and gave her the kind of kiss that definitely made for a Hollywood ending.

Once again, the passengers on the train clapped and cheered loudly. Their evening, crazy as it had been, had enjoyed a perfect ending. Besides riding the Ghost Train, they'd witnessed a wild chase, apprehension of a dangerous criminal, and an old-fashioned romantic ending.

Smiling, a little embarrassed at all the fuss, Carmela regained her footing and gave Babcock a subtle nudge. "We should take the mask back to Dallas as soon as possible. Deliver it in person to that poor man, Mr. Pitney."

"Oh no," Babcock laughed. "You're not roping me into going."

Carmela turned toward Ava and said, "How about you, girlfriend?"

Ava grinned happily. "Road trip!"

Scrapbook, Stamping, and Craft Tips from Laura Childs

✂

Scrap Your Scraps

If you have scraps of paper left over (and who doesn't?) you can turn them into bookmarks. Trim and layer your leftovers on top of each other in fun combinations, then punch a hole and thread in some ribbon or raffia. Just be sure to finish both sides!

Got Game?

If you have tokens, poker chips, or small pieces from old board games (Monopoly or Scrabble, anyone?) they can be reworked in lots of different ways. Drill your Scrabble letters and use jump rings to create a necklace. Or drill a poker chip to use as a key fob. Most of the jewelry findings you need can be found at your local craft store.

Wine Labels

You can make your own wine labels the same way Carmela does. Measure your wine bottle and create a label template. Then get creative with rubber stamps, transfer letters, stickers, and ephemera. When your label design is finished, simply color copy for however many bottles you want to decorate. Vampire Wine, Christmas Cabernet, or Valentine Blush Wine, anyone?

Design Your Own Guest Towels

Use your favorite rubber stamps to create your own unique guest towels. Just paint your rubber stamps with fabric ink and stamp carefully—you can use one signature stamp or create an entire border. Because you're stamping on terry cloth, the image is likely to be a little fuzzy, so keep that in mind when selecting your rubber stamp.

Collage Backgrounds

Create unique backgrounds on your scrapbook pages by using strips of leftover paper that are all in the same color or design family. The strips need to be as wide as your page and torn so they are 2"–3" high—and distressed edges always work best. Glue your strips onto your scrapbook page, add a glaze layer to preserve them, then go ahead and add your photos.

The Sweet Smell of Sachets

Create sachets the way Carmela did, using cheesecloth tied with ribbon. Or you can even use fabric bits that you have on hand. Cut 2 squares, about 5" x 5", using a pinking shears. Seal them on three sides using fusible bonding tape such as Stitch Witchery. Fill your sachet with dried lavender, dried rosebuds, eucalyptus, or even your favorite spice. Now simply fuse the remaining edge.

Favorite New Orleans Recipes

✂

Down-Home Chicken Corn Casserole

⅓ cup butter
⅓ cup flour
½ tsp. salt
¼ tsp. black pepper
2 cups milk
2 cups cooked chicken, cut up
1 (11-oz.) can whole kernel corn, drained
⅓ cup bread crumbs

Preheat oven to 350 degrees. Melt butter over low heat, then stir in flour, salt, and pepper. Cook until smooth and bubbly. Remove from heat and gradually stir in milk. Then cook to boiling point and let boil for 1 minute. Stir in chicken pieces and corn. Pour into a greased 1½-quart casserole dish. Top with bread crumbs and a few dots of butter. Bake for 30 minutes. Serves 6.

Super Simple Seafood Bisque

2 (10-oz.) cans potato soup
1 cup milk
½ cup cream
2 Tbsp. butter
1 (5-oz.) can shrimp, drained and rinsed
1 (5-oz.) can crabmeat, drained and rinsed

Heat potato soup, milk, cream, and butter together. Add in shrimp and crabmeat. Stir, season to taste, and serve. Serves 4.

No-Bake Peanut Butter and Cornflake Bars

½ cup sugar
½ cup corn syrup
1 cup peanut butter
5 cups cornflakes

Heat sugar and syrup together until sugar dissolves. Add peanut butter and mix well. Gently stir in cornflakes until mixed. Press mixture into a 9-by-13-inch baking pan. Cut into squares using a buttered knife while still warm. Cool until firm. Eat!

Carmela's Crazy Dump Cake

2 (21-oz.) cans blueberry pie filling
2 (20-oz.) cans crushed pineapple, about ¾ drained
½ cup sugar
1 Tbsp. cinnamon
1 box yellow cake mix
6 Tbsp. butter

Preheat oven to 375 degrees. Pour blueberry pie filling into 9-by-13-inch dish. Pour crushed pineapple over blueberries. Mix sugar and cinnamon together and sprinkle on top of pineapple layer. Pour dry cake mix on top, breaking up any lumps. Melt butter and drizzle on top. Bake for approximately 40 to 45 minutes. Top should be bubbly and golden brown.

Southern Shrimp and Black Beans

8 Tbsp. butter
juice of 2 limes
1 tsp. garlic salt
1½ lbs. raw shrimp
1 Tbsp. hot sauce
1 (15-oz.) can black beans, drained

Melt butter in frying pan, add in lime juice and garlic salt. Add shrimp and sauté quickly until cooked. Add in hot sauce and black beans, then stir. Serve over cooked rice or in pita bread pockets. Serves 4.

Baked Pork Chops in Creamed Corn

4 pork chops
2 Tbsp. oil
1 can creamed corn
½ onion, chopped
¼ cup milk
salt and pepper

Preheat oven to 300 degrees. Brown pork chops in oil, then place in baking dish. Mix together creamed corn, chopped onion, milk, salt, and pepper. Pour over pork chops and bake for about 2 hours or until fork-tender. Serves 4.

Party Shrimp Dip

1 3-oz. pkg. cream cheese, softened
¼ cup chili sauce
1 tsp. grated horseradish (or prepared)
1 tsp. lemon juice
¼ tsp. garlic powder
1 (5-oz.) can shrimp, diced

Mix all ingredients together, adding shrimp last. Chill for about 2 hours, and then serve with crackers or chips.

Baked Porcupines

1 lb. ground beef
½ cup uncooked rice
½ cup water
⅓ cup chopped onions
1 tsp. salt
⅛ tsp. garlic salt
⅛ tsp. pepper
1 (15-oz.) can tomato sauce
1 cup water
2 tsp. Worcestershire sauce

Heat oven to 350 degrees. Mix ground beef, rice, ½ cup water, onion, salt, garlic salt, and pepper together. Using a large spoon, take scoops from mixture and shape into round balls. Place balls in ungreased baking dish. Stir together tomato sauce, 1 cup water, and Worcestershire sauce and pour over porcupines. Cover with foil and bake for 45 minutes. Remove foil and bake for an additional 10 minutes. Serves 4 to 6.

Southern Spoon Bread

2 cups water
1 cup cornmeal
1 cup milk
2 eggs
1 Tbsp. melted butter
2 tsp. salt

Mix water and cornmeal in pan. Heat to boiling point and cook for 5 minutes. Beat eggs well, adding in butter, salt, and milk. Add egg mixture to cornmeal mixture. Beat well and bake in a well-greased pan for approximately 25 minutes.

New Orleans–Style Beignets

½ cup water
¼ cup butter
½ cup flour, sifted
2 eggs
1 tsp. vanilla
oil for frying
powdered sugar

Heat water and butter in large saucepan until water boils and butter is melted. Add flour all at once and stir until mixture forms a soft ball of dough in center of pan. Remove from heat and let stand 5 minutes. Add 1 egg to dough and beat well. Add second egg and vanilla and beat well again. Drop medium-sized spoonfuls of dough into about 1 inch of hot oil. Brown on both sides. Drain on paper towels and sprinkle generously with powdered sugar. Makes about 18 beignets.

Carmela's Homemade Cajun Seasoning

2½ Tbsp. salt
1 Tbsp. dried oregano, crushed to a fine powder
1 Tbsp. paprika

1 Tbsp. cayenne pepper
1 Tbsp. black pepper, fresh ground is best

Combine all ingredients, and then use mixture to spice up your meat and poultry!

Turn the page for a preview of Laura Childs's next
Scrapbooking Mystery . . .

Parchment and Old Lace

Available in hardcover from Berkley Prime Crime!

COMMANDER'S Palace wasn't just the most storied restaurant in New Orleans. For Carmela Bertrand it was pure magic.

Carmela knew this for a fact because she was sitting in their Garden Room at this very minute. And not only was she nibbling soft-shell crab and sipping an awesome Montrachet, but she was staring into the inquisitive blue eyes of her fella du jour, Detective Edgar Babcock.

Maybe it was the wine, no doubt crafted by wily Bacchus himself, that had cast such a luscious spell. Or maybe it was the soft, warm light from the gilded candelabras, the old-world charm and formality of the place, or that crazy second course of oysters baked in absinthe and buttered crumbs. Whatever the reason, Carmela was definitely feeling it. Luxuriance, exhilaration, and romance. Sweet, bubbly romance.

"This is so lovely," Carmela said, trying to pitch her voice an octave lower so it was sexy and seductive, kind of like

Kathleen Turner in *Body Heat*. Or maybe Lauren Bacall in one of those old black-and-white movies from the '40s.

"You're lovely," Babcock replied.

And Carmela really was. Her blue-gray eyes, fine features, and tawny-colored hair (this week's color, anyway) gave her an air of exuberance and creative curiosity. She was toned and fairly athletic from lots of dog walking with Boo and Poobah, but still enjoyed a few sweet curves. And, yes, she could be stubborn, but was generally quick to administer a hug or kind word.

Carmela took another sip of wine. "I have to say, this dinner has been pure perfection. If every restaurant reviewer in the universe hadn't already bequeathed four stars to this place, I would have sprinkled them on myself."

Babcock smiled and reached across the table to gently take her hand.

"Why are you talking that way?" he asked.

Carmela's eyes went slightly round. "What way?"

"Like you've got the beginnings of a head cold. Or are doing an imitation of a character from *The Simpsons*."

"Oh." Then, "I didn't mean to."

"You've just fallen completely under my spell, is that it?"

"Well . . . yeah," said Carmela, reverting to Valley-girl speak. Now she wasn't sure if he was flirting with her or putting her on.

Babcock gave a low chuckle. "You're such a little cutie, you know that? One of these days we're seriously going to have to . . ."

"Carmela!" A loud, impassioned shriek suddenly split the air.

Startled, Carmela and Babcock both whipped their heads sideways, only to find an exuberant-looking blond woman grinning at them, all teeth and gums and big Southern hair.

"Uh . . . hi," Carmela said as she scrambled to dredge her memory, to put a name to this face. "Isabelle?" She said it tentatively because she really wasn't sure that was the name of this young woman who'd just hit an earsplitting high C as she stormed their table like a pirate commandeering one of the king's galleons.

Isabelle's smile got even wider and brighter, and she said, "You remembered."

"How could I forget?" Carmela said, when she really had forgotten. Well, almost.

"Has Ellie been keeping you in the loop about all my big wedding plans?" Isabelle asked. Ellie was Eldora Black, Isabelle's sister and the tarot card reader who worked at Juju Voodoo, the little shop across the courtyard from Carmela's French Quarter apartment. The voodoo shop, a kind of funky, fun tourist trap, was owned by Carmela's very best friend, Ava Gruiex.

"Ellie *has* shared a few things with me," Carmela said, lying as gracefully as she could. She glanced over at Babcock. "With us." Now she gave Babcock an encouraging nod. "You remember Isabelle, don't you? She's one of the assistant district attorneys."

"We've met," Babcock said politely.

"Just two more weeks," Isabelle said. She held up two fingers and then fluttered her hand nervously as her engagement ring caught the light and glittered like a disco ball.

"That's some gorgeous ring," Carmela said.

Now Isabelle preened a bit. "Isn't it? Three carats, a VS2."

"Sweet," Babcock said, gamely trying to interject himself in a conversation that had suddenly turned girly.

Flustered by the attention, Isabelle took a step back from their table. "I hope you two are still planning to attend my wedding."

"Absolutely," Carmela said. She had an awful feeling that she hadn't actually mailed back her RSVP. She'd been busy and scattered lately, what with teaching a series of card-making classes at her scrapbook shop, Memory Mine. Oh well, maybe she could short-circuit things and give her reply to Ellie. Yeah, that oughta work just fine.

Isabelle glanced across the room where two of her friends waved at her, one tall and blond, the other short and dark haired. "Well, I'm afraid I have to hustle off. I've been tasting cakes with Naomi and Cynthia and a few other folks from the wedding party." She rolled her eyes. "And now I have a thousand other things to nail down."

"I'll bet you do," Carmela said. She gave a little wave as Isabelle scampered away. "Bye-bye. Good luck." Then, when Isabelle and her friends were out of both sight and earshot, she leaned across the table and said, "Do you recall me inviting you to her wedding?"

Babcock shook his head. "Nope."

"Do you want to go? Do you want to be my plus-one?"

Another head shake. "Nope."

"Come on," Carmela said. "Don't be an old poop. Weddings are exciting, romantic events filled with dancing, champagne, good food, and excellent cake." Carmela was particularly fond of cake, though champagne wasn't too far down her list, either.

"I'm pretty sure I have to work," Babcock said.

"You don't even know when her wedding is," Carmela snorted. "So how do you know if you'll be called upon to bust an international smuggling ring of ladies' designer flip-flops or chase down a homicidal maniac?"

But Babcock didn't answer. He was suddenly frowning at the check that had been surreptitiously deposited at their table, running quick computations in his head.

Hmm. He was good at dodging bullets, that's for sure, Carmela decided. Probably from all the practice he got as a police detective.

She narrowed her eyes and studied him carefully. He was quite a catch, this guy. Tall, lanky, ginger-colored hair, nice high cheekbones. A man who walked into a room and immediately projected a certain weighty presence. Plus he had a penchant for snazzy clothes. Really snazzy clothes, like Ralph Lauren Black Label and Moncler. Tonight he was wearing a Burberry Brit jacket that widened his shoulders and nipped his waist. Always a good thing.

Babcock glanced up and gave her a warm smile. "Ready to go?"

Carmela returned his smile. Her upper lip dipped in a soft Cupid's bow, a luscious, rounded lip that most women would kill for. Or pay good money for in a plastic surgeon's office.

"I could get used to this, you know," Carmela said. She meant the dinner, the togetherness, and then some. The *and then some* meaning the two of them would eventually head back to her place for a nice Sunday-night canoodle.

"So could I," Babcock said. He held out a hand and helped her up from the chair. Then, he slid both arms around her, pulled her close, and gave her a quick kiss.

"Uh-oh," Carmela cautioned. "PDA."

Babcock arched back an inch. "What's PDA? Some kind of women's political group? A new design project?"

She brushed her lips across his cheek, feeling his warmth and energy. "You know, public display of affection."

"Oh, that." He chuckled and grabbed her hand. "Come on."

OUTSIDE THE RESTAURANT, THE NOVEMBER evening had turned cool and breezy. Though it was full-on dark, the exterior of Commander's Palace twinkled with multiple strands of lights. Turrets, columns, gingerbread swirls, and balustrades were all shown off to full advantage, gilded and glittering like a Mardi Gras float. Turquoise and white awnings flip-flapped in the wind while the restaurant's trademark neon sign hummed softly.

The whole of the Garden District was spread out around them, stately and sublime, as if it were its own proud principality governed by some unseen archduke. Lush gardens and wrought-iron fences surrounded block after block of palatial Greek Revival homes, with a few Queen Annes and

Victorians thrown in for good measure. And, if you strolled down First Street, you might even encounter a fanciful Gothic home, owned by a famous author of vampire books.

Carmela and Babcock walked down Coliseum Street, heading for Babcock's blue BMW, which was parked at the end of the block. Across the scuffed blacktop, where dry leaves scritched and scratched, hurried along by little puffs of wind, stood the notorious Lafayette Cemetery. Dark and ominous-looking, this was one of New Orleans's oldest and most infamous Cities of the Dead. Here, crumbling tombs, ancient crypts, and hulking mausoleums stood shoulder to somber shoulder, more than seven thousand residents interred in a one-block area, attracting and terrifying swarms of tourists as well as locals.

A chill gust of wind suddenly blasted them, and Carmela turned her face into Babcock's shoulder.

"I was thinking that we should—" she began.

An ungodly scream suddenly pierced what felt like a fragile night.

"Heeeeeelp!"

Carmela clutched Babcock's arm. "What was that?"

"Nooo!"

Another agonizing scream rolled out, but was immediately cut off.

Babcock swiveled his head like a periscope. "Cemetery," he said sharply. He took off running, as if a starter's gun had sounded, leaving Carmela standing all by herself on the sidewalk. In the dark.

She weighed her options for all of one second. "Wait!" she cried. And took off after him.

But Babcock's longer legs had put him easily twenty strides ahead of her. And when he reached the cemetery's fence, he simply grabbed hold of the top tines, wedged a toe into a curlicue, and vaulted over it slick as you please.

"Where are you . . . ? Oh jeez!" Carmela cried. She knew

she couldn't climb over that foreboding-looking fence in her tight skirt, so she pounded down the block to the formal entrance at the corner, lost her balance and almost spun out, then ducked through the narrow entry.

"Babcock," she called out. "Where are you?" She slid to a stop and listened intently. When she didn't hear anything, she called again, "What's going on?" Then, "Are you okay?"

"Over here." Babcock's faint shout drifted toward her.

Carmela glanced around, decided that his voice had to be coming from practically the epicenter of the cemetery, and then took off at a gallop. She dodged around a row of low, flat, humpy-looking tombs, then sped down a narrow gravel walkway between two mausoleums that were iced by a finger of moonlight. The night felt even darker, more dangerous, in here. Fear trickled coldly down her spine, and the exertion of a full-out sprint made the blood pound in her ears.

Still she kept going, moving and darting ahead.

What could have happened? Carmela wondered. Had someone been attacked? That had to be it. None of New Orleans's cemeteries were particularly safe after dark, and visitors were constantly being cautioned to avoid them. Had Babcock been able to foil this robbery attempt or attack or whatever it had been? Had he given chase to the attacker?

Carmela spun around a stone angel whose upturned face had eroded away over the years from the constant onslaught of heat, wind, humidity, and hurricanes. She dashed past a row of oven tombs, stumbling as her toe caught on the corner of a marble tablet that the earth had heaved up. Righting herself, she listened again but didn't hear anything. So she ran left in a sort of zigzag pattern, still trying to get a bead on where Babcock had called to her from.

Gray clouds boiled up, and the sliver of moon, which had served as a small guiding beacon, slipped behind them. Now Carmela was practically running blind, feeling her way along, touching and grasping cold stone. If only she could . . .

She ran her fingers along the edge of a marble tomb, cool and smooth as picked bones. She glanced up—hoping that the crescent of moon might put in an appearance again. But the night seemed to turn darker, holding a hint of ever more danger.

Carmela scuffed along quietly. She figured she was fairly close to where Babcock might have called to her from. Now if she could only see . . .

A sound, soft and muffled, as if someone might be hunching themselves back into the shadows and hiding from her, caused Carmela to stop dead in her tracks. On high alert, hair on the back of her neck prickling like crazy, she listened as though her life depended on it. And maybe it did.

What was that? What did I hear?

Flattening herself against the side of a large, hulking crypt, she tried to modulate her breathing as best she could. Tried to make every sense keenly alert to what was going on around her.

But, after a few moments, she heard—and felt—nothing.

Carmela slowly released a breath. She was spooked, yes, but she wasn't going to let her emotions run wild. She was going to keep bumbling along and find Babcock. After all, he was in here somewhere.

Carmela moved ahead two steps, then three, her right shoulder still brushing against the side of the crypt, using it as a sort of touch point. She was just about to cry out to Babcock again, to try to get a fix on his position, when she heard a strange, low, creaking sound and caught a rush of something.

The initial spark in Carmela's brain told her it was a shadow coming at her—a grid of light and dark projected by a far-off passing car. At the last moment, she realized it was a rusty iron gate. The heavy, flaking wrought-iron door of the crypt had been flung open on squeaking hinges and was creaking inexorably toward her.

Shocked and totally unprepared, Carmela had barely two seconds to get a hand up in front of her face, a pro forma protest at best, before the gate struck hard against her, pinning her tightly against the crypt's outside wall.

She let loose a startled yelp as her forehead went numb and bright stars danced and flashed before her eyes. She suddenly felt like a captured butterfly pinned inside a display case. Angry, stunned, and struggling to pull herself back to the here and now, she gripped the gate with her hands and managed to croak out, "Help!"

Then she heard footsteps lightly running away from her as she was finally able to shove the heavy door or metal gate or whatever it was off her body.

"Stop!" she cried out. Now her fear had been replaced with fury.

But whoever had smacked her with the gate was long gone.

Carmela gently touched a hand to her nose, mindful of sudden tears that clouded her eyes.

Broken?

She prodded carefully. No, she didn't think so. Just sore. But whoever had tried to waylay her had been fairly successful. They'd stopped her cold. She figured she'd probably feel battered and bruised come tomorrow morning.

Deciding the smartest thing, the *safest* thing, to do right now was get herself out of the cemetery as fast as she could, Carmela scuttled left, found a sort of pathway, and hurried along it. She was angry and scared and hurt. If she could make it out to Babcock's car, she'd hopefully meet up with him there.

Boy, did she have a story to tell!

But as Carmela lurched along, her eyes scanning to either side of the path, she almost tripped again. She caught herself at the last moment, glanced forward, and let loose a startled cry.

What is that? What am I seeing now?

Someone had flung a coat across a gravestone?

Carmela blinked and struggled to focus. Wait a minute. Maybe that wasn't a coat?

Is that a person lying there? Oh dear Lord.

Carmela moved forward as if in a trance. She was suddenly hyperaware of every crunch of gravel underfoot, every looming grave, every sigh and hiss of the wind.

Who is it? Is it the person we heard screaming?

Had to be.

As if compelled to bear witness, Carmela drew closer and closer to the grave where someone—she was pretty sure it was a woman—was sprawled in a totally unnatural pose, as if they'd been hurled there by some uncaring, unfeeling giant.

Carmela was five feet away when her brain blipped out a warning message: *Be careful, be careful.*

Babcock. Where was Babcock? Now she really had to find him.

She opened her mouth to cry out, but no sound emerged. Because, by this time, she was standing directly in front of the slumped body (slumped *dead* body?), feeling not only shock, but paralyzing fear.

Get a grip, she told herself. *Try to breathe. Make a sound. Any sound.*

Carmela gritted her teeth and tried to rally her courage. She wasn't sure if this woman was dead or very badly injured. But she knew she had to try and help this poor soul . . .

Tentatively, Carmela reached out a hand. And just as the tips of her fingers were about to touch the woman . . .

"Carmela," came a harsh voice. "No!"

A WARNING TO READERS: AN ENTIRELY NEW SERIES FROM THE AUTHOR OF THIS BOOK!

If you enjoy pulse-pounding thrillers, if you like intriguing female protagonists, you're going to love the first book in this brand-new series.

FINDERS CREEPERS

AN AFTON TANGLER THRILLER

by Gerry Schmitt

Writing as Laura Childs, this author has brought you the *New York Times* bestselling Tea Shop Mysteries, Scrapbooking Mysteries, and Cackleberry Club Mysteries. Now, writing under her own name of Gerry Schmitt, she is bringing you an entirely new series of sharp-edged thrillers. Gerry has ratcheted up the suspense, set the stakes even higher, and created exciting, memorable characters that sizzle on the page.

We know you'll be intrigued by *Finders Creepers*, the first in this series that features Afton Tangler, single mom, Outward Bound enthusiast, and liaison officer with the Minneapolis PD, as she gets pulled into a bizarre high-profile kidnapping.

From *New York Times* bestselling author

LAURA CHILDS

Parchment and Old Lace

A Scrapbooking Mystery

✂

Scrapbook shop owner Carmela Bertrand couldn't imagine a finer evening than dinner at Commander's Palace with her beau, Detective Edgar Babcock—with the exception of Isabelle Black's stopping by to brag about her upcoming wedding. Resuming the romance with a walk in the evening air, the couple is interrupted once again—this time by a terrifying scream from inside the cemetery.

Having just seen Isabelle, Carmela and Edgar now find her lying across an aboveground tomb, strangled to death with a piece of vintage lace. Carmela would rather leave the investigating to Edgar, but she can't say no to Isabelle's sister, Ellie. As she untangles the enemies of Isabelle's past, Carmela hopes she can draw out the killer before someone else gets cold feet.

INCLUDES SCRAPBOOKING TIPS

laurachilds.com
penguin.com

The Tea Shop Mysteries by
New York Times Bestselling Author

Laura Childs

"A delightful series."
—*The Mystery Reader*

"Murder suits [Laura Childs] to a Tea."
—*St. Paul Pioneer Press*

laurachilds.com
penguin.com

M314AS0715

FROM *NEW YORK TIMES* BESTSELLING AUTHOR
· LAURA CHILDS ·

THE CACKLEBERRY
CLUB MYSTERIES

Eggs to go. Murder on the side…
EGGS IN PURGATORY

Don't put all your eggs in one casket…
EGGS BENEDICT ARNOLD

Sleuthing is never over easy…
BEDEVILED EGGS

A killer has the town walking on eggshells…
STAKE & EGGS

This killer is toast…
EGGS IN A CASKET

They're turning up the heat…
SCORCHED EGGS

facebook.com/TheCrimeSceneBooks
penguin.com

M1149AS0714

P.O. 0003342193